A Storm of Love

A vicious blast of wind buffeted her, and he put out his arms to catch her again. The wind was increasing, and suddenly her fear became panic. Only Chance's strong arms around her held any safety.

"Mollie—" His voice in her ear was rough, and his arms tightened.

Through the chill wetness of their bodies, Mollie felt the warm, vital length of him against her. Her heart began to pound, and she knew she should pull away. Yet his arms were stronger than the wind, and she yielded to their strength and her own hot desire.

"No, Chance—No!" But her cry was feeble against the raging elements loosed within their bodies, as well as those tearing at them from the sky...

Other Avon Books by
Ann Forman Barron

WINDSWEPT

PROUD GLORY

ANN FORMAN BARRON

AVON
PUBLISHERS OF BARD, CAMELOT, DISCUS AND FLARE BOOKS

AVON BOOKS
A division of
The Hearst Corporation
105 Madison Avenue
New York, New York 10016

Copyright © 1987 by Ann Forman Barron
Published by arrangement with the author
Library of Congress Catalog Card Number: 86-92048
ISBN: 0-380-89599-4

First Avon Printing: June 1987

AVON TRADEMARK REG. U.S. PAT. OFF. AND IN OTHER COUNTRIES, MARCA REGISTRADA, HECHO EN U.S.A.

Printed in the U.S.A.

K–R   10   9   8   7   6   5   4   3   2   1

For Doug, with love

Chapter 1

Mollie shivered, though the summer evening was not chilly, and drew a hand hard across her mouth. She closed the rear door of Stirling Manor with a soft click. Her cousin Rose, carrying the basket of leftover food that Cook had given them, regarded her sympathetically.

"He kissed you again, didn't he?" she said in Gaelic. "That suet pudding Horace."

"Yes. Speak English, Rose," Mollie added automatically. "We need the practice."

"You mean *I* need the practice, not you. Ma was right when she said one of us would catch one of them." Rose spoke with only the faintest brogue as she looked affectionately at her younger cousin.

In the fading light, the delicate planes of Mollie's oval face were exquisitely formed, from her wide-set blue eyes, fringed with inky double lashes, to her short, slender nose. Beyond her, the hills of Ireland were bright with the yellow blooms of late-June gorse.

"I can't understand why he wants *me*," Mollie declared. She cringed inwardly at being beholden for the food in Rose's basket—her whole soul cried out against accepting charity.

"Can't you?" Rose smiled. Her light hazel eyes looked into Mollie's vivid blue ones without a trace of jealousy. Mollie was taller than her older cousin by two inches, with long, slender legs and a narrow waist that could be spanned by a man's hands. But it was her mouth, with its short upper lip and full lower one, that made her unforgettable. "You're beautiful, Mollie," Rose added honestly, "not just pretty like me. Your shape's made to stir a man, and your mouth—"

"What blather, Rose! You're much prettier, with all that lovely hair so pale and fine. Not black and unruly like mine! And Aunt Kate with her red hair and green eyes—though it's skinny enough we all are now."

A searing fire was banked deep within Mollie. She meant—some day, some way—to be free of this grinding poverty, where starvation loomed, inevitable and inescapable. Yes, and to see her Aunt Kate and her cousin Rose out of it too!

"'Tis true. We are skinny," Rose said mournfully. "What with not a potato in all Ireland these past two years." She paused, then added cheerfully, "Anyway, you know so much more than Ma and me. You speak like—like the highborn ladies who visit the manor from London."

Mollie laughed. "Aunt Kate kept me at my schooling to keep me out of the way, I suspect. For all that, you always have your nose in a book when you're not working."

"That's true enough," Rose agreed. "But you've always been the favorite of Father O'Malley. And Sister Maria Theresa loved you best—willing you all her instruments and medicines and training you to be as good a doctor as she, God rest her soul." But there was no rancor in Rose's soft voice as they stepped off the coach trail from the manor and onto the main road to the village of Arderin, where Kate Brannigan's small cottage with its thatched roof stood at the outskirts.

The two girls walked more briskly as the road passed through a thick copse of trees. Halfway through, they were startled by the deep sound of a man's voice.

"Ho! Mollie and Rosie girl!"

"Ach, 'tis Clanahan O'Connor!" Rose cried, bursting into Gaelic once more. "Man, you frightened us half to death." But there was breathless pleasure in her voice.

Sean and Clanahan O'Connor had been handsome adolescents when Rose and Mollie were little girls. The O'Connors had a farm two miles from Arderin and for years had had a herd of cattle and an even larger flock of sheep. They were not only extraordinarily fair to look upon, but by Arderin standards they had been rich as well. But now all the cattle and sheep were gone, and their farm, like all farms in Ireland, barely supported them. Granny O'Connor was not well enough to keep house, so the men did it in their haphazard way.

Now, as Clan stepped out of the trees beside them, tall and handsome, Mollie spoke up.

"You should make yourself known more gently," she said coldly.

"Ha!" His laughter was quick, and in a heavy brogue he said, "Miss Mollie, ye speak our native tongue well enough. Why should I speak this ugly English language?"

"You'd better learn it well, too, sir—and with less an accent," Mollie replied tartly, "if you expect to survive, as I do."

He laughed again. "Run along home, Rosie girl. I'll see yer cousin Lady-Miss to her Aunt Kate's house."

Rose started to leave, but Mollie caught her arm. "No. Stay with me, Rose. Aunt Kate will worry if you come home alone—"

"Nay. She can tell Kate ye'll be along quickly enough. I want ter talk wi' ye, Moyennan." He was very firm, even using Mollie's full name.

Rose pulled out of her grasp. "I'll tell Ma you'll be along soon, Mollie." She smiled and darted on down the road.

Mollie resumed walking briskly until Clan reached

out and caught her arm, swinging her around hard to face him. "Ah, Mollie, slow ye down an' talk a bit wi' me," he said huskily.

Mollie stopped and faced him squarely. He and his brother Sean, who was a scant nine months older, were the handsomest men Mollie had ever seen. Their shoulders were wide and strong, their features clean-cut and regular, their hair black and unruly, their eyes as blue as her own. But Clan's temper was legendary. Once, in Arderin, she had seen him whip his nervous horse. She had winced, longing to soothe the quivering animal, and had done so as soon as Clan entered the Arderin Tavern.

"Clan," Mollie said, lifting her chin, "you well know there's a rumor in Arderin that the banns might be published for you and Megan Patrick. You've nothing to talk about with me."

He urged her to the edge of the road as a cart rumbled slowly by, the driver looking at them curiously in the gloom. Then Clan pulled her further into the copse until they were veiled by trees.

"Mollie darlin', it's you I want, an' ye know it, girl. Megan has a face like me horse. If it wasn't fer her father havin' all that land next to ours, that rumor wouldn't be about." He drew her still further in amongst the trees. "You, Mollie darlin', you're a fighter, an' I like fighters." His voice thickened as he pulled her resisting form against his hard body. "I could even love a fighter—"

He forced her face up, kissing her cheek. Then his lips found her mouth and fastened there, hard and compelling. She gasped, opening her lips for air, and he kissed her harder, forcing his tongue inside.

Fury rose within her, giving her abnormal strength. His arms were like iron, and she struggled wildly, tripping on her long skirts, and they both fell to the ground with him astride her.

Pulling an arm loose, she reached up and raked her nails down his cheek. He smothered a curse and seized her arm, but she had freed her mouth at last and screamed loudly. Drawing her legs up beneath him, she sought to buck him off her.

It was almost dark under the trees and Mollie knew real terror. She was sure Clanahan O'Connor meant to take her by force, and she fought frantically against him. Still, his mouth came down on hers inexorably.

He lifted his head and said roughly, "Mollie girl, I mean ye no harm, but have ye I will—"

Suddenly he was torn from her, half lifting her from the ground with him before he let go.

She fell back, panting. Looking up, she saw a taller figure looming over Clan. In the dimness a fist lashed out, and she heard the dull thud of a blow against flesh.

Clan reeled back and Mollie lay watching the two men, her breath coming in gasps. A deep voice drawled, "I'll deck you, mate—make a pulp of you. You'd better get going while you can."

Clan, holding his jaw, looked up at the man standing over him. He bunched his big shoulders in readiness. Then he glanced back at Mollie. In the half light, she saw the flash of Clan's winning smile as he shrugged and turned away.

Over his shoulder, he said, "Sure'n all I wanted was a kiss, man. 'Tis naught ter quarrel about." Then, pressing his hand to his cheek, which was bleeding where Mollie's nails had raked it, he spoke in a low, firm whisper.

"I'll see ye again, Mollie O'Meara. Never doubt it, colleen." And he moved swiftly away in the gloom.

Mollie scrambled to her feet and began to run. The deep voice followed her.

"Wait, miss. You'd better have an escort in the dark."

She cast a frightened glance back to see the stranger strapping a large, square pack onto his back. From the ground, he picked up two more bundles with handles on them. Seeing that his hands were completely filled, she halted.

"I'll see you into Arderin, miss," he said in that

strange but warmly penetrating drawl. "I take it you didn't care for the man's attentions?"

"No, no! I'm greatly in your debt, sir."

He said nothing more, and they walked in complete silence as stars came out and the moon rose higher, throwing its cold brilliance over the countryside. Mollie cast a sidelong glance at her companion. His strong, lean features were profiled against the night.

Soon they were passing by the old O'Meara cottage where Mollie had been born over seventeen years before. Another family lived there now.

Mollie could not remember her mama and papa. They had died when a terrible fever swept the countryside and the village of Arderin. Aunt Kate had taken her brother's child to raise.

Mollie's eyes sought the potato patch behind the cottage. It lay stark and black in the pale moonlight— like all the potato fields in Ireland in these terrible years of 1845 and 1846. Something awful had happened to the potato crops these past warm, wet summers. The bright green bushes had withered and blackened, leaving the main stems a brilliant green that accentuated the devastation of each plant's leaves. And the potatoes rotted in the ground with a repulsive stench.

People were panicky and starving now. Ireland was filled with walking skeletons. Death was stalking the land, and Mollie knew that it stood at her shoulder. Only the work she and her cousin and aunt had found could keep it at bay. Last summer, the first seeds of her desire to escape had been planted—to escape not just from Stirling Manor but from the Ireland she had always loved.

She *did* love it, she told herself. But escape this terrible poverty, this stark and deadly hunger she must, she thought with a new and wrenching conviction as she walked with this silent stranger down the old, familiar road.

As she and her companion neared the Brannigan cottage that stood alone at the edge of Arderin, she turned to her rescuer.

"Again, I thank you, sir. I live here and will leave you now."

He did not even say good-bye but watched her go to the cottage door. As she turned to close the door behind her, she saw him lengthen his stride and disappear into the night.

Aunt Kate came to her as she entered. At thirty-four Kate Brannigan was still a handsome woman, slim of figure and pert of face, with fiery red hair and flashing green eyes. She could have passed for twenty-five, so fresh was her creamy Irish complexion.

"An' what did Clanahan O'Connor have ter say ter ye, darlin'?" Her eyes were mischievous but hopeful.

Mollie hesitated. Both Rose and Aunt Kate were looking at her curiously. Even in these hard times the O'Connor men had enough to eat, and Kate would smile on a declaration of love from either of them to either Mollie or Rose.

"He just wanted to tell—" she lied slowly.

"Not about him an' Megan Patrick?" Kate asked swiftly. "Not that th' gossip in Arderin about him an' Megan's true?"

"No. He just wanted to talk, and he said that there's no truth to the rumors. 'Tis only because old Patrick's land is so close to the O'Connors'."

Kate sighed and took Mollie's worn cape to hang it on a peg in the main room. The kitchen and the main room were one; two small bedrooms opened off it on the south side, one for Mollie and Rose and one for Kate.

"Rosie tells me young Horace Stirling kissed ye, Mollie! Did he mention marriage?" Kate's eyes shone hopefully.

"No," Mollie said with suppressed violence. "He mentioned what he called 'an arrangement'—that I would come live at Stirling Manor and be his mistress." She added boldly, "I told him I'd die first, and he laughed and said, 'You Irish! You're priest-ridden. Your religion eats you alive.'"

Kate was shocked, but Rose, with an unusually

cynical laugh, said, "Now you'll have to confess that to
Father O'Malley this Sunday."

"You think that will bother me? I'll be glad to tell
him! And to speak the truth, Aunt Kate"—she looked
at her aunt appealingly—"if Horace Stirling should
ever propose marriage, I'd not be able to say yes. He
has smooth, fat white hands like great pale spiders,
and when he kisses me they roam over my body until I
push him away." She thought fleetingly of Clanahan
O'Connor's kisses. They had been even worse—devouring and insatiable. She could not speak of them to
her aunt and cousin.

"But he *is* the son of Lord Stirling, an' if ye hold out,
Mollie, ye might yet be the Lady Moyennan. Ye'd be
set fer life, lass!" Aunt Kate looked at her pleadingly.

"Ah, yes, Aunt Kate," Mollie said with a touch of
derision. "And don't forget he's Protestant English to
boot. You know how they've treated us Irish! For cen-
turies they've starved us, evicted us, and made life a
hell for us. They've their heels on our necks this minute. Why—why, I'd feel I was going over to the enemy
if I married Horace Stirling." Mollie went on passionately: "He brags he's Anglo-Irish just because they've
had the manor house and all that land—Irish land—
for over a hundred years. People from London—ladies
and lords—visit them, ride their horses, eat all that
fancy food they have brought in. If I married him, I'd
have to go with him and his papa to London regularly
for long periods." She shot her cousin a meaningful
glance. "*You* could snare his pa, the lord himself, if
you'd only try, Rose. He's a widower and no more than
forty. He's twice the man that fat, soft son of his is."

Rose shrugged. "I'm very polite to him—and com-
plimentary. But you nursed him through that fever of
his just a little while ago. Better you try to snare him
yourself."

"No matter," Kate said with determined cheer. "I've
raised good girls, an' ye'll both marry well an' things
will be better fer us."

The aroma of boiling cabbage, turnips, carrots
drifted to them from the fireplace with its hot peat fire

at the back of the room. They hadn't had a potato in over two years! But in her basket Rose had brought cold beef and mutton from the manor, as well as bread, and the girls knew they would have a good supper.

"Th' bakery needs me two days next week," Kate said as she set the food on the table. "Nobody bakes better breads an' pastries than me, 'less 'tis you, Mollie." Her eyes were suddenly thoughtful. "But yer good at everything. Yer a midwife an' a doctor, thanks ter blessed Sister Maria Theresa. 'Tis too good ye are fer th' young Stirling."

Mollie was silent through the meal, thinking of Horace Stirling's suggestion and Clan O'Connor's kisses, followed by the dark stranger's appearance. If that stranger had not happened by... She repressed a shiver as they rose and began to clear the table.

Afterward, she sat with the other two women before the low fire, mending laundry that Aunt Kate had washed for the English servants and their master at Stirling Manor. The soft voices beside Mollie faded as she looked toward a dark future, and fresh despair filled her sore heart.

"Mollie!" The word sharply penetrated her desperate thoughts. "I've spoken ter ye twice. Yer in a deep study, me girl. What about?" Aunt Kate's smooth brow was drawn.

"I—I—nothing, Aunt Kate."

"Well, I've asked about yer dress twice. There, that rip at yer waist." She reached over and put a finger against Mollie's waist. "What have they put ye ter doin' at Stirling Manor that ye should be a-rippin' o' yer seams?"

Mollie put a hand to it guiltily. Clan O'Connor had done that! "Ah, 'tis nothing, Aunt Kate. I guess I reached up for something and pulled the seam loose."

"Take it off an' I'll mend it fer ye."

When Mollie had changed into her only other dress and put her apron over it, she handed the torn dress to her aunt; then she said, "Aunt Kate, I'm going to walk into town and visit with Bet Delanty. I haven't seen her this week."

She felt she must get out, away from thoughts of Clan O'Connor, of Horace Stirling and his soft, prying fingers. Oh, if only she dared confide in Bet! Bet was her best friend, and Mollie had grown up with Bet's twin sons, Tim and Benjie. Bet would understand, and her advice was always good. Besides, it would make confession to the good father a bit easier to know that Bet had listened too.

There had to be a way out of the web in which she was becoming more and more entangled. There had been both promise and threat in Clan's voice. *I'll see ye again, Mollie O'Meara. Never doubt it, colleen.*

And what if Horace Stirling did propose marriage? Aunt Kate, who had always been so kind to her, who had actually saved her from death with her ma and pa—it was up to Mollie now to save them all, for Rose was much too shy to respond to Lord Stirling, even if he were attracted to her. Though Rose was over eighteen, nearly a year older than she, Mollie felt years her senior. How could Mollie save them here in Ireland? She must go to that far new world where there were opportunities—even for women!

"Mollie, darlin'," Kate said briskly as Mollie swung her cape around her shoulders, "might ye ask Bet fer two eggs fer us? She has those chickens left an'—"

"Yes, Aunt Kate, I'll ask her."

"An' ye won't stay long? Ye know ye an' Rose must be up before dawn an' on yer way ter th' manor by daylight."

"Yes, yes," Mollie interrupted hurriedly. "I won't stay long."

As she went to the door she heard Kate saying cheerfully, "I'll make us egg custard fer supper termorrow night."

She closed the door quietly behind her. The night air was damper now, and the vault above her shone brilliant with moonlight that paled the stars. She walked briskly down the road and into the lane of houses that formed Arderin. She passed cottages with candles glimmering at the windows and cottages that had tumbled down, their inhabitants forced to wander the roads.

She increased her pace, anxious to reach the De- lanty cottage. By the time she arrived she was almost running.

Bet's kitchen would be warm and cozy. She visual- ized the rosy-faced woman with the prematurely gray streak in her blue-black hair. Bet was so kind and sympathetic, as much a mother to her as Aunt Kate. How many times had she played in Bet's kitchen with the fair Tim and his dark-haired twin Benjie? She was bursting with the desire to blurt out her fears to Bet.

She began to smile as she lifted the latch to the cottage. In an instant she was closing the door behind her.

"Bet—" she called out, eyes blazing, cheeks glowing from her rapid walk. Abruptly she came to a halt, standing still as a statue.

The stranger who had rescued her from Clan O'Connor was leaning with easy grace against the stone mantel, seeming to fill the room with his pres- ence. He was taller than the O'Connor brothers by at least two inches, and his shoulders were wider. The eyes that narrowed on her from under black brows were pinpoints of blue fire. His face was browned from what must have been years spent under a sun much hotter than Ireland's. And the way he was looking at her—a powerful sensation shook her, and immediately she felt a flash of antagonism. Swallowing against a sudden dryness in her mouth, she attempted to hide the strange emotions this man's mere presence stirred in her.

What if he had already told Bet of his encounter with Mollie and her apparent intimacy with Clan? Perhaps he wouldn't recognize her! He had scarcely been able to see her face in the dark. Now, under his penetrating eyes she couldn't confide in Bet.

Bet, who had been sitting near the stranger, came forward and smoothed a stray wisp of hair from Mol- lie's cheek as she smiled warmly at the younger woman.

"Come in, come in, Mollie darlin', an' sit ye down here near me. 'Tis me brother-in-law yer lookin' at, come all th' way from th' New World ter see us. Chance Delanty, 'tis Moyennan O'Meara—Mollie, we call her. D'ye remember her? Just a child she was when ye left." Without waiting for an answer, she added worriedly, "Ben an' me boys are late comin' home. I expect ol' Fogarty's got thim doin' some extra chores, for which he'll pay nothin'."

Mollie could find no words under this stranger's eyes, which were not at all like his older brother Ben's warm, twinkling brown ones. She hung her cape on a peg and took a seat on the stool near Bet, wishing she'd removed her worn apron. She searched her memory but could not recall ever seeing this tall, black-haired man.

A marvelous aroma was rising from a small pot over a rack near the edge of the peat fire. Involuntarily, Mollie leaned forward, unable to keep from sniffing at the mouth-watering and exotic fragrance. Bet laughed delightedly.

"Aye, an' Chance has brought us boxes of good things from the New World! 'Tis coffee ye smell, colleen. 'Tis shipped from Brazil, Chance says—wherever that may be—to America, an' th' Americans drink it. 'Tis a wonder we'll soon taste." Her infectious laugh sounded again. "I'm so glad ye came, Mollie. Ben an' Benjie an' Tim have no idea Chance has come. What a surprise 'twill be!"

"Coffee," Mollie murmured, still looking at the pot. "I've never tasted such. Not even at the manor. They serve tea."

"Aye. An' Chance's brought us sugar to sweeten it. An' dried beef—I've a pot full of grand stew here. We'll have a feast tonight, darlin'. Ye must stay an' share wi' us. Chance, tell Mollie about th' New World—an' what yer wantin' us ter do." She looked at her tall brother-in-law with affection mingled faintly with apprehension.

"'Tis the answer to *your* problems, Bet," he said. But his penetrating eyes were on Mollie, and she felt his words were meant for her. His voice was deep and warm with that strange accent. That voice! It went over her like a tender hand over a deep bruise.

He went on, his eyes still on Mollie. "Ben and the boys and you must come with me. Famine is on this land. Thousands have died of it already, and it can only grow worse. On my way from Dublin, I saw people starving—scarecrows in their burrows, shanties thrown up over ditches. Scalpeens, they called them. And so many children with swollen bellies." His words were angry and bitter. "The British are letting in a little Indian corn from America—with their talk of soup kitchens. Why, in one village I passed through, they were evicting tenants by the hundreds, tumbling their houses and putting the people out on the road to starve and die. I tell you, the Irish are dying like flies, despite Queen Victoria's promise of aid."

His words were still directed at Bet, but Mollie felt they were meant for her. His voice echoed her desperation and his gaze was somehow intimate as his eyes seemed to bore into hers.

Her face heated up, and she knew her color was high. She saw the heat reflected in his eyes and suddenly felt as though he had touched her physically. She knew he recognized her now. It was in his eyes, his half-smile. Besides, she suddenly remembered that Clan had spoken her name as he left the copse. But somehow Mollie was certain that Chance had not told Bet about their earlier encounter.

There was magnetism in the man, force and drive that pulled at her with a power she found hard to control. It forced her to drop her eyes to avoid his intense scrutiny. It infuriated her that this stranger could unsettle her so.

"You've all got to pack up," he went on, "and return with me on my ship out of Dublin."

"Chance is first mate on a ship from America," Bet explained proudly. "He went to the New World back in 1835 when he was but a lad of sixteen. Maybe ye remember him, Mollie. Ye were almost seven when he left. Now he has a big farm in a place called Texas—a

new state in th' American Union. He says land is
cheap there an' rich in soil. No landlords, no rents ter
pay, an' food aplenty fer everyone." She paused, looking from Mollie to her brother-in-law as she added,
"Chance, me boys an' me husband are workin' fer Fogarty, ye know. 'Tis a poor wage they get doin' his
chores, but 'tis enough ter feed us now an"—her voice
became anguished—"an it would kill me ter leave me
home, fair Ireland."

"I heard in the Anderin Tavern, before I came here,
Bet, that Fogarty's buying up farms dirt cheap—for a
lord in London." His deep, drawling voice did not have
a trace of the Irish brogue. It had all been lost during
his long years in America. But that voice was part of
his charm, slow and measured and easy with the *r*'s.

Mollie had never heard a voice like it, nor seen such
a mouth, clean-cut and curved, with a hint of both tenderness and cruelty in it. She found herself wondering
what it would be like to be kissed by Chance Delanty,
to feel those lips pressed against her own. Through her
confusion she now remembered Bet's occasional references to Ben's younger brother who had left Ireland at
sixteen. And she remembered vividly the stories Father O'Malley had told her about the New World and
the books she had read herself. It was a land filled
with wild animals and Indians who killed when they
could, but it was a land of plenty too, where opportunity beckoned to all. It was a shimmering promise that
had been in the back of her mind for a long time.

"Mark my words," Chance Delanty said evenly,
"this famine means death—and all the while landlords are squeezing rents out of the survivors. Yet as
they starve, corn and grain are shipped out daily from
every port in Ireland. Hell, I *see* it, Bet. You and Ben
and the boys have got to get out."

Suddenly the old dream sent fresh flames of longing
through Mollie. *I'm going to get out!* With every fiber
of her being, she yearned to make the long sea voyage
to the New World, away from British rule and the constant, aching poverty of their lives.

"How much is it," she blurted, "for passage to the

New World on your ship?" In spite of her effort to control it, her voice trembled.

"Ten pounds would see you aboard Captain Gallagher's *Sea Nymph,* and he takes only as many as he can safely carry," Chance said, pulling a pipe and a little cloth sack of tobacco from his shirt pocket. "Some ships cram immigrants in like pigs, and they die before they ever reach New York or Boston. Gallagher won't do that." As he tamped down tobacco in his pipe, he asked with some amusement, "Are you planning to go, Miss Mollie?"

"I haven't ten pounds," she replied bitterly.

Bet stopped stirring the pot and looked at her. "Why, child, do ye really want ter go ter th' New World?"

"With all my heart," Mollie said passionately. Oh, if she could only tell Bet about Horace Stirling and Clanahan O'Connor and taking the poor leavings from the table at Stirling Manor. How she resented Chance Delanty's presence, which kept her from pouring out the whole miserable truth to Bet! And how she resented the way he made her heart pound each time his eyes touched her! She gave him a quick, rebellious glance, and his lip curved knowingly.

"A small young girl—alone?" There was subtle sarcasm in the words. "And what could you possibly do when you got there?"

"I could work. Keep some rich lady's house for her. I could even teach." Then, with a touch of hauteur, "I've a great deal of book knowledge, and I know medicine well."

"I'm impressed," Delanty said smoothly. "Your speech is certainly above average. British, in fact." He smiled at her, and the new heat he stirred burned in her.

"She's real talented, Chance," Bet said loyally; then, in distress, she turned to her young friend. "Mollie, are ye really thinkin' on it? What would Arderin be wi'out ye, Mollie—wi' all yer treatin' o' th' sick?"

"They'd get along somehow. And I wouldn't go without my kin. Anyway, Bet, where would I get thirty

pounds when I can't even find ten pounds for myself?"
she asked sadly, shoulders drooping. With forlorn
hope, she added, "Bet, I was wondering if any of your
friends in Clonygowan or Mountmellick would hire me
to work for them." The desperation in her voice made
both Bet and Chance regard her keenly.

"But ye've a fine job at Stirling Manor, darlin'! Has
somethin' happened at th' manor to set ye so?"

"Yes," she replied shortly. "I want to leave. I'm—I'll
soon be eighteen, and I'm old enough to make my own
way and take my aunt and cousin with me."

"Ach, me darlin', everyone I know is in such poor
condition they could hire no one. They couldn't even
feed ye, dearie. No one could even pay ye fer doctorin'
or nursin'—just like here in Arderin."

"I feared it might be that way," Mollie said resign-
edly. She glanced at Chance Delanty again and saw
curiosity—and something else—gleam in his blue
eyes under those slanting black brows. *He* knew part
of why she longed to leave.

"Things in Ireland are going to get worse," he repeated slowly. "Bet, I must pursuade you, Ben, and the
boys to leave now. The sooner the better. You know I'll
pay your passage and all expenses— No, no! I know
your stubborn Irish pride, but you can all pay me back
by working on the ranch. I won't stand by and see you
starve here." Then he said casually, "I think that coffee's ready. Let's all have a cup."

While Bet and her brother-in-law spoke of the New
World and the rotting potato crops in Ireland, Mollie
sat and sipped the exotic drink. It was like some richly
sweet nectar and it warmed her, mingling with the
heat Chance Delanty sent through her. She experienced a brief feeling of euphoria—a moment of knowing she could do *anything!*

She had never tasted anything so delicious. She
longed for another cup, but when Bet spoke, she set
her empty cup on the table.

"Ye will stay ter supper wi' us, Mollie? We've so
much, fer a change!"

Mollie shook her head, rising to leave. She was uneasy in Delanty's presence, for he increased the feeling that she could do anything, *would* do anything, to get away. She feared him, she disliked his effect on her, yet he drew her.

"I thank you kindly, Bet, but I've already had supper, and Kate's expecting me back." Hesitantly she asked, "How are the eggs this week? Aunt Kate wondered if you could spare us perhaps two?"

"O' course, darlin'!" Bet went quickly to the cupboard and handed two eggs to Mollie. "Th' hens are still layin'—some."

"You're so good and generous, Bet. I thank you from the bottom of my heart." Mollie brushed a light kiss on Bet's cheek.

As she hesitated in the doorway with an egg in each hand, the visitor came forward, hand extended, and drawled, "It's a pleasure meeting you, Miss Mollie."

She put one egg in one of her apron pockets and took his hand. It was big and hard, warm and dry, and her own small hand was lost in it. The feel of him gave her a curious, light-headed sensation. She flushed hotly and pulled away.

"Come," he said, smiling, "I'll see you safely home," adding under his breath, "again."

"Oh, no!" A small dart of panic shot through her. "That won't be necessary!"

"You never know," he said solemnly. "A girl as beautiful as you out in the dark night—"

"I'll be perfectly safe, Mr. Delanty," she said, her breath uneven. "I've walked home from Bet's many times after dark."

"Nevertheless," he said with authority, "I'll see you safely home, Miss Mollie." And taking her elbow, he steered her deftly out of the cottage, closing the door behind them.

As they took the narrow path that led to the uneven dirt street, Mollie could think of nothing to say. Gradually she became aware of her companion's close scrutiny. By now she had put the second egg in the other pocket of her apron and she could feel them both bump lightly against her as she increased her stride. Her cape fluttered behind her.

"Don't run. I won't let anything get you, Miss Mollie." There was buried laughter in his deep voice.

She made no reply. There was no way to explain why she felt the need to hurry, so she slowed her steps a bit.

"That's better. 'Tis a lovely night—with a moon, even. Just the night for a man to walk a beautiful girl home."

His white smile flashed in the luminous darkness. "I'm not afraid," she said abruptly.

"Of either of us?"

"What do you mean—either of us?"

"The darkness—or me, of course."

"Certainly not. As I told you, I didn't need you to walk me home," she said haughtily.

"You'll always need a man to walk you home, Mollie—even if you live to be a hundred." His voice was slightly roughened, and Mollie's wariness increased. He had not called her Miss Mollie this time. It implied familiarity. She said nothing.

When finally the Brannigan cottage was in view, she stopped suddenly. "This is far enough. There's Aunt Kate's house."

"I'll go with you to the door."

She wanted to shout, *Go away!* She sensed somehow he was the most dangerous element in the pale moonlight. But instead of voicing her qualms, she took the last few steps to Kate's cottage door and faced him.

"Good night, Mr. Delanty," she said firmly and put out her hand to the door latch.

He caught it warmly in his and pulled her around to face him. "Not so fast. I really came along to tell you something, Mollie."

"And what would that be?" She lifted her chin and her voice was filled with mistrust.

"That I will let you have the passage money for you and your aunt and cousin."

"What?" She was stunned.

"I'll be taking Ben and his three—you three will cost only a few dollars more."

"Dollars?" she asked, her voice low and hard. "You mean pounds! More than a hundred pounds!" Bitterly, she added, "I'll *never* be an object of charity, Mr. Delanty."

"It would be a loan, you little fool—"

"Loan, indeed!" she interrupted fiercely. She wanted terribly to slap his arrogant face. It took a physical effort to restrain herself. "I'll never borrow. Never! You can take your charity and your pity and—"

She was cut short as he caught her suddenly in his arms. One hand was tight about her waist, the other caught up in the thick fall of her black hair. Eyes wide, breath quickening, she saw his face blur as his mouth found hers. His lips were cool and firm at first, warming swiftly as they grew more insistent. The shock of his touch was stunningly sweet.

Behind her closed eyes, she remembered his lips as he had smiled at her while leaning easily against Bet's mantel, and involuntarily her arms went about his shoulders as she pressed herself against the long, hard length of him.

Responding swiftly to her surrender, he pulled her closer and her lips parted under his. His breath was clean and sweet as it mingled with hers. But even as his muscled shoulders tensed beneath her clinging fingers and she drowned under his kisses, cold, hard reality struggled to assert itself. She wrenched herself out of his arms, realizing all too late that the eggs in her apron pockets were crushed.

"Oh!" she exclaimed as she pulled away from him. "And I thought you were so gallant when you saved me from Clan O'Connor—"

"Why, Mollie! Don't you know that gallantry is only a man's intention to save a woman from every man but himself?" His laugh was faintly mocking.

"I should have known," she raged under her breath. It would never do for Aunt Kate or Rose to come to the door at this moment. Now she would slap his smiling face, and hard!

Her hand flew up, but he caught it swiftly and brought it to his lips to kiss her palm. The heat of his mouth sent slippery fire along her veins once again. She tore her hand from his and backed away.

"You've crushed Bet's eggs," she accused him, "and now I shall have to lie to Aunt Kate."

"*We* crushed Bet's eggs, Mollie. You did your part, and most satisfying it was too."

"Go—go back to your brother's! I hope never to see you again!"

He turned away, then halted, looking back at her. "But you *will* see me again Mollie—because my offer still stands. If you really want to get to the New World, I'll take you and yours—with me and mine."

He walked the few steps to the road; then paused, turned, and added seriously, "Think about it, Mollie."

Chapter 2

The following morning the ground was sodden. It had rained heavily during the night, and Rose Brannigan awoke with a fever and a sore throat. Aunt Kate, still mourning the loss of the eggs, now had her daughter's illness to regret as well. Rose did not receive pay when she did not work. Even the food given to them was less.

Mollie bade her cousin stay in bed and, after putting a poultice around her neck, she dosed her with mint tea laced with a spoonful of Irish whiskey. Then she went to work at Stirling Manor by herself, carrying the basket of mended laundry and a small, empty basket for leftovers.

She entered the rear door of the manor, which led to the kitchen, already redolent with the smells of baking bread and roasting meats. The tea kettle was whistling merrily and Cook, a formidable English woman named Nan Goddard, looked up from a pie crust she was trimming.

"Where's yer cousin?"

"She's ill," Mollie replied briefly, setting the basket

on the floor and donning one of the two fresh white
aprons Cook had laid on a nearby chair for Mollie and
Rose.

"Humph." Cook poured fragrant mincemeat and
brandy into the crust, then covered the filling with
pastry and crimped the edges. "Better she don't come
here, then. I'll wager it's th' fever. I heard his lordship
tell Andrew th' fever was sweepin' th' southern part o'
Ireland. 'Tis lice, th' dirty things. Comes of not washin'
proper, among ye filthy Irish."

Mollie bit back a sharp retort, knowing her job de-
pended on what this woman reported to Lord Stirling.
And Andrew, the English coachman, was even worse
than Cook. He was a haughty man who looked down
his long nose at anything Irish. He and the other English servants hated to come to Ireland when Lord Stirling and his son came for a protracted stay in their
castlelike home near Arderin.

"Dirty Irish," Cook repeated with relish.

"I notice you're glad enough for my Aunt Kate to do
your laundry," Mollie said, hiding her fury. "There are
no lice in the Brannigan cottage—nor in all of Arderin, I'll take an oath." She picked up the basket of
fresh clothing.

"If yer cousin's got th' fever, Kate'll be doin' no more
of our laundry."

"'Tis only a sore throat from so much dampness,"
Mollie said. Her own skirts felt moist from the long
walk in the wet. She put the basket back down on a
nearby chair. Dulcy, the English maid, would put the
laundry away later.

"Humph. So *you* say—you an' yer doctorin'." Cook
turned and looked critically at the coachman's mended
breeches. "I will say ye Irish wield a neat needle," she
said. "An' ye did nurse his lordship through th' ague."

Now Cook reached into the oven and drew out a pan
of hot scones; then she lifted down the tea kettle of
boiling water. In a short time, she had prepared a tray
of hot tea, scones, ham, and rich porridge.

Turning to Mollie, who was drying her dampened
skirts by the stove, she said, "Here, Mollie. Take his

lordship's breakfast ter him. He's in th' library. A
bunch o' mail come from London by special messenger." With a sharp, gloating glance at Mollie, she
added, "Besides, he said he wanted ter see ye when ye
come in this mornin'.""

Mollie took the heavy silver tray and walked carefully down the hall, past the oil portraits of dozens of
imperious Stirlings, past the drawing room, the salon,
and a second sitting room, until she came to the library. The door was open and a fire leaped and crack-
led in the fireplace. Beyond a huge mahogany desk sat
Lord Stirling, his dark head bent over a stack of
papers.

"Your breakfast, my lord," Mollie said quietly. As
always, her eyes went with envy to the walls of books
that filled this room. Father O'Malley's carefully hus-
banded little library at the rectory would be lost in
here, and she wished for the hundredth time she might
be allowed to read all these books.

Lord Stirling leaned back with a sigh.

"Ah, that looks very appetizing, Mollie," he said,
smiling. Though he was forty, with silver at his temples, and had been a widower for four years, he was
still virile, and his eyes were quick and young. Still
smiling, he added, "And so do you, my dear."

Surprised and disturbed, Mollie curtsied. "Thank
you, my lord." She turned to go.

"Don't go, Mollie. I want to talk with you."

She halted warily. That was what Clan O'Connor
had said, and in much the same tone. And she had
feared Lord Stirling was going to scold her regarding
Horace! Cook's expression had promised as much.

"Come," he said warmly, "and pour my tea for me. I
haven't thanked you properly for curing my chills and
fever with your magical leather bag of medicines."

Silently she poured his tea, then stepped back politely.

"You do that so gracefully," he said, his voice rich
with feeling. "Your speech is excellent, Mollie. In fact,
you speak like an English lady." With a laugh, he
added, "Better than many in London's drawing rooms."

"I had an excellent teacher. He studied in England at some of the best schools before he became a priest."

He looked at her over his cup of tea, his black eyes unreadable. Then, setting the cup down, he said, "Mollie, I have a letter here from my good friend, Assistant Secretary of the Treasury, Charles Edward Trevelyan. He has asked me to come and help him handle the relief measures for Ireland in this time of crisis. I must go to Whitehall in London and assist in administering the distribution of food to those here who are starving because of the potato-crop failures."

"Then you'll be leaving soon?" Mollie asked politely.

"Yes. Trevelyan says the worst is yet to come, and the Relief Commission needs my services."

"I'm sure they do," Mollie replied, unable to keep an edge of anger from her words. "I hope your assistance will come in time to save all of us."

"*You* shall certainly be saved, Mollie." He spoke earnestly, and his smile was winning. "Trevelyan has charge of hundreds of tons of government grain. Since I am familiar with Ireland and its problems, I should be able to see that such relief comes swiftly and surely."

"That's very kind of you, my lord," Mollie said. "As you know, the crop failures have rendered our people unable to pay their rents, and there are evictions everywhere—yet I learned only yesterday that corn and other produce are being shipped *out* of Ireland."

"That's true," he said ruefully. "'Tis a strange paradox, and something must be done about it. I propose to do it. And I am forgiving *my* tenants their rents until this crisis is over."

"That, too, is very kind of you, my lord." Mollie concealed her sarcasm with a smile. "Will that be all, my lord?"

He set his teacup down again and said slowly, "No. That will not be all. I understand my son Horace has been ... giving you trouble."

Mollie's eyes widened. Cook *had* been talking. Of course. And Andrew had caught Horace kissing Mollie out by the stables too.

"Nothing I cannot deal with, my lord," she said cautiously.

"You're much too good for my son," he said roughly. "He's a wastrel and a great disappointment to me. I sent him packing back to London before dawn this morning."

"I'm sorry, Lord Stirling." Mollie hid her relief.

"Don't call me my lord or Lord Stirling again, Mollie. My name is George."

She looked at him in astonishment. No servant ever addressed his lordship by his given name. Her feeling of relief fled. What had Chance Delanty said? Something about gallantry being a man's desire to protect a woman against any man but himself.

"I can't do that, my lord," she said positively.

"But you will—eventually, my dear. I'm going back to my residence in London next week, and I propose to take you with me. Not as a servant but as a companion." He looked at her with gleaming black eyes. "The companion of my heart. You shall have all the beautiful clothes you desire, and you will move in society as a lady. As my mistress, all of London will be at your disposal."

She was stunned. Disgusted first by the fumblings of the son, now she was frightened by the authority and resolution of the father. Looking back, she remembered the times he had observed her closely, the times he had caught her cool hand with his fevered ones during his illness two weeks earlier, the calculation that had been in the polished black eyes.

"My lord, what you suggest goes against all my religious training. I cannot do it."

"The hell with your priest and his doleful admonitions! I offer you a life of excitement, more money and food and fine clothing than you can dream of. Put your religion out of your mind. It's only a set of rules made by men who haven't the guts to live life to its fullest." His voice was convincing and ruthless.

He rose from the desk and came to her. Mollie stepped back, but he followed quickly and took her shoulders in his hands.

"Don't flinch, my dear. I shall not rape you—though I'd like to. Still—I can wait until we reach London. How soft and warm your shoulders are. Mollie, you fire my blood. You have from the first day I laid eyes on you."

He put a hand under her chin and tilted her face up as he bent his head. His lips went warmly and wetly over hers. His breath was bad, and she shrank away. The pressure of his lips increased and she pulled back.

"You are so sweet, Mollie, so young! I must have you!" He was breathing heavily as he caught her to him again.

"I will not do it," she said resolutely, but a new fear had invaded her, and her own breath was quick. She knew how powerful this man was and how far-reaching his influence, and she knew it with a certainty that filled her with desperation. She forced herself to breathe evenly and marshal her thoughts.

Without moving from the man's embrace, as one of his hands moved over her breasts caressingly, she spoke with false calm.

"Will you not give me a few days to consider your proposal, my lord? The wonderful opportunity you offer is so unexpected."

He released her and stepped back. "Good. You're talking sense now. I'm not closing the manor, but we leave next Monday morning for London. I will stay there just long enough to get my instructions from Whitehall before we return. We will have to be in Ireland frequently, so you will see how well cared for your aunt and cousin will be." He laughed suddenly as he sat down again to his tea. "What a stir you'll create among the lords and ladies. So beautiful and so young! Not to mention that astonishing talent you have for cures."

"I may leave now, your lordship?"

"Yes, my dear—for now, at any rate. It will be a great diversion to present you to London society. If I don't miss my guess, you will be the sensation of the season."

He was still chuckling as she left the library. Back

in the kitchen, Cook looked at her, relishing what she
was about to say.

"Master Horace left fer England three hours ago, so
ye won't get ter take his breakfast ter him."

"So his lordship told me," Mollie replied, careful to
hide her agitation. No one must suspect what had occurred in the library.

Disappointed in her reaction, Cook said sullenly,
"Meantime wash them dishes there."

Mollie saw Lord Stirling once more that day, when
she helped serve dinner in the great dining hall. He
sat alone at the head of the long, polished table, and
she kept her eyes down as she moved about him.

Once, when she placed a bowl of soup before him, he
let his hand slide across hers and up her arm.

"My dear," he whispered. "My darling—"

She did not draw back, nor did she look into his
searching black eyes, and she concealed her shiver of
real terror.

But during those long hours of the day, turning her
hand to each chore Cook ordered her to do, she made
her decision. Her position in Arderin was impossible
now. She must leave. There was no other way.

When she stepped out into the chill, damp evening
carrying a basket of food, the threat of more rain was
still upon the countryside. She walked swiftly and
nearly ran through the copse when she came to it. A
cart was rumbling by, driven by an old man, and she
took care to walk beside it all the way to Kate Brannigan's cottage.

Rose was feeling better. Her fever had left and her
throat was not nearly so sore. She remarked cheerfully
that she would be able to go to work the next morning,
and later she ate a hearty supper.

Mollie was extraordinarily quiet, for her thoughts
were racing madly. Chance Delanty's voice echoed in
her ears: *My offer still stands. Think about it, Mollie.*

Well, she had thought about it, and she had formed
a plan that would keep her honor intact and permit

them all to escape. If she could just convince Chance Delanty...

This time Tim welcomed Mollie into the warm Delanty cottage. They had all just finished another good supper, and the tantalizing smell of coffee hung in the air.

Tim caught her hand, pulling her in. "Sure'n 'tis the prettiest girl in all Ireland! Come in, come in, Mollie darlin'!"

He stooped, planting a swift, audacious kiss on Mollie's cheek.

"Oh, you!" Mollie laughed and pushed him away.

Benjie, not to be outdone, rose from the table in a flash and caught Mollie's arm. His lips brushed her chin upward, almost touching her lips.

"Now, you two let Mollie alone!" Bet admonished her sons as she took Mollie's cape from her shoulders. "Sit down, darlin'. Yer too late fer supper, but there's still some coffee in th' pot."

"I've had supper, Bet dear—Oh, but I *would* like some of the coffee!" She felt Chance's intensely blue eyes on her, but she did not glance at him. Instead she smiled at his brother, a tall, thin man with gentle brown eyes. "Hello, Ben," she said. Then she let herself look at the man who dominated the room. "Hello, Mr. Delanty."

"Mr. Delanty?" Chance's black brows lifted in mock surprise. "After drinking my coffee twice, don't you know my name, Mollie?"

"Chance, then," she answered, accepting the steaming cup from Bet. "Actually, Chance," she went on coolly, "it's you I came to see."

He laughed aloud, and she knew he was remembering her words: *I hope never to see you again!* She felt the blood rise to her cheeks as he answered.

"I'm honored." His voice was tinged with irony.

"I'm glad you feel that way," she said, taking the chair Ben had pulled up for her at the table. Mollie looked directly at Chance and finished, "I have a business proposition for you."

"Business proposition?" The drawling voice held interest.

"Yes," Mollie said, coming straight to the point. "Yesterday you offered to lend me the money to leave with all of you for the New World, and I told you I wouldn't be an object of charity. I will not take a loan from anyone, not knowing when or how I could repay it."

"You made that quite clear," he replied briefly.

"But I have thought things over since last night," she continued. "I propose that Aunt Kate, Rose, and I go with all of you to Dublin, where you and I will go to the magistrate and I will become indentured to you for whatever sum of money it will take to buy our passage and see us to the New World."

There was dead silence in the room. It was finally broken by Bet's protest.

"But, Mollie! A loan is a business proposition—"

"We have no assurance that I could pay back such a large sum in any set length of time," Mollie cut in. "But an indenture for a specified length of time is like cash in hand. I will owe Chance nothing. My indenture will cover the entire amount."

"How long do you propose to be indentured to me, Mollie?" His eyes narrowed; his rugged face was inscrutable.

"How much will it take to get the three of us to wherever your Captain Gallagher is going?"

"Counting what it will cost to keep you in Dublin until we leave, and after we arrive in Galveston, it shouldn't come to more than a thousand dollars. What do you propose to do for me as an indentured servant?"

"What is that in pounds?"

"Roughly two hundred and fifty. You didn't answer my question."

"If I'm not mistaken, you have a large farm in the New World and a house as well. You must have people who work for you there. I could help Bet keep house and take care of any who become ill. And that's all I can offer. How long would it take to be worth that much money?"

"I think a year should do it."

"If you think that, then we'll make a bargain of it— for my housekeeping and for my services as a doctor and midwife," she said firmly.

"It's enough. I have a large staff employed on my ranch, as you will see when we get there. Ministering to their ailments would take care of your debt—"

"Not debt!" she flared. "Those indenture papers will be just the same as cash in your hand. I'll owe you nothing but service!" With a tremor in her voice, she added, "How soon do you mean to leave? Could it be tomorrow?"

"Why the hurry?"

"I have reason good and enough. I don't want to go back to Stirling Manor."

"But, Mollie, why?" Bet asked anxiously.

"Lord Stirling means to take me to London with him next Monday," Mollie said flatly, "because I cured him of the ague. He wants my—he means to use my knowledge of medicine—and I cannot leave Aunt Kate and Rose." It was not all a lie, but Chance shot her a shrewd look, and she knew he was not deceived.

"That's reason enough," Bet said indignantly. "I had almost made up my mind, but that settles it. But I have to pack, little though there is. I propose next Monday, only four days—"

"I hope we can be long gone before then," Mollie said, desperation edging the words.

"You could work one more day," Bet said slowly, "so as not to let him know what you plan—an' ter give me a bit more time."

Mollie said swiftly, "Rose will be well enough to go tomorrow. She can tell them I've caught her fever and cannot be there tomorrow." Then with greater urgency, she added, "Bet, we *can* be ready to leave by Saturday, can't we?"

"I'll guarantee it," Chance drawled. "And before dawn too, if Bet will do as she says—" He broke off with a humorous glance at his sister-in-law. "She's only just now actually said she would go."

Bet sighed heavily and murmured, "I knew from

the minute you came, Chance, I'd have ter go. I've known we must leave Ireland for more than a year now. Or die here."

Mollie drained the last of her coffee and rose. "It's agreed then?" she asked Chance, holding out her hand.

"Agreed," he said soberly, taking her small fingers in his. Once again Mollie felt a powerful jolt. She withdrew her hand quickly. She must guard against these feelings for the next year. But she had fought off Clanahan O'Connor's advances—with a little help. She had put Horace Stirling off, and she had held Lord Stirling at bay—so far. She could do it with Chance Delanty.

It shouldn't be too hard, she mused, since she disliked the man personally. He was far too arrogant, too authoritative, too sure of himself—all qualities that irritated her beyond measure despite his physical appeal.

"I'll be leaving now, dear," she said, dropping a kiss on the narrow white streak in Bet's black hair. "I must tell—no, I must pursuade Aunt Kate and Rose yet. I have told them nothing of my hope for all of us to escape."

"'Tis glad I am that ye'll be wi' us," Bet said simply. "'Twill make leavin' easier fer me."

Mollie took her cape from the peg on the wall and swung it onto her shoulders. But as she reached the door, Chance Delanty was there with her.

"I'll see you home," he said.

"No." Her response was quiet but adamant. "I'll be quite all right."

"I think not. I'll see you home." His voice was low as he added, "After all, you have more than one reason to leave Ireland, Mollie."

She said nothing, but called good-bye to the others and swung hastily out the door, Chance close on her heels. He shut the door behind them as she hurried ahead. He caught up with her but did not take her arm, which relieved her.

"You're a smart woman, Mollie." There was the usual hint of amusement in the statement.

"Believe me, I meant what I said to you," she replied bitterly. "If there had been any other way, I would never lay eyes on you again."

"Yet you're willing to work for me for a year."

"That's all it will be—work. You'll keep your hands and your kisses to yourself! There'll be no repetition of last night's insult."

"Insult?" He laughed. "Why, Mollie, I meant it as the most honest of compliments. I find you irresistible."

"Insult. I don't like you, Chance Delanty. And I never shall. Furthermore, I expect you to treat me as any other lady. I want no more of your so-called gallantries."

"I won't ask you what happened at Stirling Manor with the mighty lord himself, Mollie. But I have a good idea that he didn't want just your services as a doctor." His voice was quiet and grim, which surprised Mollie. She had expected more mockery. "When I said you were a smart woman, I meant that choosing to run before he could force you was your best way out."

She said nothing, but her feet slowed perceptibly.

"In fact," he went on, "with Clan O'Connor in pursuit, as well as Lord Stirling and God knows who else, I'd say you're boxed in here, as well as certain to starve." His voice roughened, "But what makes you think there's safety in being indentured to *me?*"

She stopped in the gloom and looked up at him squarely. "You're Bet Delanty's brother-in-law, and she has long said you were an honorable man—that she trusts you."

He made no reply, and in silence they arrived at Kate's door. She did not thank him for his offer to take her and her kin with him—she would pay for that. And she did not thank him for seeing her home. But she was keenly aware of his nearness and ready to dart out of his reach at any moment.

As she put her hand on the latch, she braced herself for his attempt to kiss her again. But he made no move toward her. Instead he spoke low and rougher still. "You're a fool to trust me, Mollie O'Meara." And he turned to stride away.

* * *

She leaned against the door after she had closed it, breathing unevenly as she puzzled over the last few moments. Well, she had as good as said she trusted him! And why hadn't he tried to kiss her again? There had been no respect in his drawling voice—only a huskiness that filled her with uncertainty. She realized suddenly that Rose and Aunt Kate were regarding her with curiosity.

"What is it, Mollie?" Rose asked. "You look so strange."

"Did ye get us eggs this time?" asked Kate, ever practical.

"No," Mollie said tensely. "I did not get us any eggs. I arranged passage for the three of us to go to the New World. We leave day after tomorrow."

The two women stared at her incredulously. Rose was the first to speak.

"Mollie! How could you arrange that! It takes money—a lot of money! Where could you ever get that much?"

"And why?" Kate put in flatly.

"We're going with Bet Delanty and her family. Her brother-in-law, Chance Delanty, is taking them so they won't starve here. And he's taking us with them because I'm going to pay him for it—as soon as we get to Dublin."

"Why?" Kate asked again, her green eyes narrow and penetrating.

"Because Lord Stirling wants—*will* take me to London with him next Monday." She could not bring herself to repeat his lordship's offer, but she did not need to, for Kate's eyes widened with shock. Rose's mouth made a small O as she, too, realized the implications of Mollie's statement.

"Rose, you will go to work tomorrow and tell them at the manor that I am ill—that I caught your fever. And Aunt Kate and I will pack all our things. Chance Delanty will arrange for our departure before dawn on Saturday. I dare not go back to the manor or linger in

Arderin. Lord Stirling might change his plans and leave before Monday."

There was a long silence as Mollie removed her cape and hung it near the fireplace, then stood with her back to the low-burning peat fire and looked into the white faces before her.

"I know," Aunt Kate said slowly, "we'd starve wi'out ye, but how will ye pay fer our passage? An' get th' money to keep us before we get there an' after?"

"Chance Delanty and I will go to the magistrate in Dublin," Mollie said clearly, "and I will indenture myself to him for one year." At their obvious dismay she added swiftly, "I'll work on his—ranch, he calls it. He has many people working for him, and I shall tend the sick and help Bet keep house." She hesitated, then added hopefully, "They say there are many jobs in Galveston, and you and Rose can work there until I can join you at the end of my year of indenture."

"And I had so hoped ye'd marry th' young Stirling—" Kate began, but Mollie cut her off.

"Lord Stirling has sent him back to London—and his suggestions to me were the same as his son's, only Lord Stirling has the power to enforce them," Mollie said bitterly.

Kate looked at her for a long moment before saying in a hard voice, "Then it's go to the New World we will, an' th' divvil take his lordship an' his fat son."

Mollie smiled faintly. "So you'll both do it with me?"

"Of course we will," Rose said quickly. "But 'tisn't right for you to pay our passage. We should each pay—"

"Chance Delanty has no need for so many to keep his house in—in that new state. Besides, you and Aunt Kate can save your money when you work, and perhaps at the end of the year we can start our own bakery—and I can practice medicine there too. People will be able to *pay* me."

The die was cast. She, Aunt Kate, and Rose would leave Arderin with the Delantys in less than twenty-four hours.

* * *

Rose went to work at Stirling Manor with the story of Mollie's illness, primed to lie all the way. As soon as she left, Mollie and Aunt Kate began to gather up their meager belongings. They would have to be put in bundles, one for each of them, with a strap about each bundle. Mollie took out the precious medicine pouch she had inherited from Sister Maria Theresa and put it next to her small bundle. The fine leather bag contained little pockets filled with medicines and potions in pottery vials, a steel probe, clamps, and a scalpel, as well as small leather sacks of dry ingredients. A priceless legacy!

Even now, Mollie could see the good sister vividly. Her little black eyes brimming with life in her finely wrinkled olive face, she had said, "Use the morphine for pain sparingly, my child. It brings deep and healing sleep, but too much can be fatal."

Bet Delanty came over in the early afternoon, bringing coffee and sugar with her. She was full of news and chattered excitedly as they put a pot to brew over the fire.

"We're all packed—an' Chance went out today an' found a horse an' cart. It belonged ter a family who live two miles from Arderin and who were about ter be evicted fer not payin' their rents. They were so thankful fer the money Chance paid them. Now they can meet their rent fer a few more months."

"Then we're goin' in a cart?" Aunt Kate asked in relief. "I was thinkin' we'd have ter walk all the way ter Dublin."

"I did too, at first, Kate, but Chance says walkin's too slow a way ter travel. Th' horse is skinny but sound, he says. He's bought some good grain fer him, an' the critter's perked up a lot."

"How long will it take us to get to Dublin?" Mollie asked anxiously.

"Chance says two, maybe three days, if it doesn't rain so heavy like it's been doin'. Chance says we go through Kerry first. Then Mountmellick, an' after that Kildare, then Droichead, Naas, Tallaght, an' finally

Dublin," Bet finished, proud of her knowledge. "I made th' trip wi' me pa once when I was fourteen."

"An' have ye told anyone good-bye?" Kate asked.

"Chance says not ter do that," Bet said firmly. "Everybody's havin' such a hard time, 'tis better we go quietly." Her voice fell as she added, "So many have disappeared—so many have died."

"I'm glad our departure won't be known," Mollie said in relief. "I'd hate for Lord Stirling to follow—"

"Chance thought o' that, Mollie darlin'," Bet interrupted quickly. "If he should, Chance says he'll tell his lordship yer indentured ter him." Bet's smooth brow puckered as she added, "He says he's a citizen o' th' United States, now that th' Republic o' Texas has joined up wi' thim. His lordship couldn't do anything ter an American citizen an' his property."

His property, Molly thought ironically. Well, that's what she would be. He would buy her for a year. She added farsightedness to his other annoying characteristics, but she felt a smart dart of relief.

Molly slept fitfully that night, and she knew the same was true of her cousin and aunt. Long before dawn, they were all three up and dressed, drinking hot tea made with the last leaves in the tin box. The brew did not warm Mollie. Her hands and feet were still cold. She would not feel safe until they were miles down the road toward Dublin. Only when they were aboard ship would she feel beyond the reach of Lord Stirling.

Suddenly they heard the squeak of unoiled wheels and the quick, soft plop of a horse's hooves on the muddy road.

"They're coming," exclaimed Rose, rising from her chair and picking up the stub of the lighted candle.

The noise stopped suddenly outside the Brannigan cottage. The three women gathered up their small bundles and went to the door. Rose put her thumb over the candle, plunging them into blackness as Kate opened the door before Chance Delanty could knock.

"Glad to see you're ready," he said briefly as the

three women filed out, closing the door quietly behind them.

In the gloom Mollie could see a large, square cart. The Delantys were seated in it, surrounded by their bundles, which rested on the straw-covered floor.

Greetings were whispered as Chance took his seat on the box. Ben sat beside him, and the twins were seated on the straw just below and behind the two men.

As she pulled herself up to a seat beside Bet, Mollie sent up a fervent prayer that the old cart would last all the way to Dublin. Rose and Kate joined her, and they whispered among themselves. But a sad silence fell over them all as the horse pulled the cart forward over the worn road. They were leaving their homes and the land that they held dear. They would never return.

Chapter 3

Dublin was a gray city under a cloudy sky. The cobbled streets were filthy. Horses, drawing an assortment of vehicles, splashed muddy water upon passersby, and the riders in the Delanty cart shrank together to avoid getting even wetter.

Mollie looked up into the lowering sky and saw, tantalizingly, a forest of tall ships' masts in the harbor. A wind off the Irish Sea struck at them between the buildings as they drew nearer the harbor. Mollie pulled her old woolen cape tightly about her under the piece of oiled leather Chance had given them. She snuggled her leather medicine bag against her, but still the wind found her. No one spoke, so miserable were they.

The cart rumbled along more slowly as a dray filled with lumber clattered by. Mollie peered out and saw they were about to stop before a building with two large, mullioned windows and a bright red sign above them. It read Mulloy's Harbor.

It was the supper hour, and through the windows Mollie could see men and women inside laughing, eating, and drinking from big pewter tankards. Her mouth watered, for none of the travelers in the cart had eaten since the evening before—they had given every scrap of food they had carried away with them to the starving children they had passed. Now Mollie's stomach was crying for food, and she felt a little giddy.

"I'm going to let you out here at Mulloy's place," Chance said over his shoulder. "Ben and I will go on and stable the horse. We'll all eat here, then go to Connally's Inn to stay until the *Sea Nymph*'s ready to sail."

"Thanks be ter the blessed Mary," Bet breathed as she scrambled from under their cover and was helped to the cobbled street by her two strong sons.

"Indeed, thanks be," echoed Kate as she, Rose, and Mollie followed Bet.

As the cart started to rumble away, Chance called out, "Tell Mulloy I'll be along shortly," and he and Ben were carried away over the cobblestones toward the forest of ships' masts.

The rain grew heavier, and Mollie turned swiftly to the others saying, "Let's get inside—quickly!" The twins moved ahead of her to open the door.

Mollie, Rose, Bet, and Kate streamed inside, clutching their bags. Warmth and the fragrance of hot food enveloped them, making Mollie's empty stomach grumble. A few diners looked up briefly, then fell to eating and talking together once more.

The place was not very large. A prematurely bald man stood behind the bar slicing a long loaf of bread on a wooden tray. His small black eyes darted to them coldly. Beside him stood a woman near his age. Her hair, under a small white cap, was black and her merry eyes a bright blue. She smiled at them.

Mollie returned the smile, thinking how they must look like a pack of drowned rats. Her companions were shaking their long, wet skirts and untying the damp scarves about their heads. The twins slapped their dripping hats against their equally wet breeches. The innkeeper approached, scowling.

Kate, Rose, and Bet shrank back, slightly intimidated, but the twins began to look more belligerent as the man drew nearer. Mollie lifted her chin and stepped forward to meet him.

"We were told to look for Mr. Mulloy," she said in her clipped, almost British voice.

"Yer lookin' at 'im. What d'you want?" he asked truculently.

"We're Chance Delanty's kin. He said to tell you he'll be along shortly," Benjie said roughly.

"He says we're ter eat here," Tim added.

The man's face underwent a remarkable change. A warm smile and twinkling eyes completely transformed his forbidding mein.

"Come in, come in!" he said jovially. "Chance told me afore he left last week he'd be bringin' ye back wi' him ter sail ter th' New World. Come, I've a large table at th' end o' th' dinin' room."

As they followed him past the other diners, silence fell on them briefly while Mulloy talked about Chance.

"Ah, many's th' barrel o' white flour an' cask o' pure cane sugar me friend Chance has brought me." He continued as they seated themselves around the table. "Why, th' big warm robe me wife an' I sleep under cold nights is a buffalo skin he brought us. Kitty"—he turned to the woman with the merry smile who had followed him to the table—"these here is Chance's kin. He'll be comin' himself soon—where is he?" he asked, and Bet spoke up.

"He an' his brother Ben have gone ter stable our horse an' cart."

"Ye've come all th' way from Arderin, then? I didn't know he had so many kin there."

Mollie looked at her aunt and cousin and knew her face was pink. But Mulloy went on without waiting for an explanation.

"This is Kitty Mulloy, me wife an' helper. Kitty darlin', fetch them all a cup o' coffee, an' put a good dollop o' our best whiskey in each. They look as though they could use it. Here, ladies"—he gestured to Bet and the other three—"gi' me yer capes an' we'll hang 'em by th' fireplace in th' kitchen. They can dry while ye all eat."

In minutes they were all sipping the whiskey-laced

coffee and the warmth and fragrance of the room were soaking into them. The hot drink hit Mollie's empty stomach with a blessed heat that spread to her finger-tips. Her eyes watered slightly, but she smiled reassur-ingly at Aunt Kate, whose face still mirrored her uncertainty.

By the time Ben and Chance Delanty joined them, Mollie's apprehensions and discomfort in her wet gar-ments had eased considerably. She was able to do full justice to the roast mutton, stewed apples and carrots, and thick slices of unbuttered bread that were spread before them.

Mulloy apologized for the lack of potatoes, butter, and a sweet for dessert, and he complained bitterly about conditions in Ireland. Mollie, eating her first hot supper in days, scarcely heard him. But she was star-tled into awareness when she heard the end of Chance's explanation of the large number of his rela-tives.

"No, Bob—that one is Mollie O'Meara, to be inden-tured to me, and that is her aunt, Kate Brannigan, and her cousin, Rose."

"Chance, I didn't know ye bought indentures." There was surprise and faint disapproval in Bob Mul-loy's voice.

"I don't, ordinarily." He shrugged his broad shoulders. "But Miss Mollie insisted on it—to pay for passage for the three of them to the New World."

Mulloy's brow cleared. "Ah—that I understand. 'Tis the Irish pride, ye know, Chance." His eyes twinkled at Mollie. "An' 'tis well ye can gi' her work enough ter pay for such."

"There'll be work for her," Chance replied, helping himself generously to the mutton. "'Tis said in Arderin she's a fine doctor as well as an expert serving maid. I suppose I've bought myself a good thing."

Mollie would not look up from her plate. It angered her that they should speak of her thus. She felt their eyes on her, and a slow, hot blush suffused her face. She heard Chance's laugh as he turned the talk to the *Sea Nymph.*

"No, Bob, I don't know yet when we're sailing. Captain Gallagher's supposed to take on a load of tin in England before he comes back here for his immigrants."

"Sure'n he's a fine man, yer captain. How many will he be carryin' back wi' him from here this time?"

"Two hundred, he said."

"An' who was actin' first mate fer him while ye fetched yer people?"

"Timothy Brennan. And he'll take over as first mate when we reach Galveston. As I told you, I'll not be back after this trip, Bob—I'm staying with my ranch for good this time."

"'Tis a sad thing fer us that we'll not be seein' ye once in awhile. How long have ye been Gallagher's first mate?"

"Five years now, and I've hauled all the things I needed to make my place home to me. I've been roaming the seas and America since I was seventeen and fought at San Jacinto. I saw Texas become a republic. For eleven years I've been working for the day I could become a rancher—that's long enough."

Mollie, listening, realized there was more to the man than she had thought.

When they left Mulloy's Harbor, the rain had ceased, but the night sky was filled with scudding clouds, and a strong wind whipped at the women's skirts. Their capes were nearly dry, and it did not seem nearly so cold as it had when they'd first rumbled into Dublin.

There was little light from the houses along the street they trod, but Chance strode along confidently as he shepherded them to a large inn near the quay. Mollie knew the sea was not far away, for she could smell the salt air, wet hemp, and fish. Finally Chance pushed open a door and they trooped into Connally's Inn.

Connally himself met them, acting as friendly toward Chance as Bob Mulloy had been. In a short while the women were in a large room that held two wide beds. The clean smell of fresh straw in the mattresses filled the room.

That night Mollie slept beside Rose. Hers was a deep sleep, but she dreamed a dream that was to haunt her for days afterward.

She was back in her room in the Brannigan cottage, which was familiar and warm. She lay in the bed she had always shared with her cousin, but Rose was not beside her. The cottage was empty except for her. She was wondering where her cousin and aunt might have gone when the first sense of uneasiness struck her.

Then all at once, Chance Delanty appeared at the bedroom door. She could see him quite clearly, though it was deep night. She opened her mouth to cry out, but no sound came forth, and a frightening weakness overcame her.

In her dream, she pushed herself up on her elbows and was unable to move further. Chance approached, his towering form blotting out the background of the room. He smiled an endearing, heart-catching smile, and his teeth were white and even in his sunburned face. He wore no hat, and his broad chest was bare but for a mat of black, curling hair across it.

She shrank against the rough straw mattress, her movements slow and languid. Then all at once his big, hard hands were on her body.

Immediately she was stunned by the realization that she was naked. The knowledge sent a fluid desire through her limbs. His hands slid upward, warm and sensuous, dry and strong, to touch her upthrusting breasts, and she was sharply aware of her nipples tightening under his fingers. She could hear his quickened breath. She could smell his hard flesh—clean and warm.

Then he was over her, his weight crushing her, and she realized that he was naked too. She was sinking into a warm sea of desire. She could not breathe, so violent were the sensations sweeping her...

She awoke with a wild cry, perspiring and trembling, and sat bolt upright in the bed beside Rose.

Rose's hand was on her shoulder, shaking her gently. "Mollie, whatever's the matter with you? You've been carrying on like someone possessed! Are you ill?"

"No." Mollie's reply was muffled by her hands. "'Tis a nightmare I had, Rose. A terrible nightmare."

By then the two women in the other bed had been roused and were murmuring sleepily.

"'Tis nothing, Bet, Aunt Kate," Mollie said swiftly. "Go back to sleep. I had a bad dream." She lay down again, but Rose remained sitting upright. After the two older women had settled down to sleep again, Rose whispered to Mollie.

"Mollie, what was it? You're still trembling. Don't you want to tell me about it?"

"It was only a dream, Rose. I can't even remember what I was afraid of now." *If only she could wipe it out of her mind so easily!* she thought as Rose lay down beside her.

The window beyond them showed a clear night sky. The wind had blown all the clouds away, and stars winked brightly, reassuringly. Tomorrow would be a bright and fair July day. But how could she look at Chance Delanty again? He had invaded her mind and left her with a sense of intimacy with him that filled her with confusion.

She lay awake until dawn streaked the sky, afraid that if she slept again the dream might return. She wished now she had never laid eyes on him. But then she would still be in Arderin, and Lord Stirling would be trying to do in reality what Chance had done to her in her dream! She felt no gratitude, only animosity toward her benefactor.

Looking up at the paling sky, she thought, *Today I will ask him to take me before the magistrate and have the indenture papers drawn up. Then I shall owe him nothing. I will do his bidding for one year. After that I will go to Galveston to live with my aunt and cousin, and I will never see Chance Delanty again.*

At the thought her spirits rose. "Wake up, sleepyhead!" she called to Rose. "It's going to be a fair day!"

* * *

Mollie felt good as she and Chance left the magistrate's office. A bright, hot sun glinted off the Irish Sea and shone warmly on the quickly drying landscape.

She had signed the indenture papers, which were tucked into a leather folder Chance carried in his pocket. A thousand pounds, she thought, with grim satisfaction. It was just the same as if she had given him a thousand pounds.

She was alarmed and dismayed when, soon after they had joined Bet, her aunt, and her cousin at a table in Connally's Inn where they were having coffee, Chance pulled out the leather folder and handed Bet twenty pounds.

"Bet, I want all four of you to buy something besides those twice-turned dresses you're wearing, something sturdy enough to make the voyage between here and Galveston."

Bet looked at the money and then at her brother-in-law. His browned face showed impatience, but there was concern in it as well. Suddenly he smiled wryly. "You can pay it all back, Bet," he said coaxingly, "by being my head housekeeper. I've talked with Ben and the boys, and you'll be glad to know they've decided to buy the fifty acres downriver from me. They're going to pay for it by working at my place. Between the three of you, I'll wind up owing *you*."

"It's very good of ye, Chance," Bet said slowly, looking down at the bills. "Come, girls—we'll look through th' shops o' Dublin fer something' pretty!" Her voice was touched by excitement.

But Rose and Kate were watching Mollie, who was frowning. She looked directly at Chance, her eyes stormy.

"Go with them, Mollie," Chance said before she could protest. "Don't worry, I'll keep a careful record of every penny I spend on the three of you." He patted his pocket. "You've paid for it."

* * *

When they returned to Connally's Inn they were tired, but pleased with their purchases. Each woman had two new dresses, new slippers, and two new sets of chemises. Mollie looked down at one of her new purchases, a blue sprigged muslin dress with a white ruffle around its square neck.

"Put it on, Mollie," Rose urged. "Aren't you going to wear it to supper? 'Tis almost evening now. I'll wager Ben and Chance and the twins will be knocking on our door any minute."

Mollie wore the blue dress and put her hair up with the contents of her last purchase, a box of hairpins. The dress accented her bosom and her dark-lashed blue eyes.

"Let's go downstairs an' have tea while we wait fer th' boys," Bet said. "I've just four bob left—more'n enough fer th' four o' us!" Her blue eyes twinkled, and her smile was irresistible.

They were seated in Mr. Connally's dining room, where other people were coming in to eat, when the door was flung open and Mollie saw Andrew, the coachman from Stirling Manor, staring about the room. She shrank back in her chair, but Andrew's sharp eyes had already found her. Oddly, he turned and the door closed behind him.

"Mollie"—Bet sounded puzzled—"wasn't that th' coachman fer Lord Stirling? He looked right at ye—"

"Yes." Mollie rose quickly. "I—I'm going back to our room. Tell the twins to come for me." She moved swiftly around the table.

"But ye haven't finished yer coffee!" Aunt Kate protested.

"I'm afraid Andrew's come for me, Aunt Kate," Mollie whispered.

"Jesus, Joseph, an' Mary!" Kate gasped, rising to her feet. "He wouldn't dare!"

She broke off as the door was flung open so hard it banged against the wall. Several diners paused and looked up from their tables.

Lord Stirling stood in the doorway, cape flaring, black brows drawn, and his eyes went over the room like dark lightning. Behind him stood Andrew.

Mollie, frozen beside her Aunt Kate, could only stare at him in shocked fear as he strode forward. Reaching the table of women, he made a courtly bow, then smiled at them all.

"Good evening, ladies—and Mollie. You do look very fetching in that new blue dress. Come, you and I will return to Stirling Manor where you belong."

"I can't do that! I'm indentured to Chance Delanty for one year, and I'm going to the New World." Mollie struggled to maintain her composure.

"You are going to Stirling Manor, my dear," he said imperturbably. "I'll buy your indenture from—who is it? Delanty? For twice what he paid for it."

"You can't, I tell you! I'm going to the New World."

Everyone in the room was silent and watching. Lord Stirling's hold on her arm was like iron as he propelled her, struggling, away from the table. Bet, Rose, and Kate followed, protesting.

"Don't create such a disturbance, ladies—Mollie," Lord Stirling commanded imperiously as he and Mollie approached Andrew, who held the door open for them. "You know very well Mollie and I are going to London this week. We've just time to return to the manor and pack."

"How'd ye find us?" Kate cried desperately, trying to slow them by putting a hand on Stirling's arm.

"Take your hand off me, madame," Stirling said contemptuously. "Your neighbors, the Meeghans, told Andrew about the Delanty man visiting his brother and that you were all gone by Saturday morning. I've ridden two horses down getting here. Aren't you flattered, Mollie?"

By now he had pulled her from the room and Andrew had hold of her other arm. Two horses were hitched to the post in front of Connally's Inn. Awed by the presence and authority of Lord Stirling, no one in the inn had moved to help her.

"You will ride on the saddle before me, Mollie. I don't trust you to ride alone."

With a swift movement he hoisted her up onto the horse. She immediately slid off on the other side, crying, "You can't do this! I'm indentured! I must go with the man who bought my indenture. I will not go with you!"

Andrew turned to her and, before she could draw another breath, he had heaved her back up on the horse. Lord Stirling had mounted, and he threw one arm around her like a steel band.

She screamed piercingly as Lord Stirling wheeled the horse about. In the middle of her second scream, she saw Ben and Chance Delanty, followed by the twins, rounding the corner of the inn.

"Ben—Chance—help me!"

Annoyed, Lord Stirling struck her hard on the side of her head, hissing, "Shut your mouth, Mollie O'Meara, or I'll have you whipped when I get you home!"

But Mollie tore herself from his grasp and fell to the cobblestones. Lord Stirling's horse, alarmed by the commotion, reared suddenly, and Mollie rolled away to escape the hooves which came down perilously near her. From a safer distance she saw Chance reach up and pull George Stirling from the saddle. The twins and Ben jerked Andrew off his horse.

"Who the hell are you, and what are you doing to Mollie?" Chance asked, holding Stirling's arms in a viselike grip. "Answer me."

"I will," Lord Stirling said with icy pride, "when you let go of me, you ruffian."

Chance released the man's arms from behind him but held one in an iron grip. "You'll tell me before I let you go."

"I am Lord George Stirling, and I have come for this woman. She is part of Stirling Manor. She is a runaway servant."

"A runaway?" Chance ejaculated. "You don't own your servants, you fool. She quit your employ and she's indentured to me."

"I'll pay you twice—three times what you paid for her indenture."

"It's not for sale, Stirling. And your influence counts for nothing with me. I'm an American citizen. You have no authority over me and what's mine."

"What's yours?" Stirling said viciously and clearly. "This woman's been mine for six months. She's shared my bed with me, accepted my favors, and she's going with me to England as my mistress."

Mollie went white with shock. Dimly she realized that her aunt, cousin, and Bet stood open-mouthed in the door to the inn. Ben and the twins looked up from where they held Andrew as they heard this cold statement that carried an imperious ring of truth.

"You're lying!" she said hoarsely, pulling herself up from the cobbled street. She made no attempt to brush away the dirt that soiled her new dress as she repeated, "You're lying about me—I've done nothing but work in the manor!"

"Why, my dear," Stirling said, sneering, "I didn't know you considered those lovely hours we spent naked together in my bedchamber as work!"

"I spent no hours with you," Mollie strangled with fury on the words. She could not continue, for rage and terror mingled to choke her. Dear God, what if Chance believed him and turned her over to him?

"Get on your horse, Stirling, and get back to your manor," Chance said roughly. "Whether she's been your doxy or not is nothing to me. I've bought a servant, and I'll keep her." He gave the man a shove toward the horse, which shied nervously.

"You can't take her!" Stirling's aristocratic face was suffused with fury and frustration. "I will take her back with me! I *will*, by God!"

"You won't." Chances voice was cold and granite hard.

"I'll thrash you, you scoundrel." And he lashed out at Chance with his fist.

Chance moved aside, adroitly, and his right fist struck Stirling's jaw with a resounding thud. The man went down hard.

"Your lordship—your lordship!" Andrew cried, struggling against the twins. "Don't lower yourself to brawl with a common foreigner! The wench isn't worth it—and you've already had her!"

Stirling struggled to his feet, his icy composure regained. He dusted off his cape and hat meticulously.

"You can let my servant go," he said sharply to the twins. "And he is quite right. There's no need to exchange blows with a lowborn colonial, since the girl has been mine for six months. Keep her, Delanty. I find my taste for her is gone. Her stupidity is monumental."

He took up the reins to his horse and mounted with only slight difficulty. The twins released Andrew, who straddled his horse with less grace than his master.

Mollie, no longer frightened, was boiling with rage at George Stirling's lies. She brushed the dirt from the new blue dress with trembling fingers, her anger increasing as she turned to see the knowing, cynical expressions on the faces of the strangers.

Rose darted to her and began helping her brush off her skirts. "What a beast that man and his coachman are," she said vehemently. "What lies! I was there with you every day, except the day I was sick, and I can *prove* they lied!"

"It doesn't matter, Rose," Chance said, taking her arm and Mollie's. He glanced at his brother and the twins. "Get Bet and Kate and we'll have dinner at Mulloy's."

It was a miserable supper. The food was good, but Mollie barely picked at it. She was sick at heart. The subject of Lord Stirling was carefully avoided. There was no opening during which she could protest her innocence. Rose was the only one who looked directly into her eyes. Except, of course, Chance Delanty, and he met her glance even when she was trying to avoid it. There was a gleam in his eyes that disconcerted her. They brought sharply to mind the terrible intimacy of her dream, and she found herself studiously avoiding his gaze.

All the while, they were discussing the *Sea Nymph*. "She's in England now," Chance was saying, "but the captain said he'd be here no later than July fifteenth."

"That bein' so," Ben said to his younger brother, "when d'ye think we'll sail fer th' New World?"

"I'd guess no later than July seventeenth, Ben, but I can't say for sure. I've talked to several men on the quay, and they tell me the immigrants have gathered from far and near. Some poor souls are sleeping in doorways and under bridges while they wait."

"Ach! It makes me want ter ask them all ter Mr. Connally's place," Bet said sorrowfully.

"My dear Bet, even Mr. Connally couldn't accommodate two hundred guests. There are several times that many anyway, waiting for the *Mary Ann* and two other vessels to sail."

"An' where's th' *Mary Ann* goin'?" Benjie asked.

"To New Orleans," Chance replied. "The other two schooners are headed for New York and Boston. They'll be leaving in two more days with all they can crowd aboard." His voice was deep and contemptuous. "I know Captain Rigg and Captain Welch. Their vessels each well deserves the name of coffin ship, for they arrive with the dead and dying in their holds, bringing the fever along with them."

"An' what does it mean—Texas has been annexed, as ye say?" Ben asked.

"First, it means that Mexico has suddenly decided to ignore the fact that Texas fought for and won her independence. They're laying claim to it, saying it's always been a part of Mexico, though we've been the Republic of Texas for ten years."

"Doesn't that mean a fight?" Tim asked slowly.

"It does if Mexico starts a war. But we won't borrow trouble, Tim. Let's wait until we get home and find out what's happened over the last few months." Chance's eyes were veiled as he answered his young nephews, and Mollie, even in her concentrated misery, surmised that he was not telling them all he knew.

The others were talking and eating with relish, and Mollie eyed them coldly, but they did not notice. As they were filing out of the tavern, Chance drew up close behind her and spoke low. "Cheer up, Mollie. Who cares what such a bastard says? He'll not be troubling you again."

She made no reply.

"Doesn't it comfort you a little," he said with a touch of mockery, "that there will be thousands of miles of water between you?"

"There has never been *anything* between us!" she whispered with violence. "That's the whole point. He's a vicious liar—and so is his coachman. They said those things to shame me because I would not accept Lord Stirling's loathsome advances!"

The others, going before them, suddenly grew quiet, and Mollie knew at once that she was protesting too much.

"Of course they lied," Chance said, raising his voice so the others could hear. "All of us know that."

Bet looked over her shoulder at the two of them. "Mollie darlin', don't fret yerself over the likes o' them two. Put yer mind at ease about it an' be thankful Chance was here ter save ye when thim two would've carried ye off to th' manor, certain as death."

"And it would have been death," Mollie said with a shudder, "for I surely would have died before I went back."

They were all silent as they walked in the cool evening air back to Connally's Inn. The sun was setting over the water, leaving a trail of glittering red gold on the blue sea. Connally's Inn was right next to the quay, which was still a busy place at day's end.

When the four women reached their room, three began to make their evening preparations, but Mollie stood leaning against the closed door, watching them narrowly. Kate was the first to notice her gaze. She straightened slowly and said to her niece, "Well, Mollie darlin', ye know we don't believe it. An' even if 'twere true, ye were runnin' from it, which earns God's forgiveness for any sin."

Rose crossed the room and put an arm around Mollie. "Ma, Bet—I was there all the time Mollie was and we worked! We worked like slaveys at Stirling Manor, and Mollie *never* did anything for or with that lying Lord Stirling but cure him of the ague. I swear it!"

"I believe ye, Rose," Kate said. "It's a lie, but it's one o' thim things that leaves a dirty mark. Others heard it, and they'll not know it's a lie. 'Tis like soot from th' chimney—it sticks."

"I believe ye too, Rose. I know Mollie too well to put stock in such a rumor," Bet said, echoing Kate's belief.

"I don't care about the others," Mollie said vehemently. "I just want you and the Delanty men to know it's a lie." Most of all she wanted Chance Delanty to believe it was a lie, and of that she would never be sure.

"Ye know Ben an' our twins don't believe it! Why, Mollie darlin', we've watched ye grow up, an' a more honorable girl we never saw."

"Well," Mollie said slowly, "I just wanted to make sure you believed me. We won't speak of it again."

The following morning all of them had breakfast together at Connally's Inn, and a very good one it was too, for a land in the grip of famine. Money will buy anything, and Chance Delanty has the money, Mollie thought. Still, she did full justice to the repast, including two cups of tea and two pieces of toast. Afterward, the men went to the maritime offices on the quay to see if there was word of the *Sea Nymph*. The women went back upstairs to attend to their own chores.

After washing her hands and repinning her hair, Millie announced she was going out to watch the activity on the quay. She left the room and made her way out into the bright sunshine.

She rounded the corner of Connally's Inn and all the quay lay before her—the many ships with their tall, slender masts, the busy activity on shore. One vessel was boarding passengers, mostly gaunt emigrants. She walked on past Connally's and stopped two buildings down before the windows of a shipping office where some sacks of grain were stacked. There was a very good view of the harbor from there, and she sat down on a sack of feed to watch the pipers, clad in faded green shirts and shabby but jaunty hats, who were gathering to play the voyagers off.

Sitting there, she had been watching for about an hour when she heard her named called by a deep, familiar voice. Turning, she was surprised to see Clanahan O'Connor, well turned out and approaching her with long strides.

"Mollie!" he exclaimed again, dropping a large bundle onto the cobblestones. "I thought ye'd already be gone on yer way ter th' New World! The Meeghans told th' whole town yer family had left wi' th' Delantys like thieves in th' night! Old Lord Stirling was turnin' th' town upside down lookin' fer ye!"

"What are *you* doing here?" she asked shortly.

"Granny died th' day afore ye left, God rest her soul, an' Sean an' I had nothin' left ter hold us. We sold th' farm ter Fogarty fer some absentee landlord in England and divided th' money between us. An' we decided ter leave fer th' New World too. Where are all o' ye bound?"

"Galveston, in Texas," she said coolly. "I suppose you've decided to take passage on the *Sea Nymph* too?"

A faintly secretive look came over his face, and he said with a touch of bitterness. "No, I'm leavin' on the' *Mary Ann* wi' all those other poor creatures ye see yonder. 'Tis New Orleans we'll be sailin' ter, in a state called Louisiana. Sean, though, he's takin' passage on th' *Sea Nymph.*"

"You aren't going together?" Mollie asked, surprised.

"No. I want ter get away as soon as possible, an' I want ter leave on th' first vessel out. I'm impatient. Sean's th' one who takes his time. Besides, he wants ter farm when he gets there, an' I want adventure afore I settle down ter farmin'." There was a harried look to him that puzzled Mollie. For all his new clothes, there was something about him that reminded her sharply of the weary people she had seen on the road, hunted and longing for escape.

"It seems strange that two brothers, so close in age,

don't go together." She spoke with newly found compassion.

But a shutter fell over Clan's light blue eyes as he answered. "We just happen ter have opposite views. Th' price we got fer the farm in Arderin wasn't a fair one, but it was enough fer each of us ter make a new start."

"I'm glad for both of you," Mollie said sincerely.

"Louisiana's right next ter Texas, Mollie. Maybe I'll be seein' ye again." This last was hopeful, a strange note in the voice of so handsome and assertive a man.

"I think not."

"Now, Mollie darlin', ye know yer th' only girl in th' world fer me. I've loved ye fer months now, an' ye know it!"

"I know you took a great liberty with me." Her voice went cool again.

Clan looked quickly around and then said in a low, impassioned voice, "I wanted only a kiss, Mollie. One ye'd give me yerself. Love shouldn't go unrequited. I intend ter make ye love me one day." His voice grew urgent. "I know we've *got* ter meet again—someday. I swear ye'll come ter love me!"

"Clan, every girl in Arderin succumbed to your charm. Why do you set your mind on the only one who didn't?"

He ignored her question. "Since I'm leavin' in just a few minutes, will ye not gi' me one little kiss goodbye?" For the first time, she heard a humble plea in the arrogant voice.

She looked at him in surprise. "But I told you, I don't love you, Clan."

"A friendly kiss, then. Would ye send an old friend, a longtime neighbor, away wi'out a real farewell?" He reached down and caught her hand, pulling her up beside him. "Ye look so fair in that new blue dress wi' th' white ruffle around yer bosom. How came ye by such finery—an how is it you an' yer kin are wi' th' Delantys?"

"I'm indentured to Chance Delanty for one year to pay for our passage to Texas."

"Indentured!" He dropped her hand, his eyes widening in shock. "Ah, Mollie, Mollie," he groaned, "don't ye know that's th' same as *belongin'* ter him? Like his horse, or his house, or a piece o' his furniture." His voice broke, and she saw real pain in his eyes. Behind him the pipers began to play "Danny Boy," and the sweet, plaintive melody came to them on the wind.

Her pity for him returned with a rush. "Not me, he won't, Clan." She caught the hand he had dropped to his side. "I promise I'll not belong to him! And I'll give you a good-bye kiss!" she said impulsively.

He caught her to him, but this time he took her face gently with one hand. His lips came down on hers, softly, tenderly at first, then with increasing fervor.

Unbidden, Chance Delanty's image rose before her, and for a moment Clan's warm mouth was Delanty's mouth and the weakness was on her once more as her arms crept about his shoulders.

"Well, now," a mocking voice came from behind her. "I can see you'll not be needing me to pull him off you this time, Mollie."

She tore herself from Clan's grasp and whirled to face Chance.

"No, I'll not!" she said defiantly. "'Twas merely a good-bye kiss to a neighbor. Clan's leaving on the *Mary Ann* in just a few minutes."

"I'm glad to see you're friends again—I seem to remember you, Clan. You've a brother who looks much like you. Sean, I believe," Delanty said, surprisingly friendly.

"Yes. He's goin' on the *Sea Nymph* with all of yer group. An' I remember you, Delanty. We're of an age, but ye left when ye were a broth of a boy."

"That I did, and got caught in the middle of a war for my pains."

"Which ye won, we heard. Ben told us ye were in on the winnin' side and were paid off in acreage—the size of which I find hard to believe."

"You can believe it. But that was all I received. Texas never had any money to speak of—only debts. And now that we've been annexed to the United States,

Mexico's talking war again. You're lucky to be going to Louisiana, away from the fighting that will likely develop."

"I'm goin' to find me fortune—be it Louisiana or Texas. If I don't find it in one place, I'll find it in another. Mollie tells me she's indentured to you for a year."

"That's right."

"I'll tell ye now that I love her—an' I'll be comin' fer her eventually." The old arrogance was back in Clan O'Connor's voice.

"If she'll have you," Chance said with equal authority.

"I'll see that she does."

"I have something to say about this!" Mollie burst out. "I'm going to work for Chance for a year, and then I'm going to be independent. Marriage couldn't be further from my mind. I'll make my own way!"

Both men laughed, and Chance said mockingly, "You were born to be married, Mollie. You'll come to realize it one day."

"Thanks for the good-bye kiss, Mollie darlin'," Clan said warmly. "Ye've sent me off wi' somethin' sweet ter remember, an' ye can be sure I will remember it." He picked up his heavy bundle by its strap and slung it over his shoulder. With a wave, he headed toward the *Mary Ann,* where the last of the stragglers were boarding the vessel.

"Where are Ben and the boys?" Mollie asked abruptly, feeling awkward.

"Getting some new breeches and shirts."

"Ah, but you *are* generous, Chance Delanty!" she said sarcastically. "It must give you a great feeling of superiority to dole out money to your poor relatives—*and* the even poorer members of your party."

"It gives me satisfaction. Most especially because I know I'll get my money's worth. I always do."

"You'll certainly get it from *me!* I shall give you expert service with those who fall ill and with cleaning and cooking in your house!"

"But not with kisses?" he asked lazily. "It seems to me you pass those around rather freely."

"How can you say that?" she stormed. "You saw Clan O'Connor kissing me forcibly and you pulled him off me, for which I've thanked you."

"And Lord Stirling? He never got a kiss? Nor his fat son that Rose told me about?"

"No!" she shouted. "I never gave either of them a willing kiss! And just now I felt sorry for Clan, going off alone. The kiss was something he asked very humbly of me." The fact that she had thought of Chance Delanty all through that kiss infuriated her further. "Good day and good-bye, Chance Delanty!" She turned on her heel and left. But she heard him laughing as she walked swiftly away. She had the sick feeling that he did not respect her because of all the compromising situations in which he had found her.

She met Rose coming out of Connally's Inn as she reached it, breathing hard from her rapid pace.

"Oh, Mollie! Aren't we going to see the *Mary Ann* pull out of the harbor? I had to wait for my hair to dry and then put it up—don't go back in! I do so want to see the harbor!"

"It's time for the midday meal," Mollie said sharply.

"Mollie, has something happened? What is it?"

"Nothing, Rose. Go on and see the vessel pull out. At the American shipping office there's sacks of feed you can sit on quite comfortably."

Reluctantly Rose went out the door while Mollie, still seething, went in. Chance Delanty thought her a wanton. Worse, she was sure he had believed Lord Stirling's accusations.

Chapter 4

Mollie entered the inn, furious with Chance Delanty and the knowing look in his cynical blue eyes. She felt she could not go back upstairs and sit quietly sewing with Bet and Aunt Kate, so she went up to the bar. Connally himself was polishing glasses, and two serving maids in little white caps were stacking dishes in preparation for the noon meal.

"May I have a cup of tea, please, Mr. Connally?"

"Ter be sure, Miss Mollie," Connally said pleasantly. Turning to the maids, he said, "Tottie, you or Kathy serve Miss Mollie a mug o' tea. Go have a seat, Miss Mollie. They'll bring it to ye."

Mollie sat down beside a window that looked out on the quay. The pipers had ceased playing and were taking their leave. All the sails on the *Mary Ann* were unfurled and billowing out as the wind filled them. It was a beautiful thing to see a ship in full sail, she thought.

Tottie appeared with Mollie's tea. Mollie thanked the maid and absently took a sip from the mug, her eyes still on the ship.

"Ain't ye goin' ter pay fer it?" Tottie asked petulantly, sending a glance of wounded dignity to Mr. Connally at the bar. It was obvious that she felt Mollie should, in all justice, be serving her own tea—or, possibly, be serving it to Tottie. As Mollie started to explain that she had no money, the door opened and Chance entered. He took in the situation at once.

"I forgot to tell you, Connally, that if any in my party want service of any kind, food or drink or otherwise, put it on my bill. You know I'm good for it." He walked toward Mollie's table.

"O' course, Chance. It's me own error. I should've known it—but I was told the Brannigans an' Miss Mollie were no kin o' yours."

"True enough, but they're in my party, and I'm paying. Tottie, I'll have a cup too." With that, he sat down across from Mollie.

"Mollie," he said quietly as Tottie left, "if you hadn't been in such a hurry to get away, I'd have told you the *Sea Nymph* will arrive on the fifteenth—day after tomorrow. We sail on the morning of the seventeenth of July."

"I'm glad to hear it," Mollie said briefly, her eyes still on the *Mary Ann,* which had pulled away from the quay. She could see the water widen between it and the shore as a few lonely souls stood waving from the quay. Chance Delanty followed her gaze.

"A lot of hearts are breaking," he said moodily, his eyes on the thin figures watching the ship depart. The passengers who lined the rails of the ship, waving back, could scarcely be distinguished now.

Mollie looked at Chance in surprise. "I shouldn't imagine such things would occur to you," she said bitterly.

"And why not?" If he was stung by her implication, he refused to show it.

"Because you seem much too hardened and cynical a man to know of breaking hearts."

"If taking care of my own appears cynical and hardened to you, I suppose you may be right."

"I think taking care of your own is very commendable. It's your inability to recognize the truth that makes you cynical and hard."

He laughed aloud as Tottie set a mug of steaming tea before him.

"Thanks, Tottie," he said and slipped a coin into her hand. The girl blushed as their hands touched, and she hurried away. Mollie looked after her with cynicism. Chance Delanty was not classically handsome as Sean and Clan O'Connor were. He was bigger and his lean face harder and more rugged. But there was something in his eyes and voice that melted a woman. When he turned back to Mollie, his eyes were twinkling.

"Can it be you are still suffering from your encounter with the quick-thinking lord of Stirling Manor?"

Blood burned in her face as she said, "Yes. I think you believed his lies."

"Doesn't it matter at all that I don't care what he said?"

"Not caring and not believing are two different things."

"Then you want me to care and to believe?"

"I said they were two *different* things!" She set her cup down hard, spilling a little.

He was smiling again, a tender, amused smile, and it reminded her at once—and hotly—of the dream she'd had on the night of their arrival in Dublin.

"Perhaps it will comfort you to know that I think George Stirling is a swine who would do or say anything to get his way."

"He is certainly that. Believe me, I know."

"Then aren't you satisfied to know I don't give a damn what he says?"

Her eyes searched his and she was not satisfied, but she knew she could say nothing that would change him. She looked back out the window. The pipers were gone, and the *Mary Ann* had reached the point where the wind caught her fully. The ship would soon be out of sight.

She drained her cup and rose.

"Are you leaving?" Chance asked, rising with her.

"Yes."

"Then here. Take this newspaper. 'Tis Dublin news and very biased, but it might interest you."

"Thank you," she replied, taking the paper and moving away. She could feel her full new skirts sway gracefully with each movement. In spite of herself, she hoped Chance Delanty was watching. She still tingled from his smile and the touch of his big hand when he gave her the paper. Annoyed by her contradictory feelings, she ran up the stairs.

She was breathing hard when she entered the room. The three women looked at her curiously, and she spoke hurriedly. "I've just seen Clan O'Connor, and Granny died the day before we left. Sean and Clan have sold their farm, and both are leaving for the New World—Clan today on the *Mary Ann* for a city called New Orleans. Sean will be going on the *Sea Nymph* with us."

The three women exclaimed together over the death of the old lady. Granny O'Connor had been a fixture in Arderin as long as any of them could remember. But they were glad for Sean and Clan that they were leaving Ireland, and especially glad that Sean would be on the ship with them to Galveston.

At last Mollie and her companions stood on the crowded quay on the morning of departure. The ship had picked up a small cargo of tin in England and had returned to Dublin to take on Captain Gallagher's first mate, Chance Delanty, and the Irish passengers bound for the New World. The pipers were there too, mingling with the passengers and those who would see them off.

The morning sun shone warm and golden on the emigrants. Even the emaciated and haggard looked hopeful, though some had no baggage at all. Mollie looked down guiltily at her own fat bundle.

Turning, she saw Chance's lean, sinewy body approaching. His mate's cap was tilted at a rakish angle, leaving a shock of black hair on his tanned forehead. His strong hand suddenly cupped her elbow.

"Mollie—you too, Kate, Bet—all of you, come. I'll show you where you're to bunk." Shouldering people out of his way, he led the four women, followed by Ben and his sons, up the gangplank.

"We'll all be together, won't we?" Mollie asked uneasily.

"No, you'll be in separate quarters, Mollie."

"Why?" she asked, bewildered.

"Because I've arranged it so. I have a lot of money invested in you, and I want you to weather the trip in good shape."

"I don't understand!" She was growing angry. She should be with the other three women.

"Sometimes a passenger brings the fever with him unbeknownst to us, and we have a bit of trouble until it's cured. Occasionally, we lose a passenger."

"'Tis natural he'd look after ye first, Millie, after all th' money he's invested in ye," Kate said.

Mollie said nothing, and Delanty steered all of them toward the hold, where a large opening with steps led down into the bowels of the ship.

"Captain Gallagher's just had the hold scrubbed thoroughly with sea water and lye soap, and it's clean as a whistle. Bet, you three pick out your bunks before they let the rest of the passengers on," he told her as the three of them took the stairs down into the dimly illuminated hold.

He turned to Ben, Tim, and Benjie and added, "Most of the passengers will be in the hold. Captain Gallagher doesn't believe in mixing the sexes aboard ship, so women and children are in the fore and men and boys are in the aft hold." With a firm hold on Mollie's arm, he led his brother and nephews around to the aft, where they, too, descended into the faintly lighted depths of the huge, teeming vessel.

As they moved toward the fo'c'sle again, Mollie stopped a moment on the sunlit deck to feel the cool sea wind blowing against her. Unbidden, a sudden surge of euphoria swept through her, and she was hard put not to laugh aloud for joy. Everything was going to be all right!

"Come on—you can come back on deck to watch after I show you your quarters." Chance pulled her abruptly into a narrow, dark companionway. In another moment, he knocked on a rather small door, which opened immediately.

The woman standing there was tall and imposing and dressed in a long, black dress despite the July heat. Though she was beautiful and young—no more than twenty—her expression was grim, and she was so thin her face was gaunt, making her gray eyes look enormous, framed by lashes as thick and black as Mollie's own.

"You're to be my cabin mate?" the woman asked, frowning.

Delanty answered. "She is, Mrs. Moriarty. She is Miss Moyennan O'Meara of Arderin in the county of Leinster." With a touch of amusement, he added, "You'll have many weeks in each other's company. I suggest you become friends."

"Humph," was all the young woman said and turned away. Mollie was puzzled by the woman's hostility. She turned to Chance.

"If you trust your own kin in the hold, why not me? I'm no different!" She was growing angry at being separated from them.

"But you *are* different, Mollie. For a year you'll belong to me, and I take excellent care of my property."

"So I'm no better than your horse, or your house—or a piece of your furniture!" Clan's words came back to her with a vengeance, and her fury mounted.

"If you want to put it that way," Chance responded. "I don't want you succumbing to the fever midway through this voyage. I want my money's worth." Without further comment, he drawled, "Good day, ladies, and bon voyage."

Mollie felt utterly humiliated. She had been told she was nothing more than a bought piece of merchandise before this imperious, cold woman. All her feelings of joy left her, and only anger remained. She

looked about her. There were two bunks in the mini-
scule cabin and as the door closed on Delanty, Mrs.
Moriarty spoke authoritatively.

"I have the lower bed. The upper is yours."

Mollie continued to look around the dark, tiny
space. There was a narrow ladder at the foot of the
bunks that Mollie would have to climb to reach her
bed. At the other end was a small commode that looked
like a chest and doubled as a commode table, for it had
a pitcher and bowl upon it. The cabin was only partly
illuminated by the sunlight coming through the porthole, but Mollie could see that Mrs. Moriarty had a
number of bags and parcels, and there was scarcely
room for her own bundle and the medicine pouch.

Noting Mollie's expression, the young woman said
coldly, "You can put your things in that corner over
there." Even more coldly, she added, "How is it you're
not in the hold with the rest of the women and children?"

Mollie regarded her levelly. "Because the man I'm
indentured to had the money for a cabin."

"Indentured! Ha! I can see why he'd want you kept
from the others—to reserve your favors for himself, no
doubt." Her implication was plain enough, and Mollie's
face grew hot. With an effort she bit her tongue on a
rude rejoinder. It was beginning to look as though the
voyage would be unpleasant indeed.

As soon as she had stowed her bags and neatened
her hair, she turned to leave the cabin. She wanted to
see the ship set sail. She left Mrs. Moriarty, who had
turned back to her disheveled bunk, and made her way
to the upper deck which was thronged with passengers. Her eyes eagerly scanned the crowd, looking for
Bet and her family, but she saw no one except thin-
faced strangers, some hopeful, some desolate, some
dull and uncaring. Intending to wait for her aunt and
cousin, Mollie went to the side of the ship and leaned
against the polished brass that covered the wooden
railing. The ship beneath her strained as the wind
caught the sails, unfurling them fully. A strangely de-
tached feeling overtook her. After yearning for and

imagining this moment for so long, she could not quite believe it was happening at last.

Slowly the *Sea Nymph* moved away from the quay, and the distance widened between it and the shore. A passing sailor with twinkling black eyes said boldly, "'Tis a braw day to start a long voyage, miss. A good omen."

As the motion of the ship increased, some of the passengers paled and made their way down to the hold. But the heaving movement was pleasant under Mollie's agile feet, and she leaned against the rail, breathing the clean salt air. The sound of the pipers faded as the distance grew between the Irish shore and the ship.

Mollie was thoroughly enjoying the sun and wind in her face and the green purl of water below when a man drew up beside her and put his hands on the brass rail.

"I'll be damned—" The deep voice was familiar and held a note of pleasure.

She whirled about and looked up into the blue eyes of Sean O'Connor. Her hand moved slowly to her throat as her mouth opened in astonishment. He looked so much like his brother—they looked more like twins than did Benjie and Tim.

"'Tis the little one—Moyennan O'Meara." Sean's smile was quick and flashed white in the sunlight.

"I—for a minute I thought you were Clan!" She returned his smile. "Though I knew you'd be aboard—Clan told me so a few days ago."

"Then ye've seen Clan?"

"Only for a few minutes. He was leaving within the hour on the *Mary Ann,* bound for a city called New Orleans, in America. I told him it was a pity you two couldn't go together."

"Clan's not ready for settling down, Mollie—he balks at th' responsibilities. Me brother's fer adventurin' a bit." But there was that same closed look in his eyes that had been in Clan's. "Though I can tell ye his heart's set on you, Mollie."

"'Tis a waste," she said lightly, her smile still

friendly, "for I'm not for settling down either, though I'm indentured for a year to Chance Delanty to pay for passage for Aunt Kate, Rose, and me."

"Indentured?" His astonishment was as great as his brother's had been.

Her chin went up. "I'll not be indebted ever again. I pay as I go, from now on. When I'm through, I plan to use my knowledge of medicine and live in Galveston with my aunt and cousin. They'll find work as soon as they arrive, we're told. Why haven't I seen you in Dublin town, Sean?"

"I just got in last night. I had ter stay an' see things properly settled afore I left. Clan was so impatient he came on ahead."

Sean leaned near her, his hands on the rail beside hers, where they touched lightly.

"I'm sorry about Granny O'Connor," Mollie said softly.

"'Twas an easy goin'—she died in her sleep. Clan stayed for th' burial next day. I told him ter come on—I'd take th' next ship out fer Texas. There's so much talk of it since Chance Delanty came back for his kin—an' yers too, it seems."

Someone spoke behind them, and Mollie immediately recognized the husky, appealing voice of Chance. "Then you didn't make the *Mary Ann* after all, O'Connor. Welcome aboard."

Sean and Mollie turned to face the speaker, and Chance's brows drew together. "Ah—'tis the brother. Sean, isn't it?"

"Yes. I remember you from years ago, Chance, when we were all sixteen an' you were th' only one with th' spirit ter leave Arderin. We should have done th' same then."

"It's not too late, Sean. Your brother will find New Orleans a fair city. I've been there several times. And you'll like Texas. What are your plans?"

"Me brother an' I sold our farm—I've me half o' th' money wi' me, an' I hope ter buy some land in Texas an' raise potatoes. Maybe a few cattle an' sheep as well. Though I heard the cap'n sayin' Texas may have ter fight Mexico again."

"The Mexicans will have to fight the United States then, for we're a state in the Union now." Chance smiled at him, adding, "I think you'll find Texas a fair place for your farm, O'Connor. I've a bit of land—a ranch—there myself. On the Nueces River, about a hundred miles from a small but thriving town on the coast." He turned to Mollie and asked, "How do you like sailing?"

"I think it's wonderful," she replied, unable to keep the animosity out of her voice.

"I thought you'd be a little seasick." He laughed.

"Not I," she retorted scornfully.

"No, not you," he said with a touch of sarcasm. Then, with a lift of his cap, he added, "And good day to you both."

The two stood looking after him as he strode toward the bow of the ship, his big body moving gracefully with the sway of the ship. He wore tan breeches that clung to his muscular legs like a second skin. Mollie realized she was staring when she heard Sean's voice.

"Do ye not like yer new master?" There was mockery in Sean's question.

"No, I don't like him," she answered, scowling. "But it's worth it not to be starving and to be on my way to the New World!"

He laughed, and Mollie smiled in spite of herself.

"Sure'n ye'll work out yer time, an' I'll wager Clan'll come fer ye. I never saw him so set on a girl."

"I'll never marry Clan O'Connor," she said flatly.

"Ah, come now! A good girl could tame that divvil of a temper!"

"No, Sean. I care nothing for your brother."

"Ye don't mean that."

She turned away, and the wind whipped the deep yellow skirts of her other new dress. She put a hand to her black hair, which was coming loose. After a moment Sean's voice interrupted her reverie.

"I suppose yer down in th' hold wi' yer kin an' Bet Delanty. Do ye like th' damned hold?"

She looked up, startled, into his smoldering eyes.

"I—no." She averted her face, and her voice was muffled. "Chance put me in a cabin in the fo'c'sle."

"Ye've a cabin? Alone?"

"No, I'm in a very small cabin with two bunks in it—with another woman. A Mrs. Moriarty."

"Meg Moriarty?" His smile was slightly bitter.

Mollie was astonished. "You know her?"

"All in black? Very thin, with great gray eyes?"

"Yes."

"Aye, I know her," he replied briefly. "So ye've a near private bunk aboard th' *Sea Nymph*. It must've taken a deal of money ter set ye up in *that*," he said dryly. "I couldn't buy one wi' a twenty-pound note." With a touch of mockery, he added, "But I forgot. Ye belong ter Chance Delanty fer a year, an' he's first mate."

She was silent for a moment, looking toward the back of the ship. "Is it so bad in the hold?"

"It is if yer used ter being alone as I am," he replied somberly. "If I can do so, I'll be sleepin' on deck th' comin' nights."

"How did you come to know Meg Moriarty?"

His eyes were veiled. "She comes from Sharavogue, other side o' th' Slieve Bloom Mountains. A recent widow."

"How sad. She's so terribly thin—and bad tempered too. But where did you meet her?"

"Clan and I used ter buy sheep from her husband Bill—breedin' stock fer our flock—afore things got so bad. We didn't know her well." His voice was suddenly cold, and Mollie sensed he did not want to discuss the widow from Sharavogue.

Still she persisted. "Yet she evidently has money enough to pay for a berth on this ship. Why didn't she come to Dublin before, where she could buy food?"

"Perhaps when ye come ter know her better, she'll tell ye." There was finality in his words.

"I doubt that." Mollie laughed shortly. "She's taken a dislike to me already."

"Surely ye imagine that, Mollie. No one could dislike *you*." The light note was back in his voice, along with a faint caress.

"No," Mollie replied obstinately. "She doesn't like me."

"I should think her condition might stir yer sympathy," he said roughly. "Near starved an' with a baby daughter ter care for."

Mollie's eyes widened. "A baby? Oh, I didn't know! She didn't say—I didn't see—" She hadn't looked closely at Meg Moriarty's bunk before coming up on the deck. "Why didn't you tell me before this that she had a baby?"

"Since yer sharin' a room wi' her, I thought ye knew it."

"What happened to her husband?"

"He was a deal older than Meg. The last I heard, she found him dead in bed. Likely he starved." He shrugged, then added bitterly, "Near all Ireland is starvin', an' naught can be done about it."

"I know that, Sean O'Connor, better than you think," she retorted. "I'm going back and making friends with her. Perhaps I can get Chance to arrange for a little extra food for her and the baby."

Turning, she left Sean looking after her as she moved swiftly across the deck, her long black locks tumbling down her back and her full yellow print skirts flaring in the strong wind.

It seemed uncommonly dark in the companionway after the hot, bright sunlight on deck, and she made her way cautiously along the corridor, quickly reaching the narrow door that was hers. She flung it open without knocking and stood transfixed by the sight that met her eyes.

Meg Moriarty held a leather sack in one hand, while the other hand counted a glittering pile of gold coins scattered before a little girl who was sitting in the middle of the bunk. It was more wealth than Mollie had known existed. Indeed, they were the first gold coins she had ever seen in her life. Stunned, she realized that the young woman before her possessed a fortune.

Chapter 5

"How dare you come in without knocking?" The young woman's voice was low and menacing.

"This is my room too," Mollie retorted. "I don't have to knock." Her resolve to make a friend of Meg Moriarty dimmed momentarily. Then her gaze went to the pinched white face of the child. She was beautiful, with a tumble of thick, black curls and wide blue eyes. Her pale little mouth was parted in distress at the unfriendly exchange between her mother and Mollie. There was something about the child's features that vaguely disturbed Mollie and at the same time made her heart go out to the thin, big-eyed little girl. For the child's sake she would try hard to make a friend of this sharp-tongued woman.

Mollie said kindly, "It doesn't matter to me how much gold you have, Mrs. Moriarty. It's none of my business, but I should think you would at least buy food for your child even though you choose to starve yourself."

"You don't know anything about it," Meg Moriarty said in a half whisper. "I didn't have this gold until only a short time ago—not in time to feed us. But I shall now." Her gray eyes blazed with defiance.

"I came back," Mollie said gently, "to ask if I could get more food for you and your child. I know the first mate on this ship, and he might be able to get extra rations for you both—until you regain your strength."

"I know Mr. Delanty and Captain Gallagher too—and I've already arranged for extra food until we become strong again."

Mollie ignored her truculence. "What is your little girl's name?"

"Dierdre."

"That's a beautiful name." Mollie smiled warmly at the child, who suddenly held up her arms. Mollie looked at the mother. "May I pick her up?"

Meg was swiftly putting gold coins back into the bag. Drawing the string tight, she said, "I suppose so. She seems to have taken to you."

Mollie reached down and took the thin little body in her arms. As she lifted her up, she realized the child was just skin and bones.

"You're bonny," the child said solemnly.

"And you're bonny too, Deirdre. My name is Mollie, and I'm sure we're going to be great friends. Would you like to go on deck and see the big ocean?"

"Ocean? Water? Oh, yes, yes!"

From the size of her, Mollie had thought she was no more than two, but her speech was that of a child of three or more. Further, she spoke English, not Gaelic. Meg's speech was not only English, but uncommonly good English too.

Mollie looked at the mother questioningly, and Meg nodded her head curtly, saying, "Go on. The fresh air will do her good. I'm coming out shortly myself."

At the door, Mollie paused. "If I were you, I'd put my gold in the safekeeping of the captain, Mrs. Moriarty."

Meg looked at her from under her brows. "I'll keep it with me. I trust no one." And from the folds of her dress at her waist she pulled forth a gleaming knife, nearly a foot long, it's edge razor sharp. It glittered like a flash of lightning in a small pool of sunlight. She smiled cruelly. "Except this."

Mollie repressed a shiver as she went out quickly with the little girl's arms wound around her neck. The child was an enchanting little sprite, but the mother —Mollie didn't know if she could ever break through the wall of anger and resentment the woman seemed to have built around herself, but she vowed to try.

There was more than menace in Meg Moriarty's manner. There was a mysterious aura of violence, and something else about her—corruption? Secrecy? Mollie put aside her thoughts and stepped out onto the deck.

"Ohh," cried Dierdre. "Sooo nice!"

Mollie laughed aloud. "I agree, Dierdre." Her eyes roamed the deck, past the sailors and several men and women who had come up from the hold. Sean O'Connor was still leaning against the brass railing, facing the sea. None of the Delantys were to be seen.

Mollie walked slowly toward O'Connor. Feeling her gaze, he turned and broke into a broad smile. "I see you've made a friend," he said, and walked to meet them, balancing easily with the gentle roll of the ship.

"Have you seen Aunt Kate or Rose or Bet Delanty —any of the others?"

"Not since I boarded. They're probably getting used to it"—his voice dropped and the last word was bitter —"below."

"Hello, bonny Sean," Dierdre said, with the ease of a longtime friendship.

"Hello, Deedee." Sean laughed and reached for her, adding, "I'll hold her while you go below and find your kin and Bet." Dierdre went eagerly into his arms as he added, "We're old friends, Deedee and I."

"Thank you," Mollie said, puzzling over their familiarity. He had said he didn't know Meg well—evidently he knew the family better than he admitted. "Her mother will be coming up shortly. Watch for her so she doesn't worry about Dierdre." And she turned to make her way to the hatch that opened on the hold at the fore of the ship.

The hatch was wide open, and the sea wind was coursing up from the dark depths, carrying the odor of strong disinfectant. Dimly, the sound of women's voices came up to her, mingled with the piping of small children. The clamor increased as Mollie eased herself down the steep steps to the narrow passage between the bunks, row on row that stretched on either side of the hold. It didn't smell bad—*yet,* she thought grimly.

As her eyes became adjusted to the dim light, she saw that lanterns swung on beams above the bunks, but there were few of them and they gave poor illumination. The women and children bending over their crowded bunks working at their baggage, were so busy they did not look up at her. The sound of their voices rose and fell in the dark hold. Several women already lay prostrate on their narrow beds.

"Oh, Mollie, Mollie! Blessed Mary, I'm so glad to see you, Mollie!" It was Rose, rapidly weaving her way between bunks. Behind her came Kate and Bet, who also called her name. The four embraced as if it had been years since they'd last met.

"Ach, me darlin', 'tis so crowded an' all—an' th' light's dim an' Rose is queasy—"

"Hush, Ma. It's not nearly so crowded as the ships leaving for the east coast of America," Rose said reprovingly. "Captain Gallagher and Chance Delanty told us—there's only eighty-five of us in here."

"An' near a hundred children, I'll take an oath," Bet said.

The wind coursing between the two open hatches kept the interior of the hold from being overly warm. Mollie gulped in the fresh air, a sense of imprisonment suddenly sweeping over her.

"Let's go up on deck," she said, putting an arm about her aunt's waist. "It's so much cooler and fresher, and you can see how vast the ocean is."

Rose was clinging to a stanchion, one of the several that stood at intervals along the length of the hold. She swayed with every roll of the ship, her face pale, her hazel eyes enormous.

"I—I can't go up there, Mollie. The rocking of the boat—"

Kate and Bet each took one of Rose's arms and led her back to her bed. Silently, Mollie followed them, wishing she had her medicine bag with her. Rose collapsed on the bunk, clutching her stomach and closing her eyes.

"A cup of strong tea with a spoonful of mint syrup would help," Mollie said, her sense of guilt increasing as she thought of her own semi-private bunk. "I'll fetch it." She hurriedly made her way up to the deck.

In a matter of minutes she had begged a cup of hot tea from a sour-faced middle-aged man in the galley. She darted into her small cabin, which was empty, and poured a small measure of mint syrup into the steaming cup. Within seconds she was on her way back down into the bowels of the ship.

Drawing up beside the supine Rose, her anxious mother, and Bet, Mollie carefully handed Rose the cup.

"Sit up, Rose, and sip it very slowly. Wait awhile between each swallow." Tentatively she added, "I share my cabin with a sharp-tongued widow and her baby daughter. I've made friends with the baby, Dierdre, but the mother, Meg Moriarty, is very unfriendly. 'Tis a small room with only two bunks, and Dierdre sleeps in the lower bed with her mother. I'm to sleep in the upper. I must climb a little ladder to reach it."

Aunt Kate looked at her understandingly. "Ye shouldn't have indentured yerself fer us, child."

"Do you think I could have rested knowing that the ones I love best in the world were starving?" Mollie burst out.

"I'm glad you're not down here," Rose said in a low voice, two red spots on her cheeks. "Don't feel bad about having a cabin above, Mollie," she added with a faint smile. "I'd be as seasick in a palace, were it afloat."

"People don't die of seasickness, Rose," Mollie said gently. "You're going to feel better soon."

"We'll see ye at supper fer sure, Mollie," Bet said hopefully.

"Now you run along," Kate said firmly.

But Mollie did not see them at supper after all. Nor did she see any of the Delantys—except Chance, who merely spoke to her in passing as he went about his duties. The passengers dined in shifts, and Mollie ate before any of the others.

Supper consisted of dried fruit and the contents of four huge pots of dried beans cooked on deck. The food was supplemented with a kind of hard bread the sailors called tack. It was served on tin plates, with a heavier tin spoon. There was even a heavy pottery cup of coffee for each passenger.

After Mollie had finished eating she looked up to see Chance Delanty coming toward her with a large glass full of water, which he held by a handle at the corked top. His strong, muscled arms were bare to the elbow, and she was unable to tear her eyes from the tanned forearms covered with springy black hair.

"It's for you," he said briefly, following her gaze. "Your cabin mate and her daughter each have one and you can have another, provided you don't want it re-filled too often."

"Thank you," she said coldly, but she did not reach for the jug. "Too bad your influence didn't extend to the rest of my family."

"It did. And for my sister-in-law and brother, as well as my nephews. They have water." His deep, husky voice sent an unwelcome yearning through her.

"Then why didn't all of them get a cabin?"

"Have you examined the fo'c'sle closely? There's only one extra cabin there—you and Meg Moriarty have it. The rest is crew's quarters—including mine and the captain's." His smile was winning, and it drew her unwilling gaze. No man had ever sent fire through her veins the way Chance Delanty did.

"Then your influence in obtaining cabins extended only to me!" she said angrily.

"My money extended so far as you." His smile was

gone. "You and Meg Moriarty bought the cabin space for a hundred dollars apiece."

"Blessed Mary! I'll owe you ten years' service by the time we reach America!"

"Not quite." His grin was sardonic now. "I assure you I won't run over the amount specified."

"Rose is very ill. I'm going to offer her my bed."

"You will not," he said flatly. "You will do as I say, miss. And Rose is only seasick—and much better off with her mother."

It was the first order he had given her, and she swallowed hard. He had the papers that plainly stated she would do as he bid. She squared her shoulders.

"Will that be all, sir?" she asked with false humility, reaching for the bottle of water.

"That's better." He was mocking her now. "That will be all, Mollie. Sleep well." After handing her the jug, he strode away.

After she had gone to bed, she consoled herself with the thought that ten days of her indenture were already gone. And tomorrow, she would keep a tight rein on her fears of the hold and go down again to spend some time with Rose.

Still later, she awakened to smothered weeping, great, wrenching sobs that she could not locate at first. Then she realized they were coming from beneath her, from Meg Moriarty. The porthole was open, and the soft, rushing whisper of the sea drew the sound upward, mingling it with the wind.

Mollie pushed herself up on one elbow and listened. Meg had appeared so hard and cold that Mollie found it hard to believe she was capable of such agonizing grief. Such sobs could melt a heart much harder than Mollie's, and her first thought was to climb down the ladder and put an arm about the young widow to comfort her. As the sobs continued, Mollie rose. Perhaps a half teaspoon of laudanum...

She drew back from the ladder. Instinct, stronger than the quick desire to help, warned her that Meg would not welcome her support. There was something strange about Meg. Dierdre was untouched by it, for the child was wholly herself. But Meg harbored something dark and unspeakable.

Mollie lay back down. The anguished sobs lessened slowly, and silence filled the dark room. The waning moon peered in the porthole for a short time, its pale light spectral. The sea wind rushed in, and Mollie shivered. It was a long time before she slept.

"Ho, Mollie darlin'!" Benjie came up behind her the next morning at breakfast. "Ye come an' sit wi' Pa an' Ma an' me an' Tim."

She smiled warmly and took her place beside Bet, who was sitting on the deck. Almost all the passengers who had their meal at this hour—about forty at a time—sat cross-legged to eat, the women with their legs folded decorously beneath voluminous skirts.

"Rose an' Kate will be comin' with th' next batch, darlin'," Bet told her, taking a spoonful of porridge.

"I'm going down to stay with Rose awhile today," Mollie said. "I just hope she feels well enough to come to breakfast."

When the next group of passengers came up, Mollie saw that Kate was with them, but not Rose.

"She's terrible nauseated," Kate said in answer to Mollie's anxious question. "It's worse when she stands up."

"Wait here for me, Aunt Kate. I'm going to fetch my medicine bag." When she returned, both women went down into the hold.

"Rose, didn't the tea yesterday help?" Mollie asked. When her cousin nodded vaguely, she urged, "Then sit up and take a little of the mint syrup. Maybe it will settle your stomach enough to eat. You *must* eat something, or you'll really be ill."

Rose shook her head weakly. "Everything I swallow comes up. Just let me alone. I'll get better or die—I hope."

"Nay," Mollie said angrily. "You'll try to eat later. Now sit up and take this syrup." Rose swallowed the spoonful obediently, and Mollie added, "Lie still, Rose. I'm going to stay with you until the syrup settles."

Mollie and her Aunt Kate sat with Rose for more than an hour. Rose was even able to smile wanly as Mollie rose.

"Aunt Kate, I'm leaving the bottle of mint syrup here. Get her some bean broth, and give her a little of the syrup—not even a spoonful, just a few drops—if the nausea comes on too strongly."

Days passed. Rose did not leave the hold, but Mollie did get her to eat bowls of bean broth. With the syrup and a little laudanum to make her sleep at night, Rose gradually grew better.

Mollie also detected a remarkable change in Meg and her daughter as the days slipped by. There was color in their faces now. They had put on weight and Dierdre showed more vivacity.

One morning after more than three weeks at sea, a rap came at Mollie's cabin door, and Mollie opened it to Rose and Kate.

"Rose! I'm so glad to see you up—and Aunt Kate! You're really better, Rose!" She drew them into the narrow confines of the little room. The porthole, as always, was open, and a cool, fresh breeze poured in through it. Rose lifted her pale face and sighed.

"I still feel sick, but I might as well stand up and die as lie down and die." She handed the pottery bottle of mint syrup and its wooden spoon to Mollie.

Meg and Dierdre had been observing the Brannigan women silently from their bunk. Now Mollie turned to her cabin mates.

"Mrs. Moriarty—Deedee—this is my Aunt Kate Brannigan and her daughter Rose, my cousin."

Meg greeted them curtly, but the baby walked up to Rose and caught her hand, saying, "Wose? Auntie Kate?"

Rose stooped swiftly and kissed the child's cheek, murmuring, "What a little love you are, you wee colleen. Mollie's told me about the fun you two have on deck."

"Let's go up on deck now, dears," Mollie said. She wanted to escape from the dampening Meg, who had been glowering in silence since the women had arrived. "It's such a beautiful day, and the fresh air will do Rose a world of good."

The child, who had been listening, held up her arms. "Take Deedee too, Mollie."

Mollie caught her up in her arms, then paused. "Indeed we will—if your mother says so."

"Go on. Take her," Meg said indifferently. "She's become such a fool about you."

The four of them left the small room and made their way to the sunny, windswept deck.

The weeks passed slowly for Mollie. She saw Chance Delanty often in passing. He always smiled, the heart-catching smile with even teeth that gleamed whiter as the hot sun darkened his face. But his blue eyes remained enigmatic.

Though Mollie returned his smiles grudgingly, she was annoyed by the fact that his presence always quickened her heartbeat. She found she could not shake the unbidden sense of intimacy the dream in Dublin had forced on her. She felt he knew her too well—and there was something in his eyes that proclaimed his skepticism about her avowals of innocence.

Another thing bothered her as well: Meg Moriarty frequently sought out Sean O'Connor to talk. Why their friendship should disturb her Mollie did not know, unless it was the fact that she had admired Sean all her life—and while she was sorry for Meg, she could not like her.

As for Meg, though she no longer cried for such long periods at night, when she did cry, Mollie's heart softened toward the young widow. Meg, in keeping with her disposition, continued to ignore Mollie. Her indifference had ceased to bother Mollie, however, for the growing affection between her and Dierdre more than made up for the mother's coldness.

Mollie saw Meg and Sean together more often, with the child between them at the gleaming brass railing, where they talked in low voices. Yet when Sean sought out Mollie, and he often did so, she made no mention of his friendship with Meg and Dierdre, nor did he offer any explanations.

Early one morning, as August neared its end, Mollie asked Sean when he thought they would reach Texas.

"Chance Delanty told me we ought ter be there around th' first few days of September."

She sighed with relief. Only a few more days! "How are things down in the men's hold now?" she asked. She had noticed that Sean's clothing looked bleached and faded—and very clean.

"It's hell down there when yer used ter th' open as I am—in spite o' all th' cap'n's efforts to keep it clean." His light blue eyes reflected his bitterness. "We're all o' us crammed in like pigs in a sty. I've slept on deck every damn night but fer th' first two. Not even the squalls have driven me back down there."

That would explain his clothing, Mollie thought, looking out at the endless Atlantic Ocean.

Sean broke into her thoughts. "Cap'n Gallagher says we're runnin' ahead o' schedule."

Her eyes widened in surprise. Damn Chance Delanty! He should have told her when they were due to arrive in Galveston and how they were to reach his home in the western portion of the state.

Looking down into her troubled face, O'Connor smiled faintly. "Cheer up, colleen. It's only a few more days."

"No one told me about our arrival time," she said, scowling.

"Ye'd have heard were ye in th' men's hold even a short time. They talk of nothin' else."

Looking up, Mollie saw that Meg and her daughter were approaching in the bright, early sunlight, so with a wave of her hand, she left Sean. In passing, Mollie smiled warmly at Dierdre and in turn received a cold nod from Meg. Dierdre clamored for a kiss and Mollie, bending down, touched her lips to the rosy, dimpled cheek.

It was nearly the breakfast hour. The pots of porridge gave off fragrant steam, and the men tending them stirred them languidly as Mollie passed on her way to her cabin to wash her hands. Once again her thoughts returned angrily to Chance. He *might* have paused long enough to tell her it would be but a few days before they reached their destination!

Chapter 6

As they entered the Gulf of Mexico, the first real storm of the voyage came upon them. Mollie was on deck with Dierdre when she noticed the line of low-lying clouds on the eastern horizon. She thought idly that it might be another of the small late-summer squalls that had blown down on them recently. But before the day was half spent, the clouds covered the sky and rain began to fall heavily. The wind, growing ever stronger, set the sailors scrambling up to trim the sails.

Mollie, who earlier had gone to her cabin with Dierdre, came back alone to watch, standing in the lee of the fo'c'sle. She knew she would get wet running back to the companionway, but the wind was exhilarating, and the swelling sea with white foam breaking over mounting waves hypnotized her. All that water, she thought, and yet I've had little more than a teacupful in the basin to bathe with. Now the sea smelled wonderful, and the rushing air was cleanliness in itself. The black-eyed sailor passed her.

"Better get inside, miss. 'Tis the time o' year fer hurricanes in these parts."

It was very hard now to balance herself, and she clung to the iron trim on the fo'c'sle. Taking a last glance at the darkening sky, she picked up her blue skirts and scampered back inside. She knew a momentary sympathy for the sailors who would have to handle the ship through the turbulent night.

She was fairly damp when she entered the small, dark cabin where Meg sat on her bunk undressing Dierdre.

"Light the lamp, will you, Mollie?" she asked coolly. "It's getting so dark with the storm outside."

Silently, Mollie took down the tinderbox from the narrow wall cupboard and struck fire to the wick. She was about to get ready to retire when a delicious idea came to her.

If only she dared stand outside in that drenching rain and let it cleanse her! Though September had come, the air was humid and warm. Indeed, it was the warmth that made her blue printed muslin dress feel sticky and stale. It probably even smelled bad, she thought wryly, but she was so used to it she no longer noticed. Desire hardened to decision.

Meg looked up but made no comment when Mollie took her soap and left the room again in stockinged feet. The pitching of the ship had increased, but Mollie gave no thought to the danger of going on deck. She held onto the sides of the companionway as she carefully made her way down the short steps to the door. Closing it carefully behind her, she stepped out.

Seeing no one in the blowing darkness, she edged her way around the fo'c'sle and leaned against it, letting the heavy sheets of rain drench her. She gradually grew aware of a dim, phosphorescent light from the boiling sky.

Her clothing and hair were already soaked when she started soaping herself. She lathered her wet head and rubbed her arms, legs, and clothing. She could hear the wind shrieking in the halyars, and twice she almost lost her balance.

It was glorious, she thought joyfully, feeling the heavy streams of rain wash her clean. The wind came from every direction now, tearing wildly at her clothing and hair, and she reveled in it, even though she had to clutch the trim on the fo'c'sle when she was not holding the railing to keep her footing.

A monstrous wave rose up aft and crashed over the entire deck, swirling up above her ankles. It was then she knew her first misgivings. She stood swaying in the driving rain for a few more moments until all the soap had rinsed away.

The waves were storming across the deck with ever greater frequency when she turned to make her way back inside. As the ship lurched, bucked, and turned far over on one side, her misgivings became hard fear.

She was rounding the corner of the fo'c'sle when she met head on the looming figure of a man. His arms came out and caught her before she could spin away. The deep, husky voice was unmistakable as he shouted over the howling storm.

"What the hell—"

Trapped in his grip, she cried, "I was getting clean all over for once—there's never enough water to bathe in! I notice *you're* up here, Chance Delanty!"

"My God, it's Mollie!"

She pulled away from his arms. The dim light revealed that Chance wore no cap, and his hair was plastered to his head.

"You little fool! Don't you know better than to be on deck in a hurricane?"

"At least I'm clean, for the first time since Dublin!"

A vicious blast of wind buffeted her, and he put out his arms to catch her again. The wind was increasing, and suddenly her fear turned to panic. Only Chance's strong arms around her held any safety.

"Mollie—" His voice in her ear was rough and vibrant, and his arms tightened.

Through the chill wetness of their bodies, Mollie felt the warm, vital length of him against her. Her heart began to pound harder, and she knew she should pull away. Yet his arms were stronger than the wind,

and she yielded to their strength and her own hot desire.

In the eerie glow of the storm, he looked down into
her rain-drenched face and suddenly bent his head to
hers. His smooth, cool mouth, sweet with rain, found
her parted lips and fastened there, warming swiftly.
For a long moment they swayed together in the howling wind, with the rain beating down upon them. One
arm holding her, he grasped the iron rail of the fo'c'sle
with his other hand as both of them were deluged by
an enormous wave that crashed over the deck. Had it
not been for his grip on the trim, they both would have
been sucked into the maelstrom of the sea. But their
mouths clung together in a kiss unbroken by the
storm.

It was Mollie who finally turned from his searching
lips and hungrily probing tongue. He had taken his
hand from the rail as the wave spent itself, and now he
caught her round buttocks in it, pressing her against
his own hardness.

"No, Chance, no!" Her cry was feeble against the
raging elements loosed within their bodies and tearing
at them from the sky.

Suddenly he caught her up in his arms and, opening
the companionway door, he entered, kicking it shut
behind him. She was in a turmoil of conflicting emotions as he carried her to the door of her cabin and set
her on her feet.

"I thought you liked it," he said roughly. "Hell, I
know you liked it."

"You're wrong! You took advantage of me—you
forced that kiss on me!" How could she have let him
kiss her when she hated him?

"I took advantage of you," he mocked, reacting to
her bitter accusation. "Like O'Connor did—and Stirling—and who knows about other men?"

"You've a wicked, evil mind, Chance Delanty! I was
kissed by those men against my will. I was kissed
against my will by you!" She stood hesitating at the
doorway, unable to let the matter go. It was quieter in
the companionway, but Mollie was shouting at him.

"Are you unwilling now, Mollie O'Meara?" Before she could answer, he caught her once more against his wet body, more tightly than she had ever been held. Unerringly, his mouth found hers. She was helpless against the wild flood of emotion that shook her. The wetness acted as an electrical current between them, and Mollie was shocked anew at the frightening sweetness of his mouth on hers. No thoughts intruded on this kiss. Delanty filled her mind and every muscle; every vein in her body throbbed with him.

It took her a long moment to gather her strength and tear herself from his embrace. He opened the door to her cabin and pushed her inside with a hard laugh.

"Against your will, eh?" he said, closing the door firmly.

She whirled and swiftly swung the latch, her fury becoming cold rage. As she leaned for an instant against the door, her breath came unevenly and her breasts heaved with warring emotions. She told herself for the hundredth time that she had such an abiding hatred for the man, she did not see how she could serve him for a year as his menial.

Lurching with the violent roll of the ship, she made her way across the cabin. Swaying, she began to remove her clean, wet garments. The ship was heaving so wildly that she had to sit on the rough wooden floor to don her nightgown. She left her wet clothing in a pile on the floor because there was no place to wring the water from them or to hang them without dripping onto the dry bundles that had been tossed around the cabin by the storm.

Turning down the lantern, she attempted to climb the short ladder to her bunk and was flung bruisingly across the room. She crashed against the door, tripping over the scattered bundles. She leaned back against the door as the vessel heeled on its side. Slowly it righted itself, and she was able to make her way to the ladder once more.

For the first time, Meg Moriarty spoke. "Where have you been?" The question was angrier than usual and edged with fear.

Mollie clung to the ladder. "I went up on deck to bathe in the rain," she said defiantly.

"To bathe? You fool! 'Tis a wonder you didn't drown."

"At least I'm clean for the first time on this voyage."

"Little comfort that would be to you at the bottom of the sea."

For the first time it occurred to Mollie that the vessel might be swamped and every soul aboard drowned.

"Dierdre is sleeping through the storm?" she asked softly.

"Yes, thank God. I wish I could, but the sea is so fierce, I must hold her on the bunk." Tentatively and in a conciliatory tone, Meg added, "Why don't you light the lamp again? 'Tis certain we'll not be sleeping until this thing is over."

Mollie staggered to the cupboard and felt for the tinderbox. After several attempts at catching the swinging lantern in the dark, Mollie said, "I can't hold it still long enough to light it. And I could set the ship afire if the oil should spill and catch."

"Be careful it doesn't, then, and keep trying," Meg commanded, though her voice shook.

When at last the shuddering ship remained on an even keel for just a moment, Mollie was able to light the lantern and replace the glass chimney. Light bloomed, revealing the scattered baggage and Meg's gray eyes, wide with fear, her hands on the small body beside her.

"There's no use my trying to climb that ladder and being thrown from my bed," Mollie said, sitting down on one of her bundles, which proved to be a very insecure seat.

"You can sit here by me," Meg said grudgingly. "You can hold to the uprights."

So the two young women sat stiffly side by side, with the sleeping child held on the bed by Meg, until the porthole showed a dim gray light through the sheets of rain that poured steadily over the glass.

"It's dawn," Mollie said tiredly.

"And the storm is still on us," Meg responded dully.

"It's a little less violent though. Don't you think so?"

"No, I don't," Meg said shortly. "It's just as bad as ever. I don't see how we can get dressed—and you know they won't be feeding us anything on deck today." She looked down at her sleeping child. Dierdre stirred and turned her head.

"I hope never to be in another storm like this," Mollie said fervently. "I'm going to dress." She looked down at her sodden undergarments, petticoat, and dress still on the floor where she had dropped them during the night. Then she took her yellow print muslin dress and fresh underclothing from one of her bundles.

When she finally completed dressing, Meg said from the bunk, "And now what do you propose to do, miss? There'll be no breakfast in this weather."

"I'll wait. The storm's bound to stop sometime—and I *know* it's not as rough as it was last night."

"Mama, what's the matter with the boat?" asked Dierdre, sitting up and rubbing her eyes.

"It's a storm, Deedee," Mollie replied, "but it's almost over."

"I'm hungry, Mama. Let's put on our dresses and go eat."

Meg answered sharply, "We can't eat, Deedee, until the storm stops," Meg told her. She added under her breath, "If it ever does."

Mollie pinched the wick in the lantern, putting out the flame, and pale light from the porthole partially illuminated the little room. As they all sat down again on Meg's bunk, Dierdre said again, plaintively, "I'm hungry, Mama."

"You'll just have to—" Meg broke off as a hard rap sounded on the door.

Mollie opened it, and Chance Delanty loomed up before her. His tanned face looked tired and grim.

"Storm's lessening, and we're miles off course. The ship's suffered damage, too. But we're at the edge of the weather, and you should be able to come on deck in a while and eat." His glance at Mollie was sharp as he

asked, "You weren't thrown about—hurt in any way?"
His eyes went to her red lips for an instant, an echo of
passion in his glance.

"No," she said coldly. "Thank you for telling us."

"Don't mention it," he replied dryly, closing the
door.

Mollie stood for a moment, anger and guilt filling
her afresh. Why should she care what this arrogant
man thought of her? As long as he didn't touch her
again, she didn't care what opinion he held . . .

"That man knows you well, eh?" Meg asked with a
shrewd smile.

"He does not."

"I saw his eyes, my pretty—and he *knows* you. No
doubt you'll make him a good serving wench."

"You know nothing of him or of me, madame, so
keep a civil tongue in your head!"

"A good serving wench and a good bed partner,"
Meg finished and laughed. "Don't bother lying, Mollie
O'Meara. His eyes said it all."

Mollie turned her back on the woman, cold with
rage.

Meg's fear of the storm had finally communicated
itself to Dierdre, who sat white and still now, her dimpled hands holding fast to her mother's arm.

"It's almost over, Deedee," Mollie said cheerfully.
"In a little while you'll see the sunshine—and we'll go
up on deck to eat!"

"You give the child false hopes." Meg's eyes blazed
up at Mollie. "It is still storming, Dierdre!"

"No, it isn't, Deedee. It's only raining a little, and
that will soon be over."

In less than an hour, the sun appeared, flooding the
room with a shaft of golden light, and the ship was
riding the waves with its normal rolling motion.

Dierdre cried out at the sight. "Oh, look, Mama—
look at the sky!" She pointed her small finger at the
azure sky that glimmered peacefully through the
sunny opening. "Mollie was right, Mama."

* * *

Breakfast on the wet deck, though late, was almost merry. Mollie noted that the ship had sustained quite a bit of damage. Both main masts still stood, but a smaller one had crashed to the deck, and two timbers that held sails hung in a tangle of rigging. Some of the sails were badly torn also.

Still, everyone was so relieved to be alive that laughter came easily, and no one complained about the porridge and tough bread.

Mollie took her ration and eased through the crowd to where Rose, pallid and frail in the sunlight, sat next to her mother on a coil of rope.

"Were you terribly sick during the storm, Rose?" Mollie asked sympathetically, leaning over to kiss her cheek.

"Aye, Mollie. I could scarcely lift my head."

"An' look at me arms," Kate said, displaying the faint blue spots along their smooth sides. "Tossed about like a cork, I was. We *all* were!"

"Chance Delanty told me this morning we were miles off course," Mollie said abruptly. "There's no telling when we'll reach Galveston."

"I don't care where we are," Rose said with unsteady vehemence. "I just want to go ashore—" She rose and walked toward the rail. The other two followed her. "Just to be off this awful ship—" She broke off abruptly, and said in an awed voice, "Look—look yonder. Is it? Can it possibly be land?"

Mollie and Kate followed her trembling finger, and at that moment a chorus of shouts went up about them.

"Look!"

"'Tis land—"

"'Tis Galveston!"

"Thank God, thank God! We've made it ter Galveston!"

"An' ye thought we'd all die afore we reached it, ye did—"

Families who had been separated most of the time by the captain's edict now clutched each other and kissed in the warm wind. Then they hurried to stare greedily at the distant land.

A long strip of bare white sand glimmered on the horizon. Mollie squinted against the brilliant sunlight and saw that beyond the strip and a small inlet were palm trees and stunted oaks interspersed with huge bushes.

"That's not Galveston," she said slowly.

"How can ye know fer certain, Mollie?" Aunt Kate asked, her voice still joyful. "It *has* to be Galveston."

"No. The storm blew us off course."

"Ah—I can't believe that!" Kate's face was pink and her green eyes flashed with excitement as she caught Rose's hand and pulled her closer to the crowd at the rail. "Come on, girls!"

But Mollie stood where she was, middeck. She knew she was right. The land looked wild and desolate to her—with no welcoming quays or masts, no buildings, no smoke hanging in the beautiful, clear air.

She felt a hand on her elbow and turned to look up into the sun-browned face of Chance Delanty. His sleeves were rolled up above the elbows as usual, exposing his muscular, tanned arms. He steered her along until they reached the shelter of a tall stack of canvas.

"That's Mustang Island," he told her, jerking his head toward the land. "It's part of the Padre Islands. The hurricane blew us well beyond Galveston. And beyond Mustang Island is Corpus Christi, the small town on Nueces Bay I told you about."

Mollie recalled his mentioning the town, but the rest meant nothing to her. "Are we far from Galveston?"

He laughed shortly. "We're better off, you and I—and Ben and his family. The Delanty ranch is on the Nueces River, a couple of days' ride from Corpus. We're even closer to the ranch this way—thanks to the storm. It saves us a longer horseback ride from Galveston."

"But Aunt Kate and Rose are planning to find work in Galveston!"

"They still can. Captain Gallagher is going to put in at Corpus for repairs before he sails to Galveston. The passengers will be here a couple of weeks first. They can get their land legs back and have a change in diet before he leaves. As for you and me, we'll be long gone before the captain heads out to his original destination."

"But I wanted to see Aunt Kate and Rose well settled!"

"Nonsense. I'll give them each fifty dollars. That's enough to keep them until they find work. Galveston's hungry for workers."

"And you certainly didn't tell any of us we had a long horseback ride to your farm—ranch! The twins would've told me if Bet didn't," she said accusingly.

"Ben and the boys and Bet *do* know. I thought you'd talked with them about it. Besides, I thought Sean O'Connor would tell you plenty. He learned everything he could about the country before he came aboard and asked many questions. He knows where we're going and how to get there. And you certainly were with him enough."

She was silent at first, then she said softly, "Sean O'Connor is an old friend. We didn't talk much except about old times in Ireland."

"Old friend?" He cocked a brow and his mouth twisted mockingly. "The way he looks at you is not what I'd call friendly—more like new love."

"It isn't so. Sean's a friend, I tell you!" Her face grew hot.

"Even so, it's plain to see you enjoy his company."

"Of course I do. *He* doesn't think of me as a woman who's fast and loose. He respects me!"

"So you say," Chance replied with sudden indifference. "It doesn't matter one way or the other to me. The fact remains that we have a three-day trip to the ranch. Can you stay on a horse that long?"

"I can do anything I have to do," she retorted, "including working for you for a year."

"Remember, that was your idea, not mine. I would have loaned you the money with only your note for collateral. But you would have none of it. You'd owe no man, and you were almost nasty about it. So instead you chose to be a bondservant, and a bondservant you'll be—and to *me,* miss."

He turned abruptly and left her.

Chapter 7

By late afternoon, the *Sea Nymph* had weighed anchor in Nueces Bay and the gangplank was lowered to the long, roughly built pier. Captain Gallagher stood on the bridge and called all the passengers together.

"Mates, this ship is goin' ter be laid up here at Corpus Christi fer near two weeks. When she's repaired, I'll take all o' ye ter Galveston who want ter go. Fer all o' ye who're short on money, ye can take yer meals aboard me ship like always. If ye've th' money, ye can eat ashore."

At his words, the immigrants reacted like freed prisoners, and most of them were pouring down the gangplank almost immediately. Mollie went to her cabin and stood looking at her baggage irresolutely. Should she find a place to stay the night—before she took up her bundle and medicine pouch? Or would Chance Delanty find lodgings for her? As she stood undecided, a light rap sounded at the door. She opened it to find Rose, Kate, and Bet Delanty, their faces glowing. They all spoke at once until Bet's voice rose above the others. "Mollie darlin'! We're all goin' in ter see th' town—me boys an' their pa have already gone wi' Chance!"

"Oh, Mollie." Rose put her arms about her cousin and swung her around the room. "Do come with us!"

Mollie laughed aloud and, leaving both her large bundle and the pouch on her bunk, she followed them up on deck. Rose caught Mollie's arm as they started down the gangplank. "Mollie, Chance gave Ma and me fifty dollars each to keep us until we find work. He says we can go on to Galveston or find a job here, if we like the place." She sighed, then added, "This town's not half the size of Galveston."

"That isn't sayin' there's nothin' here fer us!" Kate grinned at the three of them.

Bet interrupted to ask, "Ye know that Mollie an' all of us Delantys are gettin' off here, Rose?"

"Yes, Chance told us that when he gave us the money," Rose answered.

"He's taking us by horseback," Mollie said angrily, "to his farm somewhere north of this town."

"I hate us bein' separated by such a distance," Kate said anxiously as the four of them strode across the hard-packed sand on the beach.

"Now, Katie," Bet said placatingly, "Corpus Christi is th' closest town ter his farm—I mean ranch. This is his last voyage, ye know. An' if Texas is at war again"—her voice took on a tinge of fear—"then he's goin' ter fight fer it wi' a man he's told Ben an' me about. He's a Colonel Almonte—Jose—an' he's got a whole troop o' men Chance called guerrilas; they're volunteers fer Texas."

"Go on, Bet," prompted Mollie. "Tell us the rest of Chance's plans. He didn't see fit to let *me* know about any of them."

"It's only that he's known this Almonte fer years. He was fer Texas independence way back in 1835, an' they're good friends."

They were silent for a moment as they entered the town. Then Rose spoke dolefully. "Ma and I will likely have to get back on that dreadful ship and go to Galveston and find jobs."

"An' maybe we won't either," Kate said half to herself, pulling the other three with her to a street lined with buildings and filled with wagons and horses. Scores of people were moving about, each intent upon some errand. An occasional loitering inhabitant leaned against the wooden uprights that stood before the stores. In the distance beyond the last building a cluster of gray tents confirmed the presence of soldiers.

"I bet this little town is growin' like a weed!" Kate said, pleased.

They walked more slowly now along a wooden platform that bordered the stores and office fronts. Lanterns were being lit in some of the stores, and they admired the wares they could see through the windows. They had stopped to look into one store window with an especially tempting display of merchandise when the door opened suddenly. Chance Delanty strode out, a coil of rope over his shoulder and a large package under his arm.

"Ah, there you are, ladies. Ben and the boys are inside, buying saddles. And you'd better watch yourselves, for part of General Zachary Taylor's army has been left in camp here to convalesce. It seems the war with Mexico began last May, after Captain Gallagher and I left for Ireland."

"War!" Mollie said in dismay. "But Texas has been a republic for over ten years."

"I told you," he said. "Mexico now says they've never recognized our independence. So it appears we have a war between Mexico and the United States."

"How many people live in this village?" Kate broke in, ignoring his remarks.

"Roughly, near three thousand right now, madame."

"Don't ye 'madame' me, Chance Delanty! I knew ye afore ye ran away ter th' New World—tall, skinny lad that ye were!" Kate replied tartly.

Bet and Chance burst out laughing. "So you did, Katie Brannigan," he replied in Gaelic. "And you were prettier than a bright red apple then, and feisty too. You haven't changed much that I can see."

"Ah, now, laddie." Kate blushed like a girl, but she answered him in English. "Don't be jokin' wi' me like that! I was only askin' because I thought p'raps Rosie an' me might find work here—make our home in Corpus Christi."

"That's Latin for 'Body of Christ,' Kate. I think that's a very fine omen for all good Catholics." He reverted to his customary deep drawl. "And the town's booming. I think it's a fine idea for you to find work here. You'd be only ninety-eight miles from us."

"And I'd be glad to know where you both are, Aunt Kate," Mollie said firmly, "so I can find you when I'm free."

"An' both o' ye might one day come an' visit us, Rose," Bet said hopefully.

"Mollie, have you any money?" Chance asked abruptly.

"No," she said frostily. "What would I do with it?"

"You may have need of it." He was curt. "Here's ten dollars. I've arranged for all of us to stay at the Cortez Inn—it's the better of the two in town."

"If you keep giving me money, my indenture will run to two years!" she said angrily as he caught her hand and put the bill into it.

"Mollie, don't be a fool," he said with exasperation. "I'm noting down all the expenditures I make on behalf of you and your kin. You three are well under the thousand we agreed on."

"You'd save money if we stayed on the ship," Mollie said obstinately, extending her hand to give the bill back to Chance.

"As my bondservant you'll do as I say, Mollie O'Meara," he said shortly, "and I've said you'll stay with the rest of us at the Cortez Inn." Mollie, mortified at his tone, stuffed the bill into her skirt pocket. His voice was suddenly gentle as he spoke to Rose. "And I know you're sick to death of the ship, Rose. You need the comforts of the inn."

"Oh, I do, I do!" she agreed, "and I'm most grateful to you, Chance."

"Where is this Cortez Inn?" Mollie asked icily, still smarting at his exercise of authority over her.

"Near the end of this street—you'll find it easily. Bet, your husband and the twins and I will see all of you there later. We're buying supplies and horses for all of us." He shifted the coils of rope on his wide shoulder and prepared to leave them, then he turned-back. "And Mollie, don't be tightfisted with that money. Buy what you need for the trip to the ranch."

"And what will I be needing," she asked, "if you're buying supplies and such?"

"Britches that fit you, for one thing."

"Breeches?" echoed Rose and Kate. Mollie stared at him. Bet was silent.

He bowed slightly. "That wounds your modesty, ladies?" He grinned as two soldiers passed and craned about to stare admiringly at the fair women. "It would wound you deeper, Mollie, to have mesquite thorns catching in all those skirts of yours."

"I'll buy no breeches with your money," Mollie said, lifting her chin stubbornly.

He shrugged as he heaved the rope higher on his shoulder. "I'll have all the baggage brought to the Cortez in an hour or so. Until later then, ladies." He smiled at them and swung away.

They stood looking after the tall, broad-shouldered figure for an instant before Kate spoke.

"Well, Bet! Yer brother-in-law's grown into a high-flown Irishman, hasn't he? He doesn't even sound Irish but fer that bit o' th' old language he spoke."

"Now, Kate, he's got a lot on his mind. But Mollie darlin', ye talk bitter ter him, almost as if ye *hated* him—an' yer not an unkind person! Ye've always been such a lovin' little body.

Mollie's heart went out to Bet. "Ah, Bet, dear, if I sound a bit short, 'tis only because I've sold myself to him. I didn't realize how much power over my own wishes that meant he'd have."

"He'll not be misusin' his authority over ye. Not as long as I'm around, darlin'. Ben an' I'll see ter that!" Bet caught Mollie's arm to squeeze it as the little group started once again down the dusty wooden walkway.

The late evening heat was intense. September, thought Mollie, and still so hot! Her throat constricted with sudden yearning to see the green mists of the Slieve Bloom Mountains, and she put the thought firmly from her. This would be her home now, this strange, hot land of browns and tans, of green palms and great green bushes covered with pink and white flowers that sent sweet, alien perfume into the warm wind.

They had passed the Javelina Inn, three stores, and several other buildings that bore such titles as J. Pinckney, Atty-at-Law; Baker's Saddle & Boot Store; Nueces State Bank; John's Barber Shop; Nueces County Land Office; and Mama Sanchez's Bakery before Mollie glimpsed a sign near the end of the street that read Cortez Inn. Across from it was a large building across whose front was the name Sawyer's Stable. Around it was a fence, behind which were more than a dozen horses.

From a block away, the Cortez Inn was an unprepossessing building, only two stories high and rectangular like the old, blocky houses in Ireland. In the fading light the inn looked weathered from the salt air, like the other wooden buildings they had passed.

"With so many places of business, Ma, there ought to be jobs for you and me!" Rose's voice was lighter than it had been in three months. Her color had come back too, and her face was rosy in the twilight. "Ma, did you notice there's a bakery?"

"Indeed I did. An' nobody bakes better breads an' pastries than me—maybe I can find work there!"

Mollie half heard them, for she was thinking of Dierdre Moriarty and realizing how much she had come to love the warm-hearted little girl. She decided suddenly that she would go back to the ship herself to fetch her bundle and medicine bag. Maybe she would see Dierdre again to tell her good-bye.

But in the next moment Mollie stopped dead still, staring at the entrance to the inn. Meg Moriarty and Sean O'Connor were coming out of the door to the inn. Dierdre clung comfortably to Sean's neck as he held the child in one arm. His tall body bent toward Meg as he listened to something she was saying. As usual, Meg appeared dissatisfied and a touch angry.

Following Mollie's gaze, Rose said, "It looks as though yer disagreeable cabin mate is very friendly with Sean O'Connor, doesn't it?"

"Yes," Mollie replied shortly. "She has been the entire voyage. It makes no difference to me."

As Meg and Sean approached, he greeted them warmly. "Ah, Mollie—ladies! 'Tis glad I am ter see ye," he said, smiling broadly as both he and Meg halted. "Ladies, I've decided ter stay here an' buy land up th' Nueces River. Chance Delanty's told me 'tis ter be had cheaply. I'm goin' ter th' land office tomorrow an' buy fifty acres."

"Fine," Mollie said casually, but Bet spoke more warmly.

"Why, Sean, I'm glad fer ye! Rose an' Kate are goin' ter find jobs here too—an' ye know Mollie's ter go up ter Chance's place wi' us."

"We may be neighbors, Mollie." Sean's smile was warm, but Meg looked at her sourly. "Meg an' Deedee have just taken a room at th' Cortez, an' so have I. Are ye ladies goin' ter stay there too?"

"We are indeed," Bet said.

"Good. I'll see ye there later, then. Meg an' I are goin' ter th' ship now to fetch our baggage."

The two moved away without a word from Meg. Mollie gazed after them for a moment, then hurried to catch up with the others who were entering the door of the inn. Behind a counter next to a stairway was a swarthy little man whose black mustache made a sharp contrast to his flashing white teeth.

"Buenas noches, senoras y senoritas! Good evening, ladies. I am Tomas Cortez an' I welcome you to my een." He bowed behind the counter.

"Good evenin'," Kate said. They introduced themselves and explained that Chance Delanty had arranged for their stay at the inn.

"Mucho gusto! Si! I have my bes' rooms reserve for friends of Senor Delanty. He ees one fine *hombre*. I am so glad to serve you." Then, in a steady stream of half-English, half-Spanish praise for Senor Delanty, he took down several keys from the wall behind him and escorted the women upstairs. He installed Bet in the first room and showed the other women to connecting rooms down the hall.

The four women were met downstairs at suppertime by the four Delanty men and an unexpected fifth man. He was tall and slender, and his thick black hair was graying at the temples. Mollie judged him to be about forty. She was struck by his eyes, which were light hazel with black lashes as thick as Mollie's own. He would have been handsome but for the perpetual scowl on his brow.

"Ladies, meet my foreman, Squint Burleson," Chance said. "He got in two days ago to buy staples for the Delanty ranch. He'll be going back tomorrow."

Burleson's clear gaze traveled over them and his scowl deepened until his eyes rested at last on Kate. He gave a curt little nod. Then Ben took Bet's arm and all of them moved toward the dining room.

When the slender dark boy who was Cortez's son seated them at the largest round table in the dining room, Mollie noticed that Sean O'Connor was alone at another table and that, oddly, Meg Moriarty and her daughter were seated at still another.

The Delanty men began talking politics. As they all took their seats, Chance said, "I heard in town from a captain in General Zachary Taylor's army that Santa Anna has again taken control of the armies of Mexico and of the Mexican government."

"An' didn't ye tell us he was th' leader o' Mexico when ye won yer independence in April o' 1836?" Ben asked.

"Hell, yes!" was the explosive rejoinder. "We captured him at San Jacinto! But Sam Houston wouldn't let us shoot him. We bargained with him for Texas independence, and he went back to his government saying he'd see that we got it." Chance spread his hands. "You can see what an unprincipled liar he is. As a matter of fact, he's led Mexico to defeat more than once—"

Cortez's son reappeared and broke in with a rapid flow of Spanish aimed at Chance, who grinned and answered, also in Spanish. Squint Burleson joined in and a three-way conversation followed. When the boy left, smiling, Burleson was laughing outright and Chance looked with amusement at his puzzled relatives. With a wink at Burlson, he spoke to the women.

"I've ordered frijoles and rice, enchiladas, and tamales." Chance grinned at them. "We might as well make real Texans out of all of you tonight."

"Sounds as if it might be too late," Mollie said, "since its status is in dispute. I thought Mexico had agreed to your independence ten years ago."

"Only Santa Anna and a few of his henchmen agreed to it—and you know now what his word is worth." Chance regarded her levelly. "He was the man who massacred a hundred and eighty-seven men at the Alamo and more at Goliad ten years ago."

"I was at Goliad," Squint Burleson said, his cold eyes on Mollie. "I saw it all—an' escaped only because I hid under a dead man. There won't be no question about Texas bein' free this time, ma'am."

"Santa Anna's been in exile in Cuba for a long time." Chance's laugh was grim. "How he got back in power must surely be one of life's greater mysteries."

Everyone around the table had fallen silent, and Mollie suddenly realized how deeply the desire for freedom ran in Chance Delanty and Squint Burleson —and how bitter was their hatred for the tyrant Santa Anna.

Finally Ben cleared his throat.

"Chance, I been feelin' like I was a Texan since ye first come inter me house with yer packs an' bundles an' told us about th' place."

"Hope you don't have t' draw a gun one day an' prove that, Ben," Squint said, still looking at Mollie with such hostility that she was hard put not to squirm.

"Reckon I'm the one who'll do that, Squint," Chance said. "I want Ben to look after the ranch with you while I'm gone."

The twins, who had followed every nuance of the conversation, spoke together.

"If yer goin' ter fight Uncle Chance, we're going wi' ye!"

"I'll take a gun an' go wi' ye, Uncle Chance!"

Bet's hand flew to her throat and she cried out, "Yer too young, both o' ye, ter be talkin' guns an' war an' such!"

"Ah, Ma, we're men grown," Tim growled.

"An' ye know it, Ma!" Benjie added.

"Let's see if you're men enough to eat a real Texican supper, boys." Chance grinned as the Mexican youth and his sister approached the table, carrying trays of smoking food.

The food was delicious after weeks of monotonous shipboard fare, and Mollie devoured every highly seasoned bite. The conversation was cheerful, but Mollie noticed that Squint Burleson conversed strictly with the men. She strained to hear what he was saying.

"—I ain't got no use for wimmen, Ben," he said, but his hazel eyes were on Kate, who blushed under his gaze.

"Ye wouldn't say that were ye a happily married man like me, Squint," Ben said, laughing.

"I ain't goin' to give myself that chance, Ben. Wimmen don't never say what they mean—and they don't mean half of what they say."

"You're a misogynist," Chance said, grinning at his foreman.

"Whatever that is." Squint shrugged.

They had finished the main course of their meal when Chance casually dropped a bombshell. "Ben, I've planned for you and Bet and the boys to go on back to the ranch tomorrow afternoon. Bet can buy the britches and things she needs in the morning—and we've already bought the horses and saddles. Squint has plenty of supplies to feed you for the three-day trip."

The twins were joyous, shouting in unison, "Hurray! We leave termorrow!"

"I'm to go with them, of course," Mollie put in anxiously.

"No, you're not," Chance replied.

"But I *want* to go with them!" Her heart began to bump unevenly. What was this man planning?

"You've already been indentured to me for three months and you haven't done a lick of work. You'll travel with me to the ranch after I've transacted my business here. On the way home you can fry my bacon, make my coffee, and wash up the dishes." He was very matter-of-fact, but those around the table were quiet.

"Besides," Chance continued, "I thought you'd want to see your aunt and cousin well settled in jobs before you left them. I can introduce them to some of my friends in town, and you'll get to see where they'll be working."

"Oh, Mollie—I wish you'd stay," Rose said, as if Mollie had a choice. "I—I—sort of dread going to look for a place. If you were with us—"

"Th' child shouldn't be travellin' alone wi' Chance," Aunt Kate said indignantly. "It's unseemly fer a young man an' a young woman ter travel tergether so far wi' no one else along."

"Why, Kate!" Chance remonstrated. "You do me a great injustice! I'll be a fine chaperone for Mollie—and aren't you forgetting she's indentured to me? If I expect her to serve me, I'm quite within my rights."

"That's true, Mollie," Kate said worriedly. "Ye are his servant."

"And she owes me only nine months' service now, for all I've spent on you three. It was her idea, if you remember."

"That's true, too," Kate said reluctantly. "Ye will look after her, won't ye, Chance?"

"I'll see no harm comes to her, Kate. She'll arrive at the ranch just a few days after Bet and the others, none the worse for wear."

Mollie was silent, her mind in turmoil. Alone on the road with Chance Delanty! A queer little catch in the pit of her stomach made her wary. She didn't want to be alone with this man who had such power over her, power not only over her life but over the wayward emotions he set boiling within her.

The others were talking now as if everything was settled, and Mollie knew with a sinking heart that it *was* settled.

Chapter 8

"Chance says we'll leave at noon, right after we eat," Bet said to her three companions the next day as they walked from the Cortez Inn toward the stores in the cool early morning sunlight.

"Are you really going to buy breeches, Bet?" Mollie asked.

"I'll feel like a goose," Bet replied, "but I'm goin' ter to do it, Mollie. If Chance says I'll need thim things, then thim are what I'll buy."

Kate laughed aloud and Rose smiled. "Mollie," she said, "you'd better buy a pair or two. What did he call those things that can get you? Cat's claws and mes— mes— Some kind of thorns."

"Mesquite thorns," Mollie supplied shortly. "I'll wear skirts."

They reached H. Williams, Merchant, the largest store in town, and Bet pushed open the door. The warm scents of feed and leather mingled with that of new cloth, and somewhere in the mixture was the smell of licorice, new to Mollie and the others. The sweet smell of sugar combined with delicious flavors of grape, cherry, and other fruits. She glanced at the counter beside them and saw a row of large glass jars containing brightly colored candies.

Mollie's interest was then caught by bolts and bolts of cloth lying on several counters toward the back of the store. There were all kinds of materials. Oh, the lovely dresses that she could make from the silks and satins! And what cool frocks the cottons and poplins would make up...

"Mollie, see what's hanging on the wall," Rose said, pinching her arm. Looking up, Mollie saw great leather collars for horses, all sorts of bridles and bits, and metal pieces made to fit on the heel of a boot, with star-shaped spurs at the curve.

There were bolts of lace and barrels emitting tasty sour odors. Mollie lifted a lid to see dark green cucumber pickles bobbing in the liquid. But all these wonders were put aside while Bet received three pairs of heavy twill breeches from a young man with a long, drooping mustache who did not seem at all surprised by her choice.

When the four women emerged from H. Williams, Merchant, Bet had bought three pair of breeches, four plaid shirts, and a pair of sturdy boots, each wrapped in a separate brown paper package and tied with heavy twine.

"How did they feel?" Rose asked.

"How did they look—or did ye not have a mirrer in that little room behind th' curtain?" Kate added.

"They looked like breeches on a lady," Bet said unhappily. "Me shape's not made ter fit such—or p'raps it's th' breeches aren't made fer me shape. Th' boots fit fine, as ye saw—an' felt better."

"And the shirts?" Mollie asked ironically.

"Now, Mollie darlin', don't ye make fun o' yer old friend! Th' shirts fit much better'n th' breeches." She paused, looking into Mollie's brilliant blue eyes, then added reproachfully, "'Tis a pity ye don't see fit ter buy some yerself. Chance wouldn't tell us we needed such if we didn't."

* * *

Mollie did make a purchase before the four women returned to the inn. In a sudden surge of rebellion, she entered an emporium and bought a dark blue sateen dress with a small, round, white collar. It had deliciously full skirts that showed off her tiny waist, and it obviously required the purchase of one more petticoat. There was also a pair of black leather slippers she was unable to resist. When she left the store, her arms were almost as full as Bet's, and she had spent nine of her ten dollars. So what if she regretted her purchases later? She was thrilled with them now.

About one o'clock, they gathered to see Squint Burleson depart with Bet and her men. Bet wore the breeches, and Mollie was forced to admit she looked very trim in them as she sat astride a little bay mare. On her head was a broad-brimmed man's hat. Squint's hat was older and the brim curled up a little on each side from age and use. He sat on the box of what Chance Delanty called a buckboard wagon, which was piled high with food staples, seed, ammunition, and crates of unknown contents.

There were hugs and tears among the women as they stood in front of Sawyer's Stable. Chance Delanty, Squint, the twins, and Ben exchanged last-minute advice and joking references to the trials that would beset their journey.

Then they were gone, the hooves of their horses kicking up dust and sand as they disappeared into the distance.

Chance turned to the three who remained.

"Rose, I've talked to Henry Williams, who owns the largest store in town, and he says he'll speak to you about a job with him. He wants the chance to size you up."

"Oh, dear! That must be the wonderful store where Bet bought her breeches—I mean, clothes—H. Williams, Merchant!"

"That's the one. He'll be expecting you tomorrow morning. And, Kate, you've passed by Mama Sanchez's Bakery, haven't you?"

"O' course—it's a fine-looking store."

"Mama is Dolores Sanchez, a fine lady. She'll be expecting to talk with you sometime tomorrow as well. I'm not guaranteeing they'll hire either of you, but at least you'll each get a chance at a job."

"Bless you, Chance Delanty! If Rose an' me can't sweet-talk Mr. Williams and Mrs. Sanchez inter hirin' us, it'll be our own fault!"

"Mollie"—he frowned as he spoke her name—"Bet tells me you didn't buy breeches or boots after all."

"No, I didn't. I told you I wouldn't wear breeches. Did she tell you what I did buy?"

"No. What did you buy?"

"A dress. And a petticoat to go with it. And a pair of nice slippers. It's a traveling outfit, and I plan to wear it when we leave for your ranch."

He shrugged and his smile was enigmatic. "I hope you don't regret it."

"If I do, you'll not hear me complain." Her chin went up and her eyes flashed. "Even though I imagine you're hoping I do."

He shook his head. "I've found it doesn't pay to imagine. I'll wait, Mollie. You'll complain." He turned and went into the stable where Sawyer was waiting to talk with him.

"Mollie darlin', why d'ye go out o' yer way ter antagonize th' man? 'Twas yer own idea, this indenture business."

"Don't tell me that again, Aunt Kate! I've heard it enough!"

The following morning, Aunt Kate, Rose, and Mollie awakened early and were dressed by seven-thirty. They took a long time at breakfast so they would find the stores open when they went out. By nine, the stores had been open for half an hour, and the three women had visited most of the shops on the main street.

They finally left the grocery counter of the third general emporium and went to Mama Sanchez's Bakery. Kate introduced herself to the comfortably fat proprietor. Dolores Sanchez was a pretty woman with smooth olive skin and deep dimples in her cheeks.

"Ah, *si!* Senor Delanty tell me about you! You look for zee job in zee bakery, *si?*"

"Yes, I do," Kate replied eagerly.

After that, Dolores Sanchez and Kate Brannigan carried on a rapid, half-understood conversation regarding the baking business and Kate's skill as a baker. They liked each other immediately, despite their difficulties in communication. Kate's heavy Irish brogue and Dolores's broad Mexican accent blended very well as the interview progressed.

Dolores found it interesting that Mollie was going to Chance Delanty's ranch on the Nueces River. She had known him for a long time and admired him enormously.

"*Es guapo, no?* One handsome *hombre*. Honest, *y rico* too."

It developed that Dolores was a widow who ran a boarding house as well as the bakery, with the help of three daughters and a son.

"But my rates are *mucho* low—'alf what zat robber Cortez charge you."

Not many more minutes passed before Kate and Rose had agreed to take a room at her boarding house.

"Senor Chance, he stay at my *pension* more zan a month once, when he build hees *casa* een zee country," Dolores told them proudly. She rattled on about Delanty, half in Spanish, half in English, until Kate cut in.

"Yes, yes, we agree wi' ye, Missis Sanchez, but about your bakery: Don't ye think 'twould be a fine thing ter have good Irish pastries an' tarts an' pies to sell to the soldiers an' new arrivals? Me breads are very good too."

"I theenk maybe you are right, Senora Brannee— Senora Kate. Eet would give many variety to my Mexican sweets. Zee soldiers boys here, zey would like zat." Tilting her smoothly chignoned head to one side, she smiled again, deepening her dimples. "I pay you five dolla' a week, senora. Ees all right?"

"What is that in English money?" Kate asked warily.

Mollie, who stood beside Rose, said, "A pound, Aunt Kate."

"A pound!" Kate's jaw dropped. So much money was astounding. "I'll take it," she said hastily. "An' I can begin termorrer."

"I bake early, senora. I am here by seex in zee morning, wiz my ovens 'ot." She glanced at Mollie with her dark, liquid eyes and added, "Maybe you want to start after your leetle niece have leave wiz Senor Delanty — zen you come een tomorrow an' meet my ovens."

"No, no! I'll be here by six in th' mornin', Missis Sanchez. I'm anxious to get ter work. I'll take time off ter say good-bye ter me niece an' Chance when they leave."

"Ees fine, Senora Kate."

Before they left, Mollie, Rose, and Kate stood at the counter and chose Mexican pastries for themselves at Dolores's invitation.

They left, munching *bunuelos*. The pastries were exotic and delicious, and Mollie wished she had another before they were two doors down the street.

Looking up, she saw Chance approaching on the boardwalk, in company of a swarthy Mexican with the customary drooping mustache. This man wore an enormously broad-brimmed hat with many decorations on it. It was instantly in his hand as they approached.

Chance drawled, "This is my compadre, Pedro Mendoza. I was going to see you ladies this evening, but I can give you my news now. I'll have finished my business by Friday, and we'll leave then, four days from now, Mollie. Agreed?"

"What else could it be, but agreed?" Mollie asked rudely. "I have no say over when you choose to leave."

"I've already got a good job at th' bakery, Chance," Kate said hastily, sending Mollie a reproachful glance, "an' I know Rosie will have one before termorrer."

"Good for you, Kate. As for you, Mollie, I'll see you again before we leave." Delanty's voice was cold. Mendoza smiled, still holding his sombrero, as Chance added, "We'll have dinner together with Mendoza before we go, Mollie."

"All right," she said with pretended indifference before the women moved on down the boardwalk.

"Now, Rose, me darlin'," Kate said, her optimism and pleasure returning, "we'll go ter Mr. Williams's store ter see if he will hire ye."

Later in the evening, Sean O'Connor sat with the three women at supper in the Cortez Inn, and they celebrated the new jobs of both Kate and Rose. Mollie observed that Meg and Dierdre sat some distance away. Meg didn't even glance toward them until Dierdre made a commotion.

"But I want a kiss and a hug from bonny Mollie!" Her piping voice came to Mollie clearly and in a moment the child was at their table and proceeded to hug each of them.

"'Tis a marvel th' child can be so sunny an' lovin' when th' mother's so cold an' distant," Kate said under her breath.

Sean's face was unreadable for an instant; then his smile was as sudden and winning as Dierdre's when he said, "Sure'n it's glad I am that you an' Rose have found such fine work in Corpus Christi, Kate!"

The conversation turned to pleasant matters, and Sean talked enthusiastically about his new acquisitions. He was as attentive and charming to Rose and Kate as he was to Mollie. Meg and Dierdre left the dining room by themselves while the others were deep in a discussion of their new life. But later, as Mollie was going to sleep, she once again wondered about the mysterious, dour woman and her winsome daughter.

Mollie had an early breakfast with Kate and Rose before the two women hurried off to their new employment. She spent the rest of the day alone in her room.

At six, she accompanied Aunt Kate and Rose as they moved into Dolores Sanchez's *pension.*

The room Kate and Rose would share was bright and pleasant, with brilliant Mexican prints on the bed and at the windows. There was a bright dyed woven reed rug on the floor. The decor looked strange to their Irish eyes, but cheerfully so. And for all of this, Rose and her mother would pay only two dollars a week. Meals would be served in the morning and evening. Mollie, Rose, and Kate thought it a sumptuous arrangement.

After sharing supper with her family, Mollie walked back alone in the pale darkness to the Cortez Inn. She passed several houses, all of which were smaller than the Sanchez dwelling, and glimpsed supper lamps gleaming in the windows. She saw no evidence of soldiers until she reached the main street, where the music of guitars and singing voices came faintly to her ears from one of the several saloons, or cantinas.

Mollie felt very lonely as she went into the inn, though Senor and Senora Cortez greeted her with the warmth of old friends and assured her she had been missed at supper.

"I 'ave zee pitcher fill' for you—but eef you want a bath, I 'ave our son an' daughter breeng you zee tub and zee 'ot water. Eez all ready een zee keetchen, senorita." Senora Cortez smiled.

"I'll have a bath in the tub tomorrow night, senora," Mollie said, remembering the wooden bathtubs she had laboriously helped fill with hot water at Stirling Manor. Then she bid the landlady good night and went to bed.

At breakfast the next morning, Sean O'Connor approached Mollie's table as she was sipping a last cup of coffee. He was carrying one of the broad-brimmed hats that the climate demanded.

"Mollie, I've come ter say me good-byes to ye an' wish ye well till we meet again—which I'm sure will be soon!"

"And I wish you well, Sean," Mollie said, putting down her cup. "I know you'll prosper."

His smile was mischievous. "I plan on growin' th' finest potatoes in th' world."

"I'm sure you will," Mollie said, returning his smile warmly.

She happened to glance at the door and was surprised to see Meg Moriarty, bundles in hand, with Dierdre beside her, obviously waiting for him.

"Mollie, I'll see ye at th' Delanty place, I swear it. After I'm settled in, I'll come callin'" Sean said huskily.

Mollie was stunned. What did Meg have in mind? Was it possible she and her daughter were going with Sean into the wilderness? Mollie couldn't believe it. As she looked at them, they came slowly forward.

"Dierdre wants to say good-bye to you, Mollie," Meg said impatiently. "She's become such a fool about you."

"Are you—are you both going with Sean?" Mollie asked incredulously.

"Of course," Meg retorted without elaboration.

Sean's face was suddenly set, but his eyes sought Mollie's with a plea for understanding. Confused, Mollie said, "I hope all of you have a safe journey."

Dierdre reached her plump arms up to Mollie. "Kiss good-bye, bonny Mollie? I love you."

Mollie caught the child in her arms. "And I love you too, DeeDee, with all my heart. I'm sure we'll meet again, and soon." She soothed the child, who was on the verge of tears. Then Meg took her from Mollie and stood her on the floor beside her bundles.

Sean said briefly, "Meg is to be me housekeeper. With a seventy-five-acre ranch, I'll be needin' plenty of help. Good-bye again. God be with you, Mollie." And the three of them turned and left.

Mollie looked after them in stunned disappointment. All that gold Meg had—Sean probably felt he could use that! He suddenly seemed so mercenary— and she had allowed herself to become fond of him. Housekeeper! With no house to keep?

Then, all at once, as she looked at the blue eyes and shining black curls of Dierdre, who was waving back at her from the doorway, it burst on her like a flash of lightning. The child was a feminine image of Sean O'Connor!

She cursed herself for a fool, for not having recognized it sooner. Whatever lay between Sean and Meg was personal and intimate, and it shattered Mollie's previous admiration for the man. Sean and Meg and Dierdre were going away together, yet he had the temerity to say he would come calling on Mollie when she reached the Delanty ranch! Cold welcome he would receive!

Thursday afternoon, after bathing and donning her new dress, Mollie went to Henry Williams's store to say good-bye to Rose.

It was a wrenching farewell. Williams himself let the girls use his office while he waited out in the store.

"Oh, Mollie!" Rose whispered, tears welling up in her fine hazel eyes. "I can't bear it. You'll be so far away—for a whole year!"

"No," Mollie said thickly, trying to ease the tightness in her throat. "Only nine months. Remember, only nine months!"

Both girls' eyes were red when Mollie finally left. Henry Williams regarded them sympathetically as Rose walked with Mollie to the door.

Saying good-bye to Aunt Kate was even worse, for she was more demonstrative than her daughter. Dolores Sanchez became almost as emotional as Kate. Just before she left, Mollie gave her aunt one more hard embrace. "You'll see me again before you know it," she whispered and hastened away.

When Chance called for her at the inn at seven that evening, he was freshly shaved and smelled faintly of soap and some kind of hair tonic. His muscled thighs and narrow hips were clad in new trousers of a dark blue material, and his fresh shirt clung to his broad shoulders and chest like a second skin. Mollie strove for indifference, but in spite of herself she was unable to tear her eyes away.

"I haven't seen that dress before," he said without preamble, his blue eyes gleaming. Mollie, in spite of her earlier tears, was beautiful in her sapphire blue sateen.

"No. This is the one I bought when Bet got her new clothes." She tried not to sound defensive.

"Then you found a use for the money I gave you after all."

"Yes. This is my traveling outfit. I told you—no breeches!"

"Ah, yes. No breeches. Well, come along—you'd better enjoy your purchase while you can, for it will be in shreds by this time tomorrow."

"I don't believe that." She lifted her chin. "You're just trying to make me afraid of the trip."

His laugh was sardonic. "I can see you gathering firewood and making a fire and frying bacon and corn cakes in that outfit. Let me see the shoes," he said, taking her arm.

She lifted the full skirts a fraction, and he looked down at the neat little black slippers.

"Good God" was his only comment as they went out the door.

He took her to the town's lone restaurant which was filled with soldiers and men who looked rough even with fresh shaves and neatly combed hair.

The Mexican boy who met them at the door showed them to a table where Pedro Mendoza sat waiting. He got to his feet at once and bowed low to Mollie, murmuring, "*Buenas noches,* senorita."

"Good evening, Mr. Mendoza," she replied as she and Delanty seated themselves and the waiter approached. Delanty turned to her.

"Will you try the chicken enchiladas? They're delicious."

"Of course," she said with feigned indifference. "Whatever you order I shall eat."

The two men ordered in Spanish, and a young girl brought them two tall glasses of pale liquid, each with a slice of lemon on its edge.

"I don't think you'll want any tequila, Mollie. It's a strong drink."

"No," she said coolly, "but I will have a cup of coffee."

Delanty ordered it, and over their drinks the two

men conversed in Spanish. Mollie knew they were talking about the war, for she heard the name Santa Anna mentioned several times. Suddenly Mendoza turned to her. "I theenk we should speak een English, Captain Chance. Senorita Mollie might be interested in what we say."

"*Captain* Chance?" She looked at Chance inquiringly.

"He ees a captain weeth Colonel Jose Almonte's Volunteers for Texas. Santa Anna weel call us guerrillas, but we plan to fight on zee side of zee Americans for zee state of Texas an' zee United States."

She sipped her coffee and made no comment as she sat thinking. So Delanty was a member of an insurgent band of men, probably unrecognized officially by the American army and thus fair prey for the Mexicans, who would consider them traitors.

"Isn't that dangerous?" she asked Mendoza.

"*Si.* Eet ees dangerous. All wars are dangerous, senorita."

"Mollie wouldn't mind if I were conveniently a casualty, Pedro. She is indentured to me for a year, and my demise would set her free."

"Ah, surely zat ees not so!"

"No, it isn't so," Mollie said coolly. "I am anxious to serve out my indenture and I wish Captain Delanty well. Is he—are you going to join this band of Colonel Almonte's, Chance?"

"I did. Over a year ago, before hostilities even started. He is a longtime friend of mine. Almonte has been in New Orleans buying munitions and supplies with his troop. Pedro tells me they are due back soon."

"*Si.* I travel to Houston tomorrow to wait their arrival, and then we come back to the Nueces country."

"You see, Mollie, while Santa Anna claims all of Texas, my land is in hottest dispute because it is so close to the border of Mexico."

Mollie looked at the Mexicans who were serving the people around her and thought of Dolores Sanchez and her family, as well as the Cortez family.

"The Mexicans here are all so friendly, I can't be-

lieve there's any friction between Texas and Mexico,"
she remarked.

"These are not Mexicans, senorita," Mendoza
smiled. "They are American citizens, even as you and
Captain Delanty."

"Is Colonel Almonte's troop made up of Americans
too?" she asked.

"No, senorita, we fight to get back our lands. They
were stolen from us by Santa Anna. Colonel Almonte
ees a don, and he has great lands and a hacienda from
which he was driven." He paused; then more quietly
he added, "And there are other, more personal reasons
for the colonel's hatred of the tyrant."

"Take my word for it," Chance said grimly, "there's
more than friction between us. It was only when Texas
was annexed by the United States that Mexico officially took the attitude that the land still belonged to
them. With my ranch directly in the center of that
most disputed territory, as soon as I can get my affairs
in order I'll be gone to serve with Jose and his men. We
can be of help to General Taylor, for we all know Santa
Anna's character and are accustomed to the terrain."
He paused, then added a touch angrily, "And Jose's
men deserve to be called patriots and volunteers
rather than guerrillas."

Mollie drank some more of her hot, black coffee.
"Then you won't be staying with Bet and Ben at your
ranch for any length of time, I suppose?"

"No, I won't." he grinned sardonically. "Does that
relieve you?"

"Yes, it does," she replied frankly. "You seem to take
a certain pleasure in making me uncomfortable, so it's
scarcely strange that I would be relieved by your absence. But I assure you, I'll work hard with Bet—beside tending any who become ill."

"Ah, senorita, you know cures?" Mendoza asked.

"I've been trained in healing since I was ten years
old."

"Zat is good. Did you know that Captain Delanty
has seven people working on hees beeg ranch? Your

friends Mr. and Mrs. Ben Delanty and their sons will make eleven—and you weel be the twelfth."

"That many?" Mollie was stunned. "It must be a very large place."

"*Si*, but you weel like it there, I think."

She caught Chance's eye on her. His expression was inscrutable, but her face grew hot.

"We leave at five in the morning. Can you be ready, Mollie?"

"I *am* ready—now. But must I ride a horse? I'm accustomed to walking very long distances."

"And to riding in carts," he added dryly. "You'll find walking in Texas different from trodding the roads in Ireland. I've had the foresight to buy you a few things you may need—and I think even you will find it better on horseback than afoot. There are no roads through the wild Nueces country."

That night Mollie went to bed overfull with rich Mexican food and depressed by the talk of war. It appeared she had left a slow death by famine only to come to a land where a sudden and violent death was just as possible.

Worse, she dreamed about Chance again. She woke up sweating and aching with desire, fear, and bitter resentment. She tried to console herself with the thought that he would surely be off to Mexico soon— for a long, long time. But she could not go back to sleep. She lay in darkness, tossing on the lumpy bed for an hour before she finally got up and went to one of the two windows that opened out on the end of the town. A faint breeze blew in through the uncurtained window and she leaned upon the sill, putting her head out to look up at the arch of glittering stars above.

She could smell the gulf, so different from the tang of the Irish Sea. It smelled wilder, mingling with the pervasive scent of the pink and white flowering bushes called oleanders that grew abundantly everywhere in the town.

Mollie turned away from the window and in the paling predawn darkness found her fine new sateen dress —now her very best—with its demure collar hanging over the foot of the bed. She took up her chemise and petticoats and dressed rapidly. She certainly wouldn't meet Bet and her men looking frumpy and miserable. Sitting down on the floor beside the window, she brushed her long, thickly curling hair, then braided it and pinned it neatly around her head. Unruly little curls that refused to be pinned she let frame her face and linger along the back of her neck.

At a store clerk's suggestion and with the last of her money she had bought a hat he called a poke bonnet to keep the sun away from her fair Irish skin on the long ride to Chance's ranch.

After replacing her comb and brush and retying one of the thick oblong canvas bundles, she tucked her skirts under her knees and sat down again beside the window to wait for what Chance called sunup.

She sat motionless until the deep blue of the sky thinned and paled and along the eastern horizon a delicate pink introduced the dawn. The town below her began stirring. Two men went into Sawyer's Stables and came out on horseback to ride away down the road that led to the army camp. Two more walked by on the wooden sidewalk across the street and continued beyond her line of vision. Breakfast fires dotted the sea of tents.

It was then she saw the tall, familiar figure of Chance Delanty stride into Sawyer's Stables to get their horses. She waited, breathing quickly, and in a few minutes he came out again, riding one horse and leading two more by their bridles. One had an empty saddle. The other was laden with baggage of different shapes and sizes—the supplies he had spoken of securing, no doubt.

She stood up, smoothing her skirts. She was already a bit too warm in the long-sleeved dress and wondered briefly if she would have been wiser to wear one of the old muslins. No, this was more suitable for travel.

In less than five minutes, there was a sharp rap at her door. She went to open it.

Delanty towered in the dark opening. Without a

preliminary greeting he said, "Are you ready?" At her nod he added, "Let's go then."

She picked up her two bundles, slung the leather strap of her medical pouch over her shoulder, and returned to the open door.

He took the bundles from her hands, and in the darkness of the hallway they descended the stairs. No one stood behind the counter. It was too early for the Cortez family to be up.

Mollie stepped out into the welcome coolness of the new day.

Chapter 9

The big gelding snorted impatiently as they approached the hitching rail. The other two horses were mares. The one that was saddled had satiny flanks and narrow ankles. The other was more broadly built, carrying all the supplies easily on her wide back.

"I'm sorry, but you'll have to ride a man's saddle," said Chance. "You can hook your leg over the pommel and maybe you won't fall off."

He laced his hands together to serve as a step for her foot and helped her mount. She crooked one knee around the upthrust pommel, readjusting her skirts to cover it, foot and all. Then she hung her medicine pouch on the pommel of her saddle above her covered knee. As Chance lashed her bundles to the packhorse, she wondered how she would manage to sit on this horse for nearly a hundred miles in such an awkward position. The pouch was heavy on her knee and skirts —and she had been on a horse just one other time in her life. Watching Chance prepare his own horse, she noticed that he wore a leather belt low on his lean hips, with a gun in a holster on his right side. A long rifle was fitted in a holster strapped to the gelding's saddle.

Delanty mounted with the swift and easy grace of long practice, and they moved off down the road.

In a short time they had passed through the army camp and into the wild country beyond. The road had narrowed to a two-rut trail.

"If you let her set her own gait, it'll be easier for you," Delanty said dryly.

Mollie made no reply but loosened the reins slightly and tried to shift her position as the mare's pace evened slightly. Chance said no more, and they traveled in silence for over an hour. When they passed a stand of trees that spread enormously wide and high, their thick black trunks slightly gnarled, she asked Chance about them.

"Live oaks," he replied briefly. "Stay green all year 'round."

They rode without speaking once more. The sun had risen in the sky and shone down hotly on them. The morning breeze had died and a stillness hung over the flat, rolling land, except for the *burring* of cicadas in the brush and the distant, plaintive note of a mourning dove. They rode north, away from the Gulf of Mexico, past clumps of trees with leaves so small and delicate they were like a green mist in the air. Unfortunately, the vegetation provided little protection against the unremittingly hot sun.

In response to her second question of the morning, Chance replied, "Mesquites," without elaboration.

Mollie was becoming increasingly uncomfortable with her taciturn companion, but she silently swore she would not speak again. If he wanted to ride all the way to his ranch without another word, she would match his reticence.

Her dress was much too warm, and the full skirts hung awkwardly about the horse. The sun penetrated the brilliant blue cloth and became trapped within its folds. The poke bonnet sheltered her complexion, but no cooling breezes could pass through its stiff sides to alleviate her misery. Light perspiration beaded her

upper lip, and she wiped it away with the back of her
hand. Between her shoulders there was a growing
ache.

Finally, Chance glanced at her. "Hot?" he asked.

"Aren't you?"

"It's much more comfortable when you ride astride
and wear a hat that lets a little breeze hit your face."
He regarded her solemnly, but his blue eyes were
twinkling.

"Which I can't do because of my skirts, and you
know it! Why not say 'I told you so'? It would make you
feel better—and I'm still glad I didn't wear breeches!"

"Not to mention that ridiculous poke bonnet," he
said amiably, refusing to argue with her.

She stiffened, and they said no more. The trail had
long ago turned east, but Delanty kept steadily to a
northerly direction, following no trail at all. There was
only a vast, untouched wild land spread out before
them. All Mollie could see were strange trees and
bushes, and, interspersed with them, wide, sweeping
prairies of rough grass. It was all so foreign to her
eyes.

Eventually they entered a thick stand of mesquite
trees and were weaving their way among them when
Mollie felt a sudden tug on her shoulder, followed by a
sharp, raking pain. An exclamation of dismay escaped
her, and instinctively she drew back on the reins.

Twisting about, she saw that the low-hanging limbs
of the mesquite trees were covered with black, wicked-
looking thorns. One had caught her shoulder and torn
her dress badly.

Chance turned and rode back to her. "Here, be still.
I'll get the thorn out." There was a further ripping
noise as she felt the release of the pressure on her
dress.

Tentatively she felt her shoulder, which was now
bare under the hot noonday sun. She winced.

"Yes," Chance said without sympathy as he dismounted. "You've a nice long scratch and it's bleeding." She felt him press something against her skin
and, looking back, saw it was a multicolored handker-

chief that he had pulled from around his neck. The scratch ached now, and her eyes watered with pain.

"Here," he said. "Hold my handkerchief to it and I'll get the liniment."

She obeyed his instructions but then asked sharply, "What is liniment?"

"Something we put on horses and dogs—and girls who get snagged by mesquite thorns or cat's claw." He strode toward the packhorse.

"You'll put none of that on me!" She threw the handkerchief at him, and he caught it deftly.

"Ah, I forgot. Well, then—physician, heal thyself."

"I certainly will!" She jerked the medicine pouch up before her and took out a vial of a medicine made from cheese mold. After shaking a few of the yellowish granules into her hand, she stretched her arm back and craned to see the wound, but she could not reach it.

"Want me to put it on the scratch for you?"

"No! Well, you could help a little, I guess."

He lifted her from the mare, and she poured a few granules into his hand. He began patting them on the open flesh with a touch that was amazingly gentle for such a big man.

"That's a deep scratch," he said matter-of-factly. "It wouldn't have happened if you'd been wearing a leather vest."

"And where would I be getting a leather vest?— Oh, it hurts!"

His touch grew lighter still, and the throbbing pain began to ease.

"What is this stuff, Doctor?" he asked, smiling.

"It doesn't have a name," she replied shortly. "Sister Maria Theresa showed me years ago how to scrape it off moldly cheese. It's very good for treating fevers and sores—prevents festering too. I've even cured pneumonia with doses of it."

"I'm impressed," he said soberly. With a touch of asperity, he added, "You'll be getting sunburned now, Doctor, since your dress is properly torn from half your back."

Embarrassed, she tried in vain to pull the torn pieces of cloth over her bare flesh.

"I'll give you my deerskin jacket. You'll be hotter than ever, but at least that fair Irish skin won't burn." Going back to the packhorse, he took the garment from one of the bundles and handed it to her, adding with a touch of sarcasm, "I hope you know as much about mending clothes as you do about medicines. By the time we've gone another fifteen miles, that dress should be in tatters, because we're coming to some rough country soon."

"Rougher than this?" she asked in disbelief.

"Mesquites aren't the only trees with thorns." Shrugging, he added, "Go sit under that big mesquite yonder. We've got to stop and eat now anyway. You can rest awhile."

"But I thought the sole purpose for my being here with you was to fetch firewood and cook for you," she said, frustrated and annoyed at her helplessness.

"We'll let that go for now. You know nothing of camping on the trail, and besides, you're a wounded soldier now, Doctor." His voice was mocking.

He set about building a fire from broken limbs that littered the ground and took pans and utensils out of a pack he lifted from the patient packhorse. Left to their own devices, the horses were pulling mouthfuls of leaves from the succulent bushes that surrounded them. Mollie had been sitting on one of the tufts of thick grass that covered the terrain, but the mesquites offered little protection from the sun. Soon she sought denser shade under a stunted live oak. She let the deerskin jacket fall to the ground behind her so the air could get to the scratch. She felt sore and dreadfully tired already, but her back was as straight as a poker. If she died in the saddle, she wouldn't let Chance Delanty have the satisfaction of seeing her misery. But she was alarmed at the destruction of her one really good dress. Why hadn't he told her to buy a leather vest?

In a few minutes their meal was well underway. Chance placed a coffeepot and a frying pan on a metal rack over the fire he had built. It was obvious from his competent movements that he had long experience in cooking on the trail.

Mollie's mouth watered. She had had no breakfast, and the ride in the open air had made her ravenously hungry. When the coffee began to boil, she sniffed it unashamedly. Soon she and Chance were eating crisp salt bacon and fried cornmeal cakes and drinking the coffee. Mollie hated to let him see how much she was enjoying it. But when he pulled two oranges from the supply sack, she felt compelled to thank him.

When they had finished and Chance had cleaned and replaced the utensils, they mounted their horses once more. Though Mollie felt rested, her shoulder ached slightly under the hot deerskin jacket as they rode under the unrelenting sun. The sky was an inverted bowl of clear, hot blue, without the relief of a single cloud.

Long before evening came, Mollie was cursing the sapphire sateen dress, no longer caring that it had been ruined. Chance had been proven right. As they wound their way through the brush, her skirts had snagged a dozen times and had a dozen tears in them. One thorn had even slashed through her white eyelet petticoat. When at last they stopped for the night, she felt like a ragpicker.

Silently she thanked God that the sun was setting at last and the air was cooling. She felt sticky and hot and longed for a bath. She feared she would have to sleep in the sateen dress and wear it without changing all the way to the ranch, where Bet and her men would see her looking a filthy, tattered disgrace.

After lifting her to the ground, Chance unpacked the necessary supplies from the packhorse. Then he unsaddled the other two horses and hobbled all three. He pitched Mollie's bundles to her, then loosened two bedrolls and spread them on the level ground at the campsite he had chosen close to a dry stream bed. As Mollie considered the unfamiliar bedding she was greatly relieved. At least she wouldn't have to sleep on the bare ground with only a blanket to lie upon. The bedrolls looked reassuringly thick, and Chance flung a cozy-looking blanket over each.

After a supper of beans and more of the corn cakes and oranges, he said, "You needn't sleep in that ragged dress. I'll leave while you get ready for the night." With these words he went into the nearby woods and was rapidly lost to sight.

For an instant, panic struck Mollie. She was alone in a wilderness for the first time in her life. She shed her dress, petticoats, and chemise and donned her long, white nightgown in no time. Then she lay down on the bedroll, pulled up the blanket, and awaited Chance's return.

Thirty minutes went by and he did not come back. Mollie sat up, pulling the blanket with her. She tugged the bottom of her bedroll closer to the dying fire. Then, taking up some of the wood he had placed nearby, she threw several small limbs across the embers. They caught and the fire blazed up reassuringly, its sparks briefly joining the brilliant stars overhead.

She restrained an impulse to call out. Though she sank back on the bedroll, she did not lie down but sat holding the blanket around her shoulders. The bedroll did not seem nearly as thick as she had first thought. There were lumps under it. Cautiously, she lifted its edge and pulled out three rocks and several broken twigs.

The landscape, what little she could see of it, seemed fearsome, she thought, peering into the blackness just beyond their campsite. She heard mysterious rustlings and an occasional snap. Was some wild animal stalking another in the unfathomable darkness? She tried to recall all the wild animals she had learned were native to the New World. Father O'Malley had showed her pictures in one of his books of the North American bear and mountain lion, as well as deer and small brown rabbits.

Gradually a faint light showed above the trees, and in a few minutes a waning moon rose reluctantly in the sky, dimming the stars and darkening the shadows beneath the trees. Where was Chance? He surely had been gone for over an hour!

Suddenly something in the brush along the edges of the creek bed moved and thudded down in the darkness.

Mollie gasped and jumped to her feet, dropping the blanket. Trembling, she took up a burning brand from the fire and raised it above her head, bracing herself to face whatever might come leaping from the arroyo. The horses lifted their heads and pricked up their ears. She stood poised, ready for battle or flight, when from behind her there came another light sound.

Her heart racing wildly, she whirled to see Chance step into the circle of firelight.

He looked at the burning limb in her upraised hand and smiled a little, dropping the armload of wood he had gathered. "You weren't afraid, were you?" he asked soberly, though his eyes gleamed with amusement.

She let the burning limb fall back into the fire, unable to conceal her vast relief. Then, suddenly aware of her long, thin nightgown, she swooped down and caught up the blanket, winding it around her. Her heart was still pounding uncontrollably, making her feel slightly sick.

"I thought you'd decided to go on without me," she said stiffly.

"Never," he said pleasantly, placing two of the heavier limbs he had brought over the fire. "I've too much invested in you. Besides, Bet would skin me alive."

He had removed his broad-brimmed hat, and his black hair shone in the firelight as he checked the horses and their loose hobbles.

"The Nueces is just a half a mile over there." He jerked his head in the direction from which he had come. "It's too curving and long to follow from town. We had to get out this far to connect with it. I found a tributary just a hundred yards from here, and we'll stop by tomorrow morning and have a washup while the horses are being watered." He glanced back to where Mollie still stood, a frozen statue. "When we reach the Nueces, we'll follow it all the way to the ranch."

Mollie slowly sat back down on the bedroll, but she did not take her eyes off Chance, who was casually removing his boots. He did not glance at her as he pulled his bedroll closer to hers until there was less than two feet of ground separating them.

He took off his leather belt, removed the pistol with its long, gleaming barrel from the holster, and laid it on the edge of his bedroll. Then he casually began unbuttoning his shirt. Mollie restrained another gasp. Was he going to undress right there in front of her?"

He folded the shirt carelessly and laid it beside the bedroll. When he turned back, the firelight revealed his muscled chest with its dark mat of wiry hair. He did not remove his snug twill breeches but instead lay back on the bedroll and stretched, yawning deeply. He made no move to pull the blanket over himself, despite the cool night wind that had sprung up.

"We want to keep the fire going all night," he said idly. "Coyotes and wolves get nosy in the dark."

Mollie watched him silently from under her thick, sooty lashes, the blanket drawn up to her chin and her hair spilling in shining disarray over her shoulders.

Chance clasped his hands under his head, moving it slightly so that he could return her scrutiny. Under his gaze her eyes dropped, but she did not lie down.

"Were you that frightened?" he asked slowly.

She nodded, realizing that she was beginning to tremble slightly despite the warm blanket. She blinked, furious at her own weakness as tears came.

Chance regarded her silently for a moment, then got to his feet and kneeled beside her, his arms going slowly around her. The trembling became more intense and his arms tightened. One hand pressed her head against his shoulder.

"It's all right, Mollie," he murmured. "It's all right—"

She gulped. "I—I thought it was a bear coming."

"You did the right thing," he said soothingly. "No bear would dare approach a little girl with a burning limb in her hand. Animals are notoriously afraid of fire."

She felt his chin resting on the top of her head and under her cheek the comforting, warm smoothness of his heavy shoulder. He held her gently, his hand stroking the thick hair above her brow, and Mollie knew the intense relaxation that comes with certain safety. She wished fleetingly that she might spend the rest of the night thus sheltered. Her trembling slowly ceased and she dragged in a deep, sighing breath.

"I'm fine now, thank you," she said tremulously.

The hand that had stroked her hair so tenderly came down to her chin, tilting her face upward. Her eyes flew open wide as she looked into his dark face. Firelight reflected the sudden heat in his eyes as the clean-cut lips came deliberately down on her own. They were hard and demanding, and a new emotion shot through her. Somehow it meshed and flowed with her freshly aroused fear, for her heart began its wild gallop and her breath came fast as the memories of her dreams of Chance swarmed over her. And as in the dreams, she was fluid with desire as well as fear.

His mouth drew all resistance from her, all strength, and filled her with a vast turbulence. She felt herself melting in his grasp even as her lips parted under his, and suddenly they were lying together on her bedroll. His hands were pulling up her nightgown, slipping warmly along the smooth sides of her bare legs in slow, gentle caresses.

But there was nothing gentle about his kisses. They were hungry, searching, stirring in her a wildness that leapt to meet them. Yet his lips were leisurely, seeking and finding each sweeping wave of emotion he aroused in her.

Mollie had never known such intense desire. Her arms went around his shoulders, drawing him closer to her, and as the long, hard length of him came down upon her, she drew a shuddering breath of hot pleasure. A gust of real passion, the first of her life, shook her, and she succumbed to the fire leaping in her blood.

This was no dream. This was what she had ached

for in those dream-filled nights, and she had not known it.

"Ah, Mollie darling—sweet—no matter how many others—" His mouth closed again over hers.

No matter how many others. The words and their meaning shocked her into the familiar terror that had come with the dreams, and she closed her legs against him, and began to fight like a wild thing.

They fought silently, rolling off the bedroll onto the rough grass toward the fire. She reared under him with fear-driven strength, throwing him half off. As he rolled onto her again, she strained away, her neck arching backward, her eyes wide. He met her gaze and recognized her look of undeniable innocence and genuine terror of the unknown. Filled with passion though he was, still Chance understood clearly.

With a sudden muffled curse, he moved away and crouched before her on his knees. His eyes never left her pale, terrified face as she clutched the nightgown, pulling it down over her knees, her breath coming in great, gasping sobs. She put her hands to her face, hiding from the accusation that burned brightly in his eyes and the furious self-reproach that showed in his face.

Finally he spoke, his voice husky with passion. "I thought you were a woman of experience!" he accused. "How was I to know Stirling lied? And when I'd found you once under Clan O'Connor and again on the quay willingly kissing the man—"

Still unable to speak, she shook her head, her gleaming black hair swinging about her shoulders. Deep within her, anger blazed hotly. Her blue eyes glittered.

"I would have been safer with any animal that had come up from the arroyo—bear, lion, or wolf," she said, her voice low and scathing. "Why didn't you go ahead and take me, like the animal you are?"

His black brows drew together. "Rape is not one of my pleasures, Mollie O'Meara—especially rape of virgins who parade as wantons."

"I never pretended to be anything but what I am! I remember distinctly telling you that I was a good girl."

He burst into mocking laughter. "A good girl! Mollie, you may be many things, but you are not a good girl." His brows lifted and his mouth turned down ironically. "I never saw such passion as I felt in your first response to me tonight—and at the other times I kissed you!"

She felt the blood hot in her face, for what he said was true, but her anger now had deeper roots. "I think you planned this, from the moment you lied to Bet and Ben and said you wanted me to cook and gather firewood—from the moment you offered to lend me money."

"You're a very desirable woman, Mollie. I mean to have you sooner or later." His voice was hard now.

"You'll never have me! I hate you! Next July tenth, I'll leave your house and we'll never meet again!" She was panting with fury.

"Yes, we will, Mollie. You want me as badly as I want you. Your lips—hell, your whole body tells me as much. And you'll learn to overcome your terror of giving yourself to me." His arrogant voice carried such certainty that she was speechless with rage.

She began to brush the leaves and grass from her nightgown, ignoring his eyes. She lay down again on her bedroll and drew the blanket over her.

"I'll admit you're ignorant about lovemaking, Mollie, but I plan to teach you—and you will enjoy it fully. I can guarantee that." He stood looking down at her, his face set in hard lines. Chance Delanty was not a man who accepted denial easily.

She turned her face away in stony silence.

"You want me," he reiterated. He moved away then and lay down on his own bedroll, turning his back to her.

Mollie's breath came more easily, but every nerve in her body was still quivering, and sleep was impossible. She turned from side to side as Chance's words echoed in her mind. She tried to think of his deceptions, but somehow she sensed a truth that lay buried deep within her heart—it was so unthinkable her mind refused to name it. She would not let herself consider it, she thought desperately. She would not!

In the midst of her turbulent thoughts, fatigue overcame her and she slept so soundly that no dreams troubled her.

It was still dark when she suddenly awakened. The moon had set, but the stars were bright. She saw that the bedroll near hers was empty. On the other side of the campfire sat Chance, his long legs crossed.

At first she refused to look at him, though she felt his eyes on her. When finally she did meet his gaze, she saw that he was regarding her with an odd expression. He was not smiling, and his brows were furrowed. She sat up as he rose to his feet.

He had put his shirt back on and over it the deerskin jacket. Now he went to one of the canvas supply bags and took some garments and a pair of soft, high boots from it. Without a word, he dropped them beside Mollie, who looked down at them dubiously. He threw several pieces of wood on the fire and set the coffee pot over it, pouring in water from one of the canteens.

Finally he straightened up and looked at her. "We'll forget last night happened."

"We can't undo what's been done by saying we're sorry," she said with sudden bitterness.

"You're mistaken. I'm not sorry, and neither are you. You're still as virginal as ever. Nothing really happened."

She made no reply, but she thought, Something happened. To me. Though I can't name it and I don't want to think about it. Outwardly she feigned indifference as she spoke.

"I'll have to go to confession, and even then I won't feel clean ever again." Her words were meant to hurt him.

A muscle in his jaw twitched. "And will you confess your eager response to me in the beginning?"

"Of course!" she replied, stung herself. "I'll confess it all."

"You'll have a long wait to unburden yourself.

Priests are few and far between in Texas. You may have to wait longer than your year as a bondservant." His voice was mocking now.

She took refuge behind the garments, holding them up and saying, "What am I supposed to do with these?"

"Those are the britches and shirt you wouldn't buy, sized for a twelve-year-old boy. They ought to fit. There's another shirt and a leather vest too. I guessed at your boot size. If you're smart, you'll give up that dress, no matter how beautiful you look in it, and wear those britches and the wide-brimmed hat. We're still a long way from my place." He began slicing bacon and laying it in the pan.

The stars were fading as the sky grew lighter. Mollie's youthful resilience helped ease her guilty conscience. In spite of what she and Chance had almost done in the night, she felt better than she had in months. It was bewildering, but she put the thought from her mind.

"I can scarcely dress in these things as long as you're here," she said coolly.

He lifted the bacon from the fire and put a bowl of batter aside. Moving away, he spoke dryly over his shoulder. "Call me when you've finished—and before you get too frightened again." He strode into the woods and was lost to sight.

She noticed a subtle change in his attitude toward her, a touch of respect where there had been none before. Well, it had come too late. He had almost taken away control of her own body. She no longer trusted herself after her response to those sweet, forbidden kisses. If he were to make love to her again, would fear rescue her once more? She told herself firmly it would, but her brain whispered, *Would it?* Who would have guessed that such feelings, such intense and blinding pleasure, lay in her body? Her face grew hot at the memory, and she vowed to keep from touching him ever again. After all, didn't she hate him with good reason? She would nurse that hatred. It was her only weapon against him.

After buttoning the blue denim shirt, she tucked it

into the close-fitting twill breeches. It was too tight across her breasts, and her nipples stood out boldly. She shrugged on the deerskin vest and looked down. That was better. Next she put on the boots Chance had provided. They were comfortable and would feel even better after some wear. How had he known her size?

Looking toward the stand of trees, she called, "I'm dressed." In a few minutes he was back at the skillet over the fire. He gave her a brief glance.

"You're better covered than you were in that tent you wore yesterday."

"That's your opinion," she replied tartly. "No *lady* wears breeches."

"There's no finer lady than Bet—and she now wears breeches on occasion."

"Oh—" Mollie was chastised. "That's true. Well, I guess since Bet wore them I can too."

Corn cakes were sizzling in the pan now and bacon curled crisply. "We'll have syrup on our corn cakes this morning," he said, opening a small jar and setting it down between their plates.

Their breakfast tasted especially delicious to Mollie. She ate four corn cakes bathed in thick, brown syrup and drank lots of coffee.

"You like coffee, don't you?" Chance drawled, his eyes twinkling as he poured her third cup.

"It's very good," she replied, slightly embarrassed. She refrained from asking for a fourth cup, and Chance himself finished off the pot.

As he had promised, they made their way to the narrow, twisting tributary of the Nueces. There they washed their faces, arms, and feet in the cool, clear water, while the horses drank noisily.

"We'll follow this fork until we come to the Nueces, then follow that until we arrive at my place," he told her.

"About how far is it now?"

"We ought to be there tomorrow evening."

She let out her breath in a gusty sigh of relief only faintly tinged with uneasiness. It was the leashed restlessness in her companion that disturbed her. She

could not be sure what he would do now. And the sharp
memory of exhaltation and dizzying delight that had
been hers at the touch of his hands on her flesh increased her anxiety. Unconsciously, she lifted her chin.
She was capable of resisting him. She *was!* And, too,
there was that subtle touch of respect he was according
her now. It showed itself in his face, his voice, in his
attitude toward her. She realized suddenly that she
probably could count more on that to save her than on
her own good sense.

By noon they came upon the Nueces River itself,
broad and clear and overhung on either side with
trees. They rode parallel but at some distance to it,
following easy bends and curves as it spread through
the land.

"The Nueces is the trail from Corpus Christi to the
settlements up north," Chance said. "Sooner or later,
as I told you, you meet every local Texan traveling
along it."

Twice along the riverbank Mollie recognized deer
which she'd read about in Father O'Malley's books.
Chance paused occasionally to fill the canteens and to
let the horses drink, for the day was as hot as its pre-
decessor. Mollie was so relieved to be riding astride
and so much more comfortable than she had been the
previous day, her naturally high spirits rose.

Today Chance spoke more too, explaining the terrain and telling her about the river: "It's a clean,
spring-fed stream that starts way up northwest of
Corpus Christi and the gulf and comes down through
the canyons to the Balcones Escarpment. From there it
drops down and flows across the coastal plain for three
hundred miles until it reaches the actual coast and
Nueces Bay. Here, where we are, it's still about
twenty-five hundred feet above sea level."

His voice was soothingly deep and drawling, and
Mollie was fascinated as much by it as by what he told
her.

"What do you raise on your farm—or ranch, as you
call it?" she asked.

He was silent a moment and then said, "A good herd of longhorn cattle and enough horses so that we can have fresh ones to ride every day—that's called a remuda. I'm breeding them. We grow corn and cotton and have a big orchard of oranges and grapefruit. It's nearly tropical in this part of Texas—not cold like it is in winter in northern Texas. Oranges, lemons, and grapefruit grow very well here and can be shipped out to other parts of the country. But cotton's the real money crop. Cotton and beef."

"Blessed Mary!" Mollie murmured. "You've done so well. I hope Bet and Ben and the boys can do the same. How wonderful that would be."

Chance's laugh was short, and his eyes held mischief. "They'll have some help—and the Delantys are workers and shrewd in their dealings. Given half a chance, they'll prosper."

"What is your house like?"

"Not at all like the houses and cottages in Ireland, I can tell you. It's in two big, square sections separated by an open-ended hallway between them. It's roughly made, with puncheon floors on the ground level."

"Puncheon floors?"

"Tree trunks sawed into flat circles and put down to cover the bare earth. They make a pretty good floor. Of course the upstairs floors are made of sawed planks. They're rough on bare feet, but Bet said she'd make hooked rugs out of wool I brought from England. And there are eight rooms, not counting the kitchen in the back. There's a fireplace in each room. You'll be quite comfortable there, I think."

"Oh, oh—look!" Mollie pointed excitedly. It was a rabbit, the like of which she had never seen before. He was enormous, three times the size of an Irish hare, and his ears were nearly as long as his grayish tan body. As she watched, he bounded out of sight into the brush, the white tag of his bobbing tail showing briefly.

Chance laughed. "That's a jackrabbit—a deal bigger than the ones in Ireland, isn't he?"

"Can you eat jackrabbits?" she asked dubiously.

"If you're hungry enough. They're a little tough and gamey."

Suddenly her horse shied and reared up. Mollie grabbed for the pommel just in time to stop herself from sliding off. At the same moment, Chance reached for her bridle. As the horse came down and backed away, an ominous rattle sounded from a nearby rock.

"Rattler," Chance said calmly. Soothingly to her mare he said, "Come on now, lady, you aren't scared." All three horses gave the rock a wide berth.

"What's a rattler?" Mollie asked, looking over her shoulder at the rock. A long, sinuous shape slid from beneath it, diamond-shaped markings along its narrow form, its flat head jutting toward the river.

"Snake," Chance replied briefly. "Trust your mare; she can smell 'em before you know they're about. That was a big one, and he's thirsty."

"There's nothing in all Ireland like that! It's beautiful."

"And deadly. Its bite can kill you. I don't know but one man who ever survived a rattlesnake bite—Squint Burleson."

"They bite?"

"You bet your life. And the noise you heard is their warning. Comes from a row of hollow rattles in their tails. Always back off quick when you hear it."

Mollie digested this information in silence. After last night, she had concluded that her new home was going to be dangerous. Now she added one more fearful creature to a growing list.

She looked speculatively at the man on the horse beside her. Of all the dangerous creatures in her life now, he was by far the most dangerous. How could she evade him when darkness fell again tonight? She adjusted the angle of the wide-brimmed hat he had given her. The thought of sleeping so near Chance preoccupied her for the rest of the day.

During their ride she glimpsed a coyote, a raccoon, two more rabbits, a small herd of antelope, and an armadillo. She also saw two wary gray wolves. Chance answered her questions seriously and concealed any amusement they gave him. As Mollie rode along, she became increasingly aware of her surroundings. She looked about wide-eyed as she and Chance traveled along a broad, nearly treeless prairie that spread out from the river. Noting her nervousness, Chance said reassuringly, "Most wild things are anxious to keep out of our way. They won't hurt you unless they feel endangered. Or unless they're hungry."

With that, he reached down for the beautiful long rifle strapped to the side of his saddle and halted the horses. He gestured for silence. Raising the gun to his shoulder, he took careful aim at a patch of rough, blowing grass of the prairie just as a covey of large birds flapped up in low, awkward flight. The rifle cracked twice, and two birds fluttered to the ground some distance away.

"Pheasants—our supper tonight," he said, dismounting. As he slid the rifle back into the saddle holster, he rubbed the stock of it fondly and added, "It's a Nathaniel Locke—brought to me all the way from New Jersey by Squint Burleson, who went there just to buy one for each of us." He grinned at her. "My pistol's a Colt-Paterson. Not another one in Texas like it except Squint's. He brought them from back East too." He turned away, striding across the prairie toward the fallen birds.

He was back in a short time with the two plump pheasants, which he tied with a leather thong to the pommel of his saddle. He remounted and they set off again.

As they wound their way slowly nearer to the river, the packhorse nickered. Then Mollie's mare whinnied softly.

"They're thirsty," Chance said, leading them to a low place on the riverbank. Clean sand formed a little beach there, and the horses bent their heads to drink.

The sun was sinking at last, and beneath the trees beside the softly murmuring Nueces the shadows were lengthening. Mollie marvelled at the Texas sky, which, unlike Ireland's September sky of soft blues, grays, and pinks, was ablaze with lurid color—bright golds

and flaming scarlets. Directly above her the colors
deepened, for clouds were coming in from the south,
their empurpled edges trailing into gold and blending
with the blood-red sunset.

"Do you think it's going to rain?" she asked in concern.

"I've brought a poncho for each of us if it does," he
said. "Time to stop for the night." He slid from his saddle and, taking all three animals by the reins, led
them, with Mollie still astride her mare, into the
woods and back from the river's edge. "We'll sleep better away from the Nueces. Too many animals come to
drink at night."

Suddenly Mollie envisioned bears and panthers
drinking from the Nueces's clear, flowing waters. It
was an unsettling thought. To push the fear from her
mind she asked, "Isn't a poncho that thing you put
over us in the cart on the way to Dublin?"

"Yes. It's a Mexican invention. A big, square piece
of oiled leather with a hole in the middle for your head.
"Keeps you nice and dry in wet weather and warm
when the wind blows cold."

"Does it ever get cold here?" she asked as Chance
decided on a small clearing about a hundred feet from
the river.

"Sometimes very cold when the northers blow in."

She slid easily from her saddle. The once-scorned
breeches had been a great comfort to her all day. She
had determined to sleep in them too—and in shirt and
vest as well. She had been far too vulnerable in that
thin cotton nightgown the night before.

Chance unloaded the packhorse, removed the saddles from the other two, and hobbled them, setting
them to graze in the little clearing.

While he went to the river to clean the pheasants,
Mollie got her bedroll from the baggage stacked under
a tree and unrolled it in one side of the clearing. Then
she took out Chance's bedroll and put it down on the
other side, with a good six feet between them. Proxim-
ity was not going to be the catalyst it had been the
previous night.

When he returned with the plucked and cleaned birds, Chance glanced briefly at the positioning of the bedrolls but said nothing. He made the fire, peeled some small saplings, and with them made a spit over the blaze; then he strung the plump pheasants on it.

"It'll take awhile to roast them, but I think you'll find it worth the wait," he said casually, readying the coffeepot and bringing out a hard loaf of bread. He spread a piece of canvas on the ground where they would eat and placed the bread and the jar of syrup on it. Then he pulled a pipe and tobacco pouch from his shirt pocket and proceeded to pack tobacco into the bowl. Taking up a burning twig, he lit the pipe, and in a moment the fragrance of apple-seasoned tobacco floated to Mollie on the light night breeze.

He sat watching the spit, turning it occasionally but not speaking. The sun had set, and there was no longer any trace of color in the sky. There were no stars either, since the sky was overcast.

The night was full of sounds. Cicadas in the trees around them were chorusing their loud, somnolent buzz. Night birds called plaintively to each other, and an eerie cry, which Chance told her came from a screech owl, sounded intermittently, along with an occasional distant howl from some animal's far-off lair.

Drowsiness stole over Mollie, and her lids grew heavy. She was completely relaxed when she happened to glance casually toward the darkness behind Chance. There, reflecting the fire in their yellow depths, were two eyes blazing through the surrounding blackness. Feral eyes, hungry and dangerous.

"Oh, Chance!" she cried. "Look behind you!"

He wheeled around, and in an instant the pistol was out of its holster and in his hand. The powerful report of his shot momentarily silenced the cicadas and night birds.

"What was it?" Mollie asked shakily.

"A wolf, is my guess," he replied succinctly. "They're very dangerous." He moved toward the darkness where the eyes had gleamed and returned in a moment to say, "Got him. They will attack a man beside a fire if they're hungry enough—and that one was hungry."

Mollie shivered. The distance between her bedroll and Chance's took on a new and frightening import. If another wolf were to come into their camp during the night and head for her bedroll, would Chance be able to shoot quickly enough from that distance? Would she be able to sleep at all, under the circumstances?

She wouldn't dare close her eyes now. She worried all through the meal, which was delicious. She ate nearly an entire pheasant. The meat was tender, juicy, and mouth-watering.

The hot food brought back her drowsiness, but it did not alleviate her concern about the wolf and being so far from Chance and his pistol. He solved her problem by bringing his bedroll within two feet of hers. At her startled movement, he spoke with asperity.

"Mollie, don't be a fool. You don't know how to use a gun, and I have to stay nearby to protect you. If it eases your mind, there will be no repeat of last night." He laughed shortly, adding, "You've convinced me you're as pure as the driven snow and not to be taken roughly, and I respect you for it. You'll be perfectly safe."

All tension drained from her, though she felt slightly deflated. Had she been anticipating his embrace? That was ridiculous! Still, she would sleep in her clothes, breeches and all.

It was quite late when they finally lay down on their separate bedrolls. Chance's pistol lay at his side, and he had built up the fire so it was burning brightly. He would have to get up in the night and replenish it more than once, Mollie knew. She looked surreptitiously at the long length of him beside her.

With his high-bridged, narrow nose he was not as handsome as Sean and Clan O'Connor, she told herself once more, but he was a handsome man nonetheless, and taller than either of the O'Connors. But it was his character, his drive and restlessness, that made him more vital than any man she knew. He was always in control of any situation, undisturbed by adverse cir-

cumstances, and that set him apart. His independence
was a tangible thing—as was his money—and with
those came a certain arrogance. How she envied him
that independence!

The thought of it stiffened her pride, made her more
arbitrary and antagonistic. She began to hope it would
be possible to rid herself of any feeling for him. No one,
she thought angrily, should be so sure of himself, so
born to command, and so arrogant.

The morning was definitely cooler. The sky was still
overcast, but no rain had yet fallen. As Mollie made
her way into the woods on her private errands, she
looked down at the body of the wolf in frightened fasci-
nation.

It was a gaunt, hungry-looking animal with coarse,
grayish hair. Its mouth was open, drawn back in a
final ferocious snarl that bared its white, razor-sharp
fangs. It had been shot neatly between the eyes.

When she returned to camp, she looked with new
respect at the holstered gun at Chance's hip. A Colt-
Paterson, he had said. In a sheath on his other hip was
what he called a bowie knife, named for the Texan who
had made the first one. It looked even more murderous
than Meg Moriarty's "friend."

And Chance had moved so fast last night! Drawing
and firing had occurred almost simultaneously. It was
very comforting. Mollie could think of bears and wild-
cats, as Chance called her lions, without a quiver now.

Her hair was still damp around her shoulders, as
she had washed it in the river. She ran her hands
through it, trying to dry it. When Chance noticed her,
he pitched her a coarse towel. She dried her face and
arms and tossed the towel back to him where he was
repacking supplies on the broad-backed mare.

A new wind had sprung up from the north, colder
than any she had experienced since leaving Ireland.
The dawn sky was so heavily overcast that no vestige
of sunlight penetrated, and in the semigloom they ate
a hasty breakfast and set off, following the winding
Nueces.

This time Chance did not seem inclined to talk, and he stepped up the pace of the horses. The muscles in Mollie's legs and back were very sore. Riding sidesaddle that first day, more than riding astride, had done it, she told herself—or might her fierce and violent struggles with Chance that first night account for some of her sore muscles? She turned resolutely from the thought of the chaotic desires that had exploded in her that night.

They had been traveling just over two hours when it began to rain. Chance drew them to a halt and dismounted to pull the ponchos from the packhorse.

"Stick your head through and put your hat back on," he ordered. "The rain will run off the brim of your hat onto your poncho."

"The weather has certainly changed overnight," Mollie said as they rode on in the light rain.

"This is the first norther of the season."

"What is that—a norther?"

"A wind that blows clear down here from the north —from up in Canada. It sweeps across the plains country in the middle of the continent and comes right on down into south Texas. But it's usually lost most of its punch by the time it gets this far south. We never get as cold as north and central Texas do. It sometimes snows up there in the winter."

The horses moved steadily forward despite the downpour. Mollie saw them twitch their ears back in the rain, but they did not seem to mind it, and their progress continued unimpeded. Still, the rain did not lessen as noon came and Chance found a spot to pause for their midday meal.

Making a fire with wet twigs and limbs was difficult, and the kindling smoked excessively before it caught fully. Chance had chosen a place under a densely leaved live oak, and although water occasionally dropped from the branches, the steady rain did not strike them. The horses cropped wet, rough grass while Chance and Mollie ate.

She was beginning to tire of corn cakes but made no complaint. Tonight, she consoled herself, they would be

under the same roof as Bet and safe at last. Her usual
three cups of coffee warmed her and instilled a feeling
of well-being that cheered her despite the dismal
weather.

When they set out again, Chance said, "We ought to
be there before dark. Yonder's old man Jenkins's home-
stead."

She looked across the river to where Chance pointed
and saw a rather small, rough log building. Smoke was
rising from its stone chimney. The land around it had
been cleared and there was another building, evidently a barn, behind the first, which faced the river.

"How much further now?" Mollie was unable to
keep the longing out of her voice.

"Less than twenty miles. We'll be there in time for
supper."

By evening the wind had risen, and the clouds were
breaking up as they turned down a trace that Chance
said led to his ranch.

"Oh, to be with Bet and Ben and the boys!" Mollie
exclaimed. "It'll be almost like being home."

"You'll be welcome—and it will be home," he replied, but his little smile was unreadable.

"Can't we get the horses to trot?"

"They've had a long journey. Be patient."

What seemed like the longest hours of her emigra-
tion from Ireland passed before they came in sight of a
big house made of logs. They approached from the side,
and she looked at it in wonder as they drew nearer. It
was as Chance had described it. There were two wings,
and both had a second floor. The hallway running between the two tall squares divided them like a tunnel.

As they circled to the front, she could see in the
twilight an even bigger building—a barn, surely.
Beyond it stood still another large building—stables?
On their way around the big house, she had discerned
four small log houses, widely separated, with smoke
wafting from the chimneys of three of them and dim
lights shining through their windows.

By now, they had completed their circle and were
approaching the house from the front. It had an air of

permanence about it. There was a fence around the
house and outbuildings made of split saplings crossed
and nailed together. It all appeared exceedingly solid
and secure—and welcoming, a feeling enhanced by
the lighted lamps that gleamed through the east windows. Mollie restrained a desire to dig her heels into
the mare's flanks.

"What do you think of it?" Chance asked curiously.

"I think it's . . . solid looking," she said cautiously. "A
house made of tree trunks—it should last forever."

"Not if an Indian could shoot an arrow with enough
burning pitch on it into the roof," he said somberly as
they drew up to the gate. Chance reached down and
caught up the metal chain that was looped from gate-
post to fence and pushed the gate open.

As they passed through into the broad yard, he let
out a great shout. "Bet! Ben! Boys, we're here!"

The door flew open as Chance vaulted from his
horse and turned to lift Mollie down from hers.

Chapter 10

"Oh, Chance! We've been lookin' fer ye all day!" Bet cried, as people poured out of the front door of the ranch house to greet the weary travelers.

Chance hitched the horses to the front porch rail. "We made pretty good time, Bet, after Mollie gave up that blue dress and put on her britches."

Bet hugged Mollie, laughing with joy. "Come in, come in, me darlin'. 'Tis chill out here in the dark, an' I want ter see ye in th' light. An' Chance, yer friends th' Dominguezes an' Gutierrezes an' Hernandezes are all waitin' ter welcome ye home!"

It was Ben's turn to hug Mollie and brush his lips across her cheek. The twins came next, giving her great bear hugs, and they did not hesitate to kiss her lips soundly. Then they all entered the house.

The main room was large and comfortable with a pleasant fire burning in a huge fireplace. The room was furnished with a combination of rough pine furniture and a few gleaming mahogany pieces that would have done credit to Stirling Manor. Near the front windows was a long pine table, sanded smooth and polished until it gleamed. The overall feeling was one of warmth and hospitality.

The puncheon floor of sawed tree trunks was fitted neatly and was much smoother than Mollie had imagined it would be. And in the air there hung the most delicious, clean fragrance of fresh air mingled with the faint scent of spice.

In the hubbub Mollie was introduced to the three Mexican couples, whose strange, foreign-sounding names slipped from her mind immediately. They were voluble people, and their welcome, half in English, half in Spanish, was warm and charming.

"Tim, you an' Benjie go unpack th' horse fer Chance," Ben told his tall sons. "An' unsaddle the other two beasts. Curry 'em down an' feed 'em."

It seemed to Mollie that both boys had filled out since she'd last seen them, less than a week ago. It was amazing what good food could do. They looked broader, taller—indeed, they had become men during their journey to America. Now, reluctantly and with smiles at Mollie, they went to do as their father bid, accompanied by the six Mexicans.

Ben, too, looked taller and straighter in these surroundings, and Mollie realized that he also had put on much needed weight during their journey. So had Bet, who kept saying, "Mollie, Mollie! It just seems too good to be true that you're here! Aye, an' it'll keep me from missin' Ireland too much! Here, darlin', let me take yer poncho," she added, helping Mollie shrug off the wet garment.

Chance had already divested himself of his and was relaxing in a pine rocker decorated with two red cushions. He took out his pipe and began tamping tobacco in the bowl.

"Any supper left, Bet?" he asked around the pipe stem.

"To be sure, Chance! I'll go heat up a plate fer you an' Mollie!"

"No, wait a bit—let's have a cup of coffee to warm and dry us out a bit. It's rained hard on us the last six hours."

By now they had all taken chairs, and Mollie drew hers close to the fire to warm her chilled hands.

The twins reentered from a rear door and Benjie said, "Ramiro an' Al an' Fernando said they'd dry an' brush down yer horses, Chance—"

"Yer just in time ter fetch the coffeepot off th' rack in th' kitchen. Chance an' Mollie want a cup o' hot coffee, boys," Bet said firmly.

The twins exchanged exasperated glances and went back through the door.

"Mollie, ye look so trim in yer breeches! I'm so glad ye decided ter buy 'em after all."

"Bet, I must confess I didn't buy them. Chance did."

"Ah, an' weren't ye glad? Did ye get as sore as I did ridin' three days on a horse?"

"Yes, I did."

"But the worst was her first day sitting with a knee hooked over her pommel and with all those skirts and petticoats to look out for," Chance said, laughing.

"An', Chance, how d'ye like Mollie's cookin'? She's a very good cook, isn't she? Kate brought up both girls ter be fine cooks."

"She's a grand cook," Chance said with a perfectly straight face. "And good at fetching firewood and making a fire too. You ought to taste her corn cakes and coffee."

"I knew 'twould be so!" Bet crowed.

"If she's as good with her medicines as she is with the skillet, my bargain was more than a good one," Chance added.

Mollie was silent with rage. He hadn't even given her a chance to cook during their journey. She glanced at him to see his amused eyes on her. She swallowed thickly and tried to speak calmly. "I think Chance will find me better at cures than at cooking."

The twins returned with a wooden tray bearing a steaming coffeepot, a stack of pottery cups, a pitcher of cream, and a bowl of sugar. Tim held the tray while Benjie passed the cups around.

Since Mollie had removed her damp poncho, her hair had fallen loose in a shining mass about her shoulders. At last she could feel the heat of the low fire creeping into her body. It was comforting, and her coffee with real cream was a gourmet's delight. She savored it slowly, feeling Chance's mocking gaze on her.

"'Tis glad I am that Chance bought ye some breeches, Mollie. Don't ye like th' freedom they give ye? I've got on one o' me pairs now, even though I've three dresses hanging in me room."

"Yes, they are convenient," Mollie said, suddenly feeling bone weary.

"Breeches are me favorite garment fer this land. I been horseback ridin' wi' th' men, lookin' over Chance's holdin's," Bet said, smoothing back the silver streak in her blue-black hair.

The men had been talking together while Bet and Mollie caught up with one another's lives. Now Mollie's ear suddenly caught a familiar name.

"—and we had supper with Pedro Mendoza the night before we left. He was leaving next morning for New Orleans to meet with Colonel Almonte," Chance was saying.

"An' ye say yer goin' wi' 'em when they go ter join Gen'l Taylor?" Benjie asked eagerly.

"Yep. They've been in New Orleans buying supplies and ammunition. They ought to be coming back any time now."

"Then yer goin' ter fight wi' th' colonel against Mexico!" Tim said enviously.

Mollie and Bet's attention was riveted to the men's conversation now.

"Sure—stop 'em before they can take all my hard-earned land back from me." Chance laughed grimly. "You don't think any Texan's going to give up without a fight, do you, Tim?"

"No," Tim answered slowly. "An' I think since Pa an' th' rest o' us are workin' fer a piece o' yer land, we're Texans too."

"Now, Tim," Bet broke in, her voice agitated, "yer just a boy. You'll not be fightin' in any war!"

"Ma, you've got ter get over this thinkin' we're still

little boys!" Benjie burst out. "We've been men grown fer over two years now."

"We're two years older'n Uncle Chance was when he left fer th' New World," Tim added.

"Now you two quit devilin' yer mother about this war," Ben ordered. "Yer Uncle Chance hasn't gone yet, an' he isn't goin' until this Pedro Mendoza he's been talkin' about comes here fer him."

"An' when d' ye think that'll be, Uncle Chance?" Tim asked.

"Could be any time next month."

"Bet," Mollie said suddenly, "I don't think I'll have any supper. I'm so tired, I just want a washup and bed."

"Ye'll have a full warm bath! That's what ye need. I took one when I got here, an' me muscles weren't nearly so sore next mornin'. Boys," Bet ordered, "carry th' wooden tub up ter th' middle south room. That's goin' ter be Mollie's."

"That's a lot of trouble for you, Bet," Mollie protested halfheartedly.

"Not at all. There are two big pots o' water we keep over th' fire in th' kitchen all th' time. Come, I'll show ye ter yer room."

Mollie caught up her bundles and followed Bet up the stairway against the far wall amid a chorus of good-nights. The wide hall that connected the two wings of the house formed a long hall on the second story where the bedrooms were.

Later, after the boys had filled the tub and Bet left her to bathe, Mollie luxuriated in the hot water. The warm water eased her aching muscles and took all the tenseness from her nerves. She had put her precious medicine bag on the washstand after noting two chairs and a pine chest at the end of the big bed that would hold the rest of her things.

By the time she had finished bathing and toweled herself dry, she was so sleepy she tumbled into bed without unpacking. She knew only that the bed was exceedingly soft and comfortable and that she was so glad to be there.

* * *

Mollie awakened with a rush the following bright morning, and after dressing in her light-blue print muslin, she went downstairs to join Bet in the large kitchen at the rear of the big house. Bet was vigorously kneading bread.

"Good mornin', Mollie!" She lifted her hands from the bowl and wiped them on a cloth, then kissed Mollie quickly on the cheek. She gestured to a pretty young Mexican woman who was washing dishes in a large basin. "Ye met Ynez last night, o' course. An', Ynez, ye know Mollie's like us, newly come from Ireland ter stay wi' us."

"To *work* with you," Mollie corrected swiftly. "I'm a servant, Bet, and I want you to remember it and put me to any chore you need done."

Ynez's smile gleamed from her coffee-with-cream face. Her hair was shining black, with no hint of red or brown.

"So glad you here, senorita. We all meet you las' night, but you too tired to remember." Ynez's smile broadened as she took two eggs from a bowl. "I like zee Irish peoples—zey so jolly!" She turned to the big fireplace and broke the eggs into a pan where they began to sizzle.

Mollie returned her smile, thinking: Here's one Irish girl who doesn't feel jolly. But Bet was chattering on.

"Ynez an' her husband, Fernando Hernandez, work fer Chance. Then there's Elena an' Ramiro Dominguez an' Josefina an' Alessandro—we call him Al—Gutierrez. An', o' course, ye remember Squint Burleson. They all help run th' ranch. All of 'em have been friends o' Chance's fer years. Why, Squint fought aside him at San Jacinto over ten years ago. Ye'll see 'em all again terday." She pulled apart the dough and deftly shaped it into three loaves. "All th' girls an' I do th' housework, but I've had a dretful time tryin' ter learn ter speak Spanish. Me Irish tongue just won't wrap around them pretty words."

"Ever'body 'ave zere breakfast already, Senorita

Mollie," Ynez said from the fireplace. Her laugh was musical, and her full bosom shook as she added, "You get to sleep late, senorita."

"Call me Mollie, Ynez," she responded, smiling. "We'll be working together. Where are all the men? Where is Chance?"

"Now, darlin'—"Bet sounded faintly worried and Mollie suspected they had discussed her after she had gone to bed last night. "I know ye think Chance is a bit of a rascal, an' maybe he is, since he has more'n his share o' th' Delanty love of a joke an' th' Delanty sharp tongue—"

"I'm learning about his sharp tongue," Mollie cut in grimly.

Bet looked up from her task and her eyes met Mollie's squarely. "Mollie, ye know full well—"

"Eggs and ham for you, Mollie," Ynez interrupted with her infectious laughter. "Come. Seet—" and she pulled out a chair at the kitchen table where she had placed the savory food. Mollie glanced wryly at Bet as she sat down.

"I take your breads an' put zem on zee shelf near zee oven to rise," Ynez said to Bet. She placed the loaves above a stone oven by the fireplace.

"Fine, Ynez," Bet replied, pulling up a chair beside Mollie where she sat before a steaming plate of food. A large slice of freshly baked bread, which had been lavishly buttered, was beside the ham and scrambled eggs. Ynez returned instantly and poured hot coffee into a big pottery cup, which she set beside Mollie's plate. "Now tell me all about Kate an' Rose an' their jobs," continued Bet as Ynez left them alone to chat in the sunny kitchen.

While Mollie slowly demolished every bite, she told Bet all about Rose's job at H. Williams, Merchant, and Kate's with the merry Dolores Sanchez in the bakery.

"Now, why don't you tell me who this Colonel Jose Almonte is that Chance is going to join," Mollie suggested.

"I only know what Ynez told me about him. She said he used to come here without his men an' spend time wi' Chance. She says he's a highborn Mexican gentleman. He's terrible angry wi' th' Mexican gover'ment there. An' a man named Santy—"

"Santa Anna," Mollie supplied. "Chance told me about him."

"This Santy Anna did somethin' so awful ter Colonel Almonte an' his family"—Bet's voice lowered—"that nobody will even tell of it."

"Ah," Mollie murmured. "That's why he's so bent on fighting the man.

"An' that's why they went ter New Orleans fer guns an' such."

"Did you know that that's where Clan went?"

"Sean mentioned it ter me on the boat comin' over. Mollie, Ynez says this colonel is one more handsome laddie-buck. Sounds like he's as polite as an English lord, bowin' an' kissin' a lady's hand! She says he speaks English good as you, without hardly any accent at all, an' Chance is a captain in his troop o' soldiers."

"Captain Chance Delanty!" Mollie scoffed. "That should make him even more insufferable!"

"Come on, colleen," Bet said cheerfully. "Let me show ye around th' place." Thoughtfully, she added, "Ye look plumb beautiful in that blue muslin, Mollie darlin', but it just isn't right fer walkin' about a ranch."

"I suppose I should have breeches on, like yours," Mollie replied with irony.

"Well, yes, ye should."

"I ruined that beautiful sapphire dress getting here. I should have known."

Just then the kitchen door swung open and Ynez came in, followed by Josefina and Elena, all wearing gaily colored skirts and white blouses and chattering among themselves in Spanish. Each had an apron full of eggs, and Bet and Ynez took bowls down from a tall shelf to hold the fresh eggs.

"We must set zem in zee spreenghouse now," Ynez said, and the other two women took up the bowls and went back outside with them, smiling at Mollie as they departed.

"I'll show ye th' springhouse, Mollie, as soon as ye change ter yer breeches," Bet said. "I'll feel better if ye save that pretty dress fer some special occasion. An' it won't matter if yer breeches get a little dirty—'t'wont show. Besides, Chance told us last night he bought ye four pair. Shirts too."

Mollie groaned silently as she left the kitchen and climbed the stairs to her room. There was no end to the omnipotent Chance Delanty's foresight. And worse, he had spent more of his precious dollars on her!

Mollie went to the chest at the foot of the bed and shook out her breeches and shirt. She peeled off the blue muslin dress and the two petticoats beneath it. She had indeed indulged herself with Chance's money, she reflected, looking down at the chemise with its modest lace and ribbons. It was another extravagance she had been unable to resist in Dublin, having never had such a garment in her life.

The breeches successfully hid the lacy chemise, and she stamped her feet resentfully into the boots. Once more her full breasts tightened against the boy's shirt as she tucked it into the breeches.

A rap sounded on the door, and Bet came in without waiting for a response, carrying two wide-brimmed men's straw hats. Her sunny smile broadened at the sight of Mollie.

"Bet, I'd like to show Ynez my torn sapphire sateen, the one I was wearing when we began the journey from Corpus Christi. I was fool enough to think I would greet you and everyone else in a dress like a lady."

"Ah, Mollie, yer always a lady, dress or breeches."

Mollie laughed shortly. "Anyway, I wonder if Ynez can mend it. I don't see how, since it's in shreds, but perhaps she can try."

"O' course, darlin'," Bet said. "Put on this hat, colleen. I want ter show ye th' ranch buildin's."

Clapping the hat on her long, thick hair, Mollie followed Bet outside. They paused at the well, which was just outside the springhouse, a sturdy structure of logs. It had a slanting roof and was covered with the same hand-hewn shingles as the other buildings on the ranch.

Bet dropped the wooden bucket with a cool *thunk* down into the dark well. The windlass creaked as she drew up the brimming bucket.

"Best water in th' southwest, accordin' ter Chance." Bet proudly held out the gourd that served as a dipper, and Mollie drank thirstily. The water was cold, clear, and sweet.

After the two had slaked their thirst, Bet showed Mollie the springhouse, which was cool and dark and contained shelves for perishables. Then they went into the smokehouse next to it. From the ceiling of the dark, windowless building, fowl of all kinds—turkeys, chickens, pheasants—hung suspended from beams along with deer, hog, and sides of beef over a low, smoking bed of coals.

"'Tis oak an' mesquite burning low," Bet told her. "Ynez an' th' girls keep it burnin' wi' that big stack o' wood outside th' door. Didn't th' ham taste good ter ye this mornin'?"

Bet closed the door, and they walked across the area, dusty with patches of sparse grass, between the smokehouse and two bigger log structures. Bet told her that the larger one contained feed, oats, bran, and hay, with stalls below for cattle. The other was a large stable for horses with a corral built around it in which several mares and colts stood, eating from troughs of hay or staring curiously at the two women.

Bet halted at the broad door at one side of the stable, and the two peered into the cool gloom. The pungent fragrances of feed and well-kept animals came to them. Mollie could make out four horses— beautiful, gleaming animals, thin of ankle and broad of chest. They twitched their ears as they fixed their intelligent eyes on the two women.

"Ye'll have ter get Squint ter tell ye about these beasties. Chance brought three studs from England some years ago an' bred 'em ter some o' th' native stock. He sets great store by his colts an' calves."

The cattle barn was as big and cool as the horse barn had been, pungent with the scent of feed and hay stacked in the loft above. Mollie eyed the cows in the stalls with awe. Some of them had tremendous horns, spreading nearly five feet across. Some had much smaller horns and were heavier set than the others.

"They're milk cows, all o' thim," Bet volunteered. "Chance keeps 'em fer milk an' cream an' butter. Josefina even makes cheeses."

"Cheese?" Mollie asked quickly. At Bet's nod, she added, "Good. I can make more medicine. I've only one bag of it left in my medicine pouch."

"Medicine?"

"'Tis what we scraped from molding cheese. We dried it for use on wounds and such. 'Tis a great healer. Sister Maria Theresa said the knowledge was entrusted to her by an old nun at the Vatican."

"Ah, Mollie, ye know so much—'tis a wonder, ye are."

"I don't know nearly enough, Bet." Mollie sighed.

Bet led the way past a fenced yard where dozens of chickens were pecking at the ground among several large geese. A flock of turkeys stood off to themselves in a corner of the broad enclosure, and among all the birds were their young, scampering, peeping, and quacking.

"See there, at th' far end o' th' fence? Them's th' henhouses an' houses fer th' turkeys an' geese too," Bet told her as they moved on to another wide, fenced area containing a wallow and a trough of feed.

"Did ye ever see such pigs, Mollie?" Bet asked, leaning over the fence to look down at a great sow, black and white but covered with dried mud. She lay just outside the wallow, suckling a dozen fat piglets. Other enormous hogs were snuffling at the trough of feed.

"No. They're huge," Mollie agreed, thinking silently they were like everything else in this country, oversized and bigger than life. There was enough ham and bacon on just one pig to feed a hundred people.

She glanced to the other side of the broad lands

about the central house and saw four smaller log houses where the three "vaqueros," their wives, and Squint Burleson lived. Smoke curled from the chimneys of two of the comfortable houses, three of which had fenced gardens around them. The one at the end looked almost uninhabited.

"That's Squint Burleson's," Bet said, following Mollie's eyes. "He's a cranky sort, Mollie. 'Tis Ynez an' Elena an' Josefina who plant th' gardens an' flowers around their houses. Ynez says they'd do it fer Squint too, but he shoos 'em off."

A lean hunting dog rose from among several who were dozing in the shade of a spreading oak and padded amiably over to Mollie and Bet.

"Most o' th' dogs have gone wi' Chance an' th' others ter th' roundup an' brandin' o' horses an' colts," Bet remarked as Mollie scratched the head and ears of the hound.

So that's where all the men are, Mollie thought as the dog looked up at her with soulful brown eyes.

"Some o' the beasties are good at helpin' to round up th' colts, yippin' at their heels an' drivin' 'em to th' men, so Chance said this mornin' at breakfast. Squint Burleson an' Al Gutierrez fix th' noon meal out in the open fer all o' them. They have a thing called a chuck wagon that carries th' food along wi' 'em, so Chance told Ben."

"Where is this roundup of horses and colts?"

"Ah, that's a long way across th' river. Out where th' prairie sets in, they say."

"Is it all fenced?"

"Blessed Mary, no, child! That's why Chance had all his stock branded. They wander fer miles. When roundup time comes, all the vaqueros have ter ride fer hours ter get 'em all together again. Alesandro an' Ramiro an' Fernando are marvelous riders, their wives told me—like th' wind, they are. Squint Burleson is sort of foreman fer Chance. Ben an' me boys are learnin' ter ride wi' 'em an' doin' very well, if I do say so meself."

As they half turned toward the house, Mollie

halted. A distant rider was coming through the trees along the river. He trotted in the direction of the last little log house.

"Who—" Mollie began, then broke off, for the man was trying awkwardly to dismount a thick barreled gelding, finally sliding to the ground. The sound of his curses came faintly on the hot September wind.

"'Tis Squint Burleson, Mollie," Bet said, anxiety in her voice. "Now why would he come back at this hour?"

"He looks hurt," Mollie said, starting toward him hurriedly. Bet followed, and both women began to run as Burleson stood trying to loop his reins over a small hitching rail with his left hand. His right hand was held close to his chest, and there was a dark stain against his shirt.

Chapter 11

"Squint! Whatever's happened ter ye, man? Yer bleedin!" Bet cried in consternation.

His right hand was bound up in a multicolored kerchief that was dark with blood, as was the spot on his blue denim shirt against which he held the hand. When the women reached him, he scowled at them fiercely. His broad hat was pushed back, showing his black hair and the faint gray at the temples. Mollie noted once more that his features were angular but handsome for a man of his age.

"Yer hurt," Bet began, but Mollie simply stood and returned his angry stare.

"Nothin' happened that wouldn't happen to a damn fool pullin' a rope the wrong way, Miz Delanty." His lean features were sharpened by pain.

Mollie went forward swiftly when she saw there was blood on his breeches and both sleeves of his shirt as well as its front.

"Let me see your hand," she said firmly.

Burleson drew back, his narrowed eyes glittering.

"Lady, I ain't lettin' you see nothin'," he spat out. I'm goin' in and tend to myself."

"You've evidently hurt yourself. I can help. I was trained in medicine by a nun in Ireland." Mollie's voice was crisp and authoritative.

Burleson gave a sudden, harsh laugh. "You're but a little mite of a thing, ma'am. I wouldn't trust you with a wart on my toe. You and Miz Delanty run along, now."

"I can stitch up a wound better than I can handle a wart, Mr. Burleson." By now she had hold of his hand and was slowly unwinding the handkerchief. Her touch was light and tender.

The wound that was revealed was an ugly gash between the thumb and the back of his hand. A flap of flesh had been torn away and now rested loosely across the entire back of his hand, and it was evident he had lost a considerable amount of blood. Mollie turned to Bet, who repressed a cry of distress at the sight of the wound.

"Bet, would you fetch my medicine bag? And is there any good Irish whiskey in the house?"

"I got some a' Dan Jenkins's good corn likker in my own place," Burleson said truculently. "An' you ain't puttin' none of your so-called medicines on me."

"Then we'll use your whiskey," Mollie said imperturbably. "Let's get at it. Bet, do fetch the bag. I'll need a needle and some thread from it."

"I got a needle an' thread too," Squint Burleson said, a little less belligerently. "What d'you think you kin do about my hand, a little bitty miss like you?"

"I can mend you like a pair of breeches, and the patch won't show near as much," Mollie said, her eyes twinkling. "Now let's set about it."

Bet had sped away to fetch Mollie's medicine pouch from her room.

Burleson's air of crusty disapproval was unchanged, but he led the way into his small house. Its one room served as bedroom, kitchen, and bath, Mollie noted. There was a large, round wooden tub that hung from a peg beside the fireplace, a polished pine table in the middle, and a broad bed with a checkered counterpane neatly spread on it. Beside the bed was a washstand holding a pitcher and bowl. The floor consisted of smooth, hardpacked earth.

Burleson went to a wall cupboard and took out one of four tall bottles of corn whiskey. From a shelf below, he produced a box and several scraps of cotton cloth and a towel. Mollie took needle and thread from the box.

"Get a candle or a lamp," she ordered.

Burleson silently took a candle in a holder from the mantel over the fireplace and handed it with the flint to Mollie. She struck fire to the candle and set it on the pine table.

"Now come here, Mr. Burleson," she said calmly, "and sit down at the table—right here beside me."

Scowling, Burleson did as she commanded. He had rewrapped his hand in the bloodsoaked kerchief. Now he propped it up on his elbow and observed Mollie with hostility. "You're takin' a lot of responsibility on yourself, miss."

As he spoke, Bet came panting in with the medicine bag, her face flushed. She hurried over and placed the bag on the table, then pulled the only other chair in the room to the table and sat down.

"Squint," she said comfortingly, "believe me, Mollie O'Meara knows what she's doin'. Sister Maria Theresa was a saint an' as fine a doctor as any in this world. An' she taught this girl all she knew." Bet's face whitened as she studiously avoided looking at the raw wound.

"I'm a Presbyterian myself," Burleson said grumpily.

"You won't object to a Catholic cure, will you?" Mollie hid a smile.

"Well— Look here! That's a great waste of good corn likker!" His voice held genuine anguish as Mollie poured whiskey over the open wound. His face screwed up with pain, but he said nothing more as she sprinkled the yellow granules on the torn flesh and then took up the needle. She held it over the flame of the candle.

"Now, take about six good swallows of that corn liquor, Mr. Burleson, because I'm going to stitch you up and prescribe that you spend the rest of the day right here in your house—preferably in your bed. I will bring your supper this evening."

While he drank, she held the steel needle steadily over the flame until the tip became red hot. After the fourth swallow, he put the bottle down and looked at the needle with apprehension. "You goin' to put that red-hot needle into my hand?"

"No. I'll let it cool off, starting now." She waited while he took two more deep pulls on the bottle and set it down with a thump.

"How do you feel, Mr. Burleson?"

"That's the quickest drunk I ever got."

"Think you're feeling up to letting me stitch now?"

"Go on, but be quick about it."

Mollie's fingers were slender, deft, and gentle, and though Squint Burleson's jaw muscles quivered, he made not a sound. No wonder he had survived the bite of a rattlesnake, Mollie thought with grim humor. When she was finished, Burleson took another long pull on the bottle as she sprinkled more amelus on the stitches.

"I may as well get blind with it," he grumbled, setting the bottle down with a heavier thump. "I ain't never been sewed up with what I sew my own britches with."

"Does it hurt awful, Squint?" Bet asked sympathetically.

"It ain't no picnic." Looking at Mollie, he added, "You done a real good job—for all you ain't no bigger'n a Texas skeeter, an' a woman to boot. Does that red-headed aunt of yours doctor people too?"

"No, but she sews and bakes expertly." Mollie took up the medicine bag and put away her smaller pouch of medicine. The little pouch was almost empty, she noted with a touch of anxiety. Well, this very day she would take steps to remedy that, using some of the cheese in the springhouse.

"I don't feel nothin' from that ame—medicine stuff —except I hurt like hell," Burleson continued, his voice faintly slurred.

"Amelus can't be felt, but you'll find your hand will heal a lot faster and without infection. 'Tis a blessed medicine. The good sister didn't know where the recipe came from, but she learned about it at the Vatican from another nun."

"Vatican? From the Pope, you mean?"

"No." Mollie smiled. "Not from the Pope, but I'm sure it's with his blessings. I'll be back to check on you this evening. Then I'll put a light bandage on it. Until then, leave it unbandaged—don't touch it, but let the air get to it."

"My God! Look at that! I've wasted damn near the whole bottle—" He was outraged. The pain had evidently numbed, but his truculence was increasing.

"When you have a good hand again, you'll feel it was worth the liquor."

"How long before I can handle a rope 'er a gun again, Miss Mollie?" he asked, still scowling.

"Two weeks, at least—depending on how fast you heal."

"Two weeks! Good God—the roundup'll be long over. What a hell of a—ah—er—beg pardon. I can't lie around for two weeks doin' nothin'.'"

"Maybe we can find something for you to do with one hand," Mollie said cheerfully. "Now, you've lost a good bit of blood and, if I'm not mistaken, you're very drunk. I suggest you lie down on that bed and sleep the rest of the afternoon."

"Wimmen!" he grumbled. "They always want to tell you what to do. Bossy, I calls 'em. I'll bet that redheaded aunt of yours is the bossiest of all."

"Aunt Kate is sweet as sugar," Mollie retorted, "and a lot of fun. As for you, Mr. Burleson, you'll feel a lot better when I bring you a good supper tonight."

"The boys at the roundup, they *said* I'd be laid up

for God knows how long. Wimmen!" He stumbled slightly as he rose from the chair.

"Come on an' lie down, Squint." Bet rose, the color back in her face. "Mollie an' I will pull off yer boots fer ye and ye can sleep comfortable."

He collapsed on the bed, and it took Mollie and Bet tugging at his boots, one at a time, with all their strength before they came off.

Mollie returned the bottle of liquor to the shelf. "You'll not be needing any more of that, Mr. Burleson. You've enough in you now to sleep straight through to supper."

Outside, the two women wrestled with Burleson's heavy saddle and removed it from the horse. They left it on the narrow porch of Burleson's dwelling. Then Bet led the horse into the corral that surrounded the stables and turned him loose.

Back in the kitchen, Mollie and Bet greeted the three Mexican women, who were busy cooking.

"Josefina," Mollie said, seating herself at the kitchen table, "have you some heavy pots with lids on them?"

When Josefina looked puzzled, Bet answered, "T' be sure, darlin'. There are several iron pots—like those on the fire now. What d' ye need 'em for?"

"I want to store slabs of cheese in them near the fireplace. They must have heavy lids, for I want the cheese to become moldy in them. It's to make more amelus."

All three Mexican women chimed in with questions.

"How long will it take it to get moldy?"

"It all depends—and the mold must be scraped away at just the right time in its development. I'll keep peeking in at it as the days go by, and I'll let all of you know when we can scrape it off to dry and become grains."

"Eez good medicine? We help you make?" Josefina asked.

"Yes." Mollie smiled. "You can all help me make it."

And so Josefina went to the springhouse and returned with four broad slabs of fresh cheese, while

Ynez rounded up four iron pots with heavy iron lids.
Soon Mollie had her medicine in the making.

As the day progressed, the household seemed incredibly busy to Mollie, and she marveled that Bet had
adjusted so easily in just a few days. Earlier the three
Mexican women had gone over the house with brooms,
mops, dustcloths, and buckets of soapy water. After a
light noon meal, they tended an enormous black pot
over a fire outside. In it, clothes were boiling in soapy
water, Mollie's own soiled things among them. Before
the afternoon was half gone, the clothes had been hung
out to dry, then gathered up, separated, and placed in
chests in various rooms of the house.

Meantime, back in her room Mollie noted the sapphire blue gown laid across her bed, delicately mended
—wearable, though never again for a special occasion.
And in the chest at the foot of her bed, she found that
one of the young Mexican women had placed the three
extra pairs of breeches and the extra shirts Chance
had bought for her.

She made a wry face. Chance Delanty and his foresight!

The men rode back to the ranch at dusk. Ben and
the twins entered first. "Chance is stablin' his horse
an' rubbin' him down hisself," Benjie volunteered, "but
Al said he'd do ours. Is supper ready? I could eat a
bear."

"We're about ter set th' table now," Bet said. "You
boys wash up, now." She smiled happily at her husband and her two tall sons. Mollie was filling a plate to
take down to Squint Burleson and told the Delanty
men about her experience with the wounded man.

"I'm surprised he let ye touch him, Mollie," Tim
said, grinning. "He's worse'n a cornered cat when he's
well—an' when he hurt his hand, I'd swear he'd run
th' devil a close second."

"I didn't give him a chance," Mollie said, returning
his grin. "I just took over and ignored his protests.

He'll have a good hand in a few weeks." She turned with the full plate and went out into the dusk.

Earlier she had put a light bandage on Squint's hand when he had been only half awake. Now she also carried over her arm a sling she wanted him to wear to prevent the hand from hanging at his side and causing pain from blood pounding through it. She saw faint lantern light in the small log house and assumed that he was awake—probably with a terrible head from all the whiskey he had consumed, she thought, smiling wryly. Well, good food would help that.

But when she entered, she saw that two men were seated at the table. One of them was Chance Delanty. They both looked up. Mollie was still wearing her breeches and boots, and suddenly she wished she had changed to the printed blue muslin dress. But she spoke cheerfully.

"Feeling better, Mr. Burleson?" she asked, shooting a cool glance at Chance.

"I feel like my head's as big as a tub."

"This good supper will help that. Here you are." She set it down on the table before him, and he eyed it skeptically.

"I ain't very hungry."

"I know. All that whiskey. But eat it all and you'll feel better. I guarantee it."

"If I can hold it down." Squint grimaced.

"Bet and I will pick up the dishes when we bring your breakfast."

"Just how long you ladies goin' to bring my food?" he asked impatiently. "I feel well enough to feed myself, an' I'm used to eatin' at the big house with Chance."

"Until that hand heals a little more you'll eat what we bring here. And here's a sling. I want you to wear it so you don't let that hand hang down. You'll be a lot more comfortable with it elevated."

The food was still steaming, and the aroma was delicious. Mollie tied the sling about his neck and put his arm through it, then turned to leave.

"When I see you in the morning, we'll change that bandage."

"Thanks, Miss Mollie," Squint said gruffly. Then to the silent Chance he said, "You see what I mean—a regular doctor she is."

"I see," Chance replied. "Hold on, Mollie—I'll walk back to the house with you."

Mollie paused at the door, checking a desire to run.

"I'll see you in the morning too, Squint," Chance said. "Glad to see you're doing so well."

It was dark as Chance and Mollie stepped outside. Mollie set off quickly. Chance caught her arm. "Slow down, Mollie. I want to talk. I've been storing up a speech I'm going to make to you."

His voice was so deep, so masculine, it went over her like oil over a burn. It slowed her step and quickened her heartbeat. No man she had ever met had a voice so appealing, so compelling. She realized anew that she had been fighting the sensations he had stirred in her since that perilous first night on the trip from Corpus Christi. No—for longer than that. Since that night in Bet's cottage when she had first laid eyes on him.

"I can think of nothing we have to say to each other."

"I can," he said carefully. "First, thank you for your expert help with Squint. Without it he might have lost the use of his right hand."

"He might have, but he won't—Let go of my arm!"

"I won't have you running away from me before I've had my say."

A little shiver of anticipation slid down the back of her neck. That morning she had wanted to face him to show him she was impervious to him, but during the day she had thought better of it. It wouldn't do to quarrel openly with him before Bet and Ben.

"Well, have your say." She lifted her chin as they stopped in the dim light. The stars were thick in the sky, and a faint night breeze carried the myriad scents of trees, grasses, and tender things that grew in damp places. The air was intoxicating, and independent of her will, intense excitement gripped her.

His hand tightened on her arm, and he swung her around to face him. Despite the darkness, she could see the clean lines of his tanned face.

"It's just this, Mollie O'Meara," he said harshly. "Those indenture papers are a farce. I burned them as soon as I reached my room that day in Dublin. You're no more indentured to me than is anyone on this place. You're a free woman, and you can do as you damn well please."

The breath went out of her. At once indignation rose. "How dared you! Those papers were as good as if I had put a thousand dollars in your pocket! I owed you nothing but one year's service when you had them!"

"You don't owe me that," he said grimly. "Ah—I'll admit I've wanted you since that night you burst into Bet's kitchen, wild to confide in her and furious with me for being there to prevent it." His sudden laugh was rough. "And I admit I meant to take you with me to America, no matter what." He paused, then added with hard mockery, "But when we were making love on the trip here, you fought me and I found...I was wrong about you." He paused again, and confusion filled Mollie. "Now that I know you hate me, this makes us even. You have your precious independence and freedom, and since I'll be going to defend my land, we'll be miles apart. That should finish the matter."

"But you—"

"Just wait. My speech isn't over. My good friend, Jose Almonte, will be sending for me as soon as he and his troops reach the Nueces. You're welcome to stay with Bet until you can make the trip back to Corpus Christi with Squint or one of the other men. That, too, should please you."

"Are you quite finished?" She spoke between her teeth, her bosom heaving with repressed fury.

"Not quite." His hand tightened on her arm, swinging her hard against him. "I'll have one more kiss for all my trouble and my wounded feelings." A hot thread of desire ran through his words.

Suddenly they were grappling together, Mollie resisting and Chance pulling her inexorably against him. With one arm about her waist and the other hand caught in the back of her thick hair, he forced her face upward.

"Just one last time, Mollie." The voice that melted her was a little huskier, and Mollie could smell his breath, clean and sweet against her face. Suddenly he was kissing her mouth.

Despite her chaotic rage, her struggling arms weakened as his mouth drew all the strength from her, and she became fluid against him. A stinging sweetness increased her powerful desire for him. As his lips traveled to her throat, she heard her futile voice as if from a distance.

"Chance, you aren't fair—you're forcing me. You're no better than Clan O'Connor!"

He laughed low. "Yes, I am. I'm bigger and tougher. And it's this damned response from you that throws me like an unbroken stallion. It's as warm as a woman in love, not what I should expect from the virginal tease you are."

His jeer sent a streak of iron resistance through her, making her suddenly strong. Unexpectedly she managed to break away from him. She stood trembling in the faint orange glow of the moon.

"Don't you ever do that again!" Her voice was low and virulent with hatred for herself and loathing for him. She spoke with a cold, quiet fury. "So you burned my indenture papers, did you? It makes no difference. I pay what I owe. You may think you've done me a favor. You haven't. You've made me hate you all the more, for your cavalier attitude toward me and my kin—thinking you could throw a thousand dollars at us and go your way." She drew a deep breath. "I'll be free only when I've finished my service to you. I signed those papers July tenth this year, and July tenth, eighteen forty-seven, I'll walk away from you free and clear."

"So you refuse your freedom now? You're a fool, Mollie. But the decision is yours, not mine. At any rate, you won't be troubled by my presence much longer, and that should be of some comfort to you."

"It is! But a thousand dollars sits very heavily on me. And I *will* repay it. Just don't ever touch me again. Not even to shake hands when we say good-bye!"

"You're that vulnerable?" He laughed suddenly.

"I'm not vulnerable to you," she said confusedly. "It's something I—I don't understand—"

"You think any man can get that response from you?" he countered derisively. "Then you are, indeed, a wanton woman."

"I am not!"

"Then how do you explain returning my kisses with such...passion is the only word for it?"

"You caught me off guard!" she accused. "I didn't kiss you with anything like passion. It was all *your* doing!"

"Mollie, Mollie." He shook his head with exasperation. "You aren't making sense. And all this time we could spend making love. I'll make you a wager, my high and mighty bondservant. I won't have to force you when the time comes—and it *will* come, if you insist on serving me for a year." He paused; then in a hard, vibrant voice he added, "And your obvious virginity won't be the deterrent it was to me before."

She wheeled around and ran from him, stumbling as she passed the springhouse. Then, flushed and still quivering with anger, she paused at the door of the main house to compose herself before going inside.

She entered to see Ben and the twins drying their hands and faces on clean towels. Mollie couldn't refrain from sniffing appreciatively the aroma of Bet's pies, which were sitting, golden brown and crusty, on a sideboard. The roast on the spit in the fireplace dripped succulent juices that sizzled deliciously as they struck the coals, sending up small puffs of smoke. Bet and Ynez had taken pots from over the fire and had already filled wide bowls with vegetables.

"Come in, Mollie darlin'," Bet said merrily. "How did ye find yer patient?"

"He has a head from all that whiskey, but he's doing

fine," she replied, hastening to help pick roasted potatoes from the ashes and place them in the metal bowl Ynez held.

She heard the door behind her open and close and Chance greet Bet and the Mexican women.

"I washed up at Squint's," he added as Josefina and Elena said good night in Spanish, leaving to eat supper in their own cabins. "He's rather taken with Mollie's doctorin'."

As they took their seats in the large front room Ben spoke up. "Mollie, Squint would ha' made a botch o' that hand o' his an' maybe had the loss of it fer th' rest o' his life, if not fer you. If ever someone was needed about th' place fer doctorin', ye are, colleen."

"I know it," she said succinctly. "I intend to make myself useful here for the next year." She looked up, defiantly meeting Chance's mocking eyes.

"Ah, Mollie darlin', don't look so sour," Tim said affectionately, lamplight gleaming on his fair head. "Ye'll come ter love this country. We have already."

"Aye—love it an' cherish it, fer it'll be our very own," Benjie echoed. "No more landlords, no more rent. We'll be our own masters."

"Benjie an' I want ter go wi' Chance an' fight fer this land o' his an' what will be ours," Tim said quietly.

"Only Ma still thinks of us as her little boys," Benjie added ruefully, looking at his mother.

Finally Ben spoke up firmly. "Boys, yer Uncle Chance says yer needed here ter help at his place."

"An' ye know it too!" Bet burst out. "Instead o' sashayin' off in a country ye knew nothin' about!"

"What's ter know?" Benjie asked angrily. "We'd be wi' Chance, an' he knows Texas *an'* Mexico like the palm o' his hand!"

"Benjie," Bet said pleadingly, "we don't own any land here yet ter fight fer."

"Ma," Benjie said evenly, "ye know well enough Uncle Chance is payin' us wages—an' ever' American dime of it will go toward th' thousand acres he's sellin' us. All that land, not five miles down th' Nueces! An' ye say we got no land here!"

"I'd say you and the boys and Ben will own about five hundred of those acres in six months," Chance said in a carefully neutral voice.

"Five hundred acres," Tim said slowly, his fork poised. "Us, th' Delantys who never owned a square foot o' land before in our lives." His blue eyes were fixed reproachfully on his mother.

"Benjie"—Ben spoke softly but commandingly—"I won't have you an' Tim badgerin' yer mother like this. 'Tis settled. As long as Chance says he needs yer service on this ranch, this is where ye'll stay."

Bet cast him a grateful glance, but Tim broke in. "It isn't settled, Pa. Benjie and I are nineteen. We're men grown, an' neither you nor Ma can tell us we can't fight fer our land."

Mollie looked at Bet, who had scarcely touched her food. This was evidently a running quarrel between her and her sons. Ben knew the boys were old enough to make this decision themselves, and for all his commanding tones, his brown eyes held acceptance of the twins' decision.

Bet turned to her husband beseechingly. "Ben, make them see what a folly it is, marchin' off to a war that doesn't concern them!"

Chance put down his coffee cup. "But, Bet, my dear, it concerns all of us, you included. If Mexico succeeds, you'll have nothing, even though you've paid dearly to come here. And I would have nothing. Santa Anna has said this land all belongs to Mexico."

"It doesn't have ter be decided now—this minute— does it?" Bet asked, her eyes glistening in the lamplight, filled with tears she would not shed.

"Of course not," Chance said softly. "The colonel isn't back form New Orleans yet. And we can't go off unarmed and unprepared for the wild country we'll be in after we cross the border."

"But Colonel Almonte did tell ye he'd send one o' his men fer you, didn't he?" Tim asked swiftly.

"Yes. Pedro Mendoza will come for me."

"An' that could be any day now, couldn't it?" Benjie's dark eyes shone.

"Well, give or take a couple of weeks."

"Then I'd say it's been decided now. When he comes—"

There was a sudden scraping of a chair as Bet rose abruptly from the table. She walked swiftly to the dark staircase and disappeared into the still darker regions above.

There was silence at the table. Ynez, who had come in with a replenished plate of beef, looked after Bet's disappearing form. She murmured something softly in Spanish as her liquid eyes went to Benjie and Tim. "You re wicked to make your poor mama cry! Zere eez zee whole United States army to fight zee evil Santa Anna!" She turned and walked stiffly back into the kitchen.

"The whole United States army," Benjie said stubbornly, "doesn't have th' stake th' Delantys have in this war."

"You've put the whole argument in a nutshell, Benjie," Chance said, his eyes going from one twin to the other. "If I had to choose, and I guess I'm going to have to, it's your pa and ma who are needed most here at my ranch. And it's your pa and ma for whose services I'm paying most. The thousand acres should be yours—if we can keep it—in less than a year."

Chapter 12

Mollie wakened as the first faint streaks of dawn showed in the sky beyond her windows. She could faintly hear the bass voices of the Delanty men breakfasting below. Burrowing her head into the feather pillow, she tried to shut out the sound. Bet would let her sleep until they were all gone.

But sleep would not return. She lay quietly in her soft bed, pulling the pillow further over her head. Through the hall and under her door crept the tantalizing smells of frying bacon and boiling coffee. Her stomach growled loudly. She was hungry, but she didn't want to go down to the big front room and eat with all of them, not while her quarrel with Chance and their kiss were still so fresh in her mind! Thank God she hadn't dreamed of him again!

Giving up on sleep, she put her bare feet to the rag rug beside her bed. Through her open windows, the male voices suddenly sounded louder. She heard the clink of bridle bits and the lighter jingling sound of the spurs as the men made ready to leave for the day's roundup. A dog barked and the sound was taken up by another, until a sharply spoken Spanish word silenced them.

Mollie went to the window and peered below. In the dim light, she could see that the Mexican vaqueros had joined the men from the house, bringing their saddled horses with them. The twins and Ben were there—and Chance himself, taller than the rest. She watched him swing easily up on his mount, and in moments the group was gone, trailed by several lean hunting dogs. She watched until they were out of sight in the thick woods that bordered the river. The wind was cool, with a faint hint of fall.

She dressed quickly and caught up her medicine bag. In a few minutes she was downstairs, where she found Josefina and Elena clearing the big polished table in the front room. A fire was dying in the broad fireplace, and Mollie knew it would not be rekindled until tomorrow morning. September's cool dawns were followed by warm evenings in this country.

"Faith! Ye just missed th' boys, Mollie darlin'," Bet greeted her with a smile. Her blue eyes had shadows beneath them that touched Mollie's heart. She wanted to hug her friend and say, Bet dear, they're grown men —older than I. Don't worry so about them! Instead, she spoke cheerfully.

"I could smell the coffee and bacon way up in my own room."

"'Tis a good smell in the morning." Bet beamed in spite of her concern over her son's plans. "Come inter th' kitchen an' sit down. Let Ynez bring yer breakfast!"

After she had eaten a hearty meal, Mollie asked Bet, "Has Squint eaten?"

Ynez took her empty plate and gave a tinkling laugh. "Ah, *si*, senorita. I took Senor Burleson's breakfast to heem, before zee others ate zis morning."

"Well, I'm going to look in on Senor Burleson for a minute right now," Mollie replied, shouldering her medicine pouch.

"I'm glad ye wore yer britches," Bet said. "When ye get back, I want ter take ye fer a horseback ride along th' river, so ye can see what a bonny place this new land is."

"I'll enjoy that," Mollie replied, going out the back door.

Arriving at Squint's house, she knocked, then opened the door to see his tray of empty dishes on the table. He sat on the edge of his neatly made bed, fully dressed and smoking a villainous-looking cigar. He took it from his mouth and gave her a reluctant smile. His stern face almost seemed to crack with the effort, and Mollie knew he was unused to smiling, especially at women.

"I poured a little bit...a durn little bit... o' whiskey over it this mornin'," he said, back to his usual grumpiness. "A waste of good corn likker."

"You'll not begrudge the liquor when you have a good hand again. Is it very sore?"

"Damn—durn right, it's sore."

"It will be better in a few days."

"An' there's very little I kin do with my left hand, miss. I'm as useless as a housefly."

"You can use that right hand if you're gentle with it and don't do heavy work. The exercise will be good for it. Just don't pull the stitches loose. I'll take them out in a day or two."

"I been wantin' to braid me a new lariat. I got the leather off the last old steer we trimmed out. Could I do that, you reckon?"

"I reckon." Mollie smiled. "But little else for a while."

His narrowed brown eyes with their thick lashes fastened on hers. "I owe you, Miss Mollie. How kin I repay you?"

"I'm already paid," she said shortly. "I'm indentured to Chance Delanty and work for him the same as you do."

His eyes widened briefly in astonishment. "I didn't think Chance went in for that sort of thing. I'm plumb surprised."

"He paid my way—and that of my aunt and cousin as well—over here from Ireland." She paused, then added grudgingly, "It was my idea. I didn't want to owe him anything—and I still don't." She flushed as she took his bandaged hand out of its sling. "Let me see this," she said, swiftly unwinding the loose cloth.

It had bled very little and, apart from some swelling, the angry red of the gash, and its neat stitches, it looked very well.

"Where will I find some clean strips of cloth like those you furnished yesterday?"

"There are some fresh ones in the cupboard on the right of the fireplace."

On the bottom shelf she found an assortment of containers on one side and on the other a stack of clean, folded white cloths suitable for bandages. She chose several and shut the cupboard door. Returning to Squint, she took up the little pouch of medicine and shook a few grains along the still moist tear in his flesh, then began to bandage it once more.

"You may be indentured to Chance, but I reckon I owe you somethin', Miss Mollie," he said, grimacing, and she knew his hand was aching.

"You don't," she said firmly, her touch very gentle on his hand as she slipped it back into the sling.

"I certainly do. Kin you fire a gun?"

"Good heavens, no!" She was taken aback by the question.

"I kin pick the eye outa' a squirrel at a hundred yards. An' in this country it wouldn't hurt none if you could do it too."

"Why would I want to pick the eye out of a squirrel at a hundred yards?"

"Miss Mollie, we've fought off Indians as recently as last month. An' ever since this here piece of country won its independence, we've had roamin' bands of Mexican soldiers—regular army soldiers—comin' into Texas on raids. We fought 'em off once less'n a year ago." He paused, looking baffled. Apparently he was not accustomed to having to convince women of the danger they lived with. "Them soldiers raid Bexar—it's really the city of San Antonio de Bexar—regular an' haul citizens off to Mexico City where some of 'em get ransomed an' some of 'em rot in prisons."

Mollie had seated herself at the small round table and she was pondering the contents of her medicine bag. Her supplies were growing smaller each day.

"You ain't heard a word I said, have you missy?" he growled.

"Oh, I have," she replied, somewhat startled. "If what you say is true, we all ought to be armed."

He laughed shortly. "We all are, includin' Ynez, Josefina, an' Elena. But you're probably just like Miz Bet. Skeered to death of the big bang thim things make,' he mimicked.

"I don't frighten very easily," she said proudly, then suddenly remembered the night by the arroyo when she had been so frightened she had fallen into Chance's arms like an overripe peach. "Not of loud noises, anyway," she amended.

"Then you oughta' learn how to use a gun."

"Are you offering to teach me?"

"Yes'm. I am."

"Too bad I have no gun. Maybe I could borrow one from the Delantys."

"No need. I got an arsenal." He pointed at a long row of shelves behind his bed that held several pistols, rifles, and boxes of ammunition. "I can't use my right hand to hold a gun, but I sure kin tell you how to hold one. Take your pick, an' we'll go practice down at the river."

"No; we'll wait four more days, Mr. Burleson," she said, excited in spite of her doubts. If she could handle a gun, it would be one more step in the direction of independence!

Three days later, Mollie peered into the pots containing cheese and saw that they were properly moldy. To the intense interest of the three Mexican women and Bet, she scraped the mold carefully from the cheeses and spread it on the clean squares of cloth that had been laid on the kitchen table.

By late afternoon, she had three newly made small

drawstring bags full of medicine and stowed them safely in the medicine bag. She recruited Ynez to help her, and together they made several more of the little drawstring bags.

"I'm running low on mint, foxglove, and half a dozen herbs. I'll have to hunt for them, and Blessed Mary only knows where I'll find them in this country."

"Josefina, she have a garden of zeez theengs. Maybe not all, but she have many—what you call—herbs."

"She wouldn't mind if I looked through her herbs for those with curative powers?"

"No, no, senorita—she be glad. I tell her." Then, puzzled, "She do weeth mos' of them—season zee foods."

"Yes. Many are used for seasonings, but some of them are good for fevers, wounds, and other sickness. We'll ask Josefina if I may look in her herb garden."

That night, as supper was being prepared and after the men had stabled their horses and washed up, a horseman came riding up to the front door. Mollie was upstairs, culling over the herbs she had found in Josefina's garden and spreading them out to dry. She heard the raised voices of the men and the shared laughter and talk below stairs. She hurried to pour water into the bowl on her washstand and quickly bathe her face and hands.

By the time she reached the big front room, the men were seated before the empty fireplace. Chance Delanty and the horseman, whom she recognized immediately as Pedro Mendoza, were conversing in rapid Spanish.

As Mollie paused on the stairs, Mendoza glanced up, saw her, and immediately rose to his feet.

"Come an' join us, Mollie," Bet said quietly. "Meet Senor Pedro Mendoza, a messenger from Colonel Almonte."

As Mollie came forward to shake his hand, Mendoza bowed. "We 'ave met before, Senora Delanty. Eet ees a pleasure to see so beautiful a young woman again." He turned and said something to Chance in Spanish, which brought a smile to Chance's lips as he shook his head.

Mollie felt the blood grow hot in her face, for Pedro Mendoza's black eyes were brimming with merriment and disbelief. "I tell Chance you are too beautiful to be weethout a 'usband, Senorita Mollie."

"Thank you," Mollie replied, but she knew he was lying. He had said something far more intimate to Chance, who was regarding her with a mischievous twinkle even as his gaze caressed her. Mollie continued swiftly, "I am a servant in this house, you know. I am indentured to Mr. Delanty for payment of my own and my relatives' passage to the New World."

Mendoza's eyebrows shot up, and he looked with bewilderment at Chance, who had evidently told him nothing of this arrangement.

"What eez zis 'indentured'?"

"It means Senorita Mollie is determined to work out the cost of her and her kin's passage from Ireland to Texas," Chance explained.

"Ah. You are very proud and honorable zen, Senorita Mollie." He bowed to hr again.

"Thank you, Senor Mendoza."

When they were all seated at table, Mendoza spoke to Chance swiftly in Spanish, then turned to the others seated there. "You weel forgive me, amigos, amigas, but I speak English not so good nor so queeck as Spanish, and I have much messages from zee colonel for Capitan Chance."

After that, the languages became mixed; Bet asked Mollie about the herbs she had secured from Josefina's garden, while the twins kept interrupting Mendoza for information. Mollie found herself carrying on a conversation that excluded the men, who for their part ignored the two women.

By the time the meal was finished, however, Mollie had overheard enough to know that Colonel Almonte was making camp at some distance south of the Delanty ranch and east of the Nueces and was ready for Captain Delanty to join him. She also knew that the twins were determined to go with their uncle and Almonte's troop of Mexican guerrilla soldiers. More devastating to Bet, her husband Ben had agreed that the brothers could go.

Bet's face was drawn as they helped Ynez clear away the dishes and put away the leftover food. Her silence spoke louder than any sobs or tears. It finally drove Mollie to confront her in the kitchen.

"Bet darling, they'll be with Chance. You know he won't let anything happen to them."

"He can't stop a bullet!" Bet whirled on her. "They've never been in any sort o' fightin', an' it's only since we got here they've learned ter shoot. Oh, if only Ben would put his foot down and tell them they could not go!"

"But, Bet, they're a year older than I am! They're grown men. I've been making my own decisions for over a year—when circumstances have allowed—and I'm not quite nineteen. Tim and Benjie are almost twenty."

Bet sat down abruptly at the kitchen table and put her head on her arms, hiding her face. "You're right, o' course." Her voice was muffled. "But I can't bear it. I love them so."

"Of course you do." Mollie put a gentle hand on her shoulder. "Chance knows that, and he'll make sure they are well trained with Colonel Almonte's troops before they see any action, I'm sure." With forced cheerfulness she added, "They'll all be back before you know it."

Bet lifted her head and smiled wanly. "I'll try ter think like that, Mollie. But ye know they're leavin' afore sunup termorrow."

"Yes, I know. But we'll fix them a good breakfast and see them off with smiles. Such things are important when they remember us later. If they leave you amid tears and lamentations, I know they'll leave some of their courage and optimism behind too, and you don't want that."

"No," Bet replied, wiping her face on her apron. "You're right. They'll need all th' courage an' hope I can give them." She straightened up and added, "Ynez, ye've done enough. Go ter ye Fernando. Mollie an' I will put away th' dishes. Josefina an' Elena are goin' ter have ter take up some o' yer chores, now yer expectin'! An' thank God we've Mollie here. She's delivered many a baby in Arderin wi' Sister Maria Theresa—an' three last year by herself."

The following morning the house was alive with activity. Mollie had risen earlier than usual so that she could see the twins off with a smile and a wave. And Chance . . . as he had jokingly said, she might never see him again. Her heart constricted suddenly, and she hurried to dress.

Pedro Mendoza, who had spent the night in one of the spare rooms upstairs, was bantering with Josefina, Ynez, and Elena as they served an enormous breakfast. Mollie was trying not to look at Chance, but she felt his gaze on her. Their eyes met briefly before she looked quickly away. She had determined to say a lighthearted good-bye to him and assure him she would work hard during his absence. She knew she would not see any of them again until the war ended one way or the other, and that might be after her year of service was over.

When the others around the breakfast table rose to go, Mollie, her eyes following the twins, got up slowly, aware that Chance had paused near her. Bet and her family and Mendoza went into the broad hall. Josefina, Elena, and Ynez followed, and they all went out into the yard, leaving Mollie and Chance alone.

Mollie started to walk past him, but his big hand shot out and closed about her slender arm.

"Aren't you going to tell me 'Go and good riddance'?"

She turned on him, her blue eyes flashing. "Isn't it what you deserve?"

"What a little ingrate you are, Mollie."

"Ingrate?" Stung, she tried to pull away, glancing fleetingly into the dark, commanding face above her. "After what you said to me?" she whispered. "What you thought of me? What you *did,* planning from the first to take me like a—a—any hussy?"

"Hussy or no, you'll still be mine." There was an undercurrent of ruthlessness in his deep, vibrant voice.

She twisted in his grasp, swinging her free hand to strike his smooth, tanned face, but he dropped his sack of provisions and caught her wrist. Pulling her hard against him, he bent his head to hers.

"I'll take a good-bye kiss on account."

She turned her head away even as she felt herself helplessly responding to the feel of his big body. "You'll *never* take me, you—" His mouth cut off her breath, and for a heart-catching moment her lips clung to his.

He released her so suddenly that she almost fell. He reached out to right her, laughing softly.

"Oh!" Her words were smothered. "I hope you never come back!"

"But I will come back—and before you leave."

Head held high, she stalked down the hall as he shouldered his sack once more and followed her.

Outside, the vaqueros and Squint had brought the saddled horses around to the front, and all was in readiness. The twins were joking with Squint, and Bet and Ben were trying hard to laugh with them.

Mollie knew her color was high, and she forced a smile as she attempted to slow her breathing. It was crisp and chilly in the October dawn, and the horses were stamping their hooves and blowing through their velvety nostrils. The clink of bridle bits and the jingling of spurs added to the sense of intense excitement as the three Delanty men and Mendoza readied to leave, their packs lashed to the back of their saddles. Ben was advising his sons to stay close to their Uncle Chance.

"Aw, Colonel Almonte'll train us. We'll be so sharp, we'll be lookin' out fer Uncle Chance," Benjie said, laughing, "instead o' th' other way 'round."

From the corner of her eye, Mollie saw Chance swing gracefully into his saddle. He had put on his deerskin jacket, which molded to his wide shoulders and hung open, exposing the strong column of his throat and dark, curling hair in the V of his shirt. Mollie tore her eyes from him as he sent her a keen, searching look. Tears stung her eyes suddenly, and her throat grew tight. Her sadness was for the twins, she told herself as she blinked the moisture away.

Bet was kissing her sons soundly as she bade them farewell, and she managed to hold back her own tears with a brave smile. The vaqueros, Ben, and Squint, his arm out of the sling now, had decided to ride the first mile with the Delantys and Mendoza. The horsemen rode out of the gate, which Ynez closed behind them, and they soon vanished from sight among the thick trees.

Mollie was rubbing away her tears as she looked over to see Bet's face suddenly crumple.

"Ah, Bet, love, don't cry!" Mollie caught her in her arms. Bet put her head on Mollie's shoulder and wept unrestrainedly. Mollie's own eyes were blurred, and her heart beat heavily.

I hope you never come back! Oh, she wished she could recall those rashly spoken words! She said a short, fervent prayer of retraction. They must *all* return safely!

The Mexican women stood looking sympathetically at the weeping pair. Then slowly they returned to the big house. It was appallingly quiet, Mollie thought as she and Bet followed. Her heart ached with a dull pain. How long would the war last? Then, pushing away the thought, she forced herself to speak cheerfully to Bet.

All that day and the next, Bet remained quiet and subdued. Ben was solicitous of her, bending to kiss her each time she paused in her evening work. Mollie, too, made a determined effort to cheer her.

Since Josefina had welcomed her the first time, Mollie took Bet with her on her second trip to the Gutierrez herb garden, where she was able to completely replenish her supply of mint. Bet helped her put some of it out to dry, and the rest they boiled into a syrup.

Mollie also took Bet with her when she went to tend

Squint Burleson's hand, which was almost entirely healed now. Since the second day after the accident he had been taking his meals at the big house, and he had begun an attempt at braiding his lariat. About three days after the men left, Mollie and Bet went by Squint's house to check on him; they heard him cursing before they knocked on the door. He greeted them with a scowl.

"This damn—durned hand ain't even fit to braid little strips of leather, Miss Mollie." With an effort he smiled at Bet. "Good mornin', Miz Bet. Hope you're feelin' better?"

"I am, thank ye, Squint," she replied with false cheer. "Looks ter me like ye've done right well. Why, look at that good long piece."

"It ain't near so neat as it ought to be."

"Looks neater'n any I could do, Squint."

"Miz Bet, I know that ain't so."

"Maybe you'll feel like giving me my first lesson with a gun this morning, Squint?" Mollie gave him a warm smile.

He grinned broadly. "You do know how to cheer a man's heart, Miss Mollie. I reckon there ain't a man alive could say no to a smile like that." Turning a dull red, he added grumpily, "I'll pick out a rifle an' a pistol for you."

Thus the first golden days of October passed, with Squint's hand becoming more and more mobile and Mollie learning to fire both rifle and pistol. She and Squint went down to the river bottom each morning and shot at limbs, rocks, and targets Squint rigged up. While Mollie hit only a few, she didn't miss the others by too far a margin.

Now that his hand had healed nicely, Squint Burleson seemed to take a dour enjoyment in dining with Bet, Ben, and Mollie. One cool November night, just as they were all preparing to seat themselves at the table, they heard a horse trotting through the front gate. Visitors were always welcome, for they brought news of the world beyond the isolation of the ranch.

By the time Bet and Ben went to the door, Ynez was already setting a plate at the table for the visitor, who turned out to be a Texas Ranger, a compactly built man with a friendly face and sandy hair.

"I'm on my way to the capitol at Austin with a message from General Zachary Taylor to the governor, an' when I saw your lights, I couldn't resist stoppin' for the night, if you'll have me."

There was a chorus of welcome from all of them. Even Squint, who greeted each newcomer with suspicion, spoke a kind word. It developed as the meal was served that their visitor had a wealth of news. Under the influence of good coffee and pleasant company, the ranger, Jim Alexander by name, talked freely to his interested audience.

"'Tis rumored," he said over his second cup of coffee, "that President Polk has had a change of mind. I heard the officers talking about it while I was with Taylor's troops. Seems the president is alarmed by what he calls Taylor's 'incompetence'—though his troops call him Old Rough and Ready and think he's doing as well as anyone could. He's certainly been victorious in every undertaking an' under some very difficult circumstances." Alexander grinned. "Personally, I think it's because Polk's a Democrat an' doesn't want to give the Whigs—Taylor's a Whig—a potential presidential candidate in the form of a heroic general. But he can't find a Democratic general to put in his place."

Ben shook his head. "All this talk o' Democrats an' Whigs—'tis hard for a newcomer ter follow. If th' man's winnin' battles, he should be left in charge o' the army."

"My sentiments exactly. But my guess is Polk'll pick another Whig general to share the glory an' dilute Taylor's popularity."

"And what of the Mexicans?" Mollie asked curiously. "How are they taking these victories by their enemies? I had heard that their leader, Santa Anna, was supposed to put new heart in them."

"I've talked to a great number of them in the villages as I passed through, and many dislike their leader. They say Santa Anna has bombarded their Congress with demands for silver and succeeded in getting them to authorize the seizure and sale of several millions in church properties. That's alienated most of the clergy, an' 'tis said some of them welcome the American invasion." He paused and took a sip from his cup as Ynez brought in a cobbler made of dried peaches.

"Actually, Miss Mollie," he said thoughtfully, "no single faction, party, or ideology can unite Mexico at this stage."

They ate the delicious cobbler and finished their coffee, then settled down in comfortable chairs before the fire. Ben lit his pipe, and Alexander took a narrow black cigar from a pocket of his heavy leather coat.

"I'd like ter hear more about this Mexico, Mr. Alexander," Ben drawled. "I've got two son's an' a brother fightin' there. They've been gone near three weeks."

Alexander turned sharply to him. "You have? Who are they? Maybe I've run into them on my travels."

"Not likely, but 'tis Chance Delanty, me brother, an' Benjie an' Tim Delanty, me twin sons. They're servin' wi' a band o' soldiers—mostly Mexican—under Colonel Jose Almonte an' all o' thim hate Santy Anna."

"I've not met 'em," Alexander said, "but I've heard of Almonte. A good man. And I can see you've a big stake in this war. The Mexican government's even more chaotic than ever an' Taylor should be allowed to penetrate to the heart an' restore order." He smiled sardonically, adding, "Most of the Americans think they're going in an' fighting to free the Mexican people from ignorance, poverty, and the landed aristocracy— of which your Colonel Almonte was one until Santa Anna confiscated his estates—and free them also from the dead hand of the Catholic church, which supposedly extorts money from the Mexican people." His voice was cynical as he concluded, "But the Mexicans are not all ignorant. They are as canny and acquisitive as Americans—I know. I fought them eleven years ago in the revolution and had ample evidence of their shrewdness and military might."

The table had been completely cleared, and the hand-rubbed pine tabletop gleamed softly in the lamplight. The company before the fire was relaxed. After Alexander had his cigar glowing, he took up the conversation once more.

"An' I must warn al of you here of the lawless who prey on either side—as in all wars—as they did over fifty years ago when this country won its independence from England. We call 'em outliers, as they did then. Outliers fight for neither side but kill and rob both soldiers and innocent civilians in the name of either army. I've killed my share of outliers." He drew on the cigar and blew out a thin stream of smoke, adding finally, "'Tis a dangerous war, and here you must watch for outliers and Indians."

"An' marauders from the regular Mexican army who are given permission by Santa Anna to raid Texas cities as well as far-outlyin' ranches like this one," Squint drawled as he rolled tobacco into a paper cylinder and lit it from a glowing red coal he took from the fireplace with a pair of tongs hanging nearby for the purpose.

"That's true. I've heard they raided San Antonio de Bexar twice in the last year, taking prisoners for ransom," Alexander said somberly. "How many men do you have here?"

"There are five o' us left, since me sons went with me brother Chance. All o' us are pretty good wi' guns," Ben said with a faint smile.

"An' you might add Miss Mollie to them as can shoot straight, Ben," Squint said dryly. "I reckon she can hold her own with both pistol an' rifle."

"That's true." Ben's smile broadened. "An' a more determined colleen ye'd not find in all Ireland—or America, now."

Mollie's face heated up. "Squint's been teaching me for some time now, Mr. Alexander, but I'm not yet what you'd call a sharpshooter."

They sat for an hour longer, discussing the war and all its aspects. Jim Alexander was succinct in his predictions of its outcome. He gave a clear description of what would happen to Texas and all Texans if Mexico were victorious. He drew a vivid picture of death and destruction and finally flight east to Louisiana. Mollie's quick imagination could envision it all, and she found her sympathies with Chance and the twins taking a new intensity.

By the time they took candles and made they way upstairs to the bedrooms, Mollie found herself deeply worried about the conflict for the first time—and more, wishing she could do something about it. Jim Alexander had given her a clear knowledge of what Chance had to lose and why he and the twins were risking their lives to save it. As she slipped into bed, she found her heart riding unwillingly with Chance for the first time.

One morning in the fourth week of November, Mollie rose early to see the sky a cerulean blue and ideal for her search for wild herbs. She wanted her pouch filled with herbs that would do her patients the most good, and Josefina's garden was inadequate for her needs.

At breakfast, she outlined her plan to Bet, who was most helpful. "Ride out on the prairies in front o' th' house, darlin'. I rode that way wi' the' twins when we first got here. Yer bound ter find almost every herb or somethin' close growin' in th' wild places."

Squint, leaving after a last cup of coffee, growled, "Miss Mollie, you'd better take the pistol I gave you. Stick it in the belt of your britches. You might run into a huntin' party of Indians, so don't ride out too far. Within a mile or two you'll find most all the kinds of vegetation Texas grows."

"All right, Squint." Mollie grinned impishly at him and, going to the front room, she picked up her pistol from the mantel and thrust it into the waistband of her breeches. In less than half an hour she was astride her mare, with her medicine pouch and a good cotton sack looped over the pommel of her saddle.

About a mile out on the prairie she dismounted in

order to investigate what seemed like a particularly promising green area. After searching carefully, she found wild sage, which she knew was good for the nerves.

The further she rode, the more she found. She was well over three miles from the house when she found wild wheat, the grains of which, when properly ground, had many beneficial effects. She gathered a good-sized bunch, placing it in the now bulging white sack.

She was so lost in her scrutiny of a small stand of trees that she failed to see several figures on horseback rising over a hill in the distance behind her. She dismounted once more to examine more closely what she was sure was a form of witch hazel, but unlike any she had seen before. She was studying its leaves, which she crushed in her palm, when the distant sound of hoofbeats came to her. As she turned, it flashed through her mind that Squint, who had become very paternal toward her, was coming after her.

What she saw instead was a troop of white-clad Mexican soldiers.

Her heart raced wildly as she whirled about to loop the drawstring of the cotton sack over the saddle pommel along with the medicine bag. The men broke into whooping yells and it seemed to her she moved slowly, as if in a nightmare, while she scrambled frantically into the saddle. The mare, sensing her panic, broke into a gallop before she caught up the reins. By that time, the troop had thundered down on her and the man in the front reached out to seize the reins of her horse.

Keeping one hand on the reins, she pulled out the pistol at her waist with the other and turned to fire at her pursuer. He swung his arm up as swiftly as a striking snake, knocking her wrist aside, and the gun fired harmlessly into the air. Cruelly he twisted her arm around. Still she clung to the pistol as he reached over and lifted her easily from the saddle. He forced her across his saddle, and his well-trained horse slowed down when he dropped the reins to hold her tightly against him.

He was laughing, and his foul breath made her gag as her wild scream rose piercingly above the shouts of triumphant glee of the other soldiers.

Chapter 13

Mollie fought against her captor furiously, snatching repeatedly at her gun until he threw it to the ground. Another soldier had dismounted to catch the reins of her frightened mare and said something in rapid Spanish to the man. He burst into harsh laughter, and Mollie clawed at him, kicking fiercely at his legs.

With sudden brutality he forced her against him, and Mollie finally looked into the brown face of the man who held her. He had a long, drooping black mustache and darkly stained teeth, and he reeked of tobacco. His little black eyes shone with pleasure as he asked her something in Spanish.

She shook her head, unable to believe that they would hold her. He spat tobacco and repeated the question, and she shook her head again vehemently.

"You let me go at once! The men at the Delanty ranch will ride after you and shoot you down!"

He shook his head and laughed again loudly. Before she knew what was happening, he pulled her up even more tightly and his rough mustache was over her mouth, his tongue pushing past her lips. She clenched her teeth against him as revulsion shook her. When he drew back, she screamed with all the force in her lungs. At this, he struck her hard on the side of the head.

Frantically she looked about, hoping for help from the others. For the first time she noticed that in the center of the troop of soldiers there were several men with their hands bound behind them. One of these prisoners called out to her. "He wants to know who you are—where you come from." The man was a Mexican, but he spoke English with little accent.

"Who are *you*, and where do you come from?" she countered.

"These men are from the Mexican regular army"— the man shrugged—"and we are captured citizens of San Antonio de Bexar. They are taking us to Mexico City."

"Why?" she asked, renewing her struggles against her captor, who was bending his head to hers again.

"We are to be held for ransom or exchange. Or they may simply kill us." With urgency he added, "You'd better tell him who you are. That's what he wants to know."

"I'm Mollie O'Meara, indentured to Chance Delanty, and everyone on his ranch will be looking for me! They are all sharpshooters—all of them!" She hoped the soldiers would believe there were many more than the five men actually at the ranch.

The prisoner translated Mollie's reply, and the soldier threw back his head and roared with laughter. A gust of his fetid breath struck her like a physical blow. Then he spoke to Mollie in Spanish, contempt heavy in his voice. She looked helplessly at her interpreter.

"He says that means nothing. That he will take you to Mexico City with us—that he finds you desirable. He is Colonel Santiago, leader of this troop."

Mollie began to struggle again, but with brutal hands Santiago forced her to stillness. The small army started to move across the wide spaces beyond the small clump of trees. Bruising herself against the wiry

hardness of the leader, she fought him with renewed
fury, and this time her hand connected with his cheek,
leaving red streaks near his mustache. He cursed her
roundly and slapped her face so hard that her head
snapped back. For a moment, her vision swam.

"Ramon!" he called, then issued instructions in
Spanish. The troops stopped while Ramon brought a
rawhide thong and bound Mollie's hands behind her.
Then, holding the reins as other soldiers held those of
the horses of the men captured in San Antonio, they
set out once more across the plain.

The November wind was cool, but under her leather
jacket Mollie was perspiring with fear and rage. She
had lost her hat, and her hair had come loose in her
struggles. It blew around her face and head, black and
shining in the afternoon sunlight.

She looked at the sky to try to get her bearings. The
sun was only halfway to the horizon, and they were
riding southwest. There would be at least three more
hours until sunset and they would not begin to worry
about her at the ranch until nearly dark.

Santiago made her ride beside him. Twice he put
out his hand to caress her thigh. When he slid it up to
touch her breast, she could not shrink away without
falling to the ground. With her hands bound, she was
helpless against these random advances, but once
when he reached over to press his hand between her
thighs, she screamed again and very nearly fell from
the mare. The desperation of her plight was driven
home by his avid eyes, which undressed her constantly.
Mollie was on her way to Mexico City—with part of
the Mexican army and a man who made no secret of
what he planned to do to her!

The air was chill and the sun was a circle of scarlet
low on the horizon when Santiago held up his hand
and his troops halted near a stand of trees. Mollie
looked at the trees, deducing from their dense growth
that the troops must be near the Nueces River. But
they had traveled many miles south of the Delanty
ranch.

Mollie studied the seven captives who rode among the Mexican squadron of about thirty soldiers. They were all educated-looking men, their clothing expensive. Three of them were of Mexican heritage, but four might well have come from Ireland or England, with their blue eyes and Anglo skin now almost as darkly tanned as that of their captors. The prisoners were parceled out among the soldiers, who were dismounting, removing packs from their horses and gathering firewood.

Mollie sat stiffly on her mare until Santiago came to her. He reached up, caught her by the waist, and lifted her to the ground. He spoke to her softly in Spanish, calling her *chiquita* and stroking her hair. She jerked her head away. He caught her to him roughly and he entangled his hand in the mass of her hair, forcing her face up. His full, wet mouth covered hers and he forced his tongue into her mouth; for a full minute the foul odors and tastes sickened her.

He spoke again to her in Spanish, but she understood the threat in his voice and knew with panicky certainty that he meant to take her before the night was over. He turned away and began unpacking his own bundle, which contained a bedroll. This he spread on the ground and with a vulgar gesture made it clear that he expected Mollie to share it with him.

The prisoners, distributed as they were among the small groups of soldiers, regarded Mollie compassionately. They all seemed to be in their middle years, and she suspected they were men of some power and influence in San Antonio de Bexar. They would probably bring large ransoms or provide bargaining power in prisoner exchanges. One of the prisoners spoke in Spanish to a nearby soldier, who nodded curtly, and the prisoner, whose black hair was touched with gray at the temples, came over to Mollie.

"Senorita, I fear Colonel Santiago will do you harm if you resist him. He is not above killing women, for he killed two in San Antonio when they sorted us out and brought us with them."

"You think he means to kill me?"

The older man looked uncomfortable. "I fear he will if you resist him."

"But resist him I will," Mollie said coldly, though her heart pounded with renewed terror, "even if I die for it."

"You are brave but foolish. If you humor him, he might turn you loose this side of the Nueces once he is tired of you. He had a young girl in San Antonio and he let her go after—"

Santiago strode back from a consultation with two of his men. Roughly he shoved the prisoner away from Mollie, and a stream of Spanish flowed from him as the man returned to the campfire. Santiago then turned to Mollie and untied her hands, gesturing that she was to seat herself at the fire where four members of his squadron were preparing food.

She looked longingly at her mare, which her captors had tied along with three other horses at the edge of the woods. If she could somehow mount her, she might make a run for it, tired though all the horses were after the long and fast-paced miles. But Santiago saw her eyes in the evening dusk and shook his head contemptuously. Mollie abandoned her plan for the moment.

Supper was sparse, consisting of thin, flat rounds of a corn bread. To Mollie's surprise, one of the soldiers brought forth eggs, which he had carried carefully in a bag with his other supplies. She gathered from the banter among her captors that these must be a last of that particular delicacy. The repast was augmented by sour dried plums, but they had good coffee, made in the American way, by boiling it in a pot over the fire.

All through the meal Mollie felt Santiago's gaze on her, and she ate as slowly as possible. Finally he seized the cup from her hand and threw it to the ground. He lit a small black cigar and half reclined on his bedroll. The sun had long ago disappeared, and now dusk was darkening into night. A somnolence had crept over the men, sitting comfortably by their dying fires. Santiago's eyes were glittering darkly on her now, and there was a small smile on his red lips under the long, black, drooping mustache.

Mollie refused to look at him. She sat close to the fire, hardly aware of the chill at her back, filled with dread. Steeling herself, she resolved she would fight until Santiago either knocked her unconscious or killed her. Glancing swiftly at his rapacious face, she knew he could do either or both without a qualm.

The men moved around them, stirring up the fires, throwing on more wood, and spreading out their bed-rolls. Mollie knew her time was growing short and she stood up abruptly. She started to walk into the thick woods, but Santiago was up like a cat, twisting her around.

"Some one tell this animal I have to relieve myself," she called out.

One of the prisoners translated her request. Santiago laughed lewdly and responded in Spanish. The prisoner told her, "He says he will follow and keep you in sight."

Mollie strode into the thick trees with her captor following at an uncomfortably close distance. She walked doggedly on, thinking he would let her put more distance between them, but when he did not, she ducked behind a thick patch of brush. Santiago could no longer be seen, but he was nearby. He shouted something in Spanish at her and laughed again loudly. If she could only get to her mare! Her precious medicine pouch and the bag of raw herbs still hung from the pommel.

Santiago strode into the bushes just as she was pulling up her breeches, long before she could make a run for the mare. Then he walked beside her, holding her arm in a viselike grip all the way back to the camp.

By now, night had fallen and the vault of stars above cast a faint light. Most of the men had retired, and she knew her moment of reckoning was at hand. She had determined to scream the entire time.

Now he was murmuring Spanish endearments as he removed her leather jacket and began to unbutton

her plaid shirt. She struck his hands away. He jerked
her back and threw her unceremoniously onto the bedroll, dropping down beside her.

"I'll die before I'll let you touch me," she whispered
between her teeth, but his contemptuous smile
gleamed dully at her.

He put a hand to her blouse once more and unceremoniously ripped it open. He had hold of her camisole
when she struggled to her feet and began screaming,
the sound of her terror breaking the night stillness.

He rose with her and tore off the camisole, leaving
her breasts bare. Then he halted suddenly as he heard
muffled laughter from the soldiers, who were watching
them from beside the low-burning fire. Bending
quickly, he put one arm around her knees, caught the
back of her neck with his other hand, and slung her
over his shoulder. Turning, he bolted into the denser
woods behind him, carrying her some distance as she
screamed steadily.

Dropping her onto her feet, his hand lashed out, and
struck her, first on one side of her head, then on the
other. She sank to the ground half conscious. She
moaned feebly with pain, dimly aware that he was
pulling her boots from her feet, unbuttoning her
breeches, and pulling them and her chemise from her
body. She lay before him nude, the rough ground biting
into her soft flesh.

Santiago stopped, putting his hands on the swelling
breasts beneath him, running his fingers slowly down
her nakedness to her hips, pressing her thighs apart,
sliding his hard hands over and between them. She
tried to press her legs together, but the effort was too
great for her remaining strength. She gave one last,
piercing shriek that faded slowly in the air.

But something had stopped him. Through her half-
open lids she saw his head lift, like a dog scenting the
wind, and suddenly he was being pulled away from her
without a sound.

She forced herself to a sitting position, her head
swimming, and saw him writhing silently in the grip
of something dark and big. She shook her aching head

to clear her vision and made out another man, dressed in black like the night. His arm was about the throat of the man who would have assaulted her.

Santiago clawed vainly at the arm and the hands that were squeezing the life out of him, but his wiry strength was useless. Slowly, slowly, his struggles grew weaker.

Gradually Mollie became aware that other shadows were passing silently among the trees, going toward the camp. She opened her mouth to scream again, but only a hoarse cry escaped her lips.

"Be still!" the man whispered, tightening his hold on Santiago's throat. "You don't want to alert the soldiers."

That familiar voice! How was it possible? Mollie couldn't believe her ears.

Santiago's movement had ceased entirely now, and he lay limply in the other man's arms. Still the dark figure gripped him tightly, until Santiago's ragged breathing stopped. The night was noiseless around them. Even the night birds, the insects, and the small furry things that lived in the woods were silenced by the intruders.

The other shadows reached the clearing and in another instant, hoarse yells sounded from the camp.

"Ma'am, did he—harm you?"

It was he! It was Chance Delanty, and he did not yet recognize her.

"No," she said, her throat raw from screaming. "You came just in time." Again she thought, without saying it.

He was pulling off his own familiar leather coat as he rose above Santiago's body. Screams floated to them from the camp, and several shots rang out.

Mollie had risen shakily and stood in the darkness, her nude body gleaming in the dim night light. She tried to find her breeches and torn chemise but she could not see them anywhere.

"Here," Chance said, "put this on and let's get out before some of the bastards come in here to hide."

She put her arms into the coat, finding it still warm

from the heat of his body. All her fear began to melt away as she pulled the familiar garment around her. Chance took her hand, and she followed him to the edge of the trees where the carnage in the camp could be seen. The broken twigs and stiff grass hurt her bare feet, but she scarcely noticed the pain because of the sight confronting her.

"I'm a prisoner!" The man's cry was taken up by others.

"For God's sake, senor, I am a captive of these men!"

All the prisoners had risen and held their bound hands above their heads. They stood bunched together in the starlight.

"Stay here behind this tree until this is over," Chance said swiftly. "I'll be back to get you, ma'am." He still had not looked at her face.

The prisoners were still screaming in both Spanish and English that they were captives of the Mexican soldiers.

"I was taken from my home in San Antonio—"

"I am not one of these scum—these raiders!"

Without their leader the soldiers seemed to lose direction. As some fell under the knives of their attackers, the others panicked. They fled to where their horses were tethered and leapt upon them. With only bridles and bits in the horses' mouths, the remainder of Santiago's squadron galloped madly away, over the prairie to the east.

"Prisoners, come together over here—quickly!" Chance Delanty standing among his men looked like part of the night.

Mollie could see men lying on the ground. The prisoners, their hands free, were laughing and speaking in both Spanish and English.

Mollie began to take stock. Her legs were cold in the November chill, and the rough terrain had cut into her soft, bare feet. She came out from behind the tree and stood shivering. Her head ached terribly, and she knew her face was bruised and swollen where Santiago had struck her. If only she had her clothes, but she dared not go back into the dark woods to look for them.

Had one of the escaping soldiers taken off on her horse, with her medicine bag and the herbs in it? It would be an irreparable loss. The possibility made her feel slightly sick.

Now Chance was organizing a burial detail, while some men built up the campfires and gathered the fire-arms that the Mexican soldiers had left behind. Mollie pulled the leather coat tightly around her and ventured toward the brightest fire, where several other men were making coffee and the newly released prisoners were describing their ordeal.

Those assigned to the burial detail had dragged more than a dozen of the dead further out on the prairie. Mollie shuddered as she watched them; Santiago's body was not among them. She wondered if Chance had forgotten both of them. She was deeply embarrassed by the nakedness of her long, slender legs, which gleamed palely as she neared the fire.

Chance was squatting next to the blaze with a cup in his hand. He looked up and spoke to her, still not recognizing her bruised and swollen face.

"Ma'am, we can take a pair of britches off one of the soldiers—but I don't know about boots," he said doubtfully. "They're so big for your feet, and so dirty."

Mollie had drawn nearer the fire as he spoke and pushed the hair back from her face. "Of course, we can look in the woods for your own clothing—" He broke off suddenly, his eyes widening. There was a moment of complete silence as the men around him noticed his shock.

"My God—Mollie! Is it—can it possibly be you?"

His recognition loosed a flood in her, and her story of searching for herbs and her subsequent capture poured out. She finished, "Colonel Santiago beat me, tore off my clothes, and probably would have killed me in the end."

The released prisoners who had drawn near corroborated her words. Chance had come to her and put an arm around her. He made no sarcastic remarks about finding her under yet another man, as she had half expected him to do. Instead, he spoke soothingly.

"Come. We'll get those britches. 'Tis too cold to stand around with bare legs." Putting a tender hand to the bruises on her face, he muttered roughly, "That son of a bitch—he didn't pay enough for it, by God. I wish I'd strangled him more slowly and made it more painful."

His hand held hers as he led her to a pile of garments and supplies that his men had gathered from the dead soldiers. Mollie followed, completely taken with his gentle voice and actions. All her defenses against him were lowered by his unexpected tenderness.

"My own breeches are back in the woods where you found me—us," she began.

"Here's a smaller pair. Still, they're much too large —and I can find no shirt here without blood on it."

"My coat," she said, as Chance threw down the pair of breeches. "It's over there near his bedroll. Santiago tore it and my shirt and camisole from me there before carrying me into the woods."

He said nothing, and together they went toward the brightening fire. Pedro Mendoza looked up from the wood he was feeding the blaze.

"Ah. The Senorita Mollie," he said, as politely as he had the first time they'd met in the restaurant in Corpus Christi, as politely as if she were fully clad. "Good evening, senorita. I am making zee coffee from zis man's supplies. Weel you and Capitan Chance join me?"

"Later, after we've found Mollie's coat and gotten her properly clothed, Pedro," Chance replied.

Mollie discovered her coat not far from the bedroll. Near it were the shreds of her shirt. Her camisole was in pieces and unwearable.

"Come, Mollie, we'll go into the trees and find the rest of your clothes."

"Oh—my feet!" she cried after they had gone a little distance. She stooped to feel her right heel, which was wet with her own blood. "I've cut it on a rock," she said.

With a murmured oath, Chance caught her up in

his arms, cradling her close. "Your boots can't be far from where I found you and Santiago."

He strode into the dark stand of trees. She held her leather coat in one hand and the other arm curled around his shoulders. Her heart was pounding as it had pounded when Santiago slung her over his shoulder, but there was an ocean of difference in her emotions. She was tingling with the feel of her flesh bared to the night where her borrowed coat had fallen open slightly, partially exposing her breasts.

Once among the trees, his step slowed, but he did not put her down. Instead, he drew her upward to him and bent his head. Mollie could not restrain the sharp thrill that coursed through her when the heat of his mouth touched one of her upthrust nipples. As his lips closed over it, she arched toward him with a small gasp. Slowly, as he kissed first one breast and then the other, he lowered her to the ground and bent over her, pulling his leather coat apart to reveal her white nakedness once more.

"Mollie, Mollie," he whispered, kissing the hollow at the base of her throat and finally fastening on her mouth.

A tide of passion carried her to a convulsive movement as she dropped the leather coat from her hand and closed both arms around him. The night chill was forgotten. Santiago's brutality and her near brush with death were forgotten. Even her vow never to let Chance Delanty touch her again was forgotten as she feverishly returned his kisses.

It was as if both her body and her spirit fused with his. His movements were slow and gently sensual as his warm, hard hands stroked her narrow waist and moved on down to her thighs. As one hand fitted itself between them, new fire coursed along her veins, and her little sigh of pleasure as he moved his body over hers was like a spoken word of love.

From the edge of the forest came a loud call. *"Capitan* Delanty! We 'ave finished weeth the burying! You 'ave found zee senorita's clothes?"

A bright torch flickered through the trees, and Mol-

lie moved swiftly, thrusting her hands against
Chance's bare chest. The thick, wiry hair almost stung
her fingers.

"Oh, Mollie," Chance groaned under his breath as
she scrambled to her feet. "Damn Hernando!"

"Capitan?" the unwary Hernando cried again as he
reached the edge of the woods.

"Come here with your torch, Hernando—we need it
to look for the breeches," Chance called out, buttoning
his shirt. Mollie picked herself up without a word and
walked ahead of Chance, looking into the darkness for
some trace of her clothing. As Hernando drew nearer,
the light from his torch caught her dark twill breeches.
She ran to pick them up and saw her own boots and
stockings scattered a few feet beyond.

"Good man, Hernando," Chance said dryly.

Mollie clutched the apparel she had found and
turned to the two men.

"If you will leave me a moment," she said, "I'll put
these on and join you. Just hold the torch high, senor,
and I will come."

"You are not afraid, senorita?" Hernando asked so-
licitously. "Zee woods are so dark, an' you have had a
bad time of eet."

"No, senor, I will be able to see even with your torch
at some distance."

"I only meant I would geeve you zee torch an' we
would leave!" Hernando said hastily, walking hurriedly away. Chance followed at a more leisurely pace.

Mollie raced to put the stockings on her bare,
wounded feet and slid into the breeches. If only her
shirt were in one piece! She slipped out of Chance's big
coat and into her own, tying the leather thongs that
ran down the front. Then, picking up Chance's coat,
she hurried to join him and Hernando.

Hernando was saying something in Spanish to
Chance. He turned to Mollie. "Senorita, I was say to
the *capitan* zat we 'ave bury all zee soldiers an' we
count our loss an' find we lose not a single man. Zat eez
good, no?"

"That is good, yes," Mollie replied. "How did you happen on us so quickly and so silently?"

"A scout—Hernando himself—located you early in the day," Chance said evenly. "His scout party had you under surveillance for the last five miles and were only waiting for dark to fall. We work best at night."

"Si, we are silent an' queek," Hernando added somberly. "We work weeth zee knives an' zee garrote."

So that was why she'd heard so few shots, Mollie thought, shivering as she looked about the camp.

"Didn't you see me with them?" she asked as they drew near the campfire.

"Si, we see you from far away, an' we see the preesoners in the middle—"

"But he had few men with him, and so they sent for me and others from Colonel Almonte's troop. We joined the scout party at dark on the other side of the woods," Chance said dryly. "Even if I'd known it was you, Mollie, I couldn't have struck until well after dark."

"Zee coffee eez hot, Chance," Mendoza said from his comfortable seat on Santiago's bedroll. "And we 'ave gathered up all zee spoils we can carry weeth us. Ah—I see zee prisoners. They come to talk weeth you before zey leave for Bexar and zere homes, Captain Chance. Shall I pour your coffee, senorita?"

"Please do, senor," Mollie responded, picking up her torn shirt from the ground nearby. As she turned the ripped garment over to examine it closely, she heard one of the ex-prisoners speak.

"I'm Allan Hamm, and these are my friends, who were also captives from San Antonio de Bexar." She glanced up to see the man who had translated for her introducing his six companions. They all thanked Chance for their release and expressed their desire to leave immediately for home.

"You are a long way from Bexar, amigos," Chance said, taking a cup of steaming coffee from Mendoza. "You could spend the balance of the night resting here, if you wished. The soldiers will not return. There are too few of them, and most are unarmed."

"I know," Hamm responded, pushing back his light

hair, "but we are anxious and our families will be too." He paused, looking at Mollie. "We were most concerned for the lady. She said she belonged on the Delanty ranch. It would be out of our way, but I'm willing to see she gets back there safely."

"I'm Delanty." Chance smiled. "I'll see that she gets back."

"Oh." Hamm was vastly relieved. "Miss, I do hope you were...unharmed by that devil Santiago." He bowed slightly to her.

"I am unharmed," Mollie replied, smiling, though it hurt to do so, since her face was still swollen from Santiago's fists.

"I can see your lovely face will be all right with time and care. We would have helped you had we been able to break our bonds."

"I know, and I am grateful." She put a hand to her eye. It was puffy, and she knew it would be black and blue by morning. Her medicine bag! She could make a poultice...She said swiftly, "Did any of you see the bags I had with me? One leather and one cloth? They hung on the pommel of my saddle."

"I have zem, Senorita Mollie," Mendoza said pleasantly. "Your mare eez gone, but your saddle and zee bags were on zee ground weeth all zee other saddles."

"Thank God," Mollie said with relief as he reached behind him and handed over her bundles. She put them carefully beside her. Then she took the coffee that Mendoza offered.

"We'd better move on," Allan Hamm said restively. "Can you spare each of us a horse? Ours stampeded after the soldiers. If you don't have enough, we can walk."

"Walk to Bexar?" Chance laughed. "I wouldn't do that to a fellow Texan."

"Then if you'll pick the horses you wish us to have, we'll leave, Captain Delanty." Hamm's voice lifted questioningly.

After the two went to see about the horses, Mollie looked again at the tatters of her shirt. It would provide some warmth against her bare skin under the coat.

She ducked behind a large tree and hastily donned the ragged shirt.

Back at the campfire, she picked up her coffee cup and sat in silence with the men. They did not stare at her, for which she was grateful as she reflected on the evening's events.

The stars were still thick as they prepared to leave later that night. Mollie guessed it was about three in the morning. Each of Almonte's men had a horse. Only she was without a mount.

"You'll have to ride double with me, Mollie," Chance said, and her heart began to pound. "Will you ride in front of me on the saddle or in back, on Beau's rump?"

"I'll ride in back," she said stiffly. She hadn't counted on being so uncomfortably close to him after their recent encounter.

He stood beside her, cupping his hands for her foot so she could mount easily. When they were both on the horse he spoke to her shortly. "You'll have to hold on."

She was aware of that, she thought angrily as she put her arms tentatively around his waist and they cantered toward the woods, the others following by ones and twos. The group slowed as they entered the thick stand of trees. After going only a few yards beyond the spot where Santiago had dragged her, they came upon a small tributary of the Nueces River. They splashed across the stream easily.

Mollie was tired and her head ached. The bruises on her eye and cheek stung. She sat stiffly upright against Chance, wincing with every jolting step of the horse.

"Why don't you relax?" he suggested. "It's a good four hours' ride to the colonel's camp, and you need the rest."

She stiffened even more. "When are you going to take me back to Bet and the others?"

"I'll have Pedro escort you back to the ranch as soon

as you've rested some. It's a good day-and-a-half trip. That is, if you want to go back—if you think you're needed more at the ranch than here by the twins and me and the Colonel's men. There'll be fighting, and we've no doctor. But it's your decision."

Although this was the first time the subject had been broached, Mollie knew instantly that she wanted to go with him. She had known it since he had rescued her the night before. If he hadn't suggested it, she would have. In the darkness she flushed.

"If you don't relax, I'm going to force you to rest," he warned.

"And how would you do that?" she asked coldly.

"I'll put you across the saddle in front of me and hold you." His voice was grim.

She slumped. She was hurting too badly to argue. Her arms tightened about his waist, and she laid her unbruised cheek against his broad, warm back. Her whole body went slack. Cushioned thus, she did not feel the jolting of the horse as much, especially as her breasts were held firmly against Chance's back.

Too tired to argue with herself, she simply let the warmth and reassurance of his big, solid body flow comfortingly through her. After a few sweet moments, she dozed.

She woke as dawn broke to find herself cradled in Delanty's arms, her aching eased. How had he done that without waking her? She must have needed sleep far more than she'd known. The horse was going at a pleasant, swinging trot, and Mollie was reluctant to open her eyes.

When she did, she looked directly into the sun-darkened face of Chance, whose blue gaze was on her. The moment light hit her eyes, her head began to throb.

"You look terrible," he said soberly.

"I know," she replied, hiding her dismay. "As soon as we reach your camp, I'll put a poultice on my face." She must look *very* terrible, she thought, turning her face away. "How did you move me from Beau's back to the front?"

"Pedro helped me, and we were very gentle with you. Feel any better for the sleep?"

"Yes, but my head aches."

"We'll soon be where you can do something for it."

"I'll sit up now," she said slowly, carefully moving her sore limbs so that she sat astride before him. She was very aware of his strong hands on her body as she straightened to a sitting position.

The sun was well up when they rode into Almonte's camp on the east side of the river. Mollie was amazed at the sight that met her eyes. Breakfast fires were burning brightly. She counted five wagons filled with supplies drawn up at the rear of the camp. The one nearest carried chickens in small barred crates stacked one upon another. Several tents had been put up, giving the campsite a deceptive look of permanence. There appeared to be as many women as men in the circles around the fires and moving among the tents. She had expected this, having had the benefit of Mendoza's descriptions of Colonel Almonte's troop.

Still, the camp and the people in it looked strangely casual to her—not at all like a troop of fighters as savage as those who had fallen so ruthlessly upon her vicious captors last night. Yet there was something comforting in the campsite too, and a wholly unexpected feeling of camaraderie filled her.

Chapter 14

The women greeted their returning men with cries of delight. When their eyes fell on Mollie, the hubbub increased. They clustered around her, chattering to her in an ebullient mixture of Spanish and English. Mollie heard over and over, "Pedro say she ees *el capitan's* lady."

"So glad you are here, senorita," said a tall, full-breasted woman with a pretty face and curving lips who spoke Spanish to Pedro Mendoza with an easy familiarity. He smiled widely and addressed Mollie.

"Senorita Mollie O'Meara, thees eez my wife, Cayetana." He added something in rapid Spanish, and Mollie caught Chance Delanty's name.

"Senorita Mollie," the women repeated. "So pretty!"

The women wore colorful dresses with full skirts and bright short coats. Some had wide, gaily colored shawls called rebozos draped over their shoulders. They were like a bevy of brilliant birds in their multicolored clothing.

Chance had disappeared into the crowd, but Mollie saw him returning with a priest in a black cassock and kirtle. His hair was snowy white, but his round face was unlined, and he was beaming with pleasure.

"Welcome, Miss O'Meara," he said, taking her hand in his. "Bless you, my child. Captain Delanty tells me you have had a narrow escape from what might have been a cruel death." He had only the faintest Spanish accent.

Mollie kissed his hand. "Yes, Father, I have. It was Captain Delanty who saved me."

"As I just told you, Father Baldemero, I have suggested to Miss Mollie that she accompany us, but she has not said yet whether she will. Sister Maria Theresa of Arderin in Ireland taught her medicine, and she would be of great help to us when we face our enemies."

"Ah, Miss Mollie—you would not deny us your knowledge and assistance? Captain Chance tells me you are great friends with his sister-in-law, Elisabeth Delanty, and her two young sons are here to fight for our cause with us."

"Oh, Father! Where are the twins?"

"They are on a scouting mission for Colonel Almonte, child." The priest sighed suddenly, and Mollie realized that he was quite old. "But I suppose you are afraid of the fighting to come. I do not blame you, since you have already had one cruel experience with the kind of men who serve the General Santa Anna."

"No, Father, I am not afraid, and I will serve with these good people. I am indentured to Chance Delanty until next July—and I will serve him here if he chooses."

A small hubbub arose among the women at her statement. Word about her status had gone through the camp like lightning, Mollie thought wryly. They knew all about her indenture to Chance and had already decided she belonged to him in more ways than one.

"You are good to choose to do so of your own accord," the priest said gently. He was evidently under no delusion about her status, though he smiled benignly at her. "That is my tent at the end of the campsite, Mol-

lie. I will hold six o'clock mass just outside it this evening—if we do not have to move before then. I hear
confession in the mornings inside my tent."

"Thank you, Father. I will take mass with you. It
has been a long time—since before I left Ireland."
Mollie was grateful for the trust she saw in the man's
keen brown eyes. *He* knew she was innocent—so far.

But as Father Baldemero turned away and left her
beside the man who exerted such power over her desires, in her own heart she knew she was guilty of
wanting Chance Delanty, fight it though she might.

"Here is your medicine pouch, Mollie," Chance said,
"and the cotton sack of herbs you were collecting before you were captured by Santiago and his crew of
cutthroats."

"Thank you," she replied politely. At least she could
try to keep their relationship a cool one.

"Now come weeth me, Senorita Mollie," Cayetana
said. "At my campfire you weel find good breakfast."
She laughed heartily. "Pedro, my husban', eez already
eat like a wolf. Captain, you are invite too."

"No, thank you, Cayetana—I must see the colonel."

"He eez out weeth your nephews. They go een zee
dark—gone a long time."

"Then surely they'll be back soon," Chance replied.
"Meantime, I will have breakfast with you."

The smells that rose from the campfires were tantalizing, and Mollie was hungry. When they reached
Cayetana's fire, Pedro was helping himself to a second
portion of scrambled eggs and bacon. He laid a thin,
flat corn cake down on his metal plate and refilled his
coffee cup while welcoming them.

"Come, Captain—an' Senorita Mollie. Eet eez good.
Nobody make zee eggs an' bacon an' tortillas like my
Cayetana." Beside him was a beautiful young girl of
about fourteen who was smiling shyly at Mollie.

"These eez my daughter Maricela, Senorita Mollie.
She cooks almost as good as her mother."

"Hello, Maricela." Mollie smiled back at the girl,
who quickly fixed plates for her and Chance. Maricela

watched Mollie with disconcerting intensity and admiration as they sat eating.

They had been eating in silence for some time when Mollie looked up to see a man step out of a tent across from her. He was clean shaven, his clothes fit his big body closely, and he was the handsomest man Mollie had ever seen. But her admiration turned to shock when she realized she was looking at Clanahan O'Connor. His cap of crisp black hair, his blue eyes, and his winning smile were all unchanged from the last time she had seen him on the quay at Dublin.

For a moment he was transfixed at the sight of her; then he strode forward, saying, "Mollie, Mollie! I can't believe it's you—an' ye've been hurt, colleen! How—who hurt ye? I'll take out after him!"

"Clan—'tis good to see you again. And the man who inflicted my bruises is dead, so I am more than avenged." She was as shocked by the sight of him as he was at seeing her.

Clan looked at Chance. "Then you an th' others must have found th' squadron that raided Bexar!"

"Found 'em and freed seven prisoners—eight, counting Mollie," Chance replied casually.

Clan was taking the plate from Mollie's hands and pulling her up beside him. As he bent to kiss her, she turned her cheek.

"Ah, now—is that any way ter greet a fellow Irishman, an' one who's an old friend at that?" he asked reproachfully, his big, warm hands still holding hers.

"A kiss on the cheek is a warm greeting, Clan. The question is, what in the world are you doing here?" Mollie smiled up at him.

"I joined wi' Colonel Almonte some weeks ago in New Orleans, an' was lucky ter do so."

"Lieutenant Clan eez being too modest," Pedro spoke up. "He saved Colonel Don Jose's life een a barroom een New Orleans. Two bad men attack our colonel over cards, an' Lieutenant Clan, he keel them both, one weeth a knife an' one weeth heez bare hands."

"Ah, then you are a hero, Clan. Congratulations,"

Mollie exclaimed. "And now you plan to fight with
America against Santa Anna?"

"Yes. The colonel has promised me a large grant of
land as pay for my services in his troop. I may be a
great don in Mexico myself one day!" His rollicking
laugh made light of the prospect. "Why are you here?"

They had reseated themselves, and Mollie took up
her plate again while Maricela filled one for Clan and
served him, her eyes worshipful. One more caught by
that irresistible Irish charm, mused Mollie dryly as
she gave Clan a shortened version of her capture by
Santiago and his squadron of Mexican soldiers.

"Had I not been out scoutin' the other direction, I
would ha' been with Chance and his men meself last
night," he said in frustration. "But at least Chance
was able ter finish off th' son of a b—th' spalpeen fer
his beatin' o' ye." He paused and added musingly, "Yer
such a little wildcat, Mollie darlin', ye would be after
fightin' th' man an' gettin' yerself knocked about."

Mollie said nothing. She had not told him of Santiago's designs on her, and Chance had sat silently
through her condensed account of the events leading to
their unlikely meeting at Colonel Almonte's camp.
Now he drained his coffee cup and gave his empty
plate to the waiting Maricela. "Mollie, I'll go to the
supply wagon and get supplies for you. You'll need a
bedroll and a blanket. And since you seem partial to
them, some new britches and shirts, as well as soap
and a towel. You can clean your teeth as we all do,
using a peeled twig with a frayed end."

"Thank you," she replied coolly. "And where will I
bed down?"

"Weeth zee Mendozas," Cayetana spoke up quickly.
"We'll be very honor' to 'ave you weeth us, senorita!"

"Thank you," Mollie said with real warmth.

"Be back in a minute with your things," Chance
said and strode away. From where they sat with the
Mendozas, she and Clan watched as Chance went to
one of the wagons and jumped up into it.

"Mollie, I offer ye th' use o' my tent. I'll sleep in the
open—"

"I couldn't take your tent from you, Clan! Thank you anyway."

"But ye can! Yer not used ter sleepin' in th' open!"

"I'm going to learn to do it."

"Eet eez not so bad," Maricela said shyly. "We 'ave our sleeping bags, an' we 'ave tarpaulins to cover us when eet rains, senorita."

"You see, Clan? Let me try my hand at it."

"But, Mollie, 'twould pleasure me ter accommodate ye!"

"Clan, I'll think about it. If I find I can't sleep in the open, I promise I'll tell you."

Chance returned and put a stack of supplies on the ground beside her.

"Two pair of boy's britches, two shirts, two pair boy's stockings, one blanket, one bedroll—all brand new—two towels, and a bar of soap. Sorry there are no camisoles or chemises, but maybe Maricela and Cayetana can fix you up." His grin was mocking, for only he knew she had no camisole or chemise on, and she felt her face heat up.

Clan noticed her color, and she felt his sharp blue gaze as Chance added, "I'm going to my tent now, Pedro, to write a report on last night's action—and maybe catch a catnap afterward. If my nephews come in, tell 'em to wake me."

"*Si*, Captain Chance." As he walked away, Pedro asked, "Weel you have a leetle more food, Senorita Mollie—Lieutenant Clan?"

"Not for me, Senor Pedro," Mollie said. "Where do you suggest I put my bedroll?"

"Under that tree." He pointed to a tall cottonwood nearby. "You weel see ours are there, weeth leetle bags to hold our clothes."

Mollie turned to Maricela and Cayetana. "Will you show me where the river is? I must bathe my bruises and treat them with medicine."

Cayetana gestured to Maricela, whose eyes were shining at the prospect of showing Mollie around.

"Follow—I take you to zee river, Senorita Mollie—" And they set off together. As they went past the thick trees, Maricela cast a smile at Mollie. "You know the Lieutenant Clan a long time?"

"Yes. He and I grew up in the same village in Ireland."

"He love you very much, I theenk."

"No. He is very fond of me—as an old friend," she lied. "Clan likes all the girls."

Maricela laughed warmly. "I theenk that eez so—but I theenk he like you best. He eez so handsome, no?" She sighed as the maids in Arderin had sighed then added, "He eez a good fighting man. He weel fight zee weecked Santa Anna who steal Colonel Almonte's hacienda an' all heez lands."

"He's a mercenary." Mollie laughed. They came to the river. "Ah. How beautiful it is!" There was a small sandy spit near the flowing water.

She walked down to the spit and seated herself with her medicine bag and a half-filled cotton sack beside her.

"What eez zis—merce—mer—"

"He is being paid by Colonel Almonte to fight."

Maricela smiled winningly. "No *dinero*. Only much land when General Santa Anna is defeat. All our men fight for zere land. My own papa fight for ours." She watched as Mollie bagan bathing. "I theenk Lieutenant Clan eez fight for *heez* land, for I hear heem talk to Don Jose, an' he say he will be a good ceetizen of Mexico when zey ween back zee land."

"Perhaps you're right," Mollie said.

Later, as she lay on her bedroll with the soothing poultice on her bruised face, she reflected on the things she had learned from Maricela. Colonel Almonte was a don and was viewed with great respect by all the people who served him. And Santa Anna had done something so unspeakably terrible to the colonel's family that no one would mention it.

Mollie had also learned that his father and mother, the old Don Jose and Dona Mercedes Almonte, had been killed when Santa Anna's men took over the hacienda, along with many of the Don's trusted servants. Don Jose and Father Baldemero, with a few of the don's longtime friends, had barely escaped. But the mystery had to do with the beautiful Dona Sarita, Colonel Almonte's wife. She had disappeared, and even Maricela's mother, Cayetana, spoke of her only in whispers.

Maricela's father, Pedro Mendoza, had been the old don's overseer for a long time. He owned a nice house where Maricela had been born, at some distance from the great Almonte hacienda. Father Baldemero had been the Almonte family priest for years and had his own chapel and rectory within the walls of the great hacienda. He had come to the Almontes from Spain and had baptized the colonel when he was born. Besides this, he was very learned and could speak five languages fluently. He had tutored the young Don Jose when he was growing up.

At last Mollie slept. She slept hard and long, and evening shadows were beginning to cast long fingers across the land when she awakened. She opened her eyes to find Maricela sitting across from her on her own bedroll, watching her admiringly. The young girl smiled radiantly when Mollie's eyes fell on her.

"Ah. You wake! I 'ave watch so no one weel disturb you, Senorita Mollie. Your face, eet is grow much much better while you sleep! Look, I have brought our mirror to show you." She handed the small round mirror to Mollie. "An here eez a canvas bag for all your theengs. Captain Chance leave eet for you before he go weeth heez nephews to Ruiz. He say he weel geeve you a horse for your own when he return. You can choose eet yourself."

"Thank you, Maricela! One day I will repay you and your mother for your many kindnesses to me."

"*De nada*—eez notheeng." Maricela shook her head and blushed at the compliments. "I mus' go help my mama weeth the supper."

Mollie could see the glowing fires with meat broiling on spits across them and pots set over stones among the coals. The mouth-watering fragrances floated to her nose, and she sniffed hungrily.

She set about rolling her new clothing into the

canvas bag Maricela had given her. Then she pulled on
her boots. Hearing deep male voices and the whinny of
horses, she looked up to see men arriving beyond the
Mendoza campfire. Chance, Mendoza, and a third figure in tightly fitted Mexican-style pants were coming
into camp. Getting to her feet, she walked slowly to the
Mendoza fire, where a large roast was on the spit.
Cayetana greeted her cheerfully as she turned the
roast and moved a pot over some rocks.

"You 'ave 'ad a good sleep, Senorita Mollie. I am so
glad. You needed rest ver' badly, I theenk."

"Yes, I did, Cayetana. And I would like you and
Maricela to call me Mollie, for I am your friend."

"Ah. That ees good. Eet will be Mollie now."

Chance and the men had disappeared, but in a few
minutes they returned and made directly for the Mendoza campfire. Chance stood tall and seemed somehow
a little threatening with the firelight playing over his
weathered face and big body.

"Hello, Chance," Mollie said briefly. "Where are the
twins?"

"They're stayin in Ruiz until later. They make
friends easily, and they're having dinner with two
girls. At the girls' homes and with their families, I
must add, so you won't think the worst." It was said as
if they were continuing an ordinary conversation.

Mollie flushed. He thought her such a prig. Damn
him anyway! He lowered his voice as he asked, "Are
you sure you want to go with my ragtag army and
serve as doctor to us?"

"I'm determined to do so," she said, lifting her chin.

"Then I'll send word to Bet and Ben, so that all of
them at the ranch won't be thinking you are lost or
kidnapped."

She felt a rush of relief. She had been concerned
about Bet and Ben, knowing they would be worried by
her unexplained disappearance.

"Thank you, Chance."

"You could return with my messenger, you know.
Remember, I've torn up those damned papers of indenture."

"You think you can tear up my word of honor like a piece of paper?" she asked in a low, furious voice. "I'm indentured to you until July tenth. I'm going with this little army. I *want* to go!"

"By God, I believe you've become a patriot!" He whistled softly, and his grin was mocking.

"Call it what you will, I want to see these people find justice. Why, they're almost as badly off under Santa Anna as we were in Ireland!"

"So they are. But after we get into Mexico, I can't send you back if you find you're unable to stay the course," he warned.

"I'm tougher than you think," she said. "And I'm not the prig you think I am—you with your double-edged remarks!"

Laughter burst from him, and those around the campfire looked up, smiling at the sound. He lifted his voice. "Cayetana, Colonel Almonte will have dinner at our campfire tonight. He wants to meet our new doctor."

"Eez always an honor when Don Jose eat weeth us," she said, obviously pleased. "Lieutenant Clan weel be weeth us too. He eez at zee river, washing up after his ride zis afternoon." As she spoke, Clan could be seen coming through the trees toward them.

Later, as they sat about the campfire after dinner with their last cups of coffee, Mollie studied Jose Almonte with secret admiration. He was at least thirty-five years old; his black hair had not a thread of white in it, and his features appeared to be chiseled in bronze. The small, trimmed black mustache made his even teeth seem as white as milk, and he spoke perfect English with scarcely a trace of an accent. He carried himself regally, and Mollie knew from the proud, graceful way he held his head that he sprang from a long line of aristrocratic noblemen. He had bent and kissed her hand when they were introduced and had remarked how glad he was to have someone so gifted and talented to serve with his troop. And his gleaming black eyes had complimented her beauty.

Clan O'Connor had seated himself by Mollie when he first joined them. Now he spoke to her quietly as the others talked among themselves.

"We've got ter help General Taylor, Mollie. I don't know if Chance has told ye,"—he glanced at Chance, who was deep in conversation with the colonel and Pedro Mendoza—"but th' rumor in Mexico has it that Taylor is greatly outnumbered. An' 'tis further said the American president, a man named Polk, does not like Taylor—fears he may be a presidential candidate later—and will send him no more troops."

Mollie remembered learning this news from Jim Alexander, the ranger who had stopped for the night at the Delanty ranch, but hearing it from Clan in these surroundings brought deeper meaning to the words.

"We have many friends and sympathizers in Mexico," Clan continued, "who keep us well informed about activities there. Ah, Mollie, there are more politics an' intrigues in America than there ever were in Ireland!"

Pedro Mendoza, who had been half listening to them, turned and spoke. "But you are not so bloody een America as we are een Mexico, my friend," he said grimly. "My peoples have not yet learned to govern themselves, an' a dictator like Santa Anna only keep zee waters boiling."

Colonel Almonte cupped his hands around his steaming cup of coffee and looked directly at Mollie. "Senorita Mollie, I will tell you what turns me against my beloved country under its present ruler." His black, gleaming eyes held a wealth of hatred, and Mollie repressed a shiver. "It is common knowledge—all my fighting men know the story well, and most have been harmed in some way by Antonio López de Santa Anna. The man has five acknowledged bastards and he smokes opium. A parade of whores passes through his bedrooms." Almonte's words were quiet, but they quivered with passion as his faint accent grew more marked. "What I am telling you, senorita, everyone knows—even the lower classes of men who have been in government. Only a few of them have sold out to the

dictator. They and the ignorant ones make up the rank
and file of his great army."

Almonte's eyes glittered, reflecting the firelight,
and in the silence about the fire, his voice was calm
but deadly.

"Santa Anna calls himself the Napoleon of the
West, senorita, but he is a messenger of death and dis-
honor for my people. His excesses are beyond belief. He
has even confiscated the property of our mother
church. And now in his greed he reaches for Texas,
which won her freedom fairly."

"I am shocked and grieved for your people," Mollie
said. "And I pray that you will rid the country of him
soon."

Chance, who had been sitting quietly in the flickering light, said, "Mollie has become a strong believer in
our cause, Jose. I must admit it surprises me that she
wants to serve with us."

"I've long been a servant and have never known
real freedom and independence," Mollie said tartly. "It
should come as no surprise that I sympathize and
identify with those who live under a tyrant."

"Then you will be glad, Senorita Mollie, when I tell
you that while Chance and his nephews and I were in
Ruiz—" Almonte paused, and his smile at her deepened. "That is a small town a little distance from the
border. There we heard that General Taylor has taken
Matamoras, Resaca de la Palma, Palo Alto, and Monterrey and is on his way to Saltillo. We plan to join him
there."

"Then we move from here soon?" she asked.

"Yes. We will follow the Nueces a little farther
south, then turn west to Mexico." He rose and bowed to
Mollie, adding, "You will excuse me. I go to Father
Baldemero for special prayers." He walked away,
speaking pleasantly to people whose campfires he
passed on his way to the priest's tent.

They looked after him silently for a moment; then
Chance said, "Tomorrow will be our last day here,
Mollie. We pack up and leave the morning after."

The others showed no surprise at this announcement, and it was obvious that Mollie was the last to learn of it.

"Why didn't you tell me before?" she asked indignantly.

"You've been asleep most of the day," Chance said, rising and yawning. He stretched and added, "If you'll come with me, I'll let you choose one of two mares for your own."

Cayetana Mendoza and her daughter began clearing things away. Pedro had given Clan a black cigar and was lighting one for himself.

Mollie got to her feet and followed Chance.

"Wouldn't it be better to look at the horses in the light?" she asked.

"We will bring them into the light of the fires. Anyway, it doesn't matter which you choose. One's as good as the other," he replied.

"In that case, why make this gesture?" she asked sharply.

"Women like a choice."

"You sound as though you've known many women."

"I've known a few. They all liked to make a choice when it came to horses . . . or men."

He had a positive gift for infuriating her, she thought, biting her lip. As they approached the horses, several blew softly through their velvety nostrils and two whinnied. Mollie noted that the stallions were tethered at some distance from the geldings and mares. Mollie was surprised at how well she could see the horses in the firelight.

Chance fetched two of the mares to show her, and together they walked back toward the campsite. He halted the horses at the edge of the clearing. Both were beautiful animals with shining, satiny coats. Mollie knew that Chance must have curried them before supper.

"They're both so beautiful, I can't choose," she said honestly.

"Take your time. Look into their faces and eyes. You'll make a choice. I supplied Almonte with twelve of my best horses."

She did as he suggested. Both mares were reddish brown, but one had a splash of white on her face. The one with the white blaze looked at her as she stroked the long, smooth neck. Most of the mare's mane hung over the far side and had been curried to gleaming smoothness.

"I think," she said slowly, "I'll take the one with the white splash on her face. She looks kind and gentle."

"They're both gentle, if not especially kind."

"Well, then I think she looks more understanding."

"Now that she may be. I told you that you'd make a choice."

"So you did—and so I have."

"And what will you call her?"

"Colleen," Mollie said instantly, and Chance chuckled softly.

"Why Colleen?"

"Because she looks Irish too."

At that he burst out laughing. "Her mother is an Irish mare. I brought the mother over on one of Captain Gallagher's trips several years ago and bred her to an English stallion. Your Colleen is her daughter and a sister to Beau, my stallion."

"Then you can chalk one up for my intuition. Is the other Irish too?"

"No. Straight English."

"You see?" Mollie was pleased with herself and with the horse. "My intuition is better than you imagined."

His face was unreadable. "I've never underestimated your intuition, or will I—all things considered."

"Now what does that mean?" she asked, stroking the mare's nose. It was finer and softer than velvet.

"Whatever you choose it to mean. Now I'll tether your Colleen with the others, and you can ride out on her in about thirty-six hours."

After the supper dishes had been washed, Mendoza, Cayetana, and Maricela sat talking around a neighboring fire. Mollie had seated herself beside Clan, who was enjoying his cigar, and she could see Chance's shadow moving in his tent by the light of a lamp he had lit. Gradually the fire burned down, and Clan moved nearer to her, speaking in a low voice, obviously wanting her to stay and talk with him alone.

"Tis a troubled country west of Texas, wi' a long history o' imprisonments an' rough treatment of Americans who venture within her borders, Mollie darlin'. If I wasn't so glad ter see ye, I could almost wish ye were safe at Delanty's ranch."

"I'd not be so safe there. I only ventured three or four miles and was set upon by the Mexican army."

"Well then, maybe ye wouldn't be so safe at his ranch. Anyway, I'm glad yer goin' wi' us."

"Are we far from the Mexican border here?"

"Not so many miles, but many Americans—an' Mexicans—have been robbed and killed on the highways o' Mexico, as well as in its cities. An' Americans have been held indefinitely when they go to Mexico on international missons. 'Tis a wild, reckless place wi' little law but what Santa Anna chooses ter make."

"It is a sad thing for a country to be torn by war," Mollie said, "but sadder still to be ruled by a tyrant."

"Ah, Mollie," Clan said impulsively, putting his hand over hers, "'tis glad I am ter be wi' ye again. I swear to ye that I'm not the light-minded man ye think me. I never pursued favors from the maids in Arderin. I swear it to ye."

"I believe you, Clan," she replied dryly. "They pursued you—but 'twas a willing victim you were."

"Mollie, I swear 'twas only a kiss or two I wanted that night outside o' Arderin when Chance Delanty pulled me away. I know I was a bit rough. Will ye not accept me apology?"

"I do accept it," she said, remembering his devouring kiss, the exploring tongue when she opened her mouth to scream. But he seemed to be truly sorry. It was hard to resist such a winning man.

"I never wanted ter marry anyone but you, Mollie," he said persuasively, flashing his warm, twinkling Irish smile. "I never told a maid I loved her—but I tell you now. For all ye consider yerself indentured ter Delanty, I want ter marry ye. An' I'm willin' ter wait fer ye."

"I don't *consider* myself indentured to him. I *am* indentured to him! And when I've served out my bond, I'll be going to Corpus Christi to join Aunt Kate and Rose. I've yearned to be independent too long to give it up for the bonds of marriage!"

Clan sighed, then went on stubbornly, "I'm goin' ter try ter change yer mind—an' by th' way, 'tis a good thing yer not going ter Corpus now, Mollie. There's a terrible scourge in th' town, so Armendariz, one o' th' colonel's scouts, says. 'Tis th' bubonic plague, an' scarce anyone who catches it survives."

"Blessed Mary! And Aunt Kate and Rose are there in the middle of the town!"

"Ye'll have ter pray hard, lass, that neither catches it."

"I shall," she said, panic in her voice. "I shall go to Father Baldemero and ask his prayers as well—right now!" She rose swiftly and hurried to the priest's tent.

When she returned, she found Cayetana and Maricela had shaken out and spread her new bedroll for her. Mollie took off her leather coat and boots and slipped into the bedroll, pulling the blanket well over her, for the November nights were cold. She had reconciled herself to having no night garments to sleep in. Slowly, weariness overcame her worry over Aunt Kate and Rose, and she slept.

Chapter 15

Two days later, the sun was well up before everyone in the camp was ready to travel. Word was passed through the band that Colonel Almonte had said they would follow the Nueces until they came to the cutoff that led to Mier and Cerralvo. This was to be done so the horses as well as Almonte's followers would have access to clear water until it was time to make the long trek to the border.

Mollie was on her mare Colleen and Chance rode nearby, while Clan kept an eye on her as well. She looked coolly and directly at Clan, who returned her gaze with a smile as bright and as warming as the sunlight spilling early morning gold over them.

Chance, taller and with wider shoulders, observed them both, and the smile on his lean, tanned face was sardonic. All Clan's handsome attributes were emphasized not only by the tight Mexican breeches, but by the fitted shirt and leather short coat he wore. He carried his Mexican sombrero carelessly in one hand and his thick black hair gleamed cleanly in the sunlight.

The trees along the Nueces, except for intermittent

live oak, were almost bare of leaves, their arching and angular limbs reaching up to the November sky. They had traveled no more than fifteen miles, some yards back from the winding river, when the most astonishing meeting took place.

Following the riverbank were two of the most bedraggled women Mollie had ever seen. They were leading two mules by their bridles, and on the mules' broad backs was strapped a motley collection of baggage. The women's dresses were ragged and torn, but their faces above their rough woolen jackets were shiny clean in the dappled sunlight.

Disbelief swept Mollie first, and she was sure her vision was playing her false. As Colonel Jose Almonte spurred his horse forward calling, *"Ola, amigas,* what have we here?" the women drew back, halting their animals, alarm showing in every line of their bodies. It was Clan O'Connor who confirmed what Mollie could scarcely believe as he spurred forward beside his leader and shouted to the strangers.

"Sure'n 'tis Kate an' Rosie Brannigan, as I live an' breathe! Me dear ladies, ye look in dire need."

"Ach!" Kate cried, her voice shrill with relief. "Tis Clan O'Connor himself! Oh, laddie, 'tis glad we are ter see ye— yo'll nivver know how much!"

Mollie put her heels to the flanks of her mare and rode through the other mounted members of the guerrilla band, crying, "Aunt Kate! Oh, Rose!" She slid from the horse, leaving the reins dangling, and flung herself at her aunt and cousin.

"Jesus, Joseph, an' Mary! 'Tis our Mollie herself!" Kate shouted, her arms closing about her niece. "An' yonder's Bet's twins wi' their uncle, Chance Delanty!"

Rose took up the glad cry, tears shining in her long-lashed hazel eyes. "And we were coming to you and the Delantys, Mollie! Mr. Williams told us just to follow this river and we would be sure to find you—but not *here.*"

The twins dismounted and kissed Rose and Kate warmly. "Sure'n we've half o' Arderin wi' us now!" Benjie said, laughing.

"An' a good thing it is too. Welcome ter Colonel Almonte's army, Kate an' Rose! They're all fine people," Tim added with a grin.

Kate, weeping openly, her voice broken and thick, said, "Ah, me boys—an' Chance, what are you an' yer nephews an' our Mollie doin' wi' all these people?"

Chance had dismounted now, and he kissed each woman on the cheek. "Dear Kate and Rose, we're off to help set Santa Anna to rights. Mollie can tell you all about it later."

By now, the entire band had clustered around them and Jose Almonte and Clan had dismounted. Mollie still clung to Rose.

"I thought you were both in Corpus Christi, Rose," she said, "but I've heard terrible things about illness there."

She was interrupted by a torrent of explanation from Kate. "Ach, Mollie darlin', Corpus is no safe place now. Nigh onter everyone in town is terrible sick. It started when a ship come in from India with dead and dyin' men aboard. They brought 'em inter town, an' soon th' sickness began ter spread. 'Twas th' plague!" Her voice fell to a near whisper. "Mr. Williams told Rose 'twas th' plague. People had swellin' lumps under their arms and in their groins; they vomited, and their fever rose sky high. Poor Dolores caught it an' I nursed her, but she died in me arms! 'Tis a dire disease!"

Rose took up the story. "And along with the plague came malaria. We left poor Mister Williams terribly sick with that, but he had his wife and daughter to nurse him." Rose stopped to wipe her eyes. "They carried people away in wagons to be buried, so many there were!"

"So Mister Williams' wife gave us these two mules an' we took what little money we had, thinkin' we could stay wi' th' Delanty's and wi' you, Mollie, until things was back ter normal in Corpus," Kate finished, her eyes pleading.

Mollie was stunned and silent. How could she tell them she must go with these people, that her allegiance to Chance demanded it? But Clan broke in cheerfully. "Ye can come wi' us, Kate, as Mollie's doin'. 'Tisn't a bad life on the move. We've plenty to eat, an' Mollie an' th' Delantys will be ridin' wi' us." He came forward and hugged each woman in turn.

It was then Mollie noticed that Almonte's eyes were fastened on Rose's delicate features and the honey-colored hair that hung down her back. Admiration ...something more...flickered in the black eyes. Rose was staring at him too, her cameo face suddenly pink as her wide hazel eyes held his. Mollie felt the electric vitality that burst between them, and she drew a sharp breath.

But Almonte was saying coolly, "Ah, Clan, you have many Irish women friends, *si?* But even if we plan that they will be far back from the fighting, fierce fighting there will be, *amigo,* and you know it well. You invite your friends along under such circumstances?"

"Fightin'," Kate cried in fresh alarm. "Yer goin' somewheres ter fight, Mollie?"

Mollie shook her head, and Almonte said soothingly, "Not Mollie, senora. Our women do not fight. They go with us on our way to join General Zachary Taylor, to rid Mexico of a corrupt man, Santa Anna. Our women will keep camp well back behind the line of fire."

"I don't see how—" Rose murmured and broke off, flushing under Almonte's brilliant eyes.

"Aye," Kate said with bitter disappointment, "but we can't go ter Bet an' Ben wi'out our Mollie bein' there, an' we been lost these two days fer sure." Kate's tears were dry now, but her face showed strain. With an appealing look at Almonte, she added, "I've got a metal oven strapped on me mule—see? I can bake th' best breads, pies, cakes, an' tarts that ever melted in yer mouth. We'd not be useless, Rosie an' me."

"And they'd be no problem to us, Jose," Chance spoke up suddenly, his deep voice authoritative. "They'd be well mounted, for those are fine, strong mules, though they're poorly groomed right now. Our women are already getting new clothing for them." He and Almonte exchanged glances of agreement.

"We been livin' from hand ter mouth, an' we're so hungry right now, Chance, we could cry," Kate said, encouraged by Chance's support. "We've eaten everything we brought wi' us."

"And my mother *is* the best baker in the world," Rose put in timidly, though her eyes flashed as they met those of Almonte again. The immediate and intense attraction between the colonel and the girl was so vital that Mollie felt its echo in her own emotions.

The black-robed Father Baldemero got down from his fat little pony and, going to the two travel-stained women, made the sign of the cross over them. He turned to Almonte and spoke softly in Spanish. Almonte nodded, turned, and issued orders in Spanish, and two of the women opened a pack on the back of one of their horses. They brought out roasted deer meat left over from supper the night before, along with tortillas and two oranges, the latter looking a bit shriveled, having been stored for over a month.

The priest and the others watched silently as Kate and her daughter fell to eating hungrily. Baldemero turned back to his pony, and Kate watched him go. Mollie saw relief and gratitude in her eyes that were even greater than her hunger.

"You ladies must ride well to keep up with us," Almonte said abruptly, then issued more orders in Spanish. Two men began unstrapping the meager bundles on the backs of the mules and repacking them more compactly. Three women came to the mules and handed the men two piles of fresh clothing, which were packed tightly with the rest of Kate and Rose's things. Kate, devouring the meat and thin corn cakes, looked at Mollie helplessly.

"Ride in our dresses?" she asked, her eyes going back to Almonte. "Why, we've walked all this way! Can't we go on walking?"

"No, Kate," Chance said firmly. "All the women ride—astride. We move faster that way. Those who do not ride horseback drive the wagons. As you can see, the women who ride are very modest. Their skirts cover their limbs. When we stop tonight, you can change to the fresh clothing the women have given you."

A stout Mexican man came up to Kate and, before she knew it and while she was still gnawing the haunch of deer meat, lifted her onto the back of her mule. The man put the bridle in her hand.

But Colonel Jose Almonte himself came to put his hands carefully about Rose's slender waist and lift her gently onto her mule.

Kate's eyes sought Mollie's, and Mollie realized that Kate was still wondering why she chose to ride with this nomadic crew. There would be time for explanations later, Mollie told herself. As they all filed past the river's edge, Mollie heard Almonte say to Chance, "It's too far from your ranch now to send an escort with them, and I can't spare the men. Besides, it will be interesting to have Irish bread and cakes on our menu."

But Mollie thought, 'Tisn't the distance from the Delanty ranch, nor the men you must spare for it—no, nor the Irish cakes and breads on our menu that have convinced you they must accompany us. 'Tis our Rose that decided you.

"You'll like them, or I miss my guess, Jose. They're very tasty." Chance's quick laughter held a trace of Mollie's own cynicism. So he had also noted the intense attraction between the two, she thought.

The band of men, women, wagons, and horses with their burdens wound their way along the banks of the Nueces for the rest of the day, turning away from it at dusk to follow a little creek that flowed from the west.

That night, Clan O'Connor insisted that Mollie, Kate, and Rose, take his tent while he slept on his bedroll in the open. Kate and Rose were completely overcome by his solicitousness and sang his praises to Mollie, who was forced to admit that the warmer confines of the tent felt good.

As they settled down in their bedrolls and extinguished Clan's oil lamp, Kate turned to Mollie. "Now tell me, colleen, why yer travelin' wi' this bobtail crew o' men an' wimmen—an' why Bet let her boys join 'em."

"You forget, I am indentured to Chance and must go where he commands, though he offered to send me back to the ranch. I feel honor bound to accompany them. When they fight alongside the American army, or even before that, I shall use my medical skills for the hurt and wounded."

They were silent for a moment. Then Rose said softly, "We have heard much of the war in Corpus. The soldiers are gone now, except for a few."

"There is a wicked man ruling Mexico—Santa Anna," Mollie began, and she told them all that she had heard from Chance, Clan, and Almonte himself. Both women were astonished, and Rose was moved nearly to tears over the story of Almonte's tragic losses.

"Oh, the poor man," she lamented. "No wonder he wishes to fight on the side of the Americans! They *must* win, so he will get his estates back. And whatever can it be about his poor wife that's so unspeakable?"

"I haven't heard," Mollie said shortly. "He's promised a large block of land to Clan O'Connor for his service," she added dryly. "And Chance and the twins, of course, are fighting for their homes. Bet and Ben have bought a large tract from Chance and will soon pay it out by working for him."

The women talked on for more than an hour until sleep overcame them. As Mollie dozed off, she realized that Rose had talked mostly about Almonte and had coaxed from Mollie all she knew about him.

The following morning, the three women woke and dressed. Kate's and Rose's new clothing consisted of full, bright red skirts with white petticoats, embroidered white blouses, and red woolen ponchos to keep them warm. When they emerged from the tent, a torrent of Spanish broke over them—all of it admiring, judging from the smiles of those who greeted them. As they approached the Mendoza fire, Cayetana turned a bright smile to them, lifting her wooden spoon from the pan of eggs she was stirring.

"Eez so pretty you are, *si?*" she said. Mollie had found that Cayetana spoke the best English of any of the women except Maricela. "Eez feet you perfectly, *si?*"

"Yes, everything fits just right," Kate said, a little embarrassed at the stir they had caused. "We thank all o' ye very much." Both Kate and Rose felt a bit self-conscious, but Mollie could tell they were secretly pleased with their appearance. Rose especially was exquisite, with her thick, honey blond hair cascading about her shoulders and down her back and the red serape around her shoulders casting a warm glow on her delicate features.

"You readee for breakfast, *si?*" Cayetana asked, filling plates with eggs, tortillas, and stewed dried plums.

Colonel Almonte came up as they were settling down. He stooped beside Rose and spoke so softly that only Mollie and Rose herself caught his words.

"You are the most beautiful woman I have ever seen." He paused and drew back the hand he had almost extended to touch her hair. "Your hair is like sunlight and shadow."

"It's these new clothes, Colonel," Rose murmured, blushing. "They are so beautiful they would make anyone look pretty."

Mollie saw Kate watching them closely, her eyes sharp with distrust and sudden dislike. But the colonel rose to his feet again and bowed to her. "And you, Senora Brannigan, are too young to have a grown daughter. You might easily be her sister." It was a gallant compliment, but Kate's eyes remained hard.

"Ye flatter me, Colonel Almonte—a poor Irish woman like me." She looked down at her plate and began eating, determined to close the conversation. Colonel Almonte watched her speculatively, then bowed again.

"I will leave you, ladies. Eat hearty. We have a long day's travel ahead of us and will eat our food cold at noon as we travel." He moved away to join the group

with whom Chance, the twins, and Clan were breakfasting.

After the early meal, everyone packed swiftly. Clan
took down his tent, and the women rolled their bedding tightly for packing on the backs of their horses.
When they got to the area where the horses were tethered, Kate and Rose found that their mules had been
groomed by the men the evening before until their
coats now glistened like satin.

When the troop was strung out, traveling the dusty
trail, Rose and Kate rode beside Cayetana and Maricela. Mollie listened to their mixed conversation.

"I bake breads—*y unos pasteles*—" Kate turned and
pointed to the small metal oven strapped with her
other baggage. "In here—I bake *unos pasteles, si?*"

"Desde luego! Cakes an' breads. I know zee Englese
too." Maricela said proudly. "My *madre* and *padre,* zey
teach me!" Cayetana looked fondly at her pretty
daughter.

"Can ye be gittin' me flour an' sugar an' eggs?"
Kate asked the two women anxiously.

"Si," replied Cayetana quickly. "Colonel Almonte
eez geeve orders to let you 'ave all you need, senora."

At that moment, Colonel Almonte and Chance trotted back to ride beside them for awhile. Both men had
obviously shaved carefully in the dawn hours. The colonel had groomed his trim black mustache, and he was
wearing his short suede jacket over an embroidered
vest. His shirt, like Chance's, was fresh and white. He
spoke to Maricela and Cayetana in Spanish, then
turned and bowed courteously to the three Irish
women. His black eyes went to Kate's little oven
strapped behind her bundles.

"My ladies will see that you get the ingredients you
need tonight, Senora Brannigan. You will have time
then to do your baking, for we will make camp for a
full day. We will all clean and repair our weapons and
rest our animals. The ladies will wash the clothing and
cook food to be eaten when we travel." His eyes went to
Rose and he smiled. "I will tell you again, you are very
beautiful in the red serape, Senorita Rose."

"Muchas gracias, Colonel Almonte," was Rose's surprisingly easy response, and Mollie looked sharply at her dainty features, into which pink was stealing.

Jose Almonte was easily fifteen or even sixteen years older than Rose, who was now giving the colonel a pert smile. He was supposed to be a widower, and he was definitely an embittered man. Mollie caught Aunt Kate's gaze, which was bright with hostility.

"I will dine with Armendariz tonight, Senora Mendoza," Almonte said. Then, turning back to the Irish women, he added, "Someday, I will entertain you in my house." His words were edged in iron.

"Ye have a house?" Kate asked coldly.

"He had a hacienda, Kate," Chance said dryly.

"What is a hacienda?" Rose asked.

"It is a little village, Senorita Rose," Almonte replied, smiling warmly again. "A cluster of small houses, often surrounding a greater one on many acres of land, as in my case."

"Ye have a great house?" Kate asked stiffly, and Mollie knew she was envisioning Stirling Manor and its hated caste system.

"I *had* a very large one, Senora Brannigan," the colonel replied grimly, "which was stolen from me by the present government of Mexico under an unscrupulous tyrant some time ago. I mean to retake my property. Father Baldemero was priest of my hacienda and family for many years. He can tell you about it, about the soldiers and men who overran the place, taking all prisoner except the good father, me, and a few of my men who also escaped."

"And you had a family," Rose murmured feelingly.

"I *had* a family. No children for them to steal or murder, thank God, but a mother and father who died in prison after I fled for my life, and a wife who was taken from me."

Mollie had the strong feeling that he was not telling everything concerning his wife.

"How tragic," Rose said softly, her eyes downcast.

"You will find the history of my country to be a

tragic one, Senorita Rose. A tragedy to which I mean
to help put a stop."

"Our blessed Ireland has suffered many tragedies,"
Kate said stiffly, her green eyes cold, "among th' worst
bein' th' famine. Before we left Corpus Christi in th'
middle o' th' plague I met a sailor fresh off a ship from
Ireland, who said more'n a million Irish will be dead
afore this famine is over."

"So my Lieutenant O'Connor has told me," Almonte
replied. "We have much in common, then. But I have
made a good Mexican out of O'Connor. Perhaps you
will join him in coming to my country to live some
day." His eyes met Rose's and held. "We also have in
common our faith. We are all good Catholics." He
smiled wryly and added, "That fact alone has led some
of your countrymen to defect from the United States
Army and form a battalion of Irish to fight on the side
of Santa Anna. A great pity, for they do not realize
they fight for a despot, a man of insatiable greed for
power and wealth." He paused and added reflectively,
"All the worse for them, for when America wins the
war, those of the Irish battalion who survive will be
executed as traitors."

"Why, they can't do that!" Kate burst out angrily.
"They're Irish, not Americans!"

"They took an oath when they joined the American
army, senora," Almonte replied, his voice cold and cut-
ting. "And they will be executed as American traitors."

"Kate," drawled Chance, who had been listening silently, "you're an American now. When you chose to
immigrate to this country, you became one."

"Colonel," Rose said, "my mother has much to learn
about America—and Mexico."

"She does indeed," was the short, cold reply before
Almonte wheeled his big stallion away and trotted
swiftly toward the head of the traveling column.

"And you, Mollie"—Chance smiled—"do you still
feel you are Irish?"

"I'm an Irish American," she said proudly.

"You're *from* Ireland, but you're an American now.
You can't be both and stay here."

"I'll be Irish 'til th' day I die!" Kate said furiously. "That high-an'-mighty colonel notwithstandin'! Him an' his hacien—big house. He's just like th' Stirlings —lookin' down on all us lesser folk."

She had been right, then, Mollie thought. Kate felt the colonel considered her and her daughter inferiors, and she feared for Rose's happiness should she become involved with a man who was so highborn.

"And you, Kate," Chance was saying, "you're as high and mighty a woman as I ever met—with the exception of your niece, Mollie O'Meara—and I think you're looking down on the colonel. You'd better come to your senses." With that, he turned his stallion and galloped after Almonte to the front of the caravan.

"What does he mean?" Kate looked at Mollie.

"Chance thinks you ought to think about what's important, now that you've left the Old World behind."

"I have. Me daughter's happiness comes first, an' I don't want her makin' sheep's eyes at that highborn 'ristocrat."

"I didn't make sheep's eyes!" Rose said, stung. "I felt sorry for him. I *do* feel sorry for him, and if you had an ounce of human sympathy in you, Ma, you'd understand and feel sorry for him too. He lost all his family at once!"

"I lost Paddy; I know about heartbreak, miss. An' I know about sheep's eyes too. Ye'd better stick ter yer own kind an' leave th' likes o' that colonel alone."

When they made camp that night along the banks of the narrowing creek, Clan again insisted that the Irish women use his tent.

"Tis much larger than I need," he said. "One o' th' wee folk must've whispered in me ear when I bought it in New Orleans. Ye ladies were meant ter have it, an' have it ye shall, from now on."

Almonte had chosen a campsite in a small stand of trees. Trees were not too plentiful in the country through which they were traveling, but the women and some of the men had been gathering sticks of wood and tying them in bundles that they secured to the backs of the extra horses.

The supper fires were lit and meals were prepared. The group around the Mendoza fire now included not only Pedro and his family but Rose, Kate, Mollie, and Clan. Chance, the twins, and Almonte sat in a circle of men some distance away.

Clan sat between Mollie and Rose and talked of the beauties of the country that awaited them in Mexico.

"I've not seen it o' course," he said. "But I've been told that th' climate, th' blue mountains an' vast plains an' th' clear, spring-fed rivers will fair win th' heart o' any Irish, man or woman."

"*Si*, eet eez a wonderful country, Lieutenant O'Connor," Pedro said, a wistful note in his deep baritone. "Eet belongs to us, who weel fight for eet. Not to zee tyrant who eez rule there now."

"I'm hopin' ye get it back, senor," Kate said uneasily, not yet quite at home with her swarthy rescuers. She had baked Irish bread with real yeast and white flour furnished by the women. She has also gotten dried peaches that were now stewing, with which she would make tarts later on. The tarts could be kept for several days and eaten along the way with the dried meats and fruit that were staples of their fare.

"Zis bread, eet taste ver' good, Senora Kate," said Cayetana.

"Call me Kate, Missis Mendoza, an' I'll call ye Caye—Cayet—Cayetana." Kate triumphantly pronounced the name. "An' I'm glad ye like me bread."

The following day the women washed clothes in the narrow stream nearby. Mollie, Kate, and Rose took the opportunity to bathe as well, shivering as they dried themselves with rough towels. Then they donned fresh clothing and cleaned everything else they owned, hanging the wet garments to dry on strange bushes that grew back from the creek.

"Clan says these here bushes are called chaparral," Kate commented. "An' these clumps o' stunted trees is called mottes. An' Cayetana says we're gettin' closer ter Mexico. Where'd ye get three pairs o' breeches,

Mollie, if ye were kidnapped by them soldiers—an' you wi' nothin' but yer medicine bag wi' ye?"

"I thought I told you. Chance got them out of one of those bottomless wagons. They're boy's breeches and fit a little too tightly for modesty, but I'm grateful for them. I learned the hard way about skirts in the brush."

"I'm learning to take good care of my skirts," Rose said gloomily. "I dare not tear them—the ladies here have all been so generous. I wish I had breeches."

"No daughter o' mine'll wear breeches, Rose Brannigan!" Kate exclaimed.

"Oh, Ma, 'tis old fashioned you are! Mollie says Bet Delanty wears breeches all the time."

"Most of the time, anyway," Mollie put in.

"Then 'tis a brazen habit she's picked up in this godforsaken country. Just as ye have done, Mollie."

"I guess it is brazen, Aunt Kate. But it's so much easier riding horseback in them, or getting about in this rough life we're leading now."

"Surely you'll agree with that, Ma!"

"I'll not be agreein' wi' that, Rose. Mollie, ye should be in skirts like th' lady ye are."

"Yes, Aunt Kate," Mollie said meekly. "When my service to Chance is over and you and Rose and I are all together in Corpus Christi, I promise I'll wear skirts."

Mollie was cheerful. That morning she had bandaged a sprained finger for one of the women, and she felt she had started to earn her keep. Chance had observed from a distance, and afterward he had approached her to compliment her deftness. The patient was doing quite well with the splinted and bandaged finger.

The following morning they left very early. Before sunup, the men and women of the band had set out in a long line of twos and threes, their pack animals trotting patiently behind them. The five capacious wagons, drawn by stolid geldings, brought up the rear.

Following behind them was the remuda, or group of extra horses, herded by three vaqueros.

At first, the twins rode beside Mollie, talking excitedly about the adventures that awaited them in Mexico and how their lives had changed since leaving Ireland. They did not want to reminisce with Mollie of their times together in Ireland. Rather, they imagined the feats they would accomplish in battle and bragged unashamedly of the crack riflemen they had become under their Uncle Chance's tutelage. When they left her, weaving their way to the head of the band where Clan rode with Chance and Almonte, Rose and Kate pulled up alongside Mollie on their saddleless mules.

"'Tis fine boys they are," Kate said, looking after the twins approvingly. "An' 'tis a fine, generous man —wi' a cheerful heart too—that Clan O'Connor is. You an' Rose could only prosper, married to any o' th' three."

Mollie noticed that Rose's eyes were fixed on the lithe, graceful body of Jose Almonte as he rode easily at the head of the column. Clan O'Connor was equally graceful beside him, and Mollie spoke before she thought.

"Any girl who sets her heart on Clan O'Connor will have it broken for her."

"Ah, now, Mollie darlin', yer too hard on th' boy. He can't help that rascally charm o' his."

"He's no boy," Mollie answered. "And have you seen how little Maricela looks at him?"

"'Tis a childhood admiration she has fer him, an' ye know it!"

"Oh, Ma, let's not quarrel over men. 'Tisn't seemly." But Rose's gaze kept following the head of the column, seeking out Almonte's handsome figure. Mollie herself looked there too often, her eyes lingering on the taller man with the broad shoulders and narrow hips. It was Chance Delanty and his vital masculinity that unwillingly drew her.

During the days that followed they rode continuously, eating the already roasted deer meat, pheasant, and rabbit on the trail. Still, Almonte did not

press the horses and stopped often for them to drink at
the narrow creek that ran nearby. They had left the
Nueces miles behind when they had turned toward the
Mexican border.

December came on, and for the first week Rose and
Kate remained uncomplaining. But by the tenth of the
month, the long hours on their mules gave Kate occasion to remark that she was stiff and sore and her
muscles were protesting her mode of travel.

Almonte had sent two scouts on ahead earlier to see
how matters stood in the town of Mier, across the Rio
Grande. Clan had told Mollie, Kate, and Rose that
these scouts would report back within a couple of days.
He had also informed them that Almonte's scouts in
the heart of Mexico would also report in from time to
time as the weeks went by.

Mollie realized that Colonel Jose Almonte had a
tight, well-organized, if small, army at his command,
all fiercely loyal to their commander and equally fierce
in their hatred of Santa Anna.

As they neared the border country, the terrain grew
rougher and their pace slowed, for the pack animals
had to be led through the thick brush. There were
times when the supplies on their backs were nearly
pulled off by brush and thorns and the bundles had to be
repacked. Mollie had many occasions to use her medical knowledge on deep scratches made by thorns, on
bruises, and twice on deep cuts. Often her patients were
women, but she also had to stitch up the cuts suffered by
the men handling the wagons over the broken and
ragged country, through which there was no trail.

The weather was unseasonably warm one day when
Clan rode up beside Mollie. Aunt Kate and Rose had
fallen behind her, arguing over Rose's acceptance of a
fine, hand-tooled leather poncho from Almonte.

"Mollie," Clan said abruptly, "have ye given more
thought ter me proposal o' marriage?"

"No, Clan. I'm not for marrying. I want to make my
own way."

"Ye never want ter marry?" he asked incredulously.

"I want to live free awhile first, I think." Then, thinking of Sean, she asked curiously, "Why didn't you buy land and build a house like Sean is doing?"

"Ah, Chance has told me of me brother—buildin' and settlin' down ter his land in Texas." He laughed shortly, then added, "Sean was ever one for bein' responsible an' steady. I was th' one fer adventure."

"Well, Sean had better take more responsibility and marry his alleged housekeeper, Meg Moriarty, who has no house to keep yet."

"Now why would he do that?"

"Ah, Clan, you know as well as I. Though Sean denied it to me, only one look at Deirdre and anyone would know he's her father. He's ready enough to admit his great love for the child."

"Yes," Clan said slowly. "Dierdre is the image o' us O'Connors. An', like I say, he's a great one for responsibility. Maybe he'll marry Meg yet." His rollicking laughter rang in the air.

"You admit you're an adventurer. Why would you ask me to wed?"

"But I plan to settle down in Mexico on the land I'll help win. Ah, Mollie, I'll build a hacienda an' ye'll reign as queen. I'll make enough money to satisfy yer every whim!"

"I can't say yes to you, Clan. I'm not in love with you, besides all my other reasons."

"I'd win yer heart, colleen, before ye knew it."

"You're a handsome man, Clan, and if anyone could win me, I'm sure you could. But the answer is no."

"I won't take no. Say maybe."

"All right, if it makes you happy. Maybe."

"That's all I ask." His gay laughter rang out again and he spurred his horse forward, riding to the head of the column.

Chance Delanty was another matter. He was not particularly courteous, and he treated Mollie with a familiarity that she found extremely galling. Despite the faint touch of respect he had shown since their in-

timate encounter on the way to his ranch, he still did
not treat her as a lady.

Over supper with the Mendozas, for which he joined
them that evening, he made matters worse, sitting beside her and speaking in a low voice. "Clan tells us he
wants to marry you. I suppose you put him off because
of the so-called indenture?"

"I put him off because I don't love him," she said
tartly.

"I think you're a cold woman, Mollie. The blood in
your veins lacks the warmth of life. I've come to believe you're nothing but a cheap tease after all. Your
apparent warmth, your incredible beauty, are facades
for a cold heart."

She was so furious she couldn't speak. He took his
plate and moved to the other side of the campfire. How
dared he accuse her of coldness, she who couldn't bear
to see a rabbit trapped or a deer shot. She who suffered
with each patient she treated!

Chance finished his meal silently and walked away
from the campsite into the still-warm evening. He took
a westward direction and vanished from view. Mollie's
gaze followed him until he disappeared against the horizon, which was still streaked with scarlets and golds.

She made no excuse to the women as they cleared
up from supper but made her way through the chaparral in the direction Chance had taken. She walked a
long distance before she saw his tall, broad-shouldered
figure dimly outlined against the darkening sky.

She meant to lash out at him for his accusations,
defend her own worth to the group. If she had not been
sharply observant, she might have lost him among the
rough, shoulder-high growth of the borderland. She
slipped between the bushes and reached his side
slightly out of breath. It was still light enough to see
his features as he turned at the sound of her approach.

At the sight of his narrowed and vividly blue eyes,
the words she meant to say left her. For a long, silent
moment they stood facing each other like the adversar-
ies they were. Then the words she thought were lost
burst from her in a torrent.

"You can't talk down to me, Chance Delanty! I'm as good as you are, and better, when it comes to medicine. And to call me *cold!* You don't really know me at all—" She broke off at the expression that suddenly came over his face.

All at once, realizing what she had done by following him, she turned away swiftly, but she was too late. He reached out and caught her arm, pulling her back to him. The force of his grip caused her to lose her balance, and she fell heavily to the dry, sandy soil under the chaparral.

In an instant his body was over hers and they struggled, she to pull free, he to subdue her. Her breath came short and hard. His strength was overpowering. He shut out the first pale stars above her as his hands pinioned her arms.

"Be still," he ground out. "This is what you wanted, isn't it?"

"No, no, I—"

"Then why did you follow me out here away from everyone?"

"I only meant to tell you—" She broke off, panting for breath.

"Tell me what?"

Rage suddenly shook her, and breath came back to her. "You've treated me like a *servant!* You've spoken to me with contempt and accused me of a terrible thing—coldness! And I'm a doctor! I'm never cold!"

"Yes, you are. And you're a servant too. You would have it no other way when I tried to give you your freedom. At least I kept away from you, didn't I?"

As he spoke, he brought his face close to hers. She twisted her head, but his mouth found her cheek and then her mouth.

Her eyes closed involuntarily under the shocking thrill of it. With his weight pressing down on her, his body hard against hers, terror went through her at the old familiar weakness.

He lifted his head, and his breath was warm and clean against her lips. "You're concerned about how I treat you? What I think of you?" he asked, holding her fast. "Let me tell you, then, what I think of you." Passion mingled with the mocking laughter in his voice. "The first stars that appear in the sky at night make me think of you. I think of the prairies in spring, furious with wildflowers, when I think of you. All the beautiful things in nature bring you to mind. Does that tell you anything?"

She had ceased to struggle against him. This was different from her old dream. She could not pull her knees up and lunge away, for his mouth was over hers once more and it moved slowly, traveling warmly from her lips to her throat and down to the rapid pulse in the hollow at its base. He lifted his head again.

"I'm making love to you, Mollie darlin'," he said, loosening his grip on her to slip off their jackets and bring one hand up to her shirt. He unbuttoned it and reached in to cup her breast, to move his warm, calloused hand over and around it. Then he slipped his hand down to her waist and unfastened her breeches, slowly, gently, one button at a time, slipping his hand inside to slide, one at a time, the straps of her chemise from her shoulders and then to pull it, along with the breeches, down over her hips.

"I'll scream," she whispered breathlessly.

The breeches and chemise caught on her boots; he lifted himself to pull off both boots, freeing her legs. Then his hand slipped up her bare leg, slowly, caressingly, reaching her thigh and circling inward to touch her tenderly inside the soft secret curls. His touch grew firmer, a thumb stroking insistently between her legs, and a wild tremor shot through her. Involuntarily her legs spread apart beneath him, and her hips began to move as the ache of desire swelled unbearably.

"Oh!" she whispered, and then from her throat came an indistinguishable sound.

"I told you once, I wouldn't let your damned virginity stop me again," he murmured against her lips. His kiss deepened swiftly and her lips parted eagerly, just as her legs were parting to him.

"Shall I let it stop me, Mollie darlin'?" he asked.

He did not stop, and he could not stop the roaring

wave of sensual craving that swept them both along. She clung to him and when their bodies joined, she scarcely felt the short, sharp pain of entry. The hard heat of him within her sent a fiery swell of pleasure through every vein.

Her fingers tightened on the tough muscles of his shoulders, pulling him closer to her, urging him to greater swiftness within her. She was sharply aware of the warm night, of the faint scents on the sultry air, of the half-heard howl from some distant lair, and all of these sensations heightened the passion that overwhelmed her.

Something within her must burst. A rapturous tension filled her. She pulled his head down to hers with a swift, sure movement and their lips clung and moved against each other once more as the power that drove them heightened.

Suddenly the night was blotted out and nothing existed any longer but the pleasure that burst within them, sending shock waves through her body, waves of such keen sweetness that their bodies became one in the fiery embrace that consumed them both. It was as if the world had exploded around them and they were suspended in a universe of their own.

Slowly, slowly the tide ebbed, leaving only warmth and a tender ease that Mollie had never known before. Chance's body was still heavy on hers, and she was filled with a passionate longing for it to stay that way, so that she might never be alone again.

"Oh—" she said once more on a great, shuddering breath.

They lay together after he lifted himself from her. She was still filled with the warmth of their shared glory in a timeless moment. What she had done with him—the finality of giving up her innocence—did not matter. For that long, sweet moment it did not matter. Something inexpressibly dear to her had become his forever.

Forever! The thought echoed, chilling her like the night air settling over them. She pushed herself upright, putting on her camisole and buttoning her shirt. Slowly she pulled on her breeches, fastening them as she sat upright.

Before she could reach for it, he had one of her boots, and, gently, he pulled it on her foot. Neither of them spoke while he buttoned his shirt and picked up the fringed deerskin jackets they had so hurriedly removed.

"Mollie, I—"

"Don't say anything, please!"

"But Mollie, I—"

"Don't talk!" She turned on him in a fury. "There's nothing you can say that will make it right!" *Or make me whole again.* "I've been a complete fool—and as you once so clearly pointed out, a wanton. But never again! You'll never make a fool of me again. I hate you for it, Chance Delanty!"

Chance rose, towering over her, and his voice was suddenly as chilly as the night had become. "You *are* a fool, Mollie, you with your closed mind. So you hate me, do you?"

"Yes, yes, yes!"

"Then watch yourself, miss"—the old jeering note was back in his words—"for on another warm night I'll let you show me again how much you hate me."

She turned blindly, pushing against the chaparral and weaving her way back toward the distant glow of the campfires, her eyes blurred by hot tears of bitter and useless regret.

Chapter 16

The caravan traveled on through the borderland chaparral over the next several days. The terrain was monotonously the same everywhere Mollie looked, but the men were able to hunt game. They brought deer, quail, pheasant, and wild turkeys back to the camp, and the supper fires cooked mouth-wateringly good meals.

Chance left Mollie strictly alone, but Clan sought her out, always respectful and always full of Irish humor and charm. She began to be very nice to him, hoping that it would send the message to Chance that those wild, sweet moments in his arms meant nothing. Under her sudden warmth toward him, Clan redoubled his efforts to win her.

He found occasion to ride beside her and talk with her every day, and his conversation was of the old days in Ireland, before the famine, and of the new country and his adventures in it during the last months. Mollie found his stories interesting and sometimes amusing as he told of his awkwardness when he first arrived and before he had rescued Colonel Almonte from his attackers in the saloon. He made light of his heroics on that occasion.

"I think what interested th' colonel in me was me brogue an' why I'd come ter th' New World. An' when I told him 'twas ter make me fortune, he asked would I fight for me fortune." He laughed merrily. "Me, who's been scrappin' ever since I can remember with one or t'other in Ireland! An' th' colonel promised ter make a marksman out o' me."

After that, Clan told her, they had become fast friends, and Almonte himself had taken Clan out among the oaks that surrounded New Orleans and taught him to use both rifle and pistol.

"I can drill a silver dollar at a hundred paces. Th' colonel says I have as good an eye as Chance Delanty, an that seems ter be th' highest compliment th' colonel can pay."

Clan was only too happy to have found his place in the New World and was not the least afraid of facing the Mexican army and Santa Anna. And Clan was mastering Spanish much faster than was Mollie, which made her redouble her efforts with the women around the campfires at night.

During these days, Kate often rode beside Cayetana and Maricela. Almonte chose to ride and talk with Rose, who blossomed under his attention. Frequently after supper he would walk with her to the far edge of the campsite, his tall body bent toward hers, and they would linger out of sight there until well after dark. This made Mollie nervous, for she knew only too well what could happen on the warm, sandy soil under the chaparral. It worried Kate even more, and she grew sharp with her daughter and was outspoken in her disapproval of Rose's relationship with Jose Almonte. Rose grew increasingly silent with her mother.

Word spread among the band that they would reach the Rio Grande about Christmas Eve. Father Baldemero said they would have a fine Christmas celebration and he would conduct special masses.

Excitement ran through the guerrilla band as the day approached. Even as they traveled, the women built special fires for smoking wild turkeys, pheasants, and deer meat. Kate, with the help of Mollie and Rose, baked feverishly in the small metal oven each night, making pastries and tarts by the dozen for the great day.

When at last they drew up before the rain-swollen Rio Grande and looked across to the other side, it was December twenty-third. The river ran swiftly far below steep banks, and Mollie, looking at it, wondered how they would ever get across. Clan, nearby, answered her question.

"Th' colonel says we'll swim th' horses across, but there's a big log raft on the Mier side and we'll ferry you ladies across, after we've ferried all th' wagons an' supplies. The colonel says we won't cross the river until th' day after Christmas. He says maybe it'll be down by then. It's been rainin' ter th' north, an' the river's high and flooding." Clan paused, looking at the boiling current below them. Then, laughing, he added, "Th' city o' Mier is just beyond there." He pointed. "See? Wait for a minute an' ye can see it from here." But Mollie knew he was teasing when she looked in vain at the skyline and could see no buildings beyond it.

That evening, as they finished supper in their camp by the Rio Grande, Mollie saw Almonte take Rose's arm just beyond the Mendoza supper fire and stroll with her toward the steep bank of the river. She observed her Aunt Kate's strained face and angry eyes as Kate watched them walk away in the unusually warm winter twilight. For a moment, it appeared she would follow and pull her daughter bodily from Almonte's grasp. Instead, she began clearing the dishes with unwonted vigor and prepared them for washing.

"Cayetana, I'll go wash 'em in th' river meself tonight. Ye an' Maricela needn't do it with us every night."

"Ah, but so many, Kate. We all wash, eh?" Cayetana smiled.

Kate argued briefly, for she knew that Cayetana would circle around Rose and Almonte where they sat on the edge of the bluff, while Kate wanted to go right up to them and see what they were doing.

Later, Mollie saw Almonte and Rose return. They stood talking for a moment; suddenly he put his hand under her chin and tilted her face up to his. They stood thus for some minutes, not touching, only looking into each other's eyes. Then he murmured something to her and they parted. Soon, light blossomed in their separate tents.

Kate spoke behind her, and Mollie whirled around, unaware until then that her aunt had returned.

"Yer thinkin' what I'm thinkin', Mollie. No good can come o' that." She gestured to Almonte who had come out of his tent and now stood talking with three of his men and Father Baldemero.

"He is to Mexico what Lord Stirling was to Ireland," Mollie said bitterly. "He might take Rose as his mistress but not as his bride." She remembered Lord Stirling's hands on her arms, warm and possessive, offering nothing but a future of uncertainty.

"Never!" Kate's voice was low and violent. Then, with a touch of hope she added, "But he has the good Father Baldemero travelin' with him, an' surely th' father'll see no harm comes ter my Rose."

Much later, in the black confines of their sleeping quarters, Mollie heard Kate's muffled voice, too low to be understood.

"How can you be sure?" It was Rose, angry and hurt.

Kate's voice resumed, patient, loving, and kind. Then silence fell. Mollie waited.

"Rose?" It was Kate's voice again, this time clear and full of warning. "Do ye understand, me darlin'?"

"Go to sleep, Ma." Rose sounded impatient and unconvinced. "I've heard enough."

This time the silence remained unbroken.

Christmas Eve was spent in celebration among the guerrilla band. Everyone had made up small gifts to be exchanged, baubles such as tiny straw dolls, tiny animals made of burrs and seeds, little decorated cookies, hand-hemmed handkerchiefs of rough cotton cloth, and wooden hairpins and figures the men had carved, all wrapped to be exchanged in the morning. Mollie guessed that the women had given Rose and Aunt Kate more clothing, for their packages were large and bulky.

Food about the fires was more than plentiful and shared by all on this evening, for the men had shot two deer and several more turkeys. Mollie knew they would celebrate for two days.

After feasting that Christmas Eve, Father Baldemero held a special mass, and a feeling of peace and contentment, of gratitude and well being, settled over his silent flock as they sat upon the cold ground under a dimming sky.

Christmas day was even more festive. Some of the men had brought their guitars with them, and the camp rang with music and dancing after the opening of gifts. Mollie had been right. Kate and Rose had two new dresses, with petticoats, and even two pairs of shoes, not new but in good condition and much needed.

There was feasting all day, with a mass at noon conducted by Father Baldemero. There was dancing after supper in the light of the campfires, with the men and women performing beautiful Spanish dances with grace and charm.

Almonte danced with Mollie, Rose, Maricela, and Cayetana, though Kate coldly refused his request to dance with her. Clan claimed most of Mollie's dances, but she had one dance with Chance. She felt stiff until his arms went around her, then she flowed with his every movement in spite of her determination to resist her attraction to him.

Bottles of tequila were passed around, and the merriment increased accordingly. By the time the evening was over, everyone had eaten most of the delicious food and all were satisfied by the day's events. They went to their tents and bedrolls, drowsy and happy, knowing that the next day they would cross the Rio Grande into Mexico and take one more long step in their journey to join General Zachary Taylor's forces at Saltillo.

* * *

They were all up before dawn and the camp was bustling. Mollie went about her packing with an uneasiness she could not dispel. Deep in her lay a hard kernel of fear that she was carrying Chance's child. Determinedly she pushed the possibility to the back of her mind, but it would not stay there. Just a day or two more, she told herself desperately, perhaps even tomorrow she would know the truth.

As she prepared to strap her bundles onto Colleen's back in the dim light of the morning fires, she felt a pang of anxiety, thinking of the dainty animal having to swim the rushing current. Just then Clan stepped up quietly beside her and put a big hand over hers. She looked up and in the dim, predawn light saw his eyes crinkle at the corners.

"Don't pack it, *querida mia*," he said softly. "The colonel has looked at th' river an' determined it's too swollen ter swim heavily loaded horses across. Here, I'll take yer bundles an' pack 'em in one o' th' wagons."

"Not my medicine pouch," she said sharply. "I'll carry that with me."

As Kate and Rose approached with their bundles and bedrolls, Clan said, "Just put 'em down there, ladies. I'll stow 'em in th' wagon wi' Mollie's. You will be ferried across on th' raft—last an' safest." He strode with Mollie's belongings to the nearest wagon, where Pedro was already loading the Mendoza baggage.

Cayetana spread her hands eloquently. "Eez bad time to cross zee river, Senora Kate." She smiled ruefully. "Eet mus' steel be rain ver' bad in zee north. Now eet eez almos' to flood."

Chance stopped by as they were cleaning up after a hasty breakfast. He was brief and to the point. "We're going to take a crossing that's long been used by travelers between Mexico and Texas. The beaches on each side are still above the flooding river, or we wouldn't risk it." He smiled briefly. "It'll be rough on you ladies, but you'll make it." With that, he strode away to join the other men.

Daylight was full on them before they reached the

embarkation point two or three miles from their campsite. The river could be seen below, the water rough
and reddish brown where the strong current had
stirred up the yellowish red mud of the riverbed.
Across the rushing water, Mollie could see a broad log
raft moored to several sturdy stakes. Intuitive fear
suddenly crept into her. The river was not very wide,
but it was treacherous, and all manner of debris was
being swept along in the fierce current.

She glanced just behind the group of milling men
and women to the wagons, which looked exceedingly
full. The tarpaulins strapped over them bulged as the
men covered all the supplies Almonte had procured in
New Orleans and San Antonio. Now their capacity was
further strained by all the baggage the packhorses and
riders would ordinarily have carried.

Mollie looked up at the bluffs that had been slowly
carved by ancient waters over thousands of years.
They were raw, jagged walls of earth, crumbling in
some places, packed tightly in others, and above them
on the far side of the river stretched the endless miles
of Mexico's chaparral and scrub.

"We'll be a long time getting across," Mollie murmured to Rose and Kate beside her. "We might as well
sit down and make ourselves as comfortable as possible," she finished as Almonte, Chance, Clan, and the
twins on their big stallions swam across the river to
get the raft. Pedro and two other vaqueros on horseback plunged in after them.

Throughout the cloudless morning, the women sat
against the bluff, watching the men ferry across
wagons, supplies, and animals. Sunlight bathed them
and the little beach on which they sat, with the towering bluff behind them, broke the sweep of the wind.

At last all the women boarded the raft and the men
poled it forward. It rocked under their feet as the cold
river wind between the high bluffs caught them directly now. The raft had no railings, and all the women
clustered in the center, as far from the swirling,
muddy water as they could get. There was a man at
each corner wielding a long pole.

"I don't like this," Kate muttered to Mollie and Rose. "What if this thing was ter tip over an' sink? Not one o' th' three o' us can swim a lick, an' we'd drown like kittens."

"Ma, let's hold onto each other," Rose said tremulously.

Several of the younger women and Cayetana Mendoza tried to reassure them in a mixture of Spanish and English.

Maricela said timidly, "Zee men—all are *muy* strong. You weel be safe, *mi amigas.*"

But Mollie was of Kate's mind as the raft swirled unevenly forward. As the distance between shore and raft grew, the river current caught them and swung them further down from the point at which they wanted to land. As they pulled farther out, debris in the water bumped unnervingly against the sides of the raft. Their progress was unsteady, and sweat gathered on the foreheads of the men as they thrust their poles far down to the riverbed. Pedro Mendoza cursed softly under his breath.

Suddenly the Mexican women, who had been talking with apparent ease among themselves, fell silent, their eyes widening. Mollie turned to follow their gaze and her own eyes dilated with horror.

The bloated bodies of two drowned longhorn cattle were rushing toward them in the current, their great hooked horns pointed forward. Riding the current easily, the carcasses were being swept along with deadly accuracy toward the raft. Mollie knew these great drowned animals could mean death to all on the raft who were unable to swim. Around her, she saw the women fall suddenly to the floor of the raft, each of them clinging to its round logs.

The men poled violently to get beyond the mindless course of the dead cattle, but the carcasses bore down on them inexorably. Mollie knew unerringly that they would strike the raft, even as the men raised their poles to seek purchase on the distended bodies in a final desperate effort to shove them away.

The men waiting for them on the far shore began to shout advice and encouragement.

"Hang on — get down!"

"Grab the logs! Lie down, Mollie!"

"Pole, men — pole!"

"Cuidado, amigas—senoras! Beware!"

Mollie was the first of the Irish women to unfreeze; she seized Kate and Rose each by the arm, pulling them down with her. She felt a jarring thud; her grip loosened and she caught again at Rose's arm—and missed.

The raft swung in a wide arc, spinning its riders wildly as they clung precariously to its logs. Mollie had a dizzying glimpse of the men manning the poles as they scrambled to keep their footing while the raft rode the pointed horn of the first animal. The raft spun away, was forcibly struck by the second animal, then whirled up and around in a violent swing.

The centrifugal force knocked Rose off balance, and before Mollie's and Kate's horrified eyes, she fell into the turbulent water with scarcely a splash. The two drowned beasts swept by the spot where she disappeared beneath the brownish yellow water.

The raft slowly righted itself under the pressure of the poles against the river bottom.

"Rose!" Mollie screamed with all the force in her lungs. "Rose!"

But the honey gold head was not to be seen.

As the raft steadied and the swollen cattle were swept on down the river, Mollie and Kate rose with the Mexican women who, now that the danger was over, were weeping and chattering. Maricela and Cayetana shouted Rose's name in concert with Mollie and Kate.

"Ohhh! She's drowned—drowned!" Kate wailed, tottering to the side of the raft.

At that instant, Rose's head came up and a strangled cry issued from her lips. Frantic now, Mollie turned on the men who had let their poles go slack as they realized they had lost one of their passengers.

"Can't you swim, Pedro? For the love of God, try to save her! She can't swim!"

"I'm sorry, senorita—I, too, cannot swim," Pedro shouted.

Mollie turned in desperation to Kate. "Aunt Kate, I'm going to jump in and grab one of those limbs going by and try to reach her."

"No, no! Ye'll both drown!" She clutched Mollie's arm tightly. "Look, look! They're ridin' inter th' river on their horses. 'Tis that colonel an' Chance an'—"

Rose surfaced once more, her cries more feeble as she thrashed about weakly. She was swept along with the current and she sank from sight a third time.

"Ach! They'll never reach her in time!" Kate moaned, lapsing into Gaelic in her anguish. The four men had thrust their poles again into the river and the raft swung forward once more.

But Almonte's great stallion had plunged ahead of those of Chance and his nephews. The big black horse churned through the water easily, and Chance was just behind the colonel. Closely following them were the twins.

Under her breath, Mollie was crying, "Hurry, hurry, hurry. Dear God, let them find her—let them be in time!"

When Almonte reached the spot where Rose was last seen, he let his stallion be carried with the force of the water, then swung the reins around so that the animal swam in a tight circle. An eternity passed and Rose's head did not reappear.

She is gone. She is dead. Mollie's leaden heart beat the words into her brain, and her shoulders slumped as the raft drew further downstream. Then Almonte gave a great shout and in an instant, his hand rose from the water. Tangled in his fist was Rose's long, dripping hair. As he pulled her up by it, his other arm went out and circled her waist. He swept her into his arms before him on the horse.

Catching up his reins, he turned the big stallion back toward shore, and the others followed suit. Rose was limp in Almonte's arms, head lolling back, arms hanging slackly. He carried her like a sack of meal in

one arm as he held the reins with the other, guiding
the horse with the strong pressure of his knees.

The raft reached the shore at last, twenty yards
down from the main body of men and only a few yards
from where Almonte, Chance and the Delanty twins
were guiding their dripping mounts to shore.

The women streamed off the rough raft and started
running toward the point where the horsemen had
pulled up on the narrow shore. Almonte was already
stretching Rose out on the sand.

Ghastly white, Rose looked drowned to Mollie and
Kate. Both of them rushed to her side as Almonte
swiftly straddled her inert body. Crouching over the
unconscious girl, he put his hands to her upper abdomen and lower chest in slow, strongly pressing movements. Carefully and evenly, he continued pushing,
releasing, pushing, and releasing only to push again.

Kate gasped in horror and ran to him, screaming.

"What are ye doin' to me child, ye crazy man! Ye'll
kill 'er, ye will!" She began tearing at Almonte's broad
shoulders, shouting in Gaelic until Chance lifted her
bodily off the colonel.

"Kate, Kate! The man will save her if he can!" he
cried.

Mollie came hurrying to where Chance held the
struggling Kate. "Aunt Kate, Chance is telling you the
truth! Though we never had need of it in Arderin, Sister Maria Theresa told me of this method to expel
water and restore respiration." She put her arms
tightly around the grief-stricken mother and soothed
her, adding, "Wait with us, dear Aunt Kate! Give the
colonel a chance to bring her back. He's stronger than
I—but I should be trying to do the same thing, if he
were not here."

It seemed to Mollie that Almonte worked on Rose
for an eternity before the girl suddenly groaned and
moved her head.

Then, in seconds, she vomited great gouts of water.
As the retching abated, Rose made feeble swimming
movements but did not speak or attempt to rise. Kate
suddenly burst into loud, uncontrollable sobbing as

Rose lay pale and breathing shallowly, her lovely features etched in marble.

Almonte was still crouched over her, but his hands were moving gently now as he pressed her chest once more. She retched feebly, but little water came forth.

"She needs rest," Almonte said, rising, "and warm blankets and dry clothing." He looked at his silent people and added authoritatively, "We will set up camp on the bluff above. I want my tent prepared for her." As they stared at him, he repeated his statement in Spanish, and a few men hastened away.

To Cayetana, Almonte added in Spanish, "Prepare some hot broth immediately. We will stay until she can recover." Then he looked at Kate and spoke with little expression. "This has been a near thing, Senora Brannigan. I regret that you misunderstood my actions."

He lifted Rose in his arms and carried her tenderly along the river's edge. Mollie realized he was making a great concession, for he was determined to reach General Taylor's army before Santa Anna could mount his offensive. But now his men were hurrying to make camp here, at an unscheduled time and place.

"Kate, don't worry," Chance said as he came up beside them leading his still-damp stallion. "She's going to be all right."

"Why aren't ye carryin' her yerself, Chance Delanty?" Kate cried, her angry eyes on Almonte's tall figure. "It should be one o' her own kind saved her!"

"Why have you got a burr under your saddle about the colonel, Kate?" Chance asked quizzically. Mollie could not help exchanging glances with him.

"That high-nosed Spaniard will do me daughter ill. I know it!"

"I heard all the things you called him in Gaelic. Though Jose speaks French as well as English and Spanish, I doubt if he understood your Gaelic curses — and a lucky thing for you," Chance answered.

"Why lucky for me?" Kate asked bitterly. "I want ter let 'im know he must leave me daughter alone — if she survives his brutal treatment."

"Kate," Mollie said, reining in her impatience,

"Rose will survive this ordeal *because* of Colonel Almonte's quick thinking and his heroic action. You should be grateful to him."

"Grateful? It should've been Chance 'er th' twins who saved 'er!"

"We weren't quick enough, Kate."

"Ye should've been quicker, then!"

Almonte had reached the steep trail to the bluff top and mounted it, swinging Rose lightly in his arms. He did not look back, though Kate had spoken clearly enough for him to hear.

They took the steep incline silently, and when they reached the top, it could be seen that the wagons were drawn up on a small open place, previously used as a campsite.

"Chance," Almonte said over his shoulder, "I'd appreciate it if you'd see to our horses. I know they're hungry and need a rubdown after two trips in the Rio Grande."

"Glad to," was the response. To Kate he added, "I'll be back to check on Rose later. I think she'll be fine by tomorrow." He turned away.

"Tomorrow," Kate muttered. "I'll not rest 'til ye've taken over th' care o' me darlin' Rose, Mollie."

"You know I'll do my best for her, Aunt Kate."

As Almonte approached his big tent with Rose in his arms, Father Baldemero hastened forward. "Here is one of the new bedrolls we bought in San Antonio and a bottle of my French brandy. It will restore her."

"Don Jose—zee blankets," Cayetana said breathlessly as she rushed up. Once Rose had been carried inside, Cayetana and Almonte wrapped three blankets around her inert form and laid her on the bedroll. Her face was still as white as alabaster and she had not spoken, though her breathing was deeper and more even now.

Kate had begun weeping again despite Mollie's murmured words of comfort. Almonte began issuing orders in Spanish to Cayetana, who answered in kind with a quick, respectful bow.

"He tell *mi madre* to take these wet dress an'—an'

underclothes off," Maricela translated with an understanding look at Mollie and Kate.

The priest turned to Kate and said, "Senora Brannigan, your daughter will be well again. God has been
good to spare her." He left quietly.

Almonte paused and stooped again over the gently
breathing Rose. Mollie caught a glimpse of his dark,
anguished eyes. They were tender and filled with what
Mollie suddenly recognized as love. Shocked, she
began to revise her opinion of the colonel.

As he bent over Rose, her lids fluttered and for an
instant the beautiful hazel eyes looked up into the
dark face over her before they closed again.

"Senorita Mollie, I leave you to care for your
cousin," Almonte said, straightening. "Here is Father
Baldemero's bottle of French brandy—I am confident
of your powers as a physician." He started to leave;
then he paused and, looking at Kate crouched over her
daughter, added, "I will be back often to see how Senorita Rose is responding."

As the colonel opened the tent flap, Mollie glimpsed
Clan, Benjie, and Tim waiting outside. Mollie went to
the opening and spoke to the anxious men.

"If you want to wait," she said. "We'll come and tell
you when she's fully conscious."

"We'll be waitin'," Tim said, speaking for the three
of them.

Mollie closed the flap as Maricela struck fire to the
lamp, augmenting what sunlight managed to penetrate the tent.

"Let's get these wet clothes off her," Mollie said
briskly, pulling the blankets away. Together, she and
Cayetana stripped the wet clothing from Rose's chilled
body. Mollie began rubbing her bare feet, which felt as
cold as the winter wind. Kate sat sobbing quietly at
one side, watching Rose's still face for a flicker of con-
sciousness.

Cayetana and Mollie slipped a long flannel nightgown over the slender, naked body. In another moment, the two of them had Rose wrapped in the warm
woolen blankets on the bedroll once more. Rose began

to shake then with cold and from the shock of her ordeal, and she spoke for the first time.

"Ma— I'm s-so c-cold. How did I c-come to be here?"

"Ach! Darlin', ye fell inter that river an' we almost lost ye—but Chance an' th' twins—"

"Colonel Almonte pulled you out just in time," Mollie cut in feelingly, with a sharp glance at Kate. She rubbed Rose's cold hands. "You frightened us, Rose, but you're going to be all right."

Mollie drew the cork from the bottle of brandy and held Rose's head up on her arm. "Here, Rose, take a swallow. Then I'm going to make you a cup of hot mint tea as soon as Maricela gets the campfire hot. They'll be making broth for you later too. You must get your strength back."

Rose took a deep swallow and broke into a hard cough, gasping for breath. "Blessed Jesus!" she said, choking, "what is that, Mollie?"

"Father Baldemero's remedy for girls who almost drown." She smiled as she replaced the cork and put the bottle down.

"I n-nearly drowned?"

"Yes—but Colonel Almonte worked over you after he pulled you out," Mollie said. "And we'll be grateful to him the rest of our lives," she added, meeting Kate's angry eyes defiantly.

Rose's lids fell once more and she murmured weakly, "Colonel Almonte—I owe him my life, then."

"Ye owe him nothing'!" Kate burst out. "Chance an' the twins were right there. It could have been any one o' them!" Her resentment and hostility were undisguised. "If ye feel beholden ter him, we'll take care o' that. I'll see we repay him by servicin' his clothes. I'm not above takin' in his laundry and mendin'. 'Tis what we do best, Rose, the both o' us."

Cayetana spoke suddenly, low voiced and stricken. "Senora Kate, you mus' not hold such hate for our don. Hees beautiful wife Sarita was stolen by Santa Anna —carried away to heez palace een Mexico City. She die a few months later—while miscarry Santa Anna's baby."

Rose's eyes glistened with tears. "Oh," she whispered. "And he never spoke once of it."

"He *never* speak of eet. But Father Baldemero have special masses for our don een hees tent." Cayetana paused, tears on her bronze cheeks. "I tell you thees thing, Senora Kate, so you let heem find a leetle happiness weeth your Rose."

But Kate's face clearly showed her stubborn animosity for the highborn Don Jose.

Mollie's throat was tight with unshed tears for the man who had borne such a terrible loss. She knew with certainty now that Rose Brannigan was hopelessly in love with him.

Chapter 17

The following day Rose was still pale, but her voice was strong and she declared herself ready to travel once more. Almonte was reluctant at first.

"You must rest at least until noon," he said.

"No." Rose was stubborn. "I feel quite well. Certainly well enough to travel."

"We will wait until ten o'clock then," he said, smiling down at her as she sat eating a hearty breakfast at the Mendoza campfire. "I have a fine little mare I wish to give you, Senorita Rose. Your mule is good transportation, but I think you would be happier with the sister to your cousin's mare."

Kate put her plate aside and got to her feet. She stood looking defiantly up into the colonel's dark face.

"Colonel," she said angrily, "we owe ye too much as 'tis. Me daughter'll not be takin' one o' *your* beasties when she has her own!"

Almonte smiled. "It is one of Captain Chance Delanty's animals that I am offering, senora. Is that not so, Chance?"

Chance looked around from where he stood shaving at a small mirror hung over a branch and grinned.

"That's right, Katie. She's one of my mares. And as Mollie says"—his blue glance at Mollie was mocking —"she's Irish—or her mother was Irish."

"Well," Kate said lamely, "if it's Chance's beast, I suppose she can have 'er. But me daughter feels we owe ye, an' God knows I feel beholden ter ye. An' since we launder an' bake by trade as do most servants,"—she spat out the words for emphasis—"we'll do yer launderin' an' mendin'—as well as bakin'."

"That's kind of you, senora, but Cayetana and Maricela do those things for me. I do not think they would look too happily on your taking the work from them."

"Don Jose pay us money—geeve us horses an' our food," Cayetana said to Kate. "My Pedro work for heem many years before our lands were stolen—like Don Jose's lands." She gave Kate a calculating, level look. "No, we do not like eet eef he geeve our work to you."

Chance wiped his razor and folded it into his bundle, turning to speak. "Kate, we're all indebted to Colonel Almonte in some way or other. Why don't you accept his kindness and be gracious about it?"

Almonte bowed to Kate and took Rose's hand, saying, "Come, Rosita, I'll show you the mare I have in mind for you." They left Kate standing speechless. Mollie sent Chance a baleful glance as she put an arm about Kate.

"Come on, Aunt Kate—we all know you're only trying to pay what you feel are your just debts. You certainly wouldn't try to take Cayetana's or Maricela's place, now would you?"

Kate's face was red as she shook her head. Then Clan O'Connor spoke up for her. "I've never heard o' Katie doin' a mean thing, Cayetana."

Cayetana smiled suddenly, and her daughter followed her as she came to put a cheek against Kate's. *"De nada,* Kate," she said. "Come, you help weeth zee dishes.

By ten o'clock, they were on their way once more.

Rose was astride Colleen's sister, a beautiful, dainty mare that was almost as pretty as Colleen, Mollie thought. Almonte had provided a hand-tooled leather saddle for Rose when he gave her the horse.

Now in Mexico itself, they traveled south on their way to the interior. They were passing through beautiful country filled with fig trees, peach trees, and giant pecans trees along rippling streams of water. The limbs were bare of fruit, but many of the trees and shrubs were thick and full and had not lost their leaves.

Mollie rode with Kate, and Rose remained beside Almonte. Kate had a bruised look in her eyes. She had tried to ride beside her daughter, but Almonte had said softly, "Senora, I wish to ride beside your daughter alone. I have much to say to her." Mollie knew Kate's dislike was growing into hatred.

Chance Delanty dropped back to ride beside Mollie and Kate. He seemed in good spirits. "You ladies will enjoy the view even more when you see the Sierra Madre Mountains," he said genially. "The Slieve Bloom Mountains back home were never so grand."

"Th' land is beautiful," Kate said grudgingly. "I will say that fer it."

"Ah, wait until we get further into Mexico. There are rivers and streams with the clearest of waters, sweeter than the burns at home. The colonel's land is some of the fairest of all—it lies at the foot of the Sierra Madres."

Mollie glanced at his chiseled profile limned against the blue sky. His crisp dark hair shone cleanly in the sunlight, and she fought down the thrill that coursed through her. How, she thought despairingly, could just the sight of the man set her heart pounding and send a weakness through her thighs?

Clan rode up beside Kate. "Has Chance told ye th' land th' colonel's goin' ter gi' me fer me services is just below th' Sierra Madre Mountains, like his?"

"No, but he's told us how beautiful it is there," Mollie said, smiling warmly. Let Chance Delanty think what he would. She would encourage Clan even more.

"Me prospects are far an' away finer than those I had in Ireland, *querida mia*. Thousands o' acres fer me own, wi' Mexican renters on that land makin' a considerable income fer me, besides th' crops I'll be raisin' an' sellin'—'tis a prospect ter cheer any man!" His laughter rang on the crystal-clear air.

"Indeed it is," Mollie said admiringly.

"An' ye can share it wi' me, Mollie darlin'," he said, his lips curling in a way to charm any girl. But there was a touch of—what? Could it be brutality about those lips? Yet somehow it increased their appeal.

"I'll be my own woman for awhile, Clan," she said. "I've told you, marriage is not for me." Oh, but wasn't it? If Chance Delanty had asked her, what would her answer be? She was suddenly confused by her own thoughts. She looked back at Chance and met his eyes. They were twinkling and full of secret knowledge meant only for her, and she knew he was thinking of those moments of shared glory between them. The blood was hot in her face.

Clan saw and seemed puzzled for a moment. Then his eyes caught hers and he smiled brilliantly. Apparently he thought her blush was for him, and he was exhilarated by it.

"Ayo—an' I'd give half me promised fortune ter know what yer thinkin', lass."

"It wouldn't be worth it, Clan. You'd do well to seek out some lovely senorita and put your affections on her. I'm for making my own way."

"We'll be passing through Palo Alto before we reach Mier," Chance said casually. "Kate, if you and Mollie have any Yankee money, you can buy shoes and clothes there—if the town's not too torn up."

"An' why would it be torn up?" Kate asked.

"Because one of Almonte's scouts who joined us an hour ago says that General Taylor captured it and camped there awhile before moving on."

But the picturesque village of Palo Alto looked as though its peace had never been disturbed. It was a lazy, sleepy little town with none of the war fever that infected Almonte's guerrilla band. The inhabitants were going about their business as if there were no war, and it was as calm as if Taylor and his troops had not taken the town and camped there before moving on.

Almonte and Chance chose for their campsite the far side of a little cluster of adobe houses with gardens in back of them, away from the center of town where the small shops were located. They stopped early enough for the women to wash clothes in the tributary that ran beside the camp. The town's inhabitants came to the camp full of curiosity, but when they learned the band was under the command of Colonel Jose Almonte, they became very respectful and offered the hospitality of the village.

Late that night, two of Almonte's lone outriders came into camp bearing news. By the time Mollie and her companions awoke and dressed and left their tent, the news had already spread through the band of guerrillas.

"What is it? What is it?" Mollie asked one of the men, who spread his hands and shook his head. He did not speak English. By the firelight she saw Chance and went to question him.

"It seems that Taylor and his army are camped between Monterrey and Saltillo in a great grove of pecan and walnut trees—and they've named the place Walnut Springs."

"What does it all mean?" Rose asked.

"It means we will soon catch up with them, Rose, and hope that Taylor will let us serve with him," Chance said grimly. "They tell us there was fierce fighting for Monterrey at the end of September. But when they marched on to Saltillo, early in November —that's the capital city of the state of Coahuila— there was no fighting at all. They occupied the city without a shot. And Saltillo guards the pass into the Sierra Madres."

"What of Santa Anna? Did they bring word of his actions?" Mollie asked.

"Jose has sent two more scouts further south as far as San Luis Potosi. They know our route and will bring

us news of Santa Anna as soon as they can." Chance
laughed suddenly. "The scouts say that President Polk
is furious at the terms of the armistice dictated by
General Taylor in Saltillo. Bad feelings between General Taylor and the president are growing."

Chance took Mollie and Kate each by the arm.
"You'd better go back to bed. It's two in the morning.
You'll hear all the details tomorrow."

Mollie hung back. "Will the colonel go now to join
Taylor's army at—where did you say he was?"

"At Walnut Springs. Yes. We'll go there. And we'll
leave very early in the morning. You won't get more
than another three hours of sleep—and that much
only if you hurry." His tone was still grim, but there
was jubilation in his eyes, and Mollie realized that he
was as eager to meet the enemy as Colonel Jose Almonte was. Mollie, Rose, and Kate went back to their
bedrolls, but they did not undress and their sleep was
fitful.

In the following days the band passed through Mier
without stopping and was now approaching Cerralvo.
It was New Year's Eve, and Mollie knew they would
see 1847 come in while they were camped outside that
small town. Father Baldemero would conduct a special
midnight mass, and the word around camp was that
they were to take a few hours in the morning to wash
and dry clothes as well as prepare food to be eaten
while traveling.

Chance came up beside Mollie just before they
reached the Cerralvo and told her they would be able
to see the Sierra Madre Mountains in the distance
from the small city. She was cold to him, for she was
increasingly certain that she carried his child. It was
three days past her time now.

"They're beautiful, Mollie. I don't think you've ever
seen anything like them."

"Probably not," she said shortly.

"You look like a thundercloud this morning," he
said, curiosity in his voice. "What's troubling you?"

Oh, if she only dared to tell him. Would he laugh

and shrug his shoulders? Probably. He had never mentioned love—if he had, she would have thrown it back
in his face—but her fears now put things in another
light. He had sweet-talked her, making love to her
without saying he loved her. Her feelings regarding
him were turbulent and unexplainable.

"I'm just counting the days," she said briefly, "until
I will have served out my indenture." And by that time
she might be seven months along. Fierce resentment
rose up in her throat like bile. "I'll be so glad when I
never have to set eyes on you again, Chance Delanty!"
She sent him an angry glance and met eyes that were
flat and expressionless. He turned his stallion
abruptly about and trotted to the head of the caravan.

They reached Cerralvo midmorning. There were
people in the town who knew Almonte, and, as in Palo
Alto, they bowed to him and called him Don Jose with
a touch of awe.

"Some of these, too, were my people—living on my
lands some years ago," he explained to the three Irish
women.

He had chosen to camp on the banks of a small,
clear stream, a tributary of the San Juan River. The
townspeople were making themselves at home in his
camp. Some had brought foodstuffs and they even offered clothing. The Mexican women were especially
welcoming and warm, chattering with the women of
the camp and laughing in a spirit of festivity because
the next day would be the first day of 1847.

That night, Father Baldemero held confession and
midnight mass. All of Almonte's band went to the long
services, as well as those who visited from the town of
Cerralvo. Even Mollie confessed, a short recitation of
trivial things such as her lack of gratitude for the
kindnesses of Jose Almonte. She said nothing about
what sat most heavily on her heart—Chance Delanty.
But attending mass eased her conscience somewhat.

After mass, Chance came to her, and without a
word, took her by the arm. At his touch, fire leapt in
her and her thighs ached.

"What is it? Where are you taking me?" she asked

as they walked away from camp. She tried to pull
back, but the heat in her veins weakened her resolve.
"Chance—where are you going?"

"Away from all this merrymaking. I want to talk to
you—among other things."

Among other things. Her mind hung on the words.
What other things were there between them but their
bodies? And she realized that hers was crying out for
his touch. Oh, if only she hadn't succumbed that first
time! It was familiar now, this longing for him.

They were far from the others. The sounds of the
camp came to them faintly on the chill wind. He halted
suddenly and took her in his arms, his head bending to
hers. The touch of his lips on hers was a sweet narcotic, which she felt course through her before she
pulled away.

"No!" she burst out. "Not again!"

"Oh, yes—again. You want it as much as I, and you
know it. I've thought about you—about having you a
hundred times since then—and so have you."

He caught his hand in the back of her thick hair,
forcing her face up, and his mouth was hard and demanding. Mollie fought against it, but she felt her lips
part involuntarily under his. She clenched her teeth
against his probing tongue and he ran it around her
lips, tenderly, softly, until her teeth parted. They stood
fused in the blowing wind.

The clouds scudded low over a full moon, letting
patches of brilliant moonlight shine through, as he
picked her up to lay her gently on the ground. Gathering all her strength, she struggled up once more.

"No, Chance, no! Not again," she sobbed, her voice
thick and strangled. "Not after mass and my promises
to keep myself apart."

He stopped suddenly, pulling her down to a sitting
position beside him.

"Something's worrying you, Mollie—something besides your hell-bent desire to serve me until July. If it's
trouble, you must let me share it."

"Why should I? My troubles are my own."

"You are mine—and your troubles are mine."

"I'm yours only until July—let me go!" She pulled hard at the wrist he held in an iron grip.

"Not until you tell me."

"No. The shame will be mine alone—and I'll have your baby!" She spoke bitterly. "I'll take it with me to Corpus and raise it without you. You'll never have to see it."

"My God, Mollie! I'll marry you—"

"Out of pity? You don't want to marry—I know that." Then, trying to put conviction into her voice, she added, "And marriage is not on my mind."

"I know," he said dryly. "I heard you tell that to Clan. But this makes it different. I won't have my child a bastard."

"I'm three days late—I'm not certain, but you must let me go. I can't take the risk again."

"No matter how badly you want to?"

"I don't want to!"

He rose, still holding her wrist. "I'll wager you aren't carrying my child at all. I'll take you back to camp now—but I'll have you again, Mollie darlin'."

"Never!"

"Yes, I will. You'll be only too willing when this scare is over—when the time and the elements are more propitious."

A few drops of rain struck them and the moon disappeared completely. He led her back toward the camp. They reached it just as the clouds broke.

That night a storm of terrifying proportions unleashed its fury over the camp. Rain fell in torrents, thunder and lightning rent the air, and no one could sleep, least of all Mollie, who was struggling with her thoughts of Chance Delanty. What was it about him that melted her bones?

The wind blowing in under the sides of the tents was bitter cold, and most of the guerrillas spent a miserable night. Yet morning brought a brilliant sun and a sky without a cloud in it. The little stream beside the camp was full to overflowing, and everything was soggy and wet. Almonte told his followers they would

have to dry all the tents and tarpaulins before they
could start for Monterrey.

Clan came to Mollie as she finished breakfast and
took her by the arm, leading her to a high spot beyond
the rushing stream.

"See, Mollie?"

There on the horizon she could see great jagged
mountains, blue in the distance, seemingly carved
against the sky. Mollie was awed. Even from so far,
they appeared huge, rough, and breathtaking in their
majesty. Chance had been right. They were far more
magnificent than the gentle Slieve Bloom Mountains.
This New World was awe inspiring in its many con-
trasts, its raw beauty and, most of all, its illimitable
vastness. Even in her vivid imagination, she could
never have conceived of this land of rich and fruitful
valleys surrounded by the giant splendor of such
mountains.

When the morning sun and wind had dried the
tents and tarpaulins and the wagons were efficiently
packed, the guerrillas set out down the wet, muddy
road for Monterrey. They would have to stop there before going on to Saltillo.

Fields of late grain spread out beyond the road.
They traveled south through two sleepy villages where
peach, pomegranate, orange, and lemon groves still
bore leaves. The fragrance that emanated from the
trees beside the small tributary along the San Juan
promised a rich and luscious spring.

It was late afternoon when they reached the small
town of Cienega de Flores, where they were to camp
the last night before going into Monterrey. A man
Mollie had never seen before galloped up to Almonte
on a lathered horse and reined to a hard stop. The entire caravan ground to a halt to listen to the man's
excited words rolling out in Spanish. Maricela, on her
horse beside Mollie and Rose, murmured, "He eez a
scout. Don Jose send heem out many weeks long ahead
of us to find where Santa Anna eez—an' what he do.
Now he tell the don."

"Tell him what?" Mollie asked, with burning curiosity.

Maricela shook her head. "Don Jose—he tell you later. More better than me. I cannot—to—theenk so many English words so fast."

Mollie could not wait. She wheeled her horse about and rode to the tight group of men, the only woman to do so. Chance sat on his horse taller than the rest of them, and she reached out a hand to pluck at his sleeve. He glanced at her sharply, then turned back to the still-gesturing scout. Angrily, Mollie pushed her horse among the men on horseback and pulled at Chance's sleeve again. He turned, annoyed.

"Go back with the others, Mollie—I'll tell you all about it later. We're going to make camp here. Tell the women."

Hot with indignation, she turned Colleen and rode back to her companions.

"We're going to set up camp here," she said shortly. "I suppose we can start now."

The others listened and dismounted, leading their horses from the road. The women began the chores of making cook fires and unpacking their utensils and bedrolls. After what seemed an eternity to the impatient Mollie, the men began dispersing. Cayetana, with the help of the others, had a good fire going and her coffeepot on the rack over it. Clan approached, followed by Benjie and Tim.

Mollie looked back and saw that Chance was still deep in conversation with Almonte and the scout. She turned her sunniest smile on Clan.

"Oh, Clan, surely you and Tim and Benjie can tell us what all the excitement is about!" Her greeting was so warm that Clan and the twins expanded visibly under it.

"Rodriguez, th' scout ye see yonder wi' th' colonel an' Chance," Clan began, "has been wi' Santa Anna's troops, pretendin' ter be one o' 'em. He tells us Santa Anna captured an American messenger, a Lieutenant Ritchie, an' promptly had him killed."

"But in his pouch was a letter from Gen'l Winfield

Scott," Benjie cut in excitedly, "strippin' Gen'l Taylor o' his regulars and requestin' they be sent ter him at Vera Cruz, where Scott'll be in command o' all armies. It's President Polk's doin's."

"He wants ter bring Taylor down," Tim drawled, "an' he's doin' it. It leaves Taylor wi' only a few regulars, all o' them inexperienced volunteers—about like us."

"What does that mean?" Rose asked, frightened.

Clan said, "It means, me dear, that Santa Anna knows all th' American plans an' is massin' an army o' more'n twenty thousand at San Luis Potosi, some two hundred an' fifty miles south o' Saltillo. He means ter run Gen'l Zachary Taylor out o' Mexico wi' his tail atween his legs."

"Taylor's got less'n five thousand troops," Tim added, "but he's goin' ter have *us*."

"Blessed Mary." Kate swallowed dryly. "Santa Anna could kill all o' us, an' from what I've heard about him, he likely will."

"No, he won't." Clan grinned. "Taylor's men call him Ol' Rough an' Ready, an' my guess is he'll stick an' fight 'em ter a standstill, even wi' his decimated troops. He's not a man ter cut an' run."

Mollie remained silent.

That night, she was roused from a light slumber by a shadow that moved silently in the tent. Stiffening, she let her eyes move to the empty bedroll beside her. Kate lay on the one beyond it, breathing deeply and slowly.

It was Rose! She met with another shadow at the flap to the tent. Jose Almonte. Mollie knew him by the tall, muscular shape of his body. The shadows melted together and vanished silently into the night.

Mollie rose from her bedroll and slipped from the tent. Her eyes picked them out immediately at the edge of the campsite. Oh, she would stop Rose before she could make a fatal mistake!

The moonlight was bright, but they vanished almost immediately among the fragrant trees along the

little stream. Mollie glanced at the people sleeping in
the glade. Stealthily she followed where she had seen
the couple disappear and soon picked them up again
beyond the campsite. It was well after two in the morning.

The two lovers stopped in a small grove of trees, and
Mollie saw Jose Almonte shake out a dark object. His
poncho or serape, no doubt, and then Rose removed her
serape and laid it on the ground beside his. Then,
reaching down, she caught the hem of her nightgown
and brought it up swiftly over her head. Her body
gleamed whitely in the pale, dappled moonlight as she
stood nude before him.

Almonte caught her to him, the movement swift
with passion, and they sank to the ground together.

Mollie had intended to stop her cousin before Rose
could make the same mistake she had, but she realized
with a flash that she was already too late. She knew
instinctively this same scene had happened many
times before—and inevitably it would continue to
happen. Too late!

She did not look at them again but turned and made
her way silently and quickly to the tent. Moving like a
wraith, she found her own bedroll and sank without a
sound upon it, pulling the blanket up to her knees. It
was well over an hour before Rose returned, and Mollie lay wakeful for some time after her cousin had
slipped noiselessly into her own bedroll.

The following morning, the wagons, the remuda,
the mounted men and women, and the packhorses all
set forth on the road to Monterrey. Once again they ate
their noon meal in the saddle. The impatience of the
men, now that they knew that actual combat was near,
communicated itself to every member of the caravan.
All of them felt the pressure to move quickly.

Mollie looked at her cousin. Rose's face was serene,
her eyes glowing with tenderness each time her gaze
fell on Almonte beyond her—and that was often. Her
cheeks were rosy as she nourished her secret in silence.

Mollie thought of Santa Anna, massing twenty

thousand men to do battle with Taylor, who had less than five thousand and most of them inexperienced volunteers. Suppose in attempting to wreak his vengeance on Santa Anna, Almonte was killed—and Rose was left carrying his child. The same thing could happen to Chance and herself.

Then there would be two of them carrying bastard children. Mollie shivered.

Chapter 18

By the time they reached Monterrey three days later, Mollie knew she was not pregnant. She felt a curious letdown along with her relief. Chance had started to say, *I'll marry you, Mollie*—but it was only because he felt responsible when he thought she was carrying his child, she told herself angrily. Resolutely, she put him from her mind as she looked at the town around her.

Monterrey was by far the largest city that Mollie had seen since Dublin. It was a dusty town, as were the others they had passed through. The adobe houses were small, but some finer residences were two stories high, with wall-enclosed patios where tinkling fountains could be heard. The main plaza of the city was quite impressive, with a tall, graceful cathedral dominating the center and businesses crowding the square.

There had been bloody fighting for Monterrey, and the citizens were bitter against the Americans. The people of Monterrey wanted Santa Anna, who was riding a wave of renewed popularity, to come from San Luis Potosi and administer a thorough beating to the

Americans. Mollie was a little unsettled by this information. There were so many people here who sympathized with Santa Anna! They could easily take over Almonte's band of guerrillas, no matter how many guns his men boasted. But the inhabitants eyed Almonte's entourage with friendly curiosity. They were under the misconception that Almonte meant to fight for the Mexican cause and accordingly were cordial in their welcome. No one in the guerrilla band told them differently.

Chance and the other men were reluctant to stop even for a day to let the women wash clothing and prepare food. They were anxious to reach Saltillo.

"Don Jose weel let us make camp," Cayetana said easily. "He weel tell them we are friends. You weel see."

And she was right. Almonte had them make camp by a stream. The townsfolk were curious about the gringos with Almonte's band, but Mollie saw him talking smoothly to them in Spanish and their eyes grew friendly again.

"You see?" Cayetana smiled at Mollie as they dismounted and began to unpack their things for the night.

After supper, Mollie asked Chance how Almonte had handled the situation.

"He explained that we were Irish, and that the Irish are good Catholics and sympathize with his cause—while carefully omitting mention of his true allegiance." His laugh was ironic. "They were ready to believe him because of the large troop of Irish-Americans who defected to the Mexican side only recently. Even now they are fighting against us."

"That's terrible!" Mollie said indignantly.

"For them it is. When the war is over, they'll be hung by the military as traitors to America."

"Why, that's such a harsh punishment."

Taking her by the arm, he led her away from the others and murmured, "Are you still the little mother?"

"No!" she said violently, jerking her hand from him.

He laughed softly. "I told you, didn't I?"

"You stay away from me, Chance Delanty!"

"I will not. By your own choice, your services belong to me until July tenth of this year."

"Not *that* kind of service, and you know it!"

"I wasn't talking about *that* kind of service. I was speaking of your talents as a physician. Or do you consider *"that"* one of your talents?" He was filled with silent laughter now.

"It's impossible to have a decent conversation with you," she said, turning away, but he caught her hand.

"Take heart. We'll be seeing action soon. We're very near General Taylor's troops now, because his camp is nearly seventeen miles outside Saltillo on the Monterrey side." He paused.

Mollie caught a vibrant note in his voice when he added, "Already Almonte has sent his scouts back along the long road to San Luis Potosi, which is far to the south and is where Santa Anna is assembling his armies. Two have gone ahead to Saltillo and will wait for us at Walnut Springs, where General Taylor and his gallant five thousand are." He shrugged, then added, "Or maybe they'll bring us news that General Scott has relented and has allowed Taylor to keep a few thousand regulars."

"If General Taylor has the sense God gave a goat, he'll march those men back to Texas and let General Scott take over."

Chance threw back his head and laughed. "Not that old bird Taylor! He'll charge on through with his five thousand—and us. Cheer up, Mollie; maybe I'll catch a cannonball and you'll be rid of me. But until I do, you may be sure I won't, as you so charmingly asked, stay away from you."

Almonte's guerrillas rode into Saltillo a tired but relieved group. The people they passed in the streets eyed them warily because of the gringos among them. The natives' brown faces were implacable but their black eyes showed repressed rage and resentment over their recent defeat at the hands of Taylor's troops, though Mollie had been told that Taylor's terms of surrender were more than liberal.

Taylor had permitted General Ampudia and his army to leave the city. The officers had kept their arms and accoutrements, as had the infantry and cavalry. Taylor had even permitted them to keep a six-piece field battery. Added to all this, General Taylor had agreed to an eight-week armistice, giving the Mexicans time to retire and rebuild their forces. It was this last agreement, Clan had told Mollie, that so incensed President Polk.

Mollie was beside Rose and Kate as they rode through Saltillo, and in front of them rode Almonte, Chance Delanty, and Clan O'Connor. Almonte was saying, "My friends, I think it will be well if we camp out toward General Taylor's Walnut Springs. My countrymen do not look happy with us, and I think we will be safer out of town, despite the American garrison that occupies the city."

"You're right, Jose," Chance responded. "And I'll wager the good men of your country fought hard, and there's no disgrace in their loss to Taylor."

"To be sure," Almonte replied dryly. "I plan to help rectify the situation in my country that makes such defeats possible. You Americans will not be able to do this again." Though he laughed easily, there was an edge to his words.

"Not with men such as you in the Mexican government, Jose," Chance replied with a touch of iron in his own voice, "but it will happen again if evil men take over once more—and, in their greed, reach for the United States."

Mollie looked about her at the city as they rode along. According to Pedro Mendoza, the city had been founded in the fifteenth century and now boasted a population of nearly twenty thousand. They passed spacious plazas, and the cathedral that loomed over the center of town was even more magnificent than the one in Monterrey had been.

"An' would ye look at that," Kate murmured in admiration as she peered up at the imposing structure.

The twins rode up beside the three women, and Benjie laughed joyously. "Sure, Katie, an' 'twould be a pleasure ter confess th' worst sins in a place like that now, wouldn't it?"

"Go along, ye two spalpeens. 'Tis sacrilegious ye are!"

"Jose—I—" Rose began; then, at her mother's angry glance, she lifted her chin and finished, "Colonel Almonte says this is the most important city in northern Mexico. It controls the best route from the plains of the Gulf Coast to the highlands of this country."

Mollie said dryly, "Then it's a good thing the Americans took it, or their way would've been blocked to the Valley of Mexico from the north."

Chance, ahead of her, dropped back after hearing her remark. "Now that was a shrewd military observation, Mollie. I'm glad you're on our side." Pressing his knees against Beau's sides, he rejoined Clan and Almonte. Mollie, embarrassed that she had been overheard, muttered to her companions, "They don't need me with *him* on our side." But her sarcasm was wasted, for the twins had ridden ahead to join the others and her aunt and cousin were again lost in admiring the city.

That night after supper, one of the two scouts Almonte had sent ahead to General Taylor's camp rode in. As before, the men gathered about him as he brought news of further troop movements. Mollie realized anew that they were drawing ever nearer to real danger.

"He tell about General Taylor losing heez troops," Maricela said to the three Irish women over their last cup of coffee. "He say we just miss zee great leaving of zem. Thousands an' thousands. He say zee general eez mos' angry an' he have but few mens left—mostly zee volunteer. Not zee regular army mens."

Mollie sighed. "Well, we knew they were going to have to leave him—probably long before he did, because of Colonel Almonte's scouts and their news of the intercepted letter."

"I don't see why Almonte wants ter stay wi' Taylor an' his men," Kate said, glaring at the group of men around the scout. "Why doesn't he have sense enough ter pack up an' go wi' this other general, Scott? We'd all be safer wi' a big army."

"Go clear down to Camargo? Or worse, to Tampico on the Gulf?" Mollie looked at her. "That's where Clan said Scott was having the the troops sent. They're miles and miles farther south."

Rose looked down, her thick gold lashes making fan-shaped shadows on her cheeks. "Jose wants to fight Santa Anna. And all his scouts say Santa Anna will attack Taylor."

"An' likely that Almonte'll be shot fer his foolishness, too," Kate said.

Rose made no reply.

Later, when the cooking fires were low and the guerrilla band was settling down for the night, Clan approached Mollie as she stood outside the tent cleaning the boots still on her feet.

"Mollie," he said quietly, "Gen'l Taylor received a second dispatch from Gen'l Scott, strippin' him o' most o' his command. Almonte's rider, Cordilla, says Scott took nine thousand men from him, with all his seasoned officers, leavin' him fewer'n five thousand men."

"Less than five thousand! Then surely he'll fall back."

"That's what Gen'l Scott suggested, but not Ol' Rough an' Ready. They say he's mad enough ter chew nails an' determined ter meet Santy Anna head on. An' furthermore, Cordilla says Santy Anna's still at San Luis Potosi, 'bout two hundred an' fifty miles away, gatherin' more an' more men ter his banner. He has near twenty-five thousand now, Cordilla said." Clan paused, then added dryly, "An' Cordilla says Taylor's not too happy ter have us guerrillas join him. Calls us a reckless, ungovernable lot, but he's willin' ter talk ter Colonel Almonte about it."

"And Taylor expects to stop Santa Anna's twenty-five-thousand-man army with fewer than five thousand men?" Mollie asked. "He's a fool, whether he accepts Almonte into his command or not!"

"Don't sell him short, Mollie. He's a tough old bird. They say he has little use fer uniforms, sashes an' plumes an' such. Goes about lookin' like an ol' farmer on his way ter market ter sell eggs, but th' men under him have a powerful lot o' faith in him."

"Faith will be poor armor against twenty-five thousand guns!"

"Ye'd be surprised what faith can do, lass. An' I have faith yer goin' ter come ter love me. Ye've been so nice ter me these last weeks." He hesitated; then in a low, husky voice he asked, "Would ye gi' me a good-night kiss, Mollie?"

It was such a humble request coming from so arrogant and brash a man that Mollie hesitated. As she moved uncertainly, his hands came out and caught her arms, pulling her up. She dropped the small knife with which she was cleaning her boots and as he pulled her against him, she could feel him tremble. He bent his head to hers.

She lifted her face and he kissed her, so softly at first she could not believe it was the same man who had handled her so roughly in the copse off the road to Arderin. His lips moved tenderly over hers and his arms tightened. Even before she could pull away, his arms fell and he caught her hand lightly, kissing the palm tenderly.

"I can wait." He sighed. "I never wanted any lass like I want you, Mollie." His voice hardened and the old Clan vibrated in it. "An' I'll have ye one day. Ye'll see!"

He turned and left her, the undercurrent of passion in his words still echoing in the air around her.

As she looked after his retreating form, she saw Chance standing beside his tent. She closed the flap to her own tent quickly and stood a moment, breathing hard, her heart beating wildly. It was not Clan's tender kiss that set her pulses pounding. It was the look on Chance's face, that half smile, and the promise that

she could not see but knew burned in his eyes like a
raw flame.

On January twenty-fourth, General Zachary Taylor
came back to Walnut Springs from Vittorio. He
brought with him a part of his decimated army.

Mollie saw him for the first time the following
morning, for the guerrillas had moved up with his
army. From a short distance she saw he was reviewing
his troops.

As Clan had reported, Taylor was out of uniform
and clad in such strange clothing she would never
have recognized him as a general. He wore an old
slouch hat, worn woolen pantaloons, and an old brown
coat. The neckerchief at his throat was a striped cotton
cloth and did not even look hemmed. There was nothing about him to indicate he was an officer of any
rank. But his men regarded him with shining eyes,
confidence written plainly on their faces. That they
trusted, admired, and revered him was obvious, and
Mollie sensed they would gladly follow wherever he
led, sure they could win any battle under his leader-
ship.

That day, Colonel Almonte, Captain Chance Delanty, and Lieutenant Clanahan O'Connor spent the
morning and most of the afternoon in conference with
General Taylor and his officer, Captain Enoch Steen of
the Regiment of the First Dragoons. It was fully dark
before they all returned.

The women had prepared supper by the time Almonte, Chance, and Clan came up to the Mendoza supper fire. Almonte smiled and asked in Spanish, "May
we join you for supper tonight, my friends?"

"*Si*, Don Jose," Cayetana responded warmly, and
Pedro moved to make room on the poncho he had put
down over the rough saw grass. Benjie and Tim, who
had eaten earlier, joined them.

When each of them had a plate of pheasant, beans,
and Kate's good Irish bread, Mollie could wait no
longer. "Tell us what happened during your day with

General Taylor's troops. Was he glad to learn we would be with him?"

Almonte's smile was wry. "We learned, Senorita Mollie, that we are not especially welcome to the general, despite his greatly depleted troops."

"As a matter of fact," Chance drawled, his eyes twinkling at Mollie, "he's heard that Mexican guerrillas are nearly as bad as outliers, and he doesn't think we'll be much better. He feels the same way about the Texas Rangers who are soon to join him."

"Sure an' I got th' impression he could do wi'out any volunteer guerrillas!" Clan added. "Especially th' ones recently come from Ireland."

Almonte shrugged. "That is because of the Irish who defected and now fight for Mexico, Clan. As for Mexican guerrillas, some of them do not always respond to orders in the way General Taylor feels they should. And he was of the opinion, of course, that my band of men would be more of the same."

"Oh—" Mollie was sorely disappointed. To have come all this way for nothing! "Then he refused your help, Colonel Almonte?"

"No, no, senorita! We talked long and earnestly with him. The fact that my Captain Delanty fought at San Jacinto where Texas won her independence gained his respect—and he agreed to let us join him."

"'Tis a fine ol' curmudgeon he is," Clan said.

"Some of his disapproval stems from the fact that I bring women along. But the guns and ammunition we have brought all the way from New Orleans helped overcome that objection." Almonte smiled. His eyes went to Rose and lingered on her face. She met his look, and Mollie read the yearning to be in his arms written plainly in her face.

"He was somewhat mollified," Chance remarked dryly, "when he found that our troop is made up of sharpshooters."

Mollie knew this to be a fact, because when any of the men hunted game, they never came back empty-handed. Then she looked at Kate beside her and saw her narrowed eyes on her daughter's lover. Almonte

was aware of it too, and he looked beyond the campfire
into the darkness.

"I told the general," he said slowly, "we will see that
you ladies are well back from any action. We will be
responsible for you."

"Right now," Chance put in, "Taylor thinks Santa
Anna will go south to confront Scott at Vera Cruz or
perhaps Tampico."

"I harbor no such illusions," Almonte said bitterly.
"The Napoleon of the West will strike where he is sure
he can win—at the weakest forces of the Americans.
And that is north—up here."

Mollie was chilled by his words, by the passionate
longing for revenge she heard in them. If Almonte
found the man who had wronged him so cruelly, would
he meet him with saber, rifle, or pistol? And if he did
not, could he learn to live with his vengeance unquenched?

She glanced at Rose's pale face in the firelight, her
eyes dilated with fear, and her heart ached for her
cousin. Rose's love for the Mexican aristocrat was as
great as his thirst for revenge. No, it was greater, for
the girl rose from her place before the fire, leaving her
half-filled plate, and walked into the darkness. Almonte was swift to follow.

Kate would have risen to pursue them both, but
Chance put out a big, tanned hand and caught her
arm.

"Let them go, Kate." The command in his voice held
her. "'Tis their business—and Rose is twenty. It's out
of your hands now."

Kate's eyes on Chance were filled with tears of
pained fury, but she stayed as a wave of talk and questions broke out among those left at the fire. The loud-
est among the excited voices were those of Benjie and
Tim Delanty.

The next few days consisted of drills, marches, and
maneuvers as Taylor attempted to train the raw re-
cruits and volunteers he had taken on. Almonte's band
did not take part in these exercises, for it had been

agreed that he would operate on his own. His men were already trained. They would help shore up the others in battle, moving in where they were most needed and firing from where they were least expected.

Clan told Mollie that, left to their own devices, the guerrillas could come to the aid of hard-pressed men whenever any action took place. But Mollie was sure Colonel Jose Almonte wanted the freedom to move about in order to seek out and fall upon Antonio López de Santa Anna.

A day later, Major Ben McCulloch with his Texas Rangers rode into camp from Saltillo. Mollie glimpsed his troops from a distance as they mingled with the dragoons. They reminded her strongly of Chance Delanty—lean, quick moving, and hard faced from years of surviving by their wits and their courage, neither asking nor giving any quarter. There had to be some basis for General Taylor's reluctance to have them under his command. She smiled grimly to herself.

"What are you smiling about, Mollie?" Rose asked curiously as she curried the beautiful little mare Almonte had given her.

"I was thinking that the Texas Rangers and Chance Delanty and all these guerrillas aren't really under *anyone's* command. And that's why General Taylor isn't anxious to have them with him. Hurry up with that—I want to curry Colleen before supper."

"They all ought to do what the general tells them," Rose said.

Mollie, still looking at the rangers as they pitched camp near the dragoons, was remembering what Chance had told her of the blood shed at the Alamo and Goliad. Both massacres had been at the command of Santa Anna. She was beginning to have a dim understanding of the rankling bitterness the Texans had toward the elusive dictator and his men.

The days of drilling and maneuvering continued, and suddenly it was February.

The guerrilla band had finished supper one evening

and all were sitting around their fires, most with a last cup of coffee. Almonte, Chance, and Clan had made a point of having supper with the Mendozas almost every night, and Mollie knew it was because she and Rose were there. A dense fog had settled over the countryside, making it impossible to see more than a few feet from each supper fire. The other fires about them glowed faintly through the mist.

Suddenly the sound of hooves moving carefully through the heavy fog came to them and a voice called out, "Colonel Almonte!"

Almonte rose to his feet. "Here, senor—here."

"Lieutenant Daniels of the First Dragoons, sir. I'm to tell you that all General Taylor's troops are pulling out tomorrow—heading south on the San Luis Potosi road, where we hope to be available to take diversionary action in the event General Scott needs it." He paused, and there was silence around the fire. "The rangers will be ready to leave at dawn with the main body of those troops remaining, sir. General Taylor sends word that your troop is to follow after them."

He wheeled his horse around and vanished into the white mist. Chance looked at Almonte, and in his deep, moving voice he said, "We'll not be taking action on General Scott's behalf, Jose. Santa Anna will strike at Taylor's forces. The action will come between here and San Luis Potosi—and when we meet him, we will either win or lose this war."

Almonte's camp was astir long before dawn. They ate breakfast hurriedly, and as Taylor's troops began to march out the rangers fell in behind them. The guerrillas were followed by their wagons loaded with everything from food supplies and clothing to the remaining ammunition and guns. It was still dark, but the fog of the previous night had vanished.

Later, Mollie on her mare watched the sun come up over the long lines of blue-clad foot soldiers, over the troops of cavalry, over the long, rumbling guns they called the flying artillery because they were horse drawn and mounted on wheels and could be rushed from one battle scene to another. Sunlight glinted on harness and guns but cast no warmth on her chilled, deerskin-clad shoulders.

As they rode on, the February day grew colder, for they were climbing into the mountains. The Sierra Madres loomed blue in the west, and the narrow, rough road wound circuitously around arroyos, ravines, and gullies in the foothills. The morning had been thoroughly uncomfortable, and it wasn't until noon that the pale sun gave any real comfort. But even as it did, clouds were gathering in the north behind them, and their ominous blue-black color filled Mollie with dread. She had been through one wild storm in Mexico and was reluctant to face another.

That night, before Father Baldemero could have prayers, the storm broke upon them, and Clan erected his tent for the three Irish women as the first drops blew in. Then suddenly, lashing winds and driving cold rains assaulted the camp. Everyone in the guerrilla band huddled unhappily in hastily erected tents, or under tarpaulins, which provided poor protection, and ate cold food.

When Chance suddenly opened the flap of their tent with his arms full of brush, Kate and Rose welcomed him warmly.

"Come in, me bye, come in," Kate said. "Ye look like a drowned rat, ye do. Surely ye don't think we can be buildin' a fire in here wi' that?" She gestured at the brush with the fitful flame of a lighted candle in her hand.

"No, Kate. It's for your bedrolls. See there? Already the rain's trickling under."

Looking down, they saw small rivulets running in under the pegged edges of the tent. Chance bent to spread the brush across the bare earth. "Lay your bedrolls over this, ladies. It'll be a bit rough, but it'll keep you raised above the dampness."

"How kind and thoughtful you are, Chance," Rose said. "I'm glad you have a tent to sleep in on a night like this."

He glanced swiftly at Mollie, who met his twinkling

blue eyes in the candlelight. "You don't know how thoughtful I am, Rose." He laughed. "The twins and I have given up our tent to Maricela and Cayetana Mendoza—and Maria Garcia. It'll be a tarpaulin for me this night, if I'm lucky."

"Aye, an' we can't have that, laddie!" Kate looked warily at Mollie. "Now, me darlin's, we can make room fer Chance's bedroll below ours. I'm a widder an' a proper chaperone fer such an emergency."

"Likely a tarpaulin will provide more shelter than a tent in this weather." Mollie spoke coldly, but her heart was beating unevenly, and panic lay just below her calm. How could she sleep so close to Chance Delanty?

"Now, Mollie," Chance said smoothly, "I saw you give Clan O'Connor that sweet kiss not too long ago. If it were Clan needing to share your tent, you might be more welcoming."

"He *asked* me for that kiss! Like a gentleman."

"I must admit it was different from the evening I rescued you from his—unwelcome?—embraces on the way to Arderin."

"That was different!" she cut in, her voice rising. "He's changed entirely since that night. And he's been a real gentleman to me ever since I joined your guerrillas!"

Rose and Kate were looking from one to the other in bewildered astonishment. "What happened in Arderin?" Kate began.

"Chance Delanty is no gentleman, Aunt Kate, or he'd not be telling you about pulling Clan O'Connor off me so long ago!"

"I apologize, Mollie," he said mockingly. "And, Kate, it appears I'm not too welcome. I'll find a tarp to share somewhere—I hope."

"Ye'll do no such thing, Chance Delanty! Mollie O'Meara, I'm ashamed o' ye. Chance has been nothin' but a fine gentleman ter all o' us, an' ye know as sure as I'm standin' here, he shouldn't have ter spend this terrible night under a leaky shelter. Get yer bedroll, Chance, an' come back."

"Thank you, Kate. You're a truly gracious lady. I'll be right back."

When he was gone, Kate scolded Mollie, who was forced to explain about the incident in the copse on the road to Arderin.

"Ye said nothin' about that ter Rose an' me," Kate said shortly. "If yer so mad at Chance an' don't like him, I'm surprised ye indentured yerself ter him."

"I was desperate to get us out of Ireland to keep us from starving!"

"Now, Ma," Rose put in softly, "you mustn't take Mollie to task. She wasn't that unwelcoming."

"Oh, blessed Mary!" Kate put the candle down on a flat rock. "'Tis a squabble over nothin'," she said in exasperation. "We'll all sleep in our clothes. Maybe that'll make me squeamish niece feel better about havin' an old friend in th' tent with us."

Old friend indeed, Mollie thought rebelliously, taking off her boots and standing them atop some of the brush near her bedroll. She pulled off her heavy stockings. If her aunt had an inkling of her abandonment to the man that night under the chaparral, Aunt Kate would revise her opinion of him! And of her niece too, Mollie thought with sudden guilt.

She slipped into the bedroll as Chance reappeared in the opening and tied the flap shut against the wind. He brought more brush and his own bedroll. His dark, curling hair was wet, and his broad shoulders and tall, lean body filled the tent with a potent masculinity that burned in Mollie's veins.

"I'll not put out the candle, me bye, till yer set," Kate said from her end of the tent nearest the flap. Rose lay between her and Mollie. When Chance arranged his bedroll, his head and shoulders were right at Mollie's feet. "I've no doubt the other ladies are makin' room fer other poor lads in this storm."

"You're wise, ladies, to sleep in your clothes. We'll probably be leaving by the time this storm blows over."

"I niver saw such a night!" Kate said, settling herself on the lumpy, prickly bedroll.

"Katie Brannigan, you're a true friend," Chance

said, and Mollie detected laughter in his husky voice. What if she had that dream about him tonight and woke them all with her moaning? Saints preserve us, she thought in anguish, he was so *near* her! She lifted her head a fraction and saw his eyes gleaming at her from under tumbled dark locks.

As Kate snuffed out the candle, blackness engulfed the tent. The sound of heavy rain drumming on the canvas above was like thunder, or was that Mollie's own heart beating in her ears?

Lightning flashed, lighting up the tent brilliantly, and was followed by a clap of thunder that shook the world. Mollie gasped, cowering under the blankets. Suddenly there was a warm, hard hand over one of her naked feet, and she drew in a swift breath.

"Don't be afraid, ladies." Chance's voice was deep and soothing; the sound slipped over Mollie like the fire that was rushing through her veins. "Winter storms in Mexico make a terrible noise but do little harm."

His hand on her foot was scalding, and she jerked her leg upward, but he merely held on tighter. Indeed, he was slipping his hand up the calf of her leg under the breeches she wore. My God! How far would he go?

"I'm not afraid!" she shouted above the noise of the storm. "You can keep your reassurances to yourself, Chance Delanty!"

"As fer me, I'm not so brave, me bye." Kate's voice lifted reprovingly. "It sounds like th' end o' th' world."

"Or the voice of doom," Rose said feelingly. "You don't suppose such lightning could strike us dead, do you, Chance?"

"I saw it strike an oak once," he said, his rough hand caressing Mollie's leg and ankle smoothly. His husky voice could be heard clearly over the drumming rain. "Cleaved it in two, like a great knife."

Suddenly his words invoked for Mollie a vision of Meg Moriarty's long, shining blade. Light had flashed from it in the ship's cabin when she drew it out and showed it to Mollie, bright as the lightning now flashing. Deadly and dangerous like the lightning. A queasy fear joined the turmoil of emotions she was feeling.

"Did you ever see—or hear of"—Rose's voice quavered—"it striking a person?"

"No, Rose. Never. Not even Jose has ever seen it strike a person." His hand continued to stroke Mollie's bare skin.

"I'm afraid I won't sleep a wink this night," Rose said anxiously.

"Ah, you will, Rose. It'll be over before daylight, I'll wager," Chance said comfortingly.

I'll be the one who won't sleep—with his hand on me! Mollie thought, jerking her leg again. His grip tightened even more, and it seemed to her that all her senses were concentrated there where his hand touched her skin. Her feet, which had been cold at first, were warming rapidly. Her whole body was growing limp, and the sensation in her thighs crept upward until she knew a melting heat between her legs.

Thus she lay awake through the long, stormy night, burning with desires that could not be realized in the crowded tent. Her body was warm and utterly boneless, while his hand caressed her bare leg, until finally, realizing she would not pull away again, he closed his fingers over her calf, gently and possessively. Lightning flashed again and again, as thunder roared and finally rumbled away in the distance. The rain that pelted the tent did not cease through the long night. But as dawn approached, the wind increased and the rain stopped at last.

Mollie was keenly aware of Chance slowly withdrawing his hand from under her blankets to gather up his bedroll and step out into the predawn darkness. Other people could be heard moving about beyond the tent. Almonte's riders were stirring. Soon they would all be getting breakfast ready.

Mollie and her companions at last prepared to rise. Climbing from their bedrolls, they exclaimed over the cold. Mollie herself was chilled as she rose and donned her stockings and boots and hastily pulled on the deerskin jacket. Kate and Rose pulled their heavy serapes around them.

They stepped out into the chill dawn and saw the sun about to rise in a sky swept clean of clouds. Mollie had faint blue shadows under her eyes. She rubbed them vigorously, wishing it was warm enough to bathe her face. The men were kindling fires, which smoked thickly at first but gradually glowed red and warm, and a hot breakfast was prepared for the hungry travelers.

Later, as they made their way due south on the San Luis Potosi road behind the army, the sun warmed and dried their damp clothing. The increasing warmth from the clean-swept sky made the march almost comfortable.

On February fifth they reached Agua Nueva, where General Zachary Taylor decided to encamp. His men hauled in supplies and began to throw up breastworks. Within two days, the camp took on an air of permanency. As always, the guerrillas camped off by themselves, as did the contingent of Texas Rangers. There were a few stunted trees in the area and much thick brush, most of it still green. Each evening, Father Baldemero conducted mass.

On the fifth evening at Agua Nueva, they were all seated around the Mendoza supper fire, and Chance was telling them about his day with the soldiers.

"There's much apprehension among the men because our camp here on the flatlands is so vulnerable," he said slowly. "Jose and I mingled with the officers of Taylor's staff and, though the general expects no attack, they want to fall back to a more defendable position."

Clan began filling his plate with beans, bread, and venison. "Ol' Rough an' Ready is a powerful stubborn man," he said. "He don't like retreat an' he won't budge."

"But both flanks of the army are exposed here," Chance went on, filling his own plate, "and they could surely be turned by an enemy with superior numbers."

"Even the colonel had an audience wi' th' general," Clan added, "tellin' him we're too exposed here, an' he's had no more success than th' general's own officers in gettin' Taylor ter fall back ter a place that'd offer more protection—just in case we see some action wi' Santy Anna's army."

"And there will be action. I'm certain Santa Anna will not turn south to face Scott." Chance sat down cross-legged on the tarpaulin that had been placed on the ground. His blue eyes were on Mollie's as he added quietly, "I know Santa Anna from the old days— eleven long years ago—and he's unscrupulous and corrupt, but he's also shrewd. He'll hit hard and fast and where he can best slaughter his enemies."

Just then Almonte strode toward them. His polished black eyes went to Rose, and the expression on his face was unreadable to Mollie. But Rose flushed a delicate pink and lowered her thick lashes. Her breast rose and fell rapidly, and Mollie knew something was happening. Mollie had a wild, erratic desire to thrust herself between Almonte and her cousin, but instead she looked down into her plate of food.

"Well, th' colonel's got scouts down around th' city o' San Luis Potosi," Tim said, "an' any day they could bring news of which he'll do—turn south or come north ter face us."

"An' my money's wi' Chance," Benjie said confidently. "Santy Anna will come north. After all, th' colonel knew ol' Santy Anna intercepted Scott's order strippin' Taylor o' his army long afore Taylor knew it. I'll take Chance's word over Taylor's."

"You are a wise young man." Almonte smiled, taking the plate Cayetana had just filled for him and seating himself beside Chance. Then he looked up, black eyes directed at Kate. "Senora Brannigan, after supper, Father Baldemero wishes to speak with you in his tent."

The words fell heavily in the group, and there was a long moment of silence before Cayetana and Maricela hurriedly turned the talk to what the women would do if fighting took place.

"The colonel and I have spoken," Chance said in a low voice, "and when the fighting begins, I want you, Mollie, with Kate and Rose and the rest of the women well back from it."

"I will see to that," the colonel said quietly. "In a fight such as this will be, there'll be no distinction made between men and women in the killing."

Kate sat silent and pale, her agitation communicating itself to Mollie. She picked at her plate, finally putting it down, half finished, her eyes going to Father Baldemero's tent.

Finally, Kate excused herself, and Mollie saw her slender figure striding toward the priest's tent.

Mollie fought down a feeling of dread. She would have offered to go with her aunt for this audience with the priest, but Almonte's words had been so curt and clear-cut, there was no mistaking that Father Baldemero wanted to see Kate alone.

The hour of cleaning up after the meal dragged by, and Kate did not come out of Father Baldemero's tent. It was nearly two hours before she emerged, and in the late dusk Mollie could see that her eyes were red and swollen, her face blotchy from tears. Her red hair had come loose and swung about her shoulders.

Mollie ran to her. "Aunt Kate—Oh, Aunt Kate darling! Whatever is the matter? You're crying! What has Father Baldemero said that upset you so terribly?"

Kate laid her head on Mollie's shouder.

"Oh, Mollie," she sobbed, "me daughter married that man—last night after we were all asleep! Th' father said he thought 'twould hurt me less, knowin' it was done." She lifted her head, her green eyes swimming in tears. "I told him I could've changed her mind if only I'd known ahead o' time, but he just shook his head. He said that's what Rose an' that ol' Jose said I'd do. Rose—me own Rose—is lost ter me!"

The sobs began again. Others in the camp watched her with pity.

"Hush, Aunt Kate," Mollie whispered. "Let's go to the tent where you can cry all you like."

Kate drew back. "I can't! Rose is in there gatherin'

up her things. She's goin' ter sleep—ter live in *his* tent now! Oh, Mollie, me darlin' is goin' to have his—that terrible man has made her pregnant!" This last was whispered, but Mollie had the feeling that the entire camp knew Rose's secret. "I knew somethin' would happen ter me Rose wi' him, th' minute he clapped eyes on her, that first day. I saw it in his face."

It was in Rose's face too, Mollie thought silently.

"Just the same, we must go to the tent and help her—"

"I don't know if I can speak ter her!" Kate's eyes flashed through her tears.

"Ah, but Aunt Kate, it will be your grandchild! You haven't stopped loving Rose, have you?"

"No. But I'll never accept or love that man ner his offspring!"

Mollie had her arm about her aunt's shoulders now, leading her to the tent. Inside, Rose stood up quickly, her great hazel eyes on her weeping mother. She hesitated a moment, then in a rush embraced Kate. They clung to each other desperately, both crying now. Mollie tied the tent flaps together and sat down on her bedroll, which Rose had spread beside her mother's.

Mother and daughter separated and Kate blew her nose on a kerchief she pulled from a pocket in her skirt. She flung off her serape and stood looking at her daughter.

"How could ye do such a thing, Rose?"

"Ma! Please don't quarrel with me about it when I'm so happy—"

"Why couldn't ye have waited—at least until we got back ter—ter home. An' ter think ye let him have his way wi' ye afore—afore—"

"Look, Ma." Rose fumbled at a gold chain around her neck and pulled it from inside her blouse. On it dangled a man's ring. Light from the lantern caught the big diamonds and the blood-red ruby, flashing fire from them. "See, Ma? Father Baldemero gave me the chain so I could wear the ring until I can have it made to fit. 'Twas Jose's and his father's and his father's father, back over a hundred years. It came from Spain!"

Kate was silent, her accusing gaze on Rose. Even her lips were bloodless now, as if all her color had gone up into her bright hair. She shook her head slowly and wordlessly, and her pale lips moved in what could only be soundless prayer.

"Oh, Ma—say it's all right. I'm so happy."

"How old is yer husband?"

"Thirty-seven. Seventeen years older than I," she said defiantly. "His father was twenty years older than his mother, and Jose said they were the happiest people he knew until Santa Anna took them prisoner— and took Jose's wife, Sarita, prisoner too—and carried them all off to Mexico City. And in the end *killed* them! Have you no pity?"

"An' yer carryin' his child, conceived out o' wedlock. Has Father Baldemero given ye absolution fer *that?*" Kate's eyes narrowed to green slits.

"Ma, we'll do penance for that—but Father Baldemero says we will be forgiven." She squared her shoulders resolutely and picked up her bundles. She started toward the tent opening and Mollie untied the flaps. Rose paused beside her cousin, eyes shining with unshed tears, and pulled the bright serape tightly about her slender shoulders.

"Be happy, Rose," Mollie whispered. "Aunt Kate will change her mind about your husband." But in her heart, Mollie had serious doubts.

Rose brushed Mollie's cheek with a kiss and smiled uncertainly before she stepped out into the darkness.

Chapter 19

Late in the afternoon of February nineteenth, one of Almonte's scouts rode into camp from the south. He was travel stained and unutterably weary, but his report was clear and concise. In minutes, his news had spread through the entire guerrilla camp.

Santa Anna was on the march. And he had not turned south to face General Winfield Scott's well-outfitted and well-trained army. Instead, as Chance Delanty had predicted, he was coming north with a vast army estimated at over twenty-five thousand men.

So Santa Anna had rolled out of San Luis Potosi on the second day of February, clad in the fine apparel of the Mexican military and seated in a chariot drawn by eight mules, followed by a bevy of wanton women and many fighting cocks. The erratic liberator left the city accompanied by the songs of its newly inspired people.

Ahead of his convoy stretched the sands of the Mexican desert, with the triple threat of starvation, illness, and desertion staring the rag-clad rank-and-file full in the face. But Santa Anna, chewing his opium, was supremely confident that he would meet the Americanos

and slaughter them. Now he and his army were less
than twenty-four hours away from Agua Nueva.

Almonte, Chance, and Clan showed the guerrilla
scout to General Taylor's headquarters, where they
were granted an interview with the sturdy old soldier.
The upshot was, the guerrillas learned later, that they
were immediately to fall back about eleven miles.

It was a hasty withdrawal, and many supplies were
left behind by Taylor's army—though not by the guerrillas. A few men remained in the night to burn those
supplies and equipment that could not be carried with
the hastily retreating troops, thus preventing them
from falling into Santa Anna's hands. The rest of the
army, the rangers, and the guerrillas retreated eleven
miles to a strong position called La Angostura, "The
Narrows," just south of the hacienda of Buena Vista.
Here the road ran through a mountain pass some three
miles wide, divided almost in half by a small but clear
river. The field was further narrowed by a network of
deep and impassable gullies, which rendered the western half of the pass quite unusable for artillery and
cavalry. Men on horseback could never negotiate these
raw and ragged slashes in the earth. And if one of the
big guns on wheels fell into the gullies, it would be
completely disabled.

East of the road, the ground rose gradually toward
the base of the mountains, forming a tableland inter-
sected at several points by ravines and gorges eroded
by the torrents of water that gushed down the moun-
tainsides during the rainy season. Some of the ravines
extended to the very foot of the mountains, others only
partway. At most points these ravines were quite precipitous and almost impassable, but near the foothills
their sides were sloping and they could be climbed
without great difficulty. At the base of the mountains
that formed the eastern boundary, there was a rough
passageway, generally parallel to the regular road, by
which troops could advance from south to north.

Mollie surveyed The Narrows with awe. The great
gashes in the earth appeared to have been clawed out
by some giant prehistoric beast that had scattered

boulders about like pebbles. Some of the gullies were vastly deep and wide enough at the bottom to conceal an army. The mountains rising so high, the raw slashes in the earth, the desolation of The Narrows—all made Mollie uneasy.

How could five thousand volunteers, barely trained, turn back over five times their number? What would happen to her, her pregnant cousin, and her aunt if the Mexicans captured them? Mollie knew what the Mexicans did with their prisoners—especially their women prisoners. The terrifying fate of Almonte's wife leapt into her mind. Chance's stories about Santa Anna's tortures and his treatment of the men—his burning of the stacked bodies like cordwood at the Alamo and the slaughter at Goliad—added to her fears.

She knew the American soldiers would fight to the death for their commander and their country. She had met enough of them to know their character and tenacity. But then, thinking of the man who was marching on them, she shivered. It would be a bloody battle against great odds.

That morning, before Taylor's troops had formed, Almonte ordered his guerrillas back to the entrance to The Narrows, toward Saltillo. He led them to one of the first broad, deep ravines on the north.

"We'll make camp down in there, where all our women will be out of the line of fire. The fighting will be just beyond this," he announced reassuringly in both English and Spanish. Slowly, the guerrilla band drew up to the edge of the gorge.

Mollie peered down into the purple-shadowed depths and saw the faint gleam of running water. So there was a burn down there! At least they would have fresh water.

A detail of men hastened with sabers and axes to chop out a rough pathway down into the gully. The men were feverish in their hurried efforts as others let the emptied wagons down by rope. One wagon fell, splintering to pieces as it struck the floor of the canyon. But the guerrillas were not dismayed by the loss of the wagon. Pedro Mendoza even laughed, albeit grimly, as he turned to Mollie astride her mare.

"Lucky for us zee wagons have been mos' emptied. Now we repack zee ones left more fuller, senorita."

Getting the horses down the steep path carved out by the men posed a greater problem. Mollie's mare was skittish at the nearly perpendicular angle, and Mollie led her down a step at a time, speaking soothingly to her.

Slowly the others came down, as well as the entire remuda. Only the mounts of the guerrillas who would fight at the side of Colonel Almonte stayed at the edge of the ravine. They formed a small remuda above the ravine, the guerrillas tying the horses to the scrubby brush that grew in patches across the tableland.

From the bottom of the gorge, Mollie gazed back up at its precipitous slopes where small, twisted bushes clung desperately to the soil. She looked at the great primeval boulders clawed from the mountains and flung along the canyon floor. A feeling of claustrophobia swept her.

Apparently Rose felt it too. "How can we get out of here fast, Mollie?" she asked. "If a storm with heavy rains comes, we're likely to be under water down here."

"We'll have to chance it, for there is no protected spot for us at La Angostura. There'll be fighting in The Narrows."

Late in the evening, O'Connor was the first man to come down again along the steep path from The Narrows above. He sought out the Mendoza campfire, his grin gleeful.

"Another o' Jose's scouts came in with word that Santa Anna's come on Agua Nueva an' seen th' burned supplies. Sure an' he thinks we're runnin' from him in disarray." He laughed aloud and slapped his thigh. "So he's drivin' his men—some of 'em have deserted an' some have dropped by th' wayside—ter catch us afore we can pull ourselves together. He's in fer a big surprise!"

"Then he'll be here tomorrow?" There was dread in Rose's question.

"Yes. In fact, he's camped just outside o' cannon shot, an' he's driven his men more'n fifty miles in twenty-four hours." He half turned, and his eyes sought Mollie's.

In spite of herself she was looking at him, as were most of the women in sight. Maricela's mouth was slightly open, and her dark, liquid eyes gazed dreamily at him.

"Mollie darlin', aren't ye goin' ter offer supper ter me—fer termorrow I'll be fightin', 'tis certain."

"I'd think you'd want to be with your men up there."

"Nay, Mollie, 'tis you"—he smiled fleetingly at the other women—"'tis you ladies I'd rather be with, me last night."

Me last night. Premonition wrenched Mollie, and she told herself she was a fool. He was playing on just that, her Irish superstition. Still, she said, "There's plenty. I'm sure you're welcome to stay."

"They had cold venison an' hot coffee up there, but some men'll be comin' down later, I'll wager."

Mollie noticed now that several dark shapes had drifted down into the canyon and found their way to the women's fires. Plenty of other men were thinking it might be their last night, she thought. And well it might.

Out of the darkness stepped Chance and Jose Almonte. Rose was on her feet instantly, and swiftly as a shadow she was in Almonte's arms.

"Have you eaten, my darling?" she asked huskily. He nodded as he tipped her head back for a deep, long kiss.

As the others watched, Pedro Mendoza joined the silent circle. He and Cayetana looked at each other across the fire, longing in their eyes.

"Seet down," Cayetana murmured to the men.

Mollie cut Kate's hot, fresh bread and Kate put steaming slices of it beside hot pinto beans on each plate. Rose stooped to serve stewed apples and slices of javelina, a piglike animal, that Pedro had killed the day before.

They talked as they ate. Kate mentioned the Delanty twins and how young they were.

"They're so keen to scrap, they won't come down here." Chance smiled. "They're eating cold venison and drinking hot coffee."

"An' they've their uncle ter look after 'em termorrow." Clan laughed, his black curly hair gleaming in the firelight. "Sure an' I'd like ter have someone like that behind me ter shore me up."

"You will." Chance slanted a smile at him. "All of us Irish stick together, Clan."

"That's good," Clan replied soberly. "Ye can throw that big bowie knife o' yours fifty yards an' nail a squirrel afore he twitches his tail."

"What is a bowie knife, Clan?" Rose asked. Her plate was scarcely touched and she sat with her hip and thigh against Almonte's, her arm touching his. Kate glanced at them once, her eyes a hard green.

"'Tis a great long sharp thing. The first one was made by a man named Bowie, th' rangers say. He came ter Texas from somewhere in Louisiana an' he carried his knife ter th' Alamo. Died there wi' it in his hand." Clan chewed his food reflectively. "'Tis monstrous sharp an' most o' th' rangers carry one. Chance, I'd like ye ter help me make one fer meself." He glanced at Mollie before adding, "If I make it through termorrow."

"I'll do that, Clan,"—Chance grinned—"and you'll more than likely make it through tomorrow." His warm voice suddenly put things in perspective for Mollie.

"You will *all* make it," she said with certainty.

Almonte's black gaze touched her, and under his neat mustache his white smile showed. "Senorita Mollie, if you say so, then it must be." He got to his feet. "Come, my Rosita." He pulled her up with him before turning to those around the fire. "We will meet before dawn."

For a moment silence held them as they watched Rose and Almonte make their way to their tent. Then

Cayetana began gathering up the plates. Kate, Mollie, and Maricela joined her silently.

As the women finished cleaning away the supper things, Kate said good night quickly and left. Mollie rose. "Cayetana, I'll help wash the dishes."

"No, Mollie—Maricela an' I weel do eet."

"Then I'll tell you all good night."

Clan was beside her swiftly. "I'll see ye ter th' tent, Mollie," he said softly and swung into step beside her, lighting a thin cheroot as they walked. Looking back, Mollie saw that Chance and Pedro still sat before the fire, smoking.

"Mollie," Clan spoke tenderly, "ye remind me o' th' city o' New Orleans. A city o' fair houses, wi' ironwork like lace about 'em. Dainty houses they were—tall, wi' three stories, some o' them, wi' balconies an' fern spillin' from them an' blood red flowers. All on a great river called th' Mississippi. An' ah! Th' wimmen o' New Orleans." As they stopped before the tent, he blew a kiss into the darkness and winked broadly at Mollie, who had been unable to keep from staring at him as she herself visualized that far place.

Her glance fell and Clan laughed aloud, throwing the cheroot to the ground. "But none o' that—an' none o' th' wimmen were as fair as you, Mollie darlin'." He caught her arms and swung her up and around, then let her feet touch the ground once more. "An' will ye gi' me another kiss, Mollie? One fer luck termorrow—it may be th' last I'll ever have o' ye."

"Clanahan O'Connor, you're shameless! Trading on tomorrow and my superstitious nature!" Mollie exclaimed. "I kissed you once before—and you *took* kisses before that. And that's enough?"

"'Twill never be enough, Mollie," he said sadly and turned from her. "Good-bye."

She stood at the tent flap, watching him stride away. What was there about Clan O'Connor that both touched and repelled her? She shook her head and took a deep breath of the clean, pure air. The cooking fires were dying to red embers beyond her.

Where had Chance gone? She knew everyone had

gone to bed, for there were only a few hours to rest and tomorrow would bring death for some, terrible injury for others. Her eyes sought the top of the gorge. By the light of the brilliant stars she dimly could see the path the men had hacked out for the horses. All the single men had stayed up there around two fires, and with them were Tim and Benjie Delanty. In her mind's eye she saw their handsome young faces, heard their laughter.

"Mollie," came Chance's dark, quiet voice at her shoulder, "thinking about it won't help. Whatever tomorrow brings, it brings. Even prayer won't alter what's to be. Only one thing's certain, Mollie. Time flies. The moment you allow to pass when you could be taking happiness is forever lost. All we have is now." He reached out and caught her shoulders, pulling her against him.

"Oh," she said poignantly, "you're so right." And in the cold night the warmth of him was comforting and filled her with longing.

"Let me kiss you, Mollie," he said huskily. She turned her face up to him. He let his hands fall only to reach up again as slowly, almost reverently, he took her face in them and brought his lips, smooth and cool, to hers. Instinct told her to draw away, but his arms pulled her ever closer. Exploding within her were the wild emotions she had known before as their lips clung, warming to quick heat. All we have is now, she thought.

What better way to spend this moment than in his arms? What better way to seize this brief moment of existence than to spend it in the arms of the only man who could satisfy the turbulent desire he provoked in her? She could refuse and remain an empty vessel, unfulfilled for the rest of her life, but her soul rebelled at the thought.

As he sensed her surrender, his hand slipped under her knees while the other went around her shoulders, and he swung her up in his arms. Her arms were about his neck, her head back, looking at his strong, masculine profile etched against the star-studded sky.

He carried her to his tent, which was empty now that the twins had elected to stay with the other men. It was warmer inside, but still cold, and he did not light the lantern. In the dark, they helped each other disrobe.

When they lay together, naked on his bedroll, she pressed herself against him. With the feel of his flesh against hers, the pulsing hardness against her, she did not care that she might be doing something wrong. She wrapped her arms about him, drew his head to hers, and kissed him with parted lips.

He took their pleasure leisurely, kissing her throat, her breasts with their upthrust and eager points. He kissed the bones of her hips. And when he kissed the tender skin of her inner thighs, she caught her breath and cried his name. Then swiftly he kissed her mouth once more, deeply, movingly.

When at last he joined her, she was twisting with urgent desire for him. Their final coming together sent a shower of wild tremors through her. The slippery fire between them rose hotter and higher until a thrilling delirium seized her. For a brief eternity their bodies mingled as one, and when at last the final explosion of pleasure shook them, they clung together like drowning swimmers.

They lay thus, their breath slowing, their bodies still entwined, for a long time. Finally Chance ran a rough hand over her naked body slowly and sensuously. She moved restlessly.

The narcotic of desire was leaving and her conscience was reasserting itself. Why was it always this way? she thought angrily. She could not resist the man when he made love to her. Yet she wanted nothing more than to leave him, she swore silently, even as he caressed her. But she did not draw away from his touch, for it sent shivers of pleasure over her, mocking the conscience that struggled to be heard.

She sat up suddenly. "I must go back. Aunt Kate will be worried," she said thickly. "You'll have to light a candle. I can't find my clothes in the dark." Her voice became clear and curt, and Chance seemed to sense the difference immediately.

"What's the matter? You enjoyed it, didn't you?"

"'Time flies,'" she quoted bitterly. "'All we have is now.' Well, 'now' is over, and as before, you'll ride off to fight and I'll stay and wonder until the month is out."

"That seems to be the way you want it," he said stiffly.

She was silent a long moment, waiting for something. When it did not come, she said icily, "There must be love between two people for happiness." She paused, then added bitterly, "And I don't love you, Chance Delanty."

"You make love to me as if you do," he said quietly.

"That's your opinion."

"And I know you don't love either of the O'Connors."

"How do you know that?" She wanted to hurt him now. He hadn't said he loved her!

"I know," he said flatly, pulling on his breeches. His broad chest, dark with curling hair, drew her eyes unwillingly. Oh, he was appealing, he stirred her blood like no other man in the world could. And he confused her. Clear-thinking, concise, self-sufficient Mollie was confused by an arrogant, careless—no, reckless—Irishman who'd made his way in the New World!

"If you know so much, you must know that I don't want this to happen again," she said. "And if you come sweet-talking me just once more, I'll give you the back of my hand!" Rage filled her as she said the words.

"And if you are pregnant?" he asked coolly.

"Same thing goes," she said shortly, tugging on her deerskin jacket. "I'll have the child and raise it. It'll be *mine*, not yours!"

"You're a fool, Mollie, throwing away happiness with both hands."

"Happiness! What happiness could there be between two people who don't love each other except like ...like animals in heat!"

"Is that the way you think of it?" His tone was remote and cold now.

"That's the way it *is*," she retorted and bolted from the tent. As she ran to her Aunt Kate's tent, she felt her heart would burst. The lantern still burned there, and Mollie wondered guiltily how long she had been gone.

"Mollie darlin'! Where have you been?" Kate's green eyes were wide and fearful.

"Just talking with Chance Delanty about the plans the men are making. We walked a long way," she lied.

"Ye've been gone over an hour! An' with Rose in that man's tent, I get nervous fer you at night, Mollie."

"Ah, you're a born worrier, Aunt Kate," Mollie said soothingly, removing her clothes once more and slipping the long, white flannel nightgown over her nude body.

Only Colonel Almonte came down into the canyon the next evening after the fighting. After a long conversation in Spanish at another campfire, he came to Mollie and her companions at the Mendoza fire. Cayetana fixed a plate of food for him while he talked about the day's events.

"There was little exchange of fire," he told them, his dark eyes on Rose. "General Taylor is worried about Saltillo and the small garrison there, so he has left to go back and encourage those troops and shore them up." He took the plate from Cayetana, adding, "He's worried about General Vicente Minon and the three thousand troops that are operating near Saltillo."

"How could he leave his command where there are over twenty-five thousand Mexican troops about to fall on us?" Mollie was aghast.

"He's of the opinion there'll be no fighting until tomorrow morning. He'll be back by then."

"What are the soldiers doing with no commander?" Mollie asked apprehensively. "What's to stop the Mexicans from overrunning them even if La Angostura is the best terrain for defense?"

"General Wool is in command. All troops here at The Narrows are remaining under arms, and we've all bivouacked on the ground we occupied today." He put down his untouched plate and took a deep gulp of hot coffee. "Tomorrow we will see real battle, and I fear it will be bloody." His voice became grim. "I mean to see Santa Anna defeated."

He got to his feet. "Forgive me, Cayetana, if I do not eat. Come, my Rosita—I have much to say to you and little time to say it."

Rose took his hand and they vanished into the darkness. An hour later, she rejoined them.

"What did he tell you, Rose?" Mollie asked anxiously. "Anything more about the fighting to come?"

Rose shook her head. Unshed tears were bright in her hazel eyes. "He told me he may not come back, and if he doesn't, to remember him and that he loves me and our child to come. That I am to go to his hacienda with Pedro and Cayetana, where as his widow I will be mistress of his house."

The following day dragged; fighting was light and sporadic. But as evening drew on, the sky became overcast with the blue-black clouds that Mollie had come to dread. As she feared, another wild storm broke over The Narrows, with lashing rain and all the thunder and lightning of the previous storm. The troops above were exposed to its full fury.

Down in the gorge, the women of the guerrilla band watched the little stream of water widen until it was almost up to the level of their tents. As they hurriedly stacked their supplies high in the wagons, Mollie silently thanked God that Almonte had distributed all the extra guns and ammunition they had brought among General Taylor's troops.

Rose approached Mollie and asked, "Do you think I might sleep here in this tent with you and Ma? It's so stormy."

"Of course!" Mollie said warmly and shot Kate a challenging look. Kate said nothing. Then the women went out into the storm and gathered up all the brush they could find, spreading it in the tent to keep their bedrolls off the ground, as Chance had shown them.

316 Ann Forman Barron

They slipped out of their dripping ponchos, pulled off their soaked hats, and sat down on the brush.

A little later, Mollie peered out of the tent at the driving rain and she saw to her horror that the stream had grown into a veritable river. Peering over her shoulder, Rose gave a low sound of dismay.

"Do you think it could fill up the gorge and drown us all?"

"No," Mollie lied sturdily. "It won't even reach the tents."

But it rained all through the night and remained bitterly cold. Despite their heavy woolen blankets and the brush on the ground in each tent, all the women's garments became damp and chill. Mollie lay wakeful, thinking of the men suffering in the driving wind and rain on the tableland above. A cold knot of fear formed in her breast. How could they win, when even the elements were against them? Toward dawn she finally slept briefly.

Mollie was awakened in the early morning by the thunder of cannon and the constant musket and rifle fire. She peered out of the tent to see a sunlit, blue sky. The river that had risen in the night had magically receded. The stream was broader than when they had first arrived, but it was contained once again between its low, narrow banks. The floor of the canyon showed where water had swept over most of it. Only the higher portions, where the men had pitched the tents, had escaped.

As the three women silently dressed, each preoccupied with her own thoughts, Mollie had a slowly mounting desire to climb the steep path to the scene of battle. There were men being wounded, men she could help. Sister Maria Theresa had said, "Medicine is holy work, Moyennan. Remember that. When you help the sick or wounded, you are serving God."

When Mollie mentioned her plans to Kate over breakfast, Cayetana and Maricela stopped to stare at her. Kate and Rose looked horrified.

"No, no, Mollie!" Kate cried. "Can't ye hear th'

fightin'? Them cannons an' guns? Ye'd be hit by one or other. Ye can't go up there!"

"But our men are being wounded, Aunt Kate. I could help. I could remove bullets, bind their wounds. I must go above and help."

Kate clutched her arm. "War is men's business. They've got men ter take care o' th' wounded." Her green eyes were wide and imploring. "No, no! Ye mustn't go above!"

So while the women waited impatiently, the battle raged above them, beyond their view. The day dragged on interminably, and Mollie grew more and more restless, thinking of the wounded and the care they needed.

Father Baldemero held a mass, then went above. He returned within a very short time, bringing word that many men were wounded. He had administered the last rites to three before Almonte had come upon him and asked him to return to the canyon to look after the women. They now clustered about him as he conducted prayers, but Mollie stood apart.

Her throat grew tight when she thought of Chance locked in the ebb and flow of fierce combat. She reminded herself of his deadly aim with the long rifle and the bowie knife, the strength in his hard-muscled hands. And could Chance protect Bet's boys? Then Clan O'Connor intruded on her thoughts, with his reckless blue eyes and ready smile that transformed his dark, intense face. What if they all lay upon the ground somewhere up there, their life's blood slowly seeping into the earth?

About noon, a figure appeared at the top of the tortuous path and scrambled down. Cayetana gave a little cry and ran forward, Maricela close behind her.

It was Pedro Mendoza. And he was whole—unwounded! His smile gleamed under his black mustache as he clasped his wife and daughter in a quick embrace. Mollie ran forward as all the women and Father Baldemero clustered around him.

"*Hola*, Senora Kate, Senora Rose. Zee fight, she eez

fierce, Senorita Mollie. I come only for to eat an' tell you zee Americans, zey do what you call 'old zere own.'"

Hold their own! But who had been wounded, who killed? All the women gathered around Cayetana's fire and watched every bite Pedro wolfed down. He kept up his rapid Spanish until Mollie wanted to shake him. So intense was her gaze that he finally became aware of it and looked up at her over Cayetana, who was kneeling to refill his tin plate.

"Ah, Senorita Mollie, do not be afraid. Zee general heemself eez wiz us now. He seet on heez horse call Ol' Whitey, een zee meedle of zee fighting." He laughed grimly and added, "I tell zee womens here zat a bullet ripped through heez sleeve an' one more through heez hat, but he seet there like a rock! All of us, we take heart from heem."

"Is—are—any of our men wounded?" Mollie asked.

"*Si*, senorita. Many." His face darkened. "Zere are so many men weeth Santa Anna. No matter how many we shoot, more come."

"Is any—anyone we know hurt?" Rose asked in a low voice.

"Our Colonel Almonte eez fine. He lead us from one place to zee other, where we needed most." Pedro's dark eyes held sympathy.

"Chance," Mollie blurted. Then she added hastily, "And the rangers?"

Pedro grinned wryly. "Ah, zee rangers. Zey do not fight like zee others. Zey are like *Capitan* Chance. Zey ride like zee wind, an' zey are all *bueno* wiz zee guns an' zee big knives. Zey are everywhere at once. I do not know eef zey have any wounded, but Capitan Chance eez not." He gave her a knowing look.

Cayetana began speaking to him in Spanish again, and in a short time he was taking long, angular strides up the perpendicular path, where his horse waited tethered to a scrub bush.

Everyone was quiet after he departed. Father Baldemero went to the small altar before his tent to pray once more. One by one, the women fell to their knees before the altar with its cross and a candle on either side. Rose and Kate were the last to join them as the shadows began to lengthen.

Mollie looked at the bowed heads, then silently made her way to her tent, picked up her medicine pouch, and proceeded to the wagon where the medicines and bandages were stored. She took as many of the folded strips of cloth as she could carry and made her way to the path. The women and the good father, heads bowed in prayer, did not see her as she quietly took the rough-hewn pathway. She leaned far forward to keep her balance. Once, near the top, her boot slipped and she almost fell, but she caught herself in time.

In another moment she had reached the tableland, with all the violence and firepower of the battle spread out before her, the men shouting, running, and kneeling, the fallen and the faltering. It was all less than a quarter of a mile from where she stood.

With sudden clarity she realized that it was Chance for whom her eyes searched in the sea of fighting men. It was Chance for whom her heart beat and for whom her prayers were most fervent. As lightning reveals a dark landscape, so did the realization that she loved Chance Delanty light up the corners of her mind.

But she loved a man who did not love her, an arrogant man who was as prideful in his wealth, power, and freedom as she herself was in her own search for independence.

Chapter 20

She could not find Chance's tall body in that confined scene as she stood holding her medical supplies, surveying the chaos.

Thundering toward her were two guns of the flying artillery, each pulled by four horses. She caught her breath as the guns rumbled past the blue-jacketed American soldiers who were firing into a dense number of white-clad Mexican soldiers. The latter's multiple firepower was taking a fearsome toll among the Americans, and her heart began to thunder as loudly as the cannons.

The flying artillery rolled to a halt. The Americans swarmed over the guns and unharnessed the horses, and in an incredibly short time they were firing grapeshot and canister into the approaching Mexican soldiers. The enemy fell like wheat cut down by a scythe. The artillery fire was withering, and after a very few minutes, those white-clad soldiers who were able to, turned and fled. The artillery was quickly reharnessed and in minutes was rumbling away to deliver fire on the far side of the battlefield.

Mollie became aware of groans and cries from the wounded men on the ground nearby. She saw able-bodied soldiers pick up their fallen comrades and carry them from the scene of combat. Some were attempting to pull the injured along upright. Some hoisted them onto their backs and staggered away toward the eastern entrenchments where they would be safe from the increasingly sporadic gunfire.

Approaching the exhausted and wounded soldiers, she called out: "I can help! I know healing! I have medicine with me, and bandages."

The rescuers stopped in their tracks at the sound of her light voice. They looked at her trim breeches hugging her slender, feminine legs; at the deerskin jacket open to reveal the swelling of her breasts beneath the shirt; at the brown felt hat jammed over her long, curling black hair. Some stared in disbelief and some with dull, uncaring eyes as she stooped over the first man who lay moaning at her feet. His shoulder was dark with blood and he appeared very weak.

A tired soldier above her said, "He's my buddy, ma'am. He's taken two balls from an escopeta musket, one in his shoulder an' one in his ribs."

Mollie gave the injured soldier a pinch of foxglove and then a sip from her bottle of bloodwort before she loosened his coat and shirt. Her precious morphine she would save for those in the agonies of death. She worked furiously, removing one bullet with her sharp probe and bandaging the ribs that the bullet had penetrated.

From then on, she worked without ceasing on one man after another as word spread that she knew medicine. She wept silently for those she could not save and fought hard to save those whose wounds were not fatal.

After about two hours, a young medical officer drew near. He carried an open satchel; earlier, from the corner of her eye, she had seen him ministering to the wounded. When the young officer was near enough to be heard, he spoke to Mollie: "At first I thought you were a boy in your breeches. But the men say that you have removed bullets and bound their wounds as well as any doctor. How is it that you, a woman, are in the field?"

"I had to come," Mollie said simply. "I learned medicine from a nun in Ireland, and I could not stand by and see men die from lack of help."

"Well, you're damned good," he said tersely, working beside her. "I'm Doctor George Rogers, a graduate of Kemper Medical College in Missouri, and I must confess you're as good as any doctor I've seen in handling the wounded. Where do you come from, besides Ireland?"

"I am with Jose Almonte's band of guerrillas, who fight on the side of the Americans. The other women are in that canyon over yonder." She gestured behind them. "I slipped away to help."

"Good thing you did. Between us we'll save many a man. But we must work farther back from the fighting. Come. Let the soldiers bring the wounded to us."

Mollie and the medical officer moved nearer the eastern entrenchments, and more and more men were brought to them. All across the wide plateau between the gullies and gorges, she saw small groups of American soldiers, Texas Rangers, and Almonte's guerrillas standing up to the overwhelming numbers of the enemy. If it were not for the flying artillery pouring grapeshot and canister into the masses of Mexican soldiers, there would have been sheer slaughter of the Americans and their allies.

But the artillery galloped from one battle area to the other with such speed and efficiency that they wrought havoc among the enemy. From her hurried and occasional glances away from her patients, she could see that the dead and wounded Mexicans now far outnumbered the American casualties.

All the long afternoon, the light artillery swept from one bitter contest to another as Mollie and Dr. Rogers worked side by side. Once, from a distance, Mollie glimpsed General Zachary Taylor on his white horse on a small hillside well within the battle lines.

Horse and man stood unmoving as soldiers dashed up on horseback to consult with the general.

Gradually, the firing grew even more sporadic and the galloping horses of the light artillery slowed their pace, lingering at the last outpost where firing continued. Now Mollie could see the dead and wounded enemy lying everywhere far beyond her. Two black-robed priests passed among them, giving the last rites.

As the light faded, Dr. Rogers said, "You'd better go back to your canyon, ma'am. There'll be no more fighting tonight. Get some rest for tomorrow."

Mollie was exhausted, and the walk back to the lip of the canyon seemed interminable. When at last she reached the steep path, she made her way down carefully, seeking a firm footing on the rough path. As she stepped below the rim, she looked back one last time to see campfires being lit on the plateau. There seemed to be thousands where the Mexicans were making camp. Tomorrow...ah, tomorrow the slaughter would begin again! Nowhere had she seen Chance Delanty. Her heart ached as she wondered if he lay among the dead or wounded.

When she reached her tent, she found her aunt and cousin sitting on their bodrolls in tears. "What's happened?" she asked apprehensively.

Kate leaped up and flung her arms around Mollie, crying even harder. "'Tis you, Mollie darlin'! Thank God, yer back safe an' sound. We've been cryin' off an' on all afternoon fer worry about ye!"

"At least it's brought you two together," Mollie said wearily, dropping her medicine pouch on her bedroll.

"Mollie," Rose half whispered, "did you see...do you know if Jose is all right?"

"I didn't seem him among the wounded, Rose, and I saw none of the men we know during the battle, what little chance I had to look."

" 'Tis *you* I was sick about," Kate said. "What madness took ye up there in th' thick o' it?"

"Aunt Kate, I would have been false to all Sister Maria's teachings—and all of Father O'Malley's as

well—had I stayed here. You wouldn't have me for-
sake all my beliefs just for my safety."

"No, no! But ye mustn't go back termorrow."

"There are thousands of Mexican campfires up on
the plateau, and I expect our own men will soon be
down, bringing any wounded with them. Of course I
will go back tomorrow." She sank down on the bedroll.
"Just let me have a quick nap. Wake me when they
come." She stretched out, and in less than a minute
she was asleep.

Though it seemed only moments before Kate was
shaking her awake, nevertheless she felt refreshed.
Her muscles no longer trembled with fatigue, and she
was hungry.

"Th' men are comin' down!" Kate said, "You said to
wake ye..."

Mollie sprang to her feet, seized her medicine
pouch, and ran out of the tent. The low fires cast a
flickering light on the tattered file of exhausted men
coming slowly and haltingly down the steep path.
Those not too badly wounded carried on their backs
and in their arms those who were unable to walk.

Mollie looked frantically among them for Chance
Delanty. He was nowhere in sight.

The women of the camp were gathering at the foot
of the path, curiously silent as they met the men coming laboriously down the path. Then Mollie recognized
Chance carrying a man on his shoulders. Behind him,
Jose Almonte carried another, and she realized with
sweeping feelings of relief that both men had come
through the fighting unscathed. Then Clan, too,
passed by, carrying a man in his arms.

With a sense of shock, Mollie saw in the flickering
light that Chance was bearing a white-faced Tim Delanty on his shoulders. And as Clan O'Connor passed,
she realized he was carrying Benjie. Mollie's heart
stopped with grief and fear. Both of Bet's sons
wounded!

Following them to the Mendoza fire, Mollie swallowed back tears as the twins gave her their irrepress-

ible Irish grins, before Tim's face contorted with fresh
pain. Mollie hastily spread bedrolls with the help of
Kate and Rose.

"We had to fast-talk a 'merican colonel ter let Clan
an' Chance bring us ter you, Mollie," Tim said faintly
as Clan put him on one of the bedrolls before the fire.
"An' then he wouldn't of let us, 'cept'n a young doctor
George Rogers, said he'd worked all day wi' ye and ye
were as good as him."

"I took a ball just above me knee," Benjie said, grimacing. "Can ye dig it out, Mollie, even if I yell?"

"You won't yell, Benjie. I've some medicine that's
going to make you and Tim feel much better right
away." Mollie's smile was strained, and her chest was
tight with tears. She had seen that Tim the fair, Tim
the lighthearted, had taken his wound in the abdomen.
His hands were clutched tightly over his stomach,
dark blood seeping through his fingers, his face white
in the firelight.

She bent down, her face close to his, and said softly,
"Where is it, Tim?"

His smile was fainter. "Right through me middle,
Mollie, an' there's one in me chest." He coughed suddenly, and a bloody froth moistened his lips. Mollie's
heart sank.

"Did the bullets go clean through, Tim? Do you
know?"

He shook his head. "No. They're both in me. I'm
afeared I'm a lost cause fer ye, Mollie darlin'.'"

"Don't you say that," she whispered fiercely. "I'll get
them out, and you'll be a new man in a few days."

The faint smile showed again and the Irish eyes
twinkled. "Ah, Mollie ye always were a fighter—even
when we were little. Ye don't lose very easy, colleen."

"And I'm not going to lose this time." The crisis
brought new strength flowing into her. She would have
to work all through the night, not only with the Delanty twins but also with the other guerrillas who had
come to look upon her way with medicines as a minor
miracle.

Taking some of her precious morphine crystals, she

put them in water and gave both men a potent drink. In minutes their faces relaxed. They looked at her gratefully.

Chance had returned and squatted by the fire, his eyes on his nephews. He said nothing, but Mollie could feel his presence, solid, masculine, and reassuring.

"I'm going to work on you first, Tim," Mollie said, stooping over him, "because you're hit hardest." She probed for the bullet in his chest. "That doesn't hurt too much, does it, Tim?" she asked.

He shook his head. "I feel like I'm floatin', Mollie. Whatever ye gi' me took away nigh all o' th' pain."

"That's good," she replied grimly as she managed to remove the bullet from his chest, sprinkled medicine on the wound, and bandaged it tightly. But when she looked at his abdomen, her heart sank even lower. Across the fire, her anguished eyes met Chance Delanty's. Slowly, delicately, she probed for the bullet and pulled it out, but it had severed an artery near the liver. She knew Tim could not survive. Tears filled her eyes, and she blinked furiously as she wound bandages about his waist. Even as she wound them, the red life's blood of him stained their thick layers.

He smiled at her and said sleepily, "Mollie, I feel good. Dyin' won't be so bad if I don't have to hurt like I did at first."

"Hush that talk of dying! You're going to be all right," she lied. Her heart ached unbearably. "Now, I must get that ball out of Benjie's knee. We can't have him limping home. Your ma'll say I'm a poor doctor after all if I don't have you both on your feet when we go home." At her words, "When we go home," Chance gave her a piercing look.

Other women who had done all they could for their men were approaching her now, and she told them she would work all night after she finished with Benjie.

She found the bullet just above his knee. It had torn tendons and ligaments that would make him limp slightly for the rest of his life. But she tightly bandaged the knee halfway up his thigh and the bleeding was already lessening. Benjie was going to be all right.

Hastily, she gave each of them a few more crystals of morphine. At least Tim would die in peace and comfort. It was grim satisfaction. Then she went with the other women to work on their wounded men.

Chance sat by the fire beside his nephews all the long night.

As dawn crept over the canyon, Chance awoke her and said, "Mollie, Tim wants to talk to you. Father Baldemero has already blessed him and given him the last rites. I think you'd better come."

In moments, Mollie was kneeling beside Tim. She saw at once that his breath was short and shallow, but his blue eyes were unclouded as he looked up into her face. He smiled faintly and reached for her hand.

"Ah, Mollie darlin', ye know I've loved ye fer years. Now I must tell ye good-bye."

"No, no, Tim! You must hold on—you can't give up now!" But she saw the bandage over his abdomen was red and wet.

"Mollie, will ye hold me fer a minute...only a minute?"

She sank to the ground and lifted his head into her lap, putting her arms around him and laying her cheek against his. "You know I love you too, Tim. You *know* it."

"Like a brother, an' I'm grateful fer that." His voice grew breathy and fainter. "Mollie, tell Ma an' Pa I love 'em. They were always so good ter me. Tell 'em they an' Benjie are goin' ter have a fine house and land on th' Nueces. Tell 'em"—he drew a quick, hard breath— "tell 'em nothin' can beat the Delantys."

Mollie could not see his face clearly through her tears. She blinked furiously and cried, "Tim, you must hold on!"

The light movement of his chest finally stopped. His eyes were open but unseeing. Her childhood friend had slipped away even as Mollie clung to him.

Chance had squatted down, and as Mollie gently laid Tim's head back on the bedroll, they rose together. She looked into his impassive face, into eyes that were filled with unspeakable grief, and she went into his arms. They stood clinging to each other, taking comfort from the warmth of their bodies together. His arms tightened around her.

"You did all you could, Mollie. Bet'll be grateful for that," he said huskily into her tumbled hair. "And thanks to your medicines, he died without pain."

Mollie's shoulders shook uncontrollably as she fought her grief. "I wasn't good enough," she whispered. "I just wasn't good enough to save him."

"No one could have saved him. I knew it the minute he took the bullet in his stomach. You're not to blame yourself." Chance's voice was kind and filled with an emotion that Mollie did not recognize.

She looked up at him through tear-blurred eyes and saw the resemblance to Tim and Benjie plainly written there. The Irish go on, she told herself silently. Nothing will beat us. Not privation, nor poverty, nor famine...not even death. They would pick up and go on, rising above it all. Tim had known it and even in death he was unquenched. He had seen their fine home on the Nueces even as life slipped away.

"I'll bury him here in the canyon," Chance said, his voice thick. "There'll be other graves to keep him company. Six of Jose's brave men will have to be buried today." He paused, then added, "I've put Benjie in your tent. Kate's watching over him. He needn't know about his brother yet."

She turned from him, reluctant to leave his arms, and murmured, "I'll check on him."

"You'd better get some sleep," he said roughly, "and something to eat. You're white as a ghost."

Silently she went into the tent, where Kate looked up at her helplessly. "He's got a fever," she said, as Benjie groaned and tossed on the bedroll.

"I'll watch him while you go eat breakfast, Aunt Kate," Mollie said.

She had no sooner stretched out on the bedroll beside Benjie than she was asleep. She wakened when Kate reentered the dark tent with a plate of eggs and bread. She held a cup of coffee in her other hand.

"Ye must eat, Mollie. Ye'll need strength fer th' day. 'Tis almost sunup. They've buried Tim an' six o' th' men, an' Father Baldemero has said a mass fer 'em."

Mollie sat and drank hastily and then went through her medicine bag. She would need all her medicines today.

A small ray of sunlight slipped over the canyon wall and touched the tent flaps. That would be the signal for the fighting to begin, she thought, and strained to hear. The silence beyond the camp seemed eerie. No sound of cannon or gunfire came from the plateau above.

"Put cool, wet cloths on Benjie's forehead for the fever," she said hurriedly, "and I'll come down to see him about noon." She pushed out of the tent, her pouch slung over her arm, and ran to follow the men climbing the path to the top of the ravine.

There at the top, they all stopped in astonishment. A stunned silence fell over the company, matching the silent emptiness that stretched before them. There were no living Mexican soldiers to be seen. The thousands of campfires from last night had died out, and there was no one but the dead Mexicans to be seen on any part of the plateau.

"By God," Chance said softly, "they left their campfires burning last night to fool us. They've retreated—south."

Almonte began cursing softly in Spanish. "He can't escape so easily. We'll follow. We'll join General Scott."

Mollie turned and started back down the path.

It was late evening when Chance put his head into Mollie's tent. She looked up at him from where she sat bathing Benjie's head. His fever was raging, and he was delirious. The need to tell him of his brother's death was put off indefinitely.

"Mollie, I must talk with you. Rose is here and she says she'll bathe Benjie's head."

Rose had been weeping. Mollie reached over and caught her hand as they passed.

"What is it, Rose?"

But the girl only shook her head and reached over to brush a light kiss against Mollie's cheek. Outside, the fragrance of roasting meats was carried on the breeze, mingling with that of boiling coffee, and Mollie realized how hungry she was. Chance took her arm.

"Would you like to eat before we talk?" he asked.

"Yes." She looked up at him in the dusk and smiled. "Can't we eat and talk too?"

"We can talk. But what I have to tell you is better said in private." His slow smile was visible in the gloom, and Mollie's tired heart stepped up a beat in apprehension. She ate very little, anticipating the private talk with Chance, despite his urging that she have some of Kate's apple pie.

"I've noticed you're having to draw that belt tighter these days, Mollie. I have two more pair of breeches and two new shirts to give you before—" He broke off abruptly.

Before what? Mollie's hands began to perspire lightly. "We can go now, wherever you think it will be private enough."

"My tent's private enough. The extras I want you to have are in there anyway."

His tent! Mollie remembered vividly what had happened the last time she had been in his tent when the twins were elsewhere.

They walked toward the tent, passing the other campfires. There were two new widows among their numbers, and all were quietly grieving their losses.

When they entered Chance's tent, he struck fire to the lantern placed in a small niche dug in the ground. He seated himself on one of the bedrolls and caught Mollie's hand, pulling her down beside him.

"Well?" Her breath grew short, and she moved reluctantly to put a little distance between them. Her love for him rose up, tightening her throat.

"You, Kate, Rose, and Benjie will be heading back to my place on the Nueces tomorrow morning," he said abruptly.

"Alone?"

"Cordilla, Jose's best scout, will guide you, and Clan

has agreed to ride escort. He now says he wants to help his brother more than he wants to settle in Mexico. I think you have something to do with it too. He wants to marry you." He laughed shortly, adding, "Now that's a lost cause, isn't it?"

"I'll never marry Clan O'Connor."

"Nor any man fool enough to love you," he said roughly. "Independence is too sweet a goal."

"Yes, it is." She felt cornered. Why couldn't he have loved her? She would never let him know he held her heart. He would break it without a second thought, if she let him!

"No matter. At dawn the men will lift the wagons up to the plateau and make ready to roll. You'll go northeast, and I'll head south with Jose. And Jose is worried about Rose. She's almost four months along, and he wants her to have their baby in safety."

"Even if it's born with its father dead? This idea of his to meet Santa Anna face to face could end in his death!"

"It's not just that. Jose Almonte was influential in government circles before Santa Anna took over. The tyrant must be defeated for Jose to regain his home and his position in Mexico."

"The baby will come in July."

"Yes. Just in time perhaps for you to perform one more service for me." He laughed cynically. "On July tenth you can tell Stretch Burleson to see you safely to Corpus Christi. Maybe Kate'll go with you, since she's determined to turn her back on her daughter's marriage."

"You'll likely be back by July."

"I probably won't. I'll be seeing this through to the end with Jose." He turned and in the dim lantern light reached for a dark bundle. "Here's the extra breeches and shirts. There's an oiled leather poncho in here too. And a pair of boots, the same size I bought you the first time."

"Thank you." Her voice was muffled because her throat was achingly tight.

"And since you admired it so, there'll be a hand-

tooled Mexican leather saddle like Rose's for you in the
wagon. I imagine Colleen will appreciate it too. It's
lined with suede."

"That's too much. I'll owe—"

"It's for saving Benjie's life and making Tim's exit
from it easier. Don't argue about it, Mollie," he said
wearily. "Jose and I will see that you have plenty of
supplies to last the two months it'll take you to get to
the ranch with a wagon, a sick man, and a pregnant
woman. Cordilla and Clan are excellent marksmen.
They'll add game to your menu." He paused, then
added slowly, "And I want you to carry a message to
Bet and Ben. Tell them the land is theirs, the same
way I got mine, in payment for the services of their
sons in time of war. And if I don't come back, the whole
ranch is theirs."

"Don't *say* that!" Mollie exclaimed, crossing herself
swiftly.

His lips twisted in a sardonic smile. "Why, Mollie, I
should think the prospect would please you. You've
said you hated me often enough."

"I want to hate you *alive!*" She felt perverse and
angry. And worst of all, she wanted to cry.

"Now there's a paradox!" His eyes gleamed and
curbed heat was behind them. Mollie knew what the
look meant.

"I want you alive," she said recklessly. "Is that so
strange, when saving lives is my business?" God, don't
let it show in her eyes, not to this man so ready to take
her without returning her love!

"Ah, yes, your *business*. That comes first, always."

"Always."

He shook his head. "O'Connor hasn't a chance."

Their eyes met in the dim light. Mollie's deerskin
jacket was unbuttoned, and her tight boy's shirt was
open at the neck. Lantern light threw a little shadow
into the hollow at the base of her throat, showing her
pulse beating there, swift and hard. Her breasts
strained against the denim shirt, and her nipples cast a
faint shadow where they thrust upward. Chance could
have spanned her narrow waist with his two hands, so

slender had she become from hard travel and work, but her thighs were still rounded and her long legs, outlined by the tight breeches, were still beautiful.

He lifted his hand and put a long finger to the hollow in her throat where he felt the pulse beat faster. She said nothing, but stood and gazed at him.

"Mollie," he said huskily, letting his hand slip down into her shirt to cup one of the inviting breasts. "Either way, you'll never see me again. When I come back, you'll be gone. And if I don't come back, you'll be gone anyway." He leaned forward, his lips brushing hers. "Tell me good-bye as if you loved me. Can't you pretend?"

His other hand came out, and circled her shoulders with his arm, pulling her to him. Pretend? She flowed against him without restraint, fighting back tears. All that she had endured during the last twenty-four hours filled her with an aching need for comforting, and there was such comfort in his touch, in his big, hard body. Comfort and blissful fulfillment, a sweet torment that satisfied every fiber of her body. Loving him as she did, she could not tell him of it—even though she knew he was trading on her love.

In the dim lamplight she could see the hard planes of his face, the endearing curve of his manly mouth. She could not stop herself. She leaned into him, putting her own mouth against his, warmly and fully.

He caught his breath, and suddenly she was beneath him. He unbuttoned her blouse swiftly, spreading it open so that he could kiss her breasts, take her rosy nipples into his avid mouth. Mollie felt her need for him rising like a furious tide that swept away every rule, every teaching, every promise of regret, like straws in the wind.

She clung to him as the tide of desire swept over them both. They did not even stop to remove their clothing, for the sweet fury would bear no waiting.

Tell me good-bye as if you loved me. Can't you pretend?

Her kisses grew more fervent, her hands stroking

the curling black hair of his chest, bared by the open shirt, stroking his back, holding him ever nearer.

As his hips moved and they were joined, shudders of delight coursed through her. Wave after wave of exquisite pleasure swept her, and he murmured against her mouth, "Ah, Mollie! Mollie, you're too sweet to lose— yet I must lose you."

Yet I must lose you!

At his words, a frenzy of desire seized her, and she flung herself against him with wild abandon, increasing the finely tuned delight, the stunning sweetness of their union.

When at last the final, glorious explosion shook them, it lingered as if reluctant to leave their bodies, and Mollie lay beneath him, drowned in the radiance of the afterglow.

They lay together, their bodies still in communion. For that little while, she forgot the future and was blindly happy in the moment. Chance kept his arms about her, and she felt safe and filled with the comfort she had sought. Neither of them spoke for a long time.

When at last she moved from the circle of his arms, she sighed. "It must be very late. Rose will wonder what's keeping me."

He pulled her back. "Stay a little longer."

"You know I can't."

"Ah, Mollie." He pulled her down to kiss her lips once more, softly, lingeringly. "If I live to be a hundred, I'll never forget this good-bye. You pretend better than most women who mean it."

"Most women?" She was startled. She had never thought of Chance with other women. It was a bitter and hurtful thought now. In her imagination she saw him in the arms of dozens of girls, and anger burned through the hurt and her unreturned love for him.

"It was good-bye," she said curtly. "And I did it only because I owe you more than I can pay by July tenth."

"Why, Mollie! That's prostitution!" He laughed as he buttoned his shirt.

"How dare you! It was nothing of the kind. You seemed to have an—a—an urgent need for a loving good-bye." She was deeply angry now. "It meant no more . . . not as much as my kisses from the twins!"

"Ah. Still, I'll cherish it as long as I live. I don't know when I've known anything so satisfying. Not since the last time we made love."

Mollie finished buttoning her breeches and tucked her shirt inside. She sat on the bedroll to smooth her tangled hair.

"Here." He handed her a comb. "Sorry I haven't a ribbon so you can go out looking every inch the lady."

"I *am* a lady. You're the only man I ever—and I'll never do such again!"

"Ah, Mollie, no rash promises. Suppose I do come back after all? Would you give me such a welcome?"

"I would not! You and your other women! I'll not give you another chance to sweet-talk me. Even if you do get back before I leave!"

"Try to remember me, Mollie . . . kindly," he said, his eyes twinkling.

As if she could ever forget him! This man had put a mark on her that would never be erased. She got up to return to her tent.

"Let me carry that to your tent," he said, catching up the heavy bundle. "There's a mirror in it too."

"You're too generous!" she said sarcastically.

"No," he said judiciously, "you've paid for it—and more."

"With work!" she burst out. "And you know it, Chance Delanty."

"Oh, I do know it," he said blandly as they walked out into the dark. The campfires had burned down and the sky above the canyon was thick with stars. In the starlight she could see his face, lean and hard, as he walked beside her.

As they came to her tent, she halted before the flaps and took the heavy bundle from his hand. "Thank you for everything."

"For everything?"

"Everything in the bundle," she said, feeling her face heat up.

"You're welcome. And we'll all be too busy in the

morning for any good-byes, so I'll say *vaya con Dios,* Mollie." He turned and walked away.

She stood a moment looking after him. He had said she wouldn't see him again. If he came back, she would probably be gone—and if he didn't come back, she would still leave as soon as Rose had her baby. As she entered the tent, Rose looked up from the flushed delirious Benjie.

"You've been gone so long!"

"Chance had to explain tomorrow's plans—and he gave me some new breeches and other things. I suppose you know about tomorrow?"

"Yes," Rose said, her tears starting once more. "Jose told me. Mollie, I must go to him. It is our last night together."

"Go ahead, Rose. I'll take over."

As Rose was leaving, Kate joined Mollie in the tent. They did not speak, but Kate's hard feelings toward Jose and Rose were almost tangible.

Rose's words, *It is our last night together,* lingered. And Mollie had a sudden, terrible feeling that perhaps it had been her and Chance's last night together too. She had accepted the fact that her love for him was deep and hurtful, but she pushed it fiercely to the back of her mind. There would be time enough later to think of it, to try to make sense of it, to pick up the pieces of what had suddenly become an empty life and go on.

Chapter 21

The sun was bright on the eastern horizon as the last wagon was pulled out of the ravine. It had been difficult getting Benjie up to the plateau on an improvised stretcher. But now he lay in the wagon Almonte had given them, still tossing with fever.

General Taylor's troops had buried the Mexican casualties the day before and were themselves preparing to pull out. Earlier, Almonte and Chance had gone to Taylor's headquarters to confer with him about future movements.

Now the main body of the guerrillas and the small group returning to Texas had separated. Last farewells had been said between the Mendozas, the Garcias, and a dozen others and their Irish friends.

As the other wagons rumbled away, Mollie, riding beside her wagon, turned in her new saddle to look back. Her eyes searched for the tall, broad-shouldered figure she knew so well, and picked him out unerringly at the side of Almonte, leading the caravan southward. She gazed steadily, willing him to look her way.

When he did not, something sealed itself off within Mollie. She lifted her chin and faced northward and did not look back again.

They had been traveling for two days before Benjie's fever broke. Clan and Mollie had rigged a makeshift tent over him in the wagon to shield him from the sun during the day and the dampness at night. It was early evening and they were camped outside Saltillo when he called for Mollie. She was helping Clan start the supper fire, but she went to Benjie at once. The others hurried after her.

Benjie was sweating profusely and had thrown back his blankets. Mollie pulled them up over him again.

"Mollie! I've got ter see Tim. I know he was bad wounded, Mollie, but I got ter see him!"

When she made no reply, he grew impatient. "I know I can't walk an' I can tell it's gettin' on ter evenin', but Chance 'er you there, Clan, can carry me ter Tim—right now! My God, how long have I been out o' me head?"

"Three days," Mollie said quietly, "and we've left The Narrows. We're on our way home to Chance's ranch. Aunt Kate, Rose, Clan, you, and me. Jose Almonte's best tracker and scout is guiding us."

Benjie gave a vast sigh. "I guess it's best we go home ter get patched up." He rose again on his elbow, his eyes flashing. "But Tim an' me wanted ter be with them when they joined wi' Gen'l Scott ter see this thing ter a finish."

Mollie gathered her courage. "Benjie, Tim was shot once in his stomach and once in his chest. It cut an artery and it...it was more than he could survive. We lost him the night you were brought down from the battle at Buena Vista." Her eyes held his, and she felt tears burn in hers.

He stared at her in disbelief. "Aww! Mollie, that's not a good joke. Where is he?"

"I wouldn't make a joke of something like that, Benjie. I've cried my heart out over Tim. I loved him like a brother and I did everything in my power to save him."

"But you didn't save him!" Benjie's voice was suddenly shrill with anguish. "You didn't save him! Mollie, Mollie, why didn't you? How could ye let him—" He choked over the word. "How could ye let him *die?*"

"I fought hard to save him. I removed the bullets and bound his wounds, but the bleeding wouldn't stop." Her voice grew huskier. "Benjie, dear, I gave him morphine. I swear by my faith in God that he died easy. He didn't suffer." She ran her hands across her eyes, trying to dry her own tears.

Benjie turned his face away from her and said nothing. His face was white and stricken, and his dark eyes were dry with a grief too deep, too overwhelming for tears. The others turned and melted away. There was nothing they could say to comfort either Mollie or her patient.

Mollie stood looking at him silently for a long time. Then she said slowly, "I must go help with the supper. I'll bring you some bean broth later. You must eat something now to gain strength. You've had nothing but water for three days."

Still he said nothing, his white face averted. He did not look at her as she put the folded tarpaulin in the seat so that he could look up at the sky.

For the next two days, Benjie did not speak. He drank the broth spoon-fed him and endured Mollie's ministrations, but he remained silent.

Cordilla and Clan kept the larder well stocked with game, and the chickens that Almonte's people had given them supplied eggs. Kate had appointed herself chief cook, but all of them helped with the mealtime chores. Mollie slept in the wagon beside the wounded Benjie to tend him in the night.

As they traveled during the day, the wagon jolted over the rough terrain, and Mollie knew Benjie would bite his lip to keep from crying out. She worried about his pallor, fearing he might grieve himself to the point of following his lost brother.

Rose was another source of worry to her. Kate spoke to her daughter, but distantly, with none of the motherly love that Mollie knew was bottled up inside her. And Rose wept when she thought no one could see her. Though she and her mother shared a tent, the closeness the two women had was gone. Only Mollie sympathized with Rose and advised her on her condition. The girl was so slender, her pregnancy scarcely showed even into March, her fifth month. Mollie urged her to eat more dried fruits, raisins, peaches, and apples. Each night she looked for edible greens to cook but found none.

One balmy March morning, as Mollie readied Benjie for the day's travel, he spoke to her at last.

"Benjie," she had said to him, "I'm going to change the dressing on your leg and knee again. And I want you to take a little laudanum now that you've finished breakfast—I'm so glad you're eating better! With this" —she held the spoonful to his mouth—"perhaps you can sleep a little while we travel."

He looked up at her and said in low, hoarse tones, "Mollie, yer a very angel. I—I'm sorry I said ye didn't save Tim. I know ye tried." Tears welled up in his eyes at last. "An' I'll tell Ma too."

"We'll both tell her about Tim, Benjie. You won't have to do it alone," Mollie said gently, thanking God that he had accepted his loss at last. She tenderly removed the bandage from the ragged wound above his knee. She cleansed it carefully with soap and water, smeared an emollient and medicine on it, and carefully put a new bandage on the ugly wound. She feared Benjie would walk with a limp the rest of his life, but she comforted herself with the thought that many men who limped were extremely active. And there was no reason why this leg should not be as strong as it had ever been, despite a limp.

Crssing the Rio Grande the last of March was something Mollie had dreaded for weeks. It proved to be relatively easy, however, for Cordilla took them to a point further south than the one at which they had crossed the first time. The water was still an angry red, but the banks sloped gently, and the water was so shallow the wagon could be pulled across it.

Mollie expressed her astonishment to Cordilla, and he smiled brilliantly. "Eez easy at this place and weeth no rains. But now we mus' travel farther north to reach *Capitan* Delanty's ranchero."

Clan was unfailingly courteous and helpful to the three women. He took his turn at cheering up Benjie and distracting him from the loss of his twin brother. Mollie was grateful that Clan made no overtures to her. It was as if he sensed the withdrawal she had experienced when Chance had failed to look back at her as they left The Narrows. Nevertheless, she was surprised to feel his gaze on her many times, and there was a waiting look in his eyes—and something more —that disturbed her. Thus when they came upon the Nueces, she drew a long breath of relief.

"Cordilla says we're about halfway between Corpus Christi an' Chance's ranch," Clan told her as he handed Kate two cleaned and plucked pheasants.

"And that means we're close to Sean's place too," Mollie said, her heart lighter than it had been in months. "I'm sure his house must be nearly complete by now, but perhaps you can help him with the last of the construction. I wonder how Dierdre is. She's such a bright and loving little girl."

Clan laughed lightly. "Sean ought ter adopt her. She needs a father, I'm sure."

"Or marry Meg Moriarty. I know she loves him."

"Ah, Mollie, oftentimes we're most certain about things that aren't true. If he hasn't married her yet, he likely never will."

As they made their way slowly along the Nueces trail, April came with sudden sweet rains, and the prairies beyond the river burst into furious color. A thousand varieties of flowers sprang up everywhere, in blues, crimsons, corals, purples, and pale lavenders. There was a blood red poppy that Mollie picked to show Benjie, who had pulled himself to a sitting posi-

tion so he could look at the beauty flaunting itself for
them.

But something had gone out of Benjie with the
death of his twin. Even as the healing warmth filled
the air and trees put on their green leaves, Mollie was
unhappily aware of the change in his personality. Gone
was his old mischievous, joking manner, the twinkle in
his dark eyes, the quick response and ready wit. His
transformation was driven home with heartbreaking
clarity in one sentence he spoke to Mollie when they
were less than a week from home.

"I'll never be whole again, Mollie. Half o' me is gone
forever."

Despite her protestations that Tim himself would
not have it so, Benjie rode in stoic silence, lying on the
bedrolls in the rough wagon most of the time. He sat
up more often now, however, and his knee and leg hurt
him less. Mollie and Rose had taken turns shaving
him on the long journey, but the morning came when
he reared up and spoke sharply.

"I can bathe an' shave meself now, Mollie O'Meara.
I'm much stronger, an' I don't want ye tamperin' wi'
me." He scowled and added, "I plan ter ride me horse
the day we reach home. Me knee's fine now, an' I don't
want Ma an' Pa thinkin' I'm hurt."

Mollie drew a long breath, and her smile was radi-
ant. "Now you sound like the old Benjie!"

But Rose and Kate still worried her. They had little
to say to each other when they sat around the fire during meals, and Mollie found it increasingly hard to get
either of them to talk to the other. Kate put an end to
her efforts the day before they reached the Delanty
ranch.

"Mollie," she said finally, "'tis no use yer tryin' ter
make me accept me daughter an' her high-nosed husband. No, nor their child!"

"And my mother has made it plain her love was
easily lost," Rose said with sudden fire. "I'll not be giving love like that to my little one, you may be sure. I

will love my baby as long as I live. Nothing my baby
does will change that."

Kate looked down at her plate and said nothing.

At breakfast the following morning, Benjie insisted
on joining them, and with Clan's help, he left the
wagon for the first time. He tried hard not to cry out,
but he winced as he laboriously made his way to the
fire. He did not eat as much as he usually did.

Over their last cup of coffee, Cordilla beamed at
them. "Doña Almonte"—he bowed to Rose with the exquisite courtesy he had accorded her throughout the
trip—"I have zee honor to tell you an' your peoples zat
we well be at zee Delanty ranch zis afternoon."

They all spoke at once, but Benjie's voice rose above
the rest. "I'll mount me horse ol' Tobey now. I can't
walk yet, but I bet I can ride!"

Mollie caught his arm. "Wait until we're within
sight of the house, Benjie," she said swiftly. "Your leg
will have to hang down when you mount Tobey. You
don't want to tear the wound loose again and do more
damage to it."

His lips twisted. "*More* damage. How could that
be?"

"You could have lost that leg!" Mollie retorted.

"I know," he said huskily. "'Tis thanks ter you I
didn't."

"That isn't what I meant!" she said, angered that he
thought she wanted credit. "I mean you could reopen
the wound. It was deep, Benjie, very deep."

He was silent a long moment, and Mollie realized
she had won, even though he said implacably, "I'll
wait, but Clan an' Cordilla must put me on Tobey afore
we get there."

"All right," she replied and turned away.

It was late afternoon when they came within sight
of the Delanty ranch. Mollie felt a queer tug at her
heart as she looked at it through spring-green foliage.
Rose, driving the wagon, and Kate, on her horse, were
ecstatic.

"Look at the size o' it!" Kate exclaimed. "So many buildin's! Why, 'tis big as a village, it is. It must take a gaggle o' people ter run it, Mollie."

"It does," Mollie replied shortly, wheeling her mare about.

"Where are ye goin', lass?"

"I promised Benjie I'd get Clan and Cordilla to put him on his horse before we meet Bet and Ben."

Benjie was upright, his back against a sack of corn-meal, when she stopped beside him.

"Hurry, Mollie—they may hear us comin' an' come out afore we get there!"

Clan had already saddled Benjie's horse, which was tied to the back of the wagon with the other two animals. When Clan and Cordilla reached over and caught Benjie under his arms, his face went white. Then, as Mollie held the gelding's reins, the two men heaved Benjie into the saddle. The animal moved nervously, but quieted as Benjie spoke soothingly to him. Mollie noted that his face was still grayish white and his lips were pulled tight against the pain of his hanging leg. She moved her horse beside his and spoke softly.

"It hurts, doesn't it?"

"It's like ter kill me, but, by God, I can stand it." His chin was thrust out stubbornly as he fought to keep from wincing with each jolt of the now trotting horse.

"I'll ride t'other side o' ye, Benjie," Clan said, and Mollie was secretly glad. If the pain proved too much and Benjie were to faint from it, she would need Clan's help.

They drew up in front of the house and Mollie dismounted. She walked into the yard with the split-rail fence around it, calling, "Bet! Ben! We're home!" The dogs had already run barking from the back to the front of the house, and now a troop of four women erupted from the broad passageway that ran through the center of the big house. It was Bet, followed closely by Ynez, Josefina, and Elena.

Benjie kicked Tobey's flank with his good leg and moved forward as Bet caught sight of him at last.

She ran toward her son with arms outstretched.
"Oh, Benjie, Benjie, I can't believe 'tis you! Where's
Tim? Oh, blessed Mary, yer leg's—what?"

"Now, Ma, 'tis nothin'. I'm all right. 'Twas only a
nick. Where's Pa an' Squint an' th' rest o' them? Hello,
Ynez...Josie an' Lena!"

Bet turned distractedly to the women. "Oh, Ynez—
Josefina—won't some one go ter the stable an' get th'
men? I saw 'em come in half an hour ago, an' supper's
nigh ready."

As Josefina left at a run, Bet turned and looked first
at Mollie and then Clan, and she burst into tears as
she saw Rose and Kate. "Ah, me dears, me very dears!
How wonderful ter have ye here—" She wiped her eyes
hurriedly on her apron as Kate, gathering her ruffled
Mexican skirts, slid from her horse and ran to embrace
Bet warmly.

Rose, Kate, and Mollie all spoke at once, each one
trying to answer Bet's flurry of questions. Mollie's eyes
sought Benjie's, and there was understanding between
them. The moment had been put off a little longer.

"How come ye ter leave th' others?" Bet asked, her
eyes taking in Clan and Cordilla but seeking Chance
and her other son.

"Benjie was wounded, Bet," Mollie said quickly.
"And as Chance and Colonel Almonte said, there was
no need for us to go on south with them as they pursued General Santa Anna."

"Then Tim decided ter stay wi' Chance an' Colonel
Almonte an' his men?"

"Ma," Benjie leaned down from his saddle, forgetting the pain of his leg and knee. His voice was choked.
"Ma...listen ter me. Tim was bad wounded, but he's
not hurtin' now. He's—he's restin' easy."

Mollie came up and took Bet's arm in the crook of
her own. Her fingers closed over Bet's and she felt
them chill in her grasp as Bet's eyes swung from Benjie to Clan to Mollie. In a barely audible voice she said,
"What are ye tryin' ter tell me? Ye can't mean—"

Benjie slid from his horse, putting weight on his
cruelly hurt leg, and his mouth was tight as he limped

to his mother and caught her in an embrace. He was big and broad, and his arms enveloped the small Bet.

Cordilla, Clan, and the women had fallen silent and stood watching Benjie and his mother.

"Ma," Benjie whispered into her hair, "Ma, ye got ter understand. Tim died fer all o' us—fer th' new home on th' Nueces, fer you an' pa an' me. Aww, Ma—"

For a long minute her head was buried in Benjie's shoulder; then she raised it slowly and turned to Mollie. Her face was white and devoid of expression, her blue eyes dry, as Benjie's had been dry with a grief too deep for tears.

"Come on in, all o' ye—Mollie, Rose, Kate—all o' ye." Bet gestured to Clan and Cordilla. "Clan, ye must stay fer dinner afore ye ride on ter yer brother's house. Sean happens ter be here this evenin'. No doubt he's in back wi' Ben an' the men." She wiped her face on her apron and squared her shoulders. "I bid all o' ye welcome here. Chance would offer ye the best o' his house, were he here."

"I take zee wagon and all zee horses, Senor Clan... ladies." Cordilla said, gathering the wagon reins in his hands.

As they all walked to the house, Bet took Mollie's hand, and they fell behind as the others went on.

"Ye were wi'—" She swallowed hard. "Ye were wi' me Tim when he—when he went?"

"Yes. And our priest, the good Father Baldemero was too. I swear to you, Bet, he didn't suffer. I gave him some of Sister Maria Theresa's morphine, and he talked and smiled before—before he left us."

"I know ye did th' best ye could ter save him, Mollie. An' if you couldn't, then no one could."

Benjie had paused to wait for them, and now he said, "Ma, he was shot in th' stomach an' the' chest—"

"Benjie, don't!" Her voice was piercing. "Don't tell me all that yet. Wait until I've talked to yer pa." Then she added worriedly, "An' I can see ye have no business standin' on that leg o' yours."

Clan, who was helping Cordilla with the wagon and the horses, heard this last and came forward swiftly.

Putting his shoulder under Benjie's arm, he helped him slowly to the house. Rose and Kate had dropped back to walk with Mollie and Bet.

"Sean's goin' ter Corpus termorrow fer supplies," Bet told them as they fell in beside her. "He lives but a couple o' miles from us an' he's brought his house-keeper, Meg Moriarty, an' her little daughter ter stay wi' us until he can get back—a week 'er so, he said." As the women caught up with Clan and Benjie, she added, "Clan, you an' Sean must have supper wi' us. I know it's been a long time since ye've seen each other."

"That it has," Clan rejoined. "An' I'm anxious ter lay eyes on th' spalpeen! I've missed him more'n I'll admit."

"I know how close brothers can be," Bet said in a choked voice. "Ye know, me boys always won their fights in Arderin. It took a famine ter run 'em off their homeland."

"Ah, Bet," Clan said kindly, "it didn't run them off their homeland; instead it *sent* them to their home-land. They earned title to it at The Narrows."

Mollie cast him a grateful glance; he was an adroit and tactful man when he chose to be. Suddenly she felt her gaze drawn down the long path to the house as they all neared it. A woman and a child stood in the open middle hall. The child pulled against the woman's hand, laughing happily. Mollie met the clear gray eyes of Meg Moriarty.

Meg had filled out over the months. Her face was more strikingly beautiful and not so harshly chiseled. Deidre was plump and dimpled and had grown at least two inches. Now she called to Mollie, still pulling her mother's hand.

Bet, following Mollie's eyes, called, "Come, Meg— ye should have joined us. Let the child go." And Deidre flew over the flowered grass to throw her arms around Mollie's knees.

"Mollie, Mollie, you been gone so long!"

Mollie stooped, and the chubby arms went around her neck, hugging her close. Over Deidre's curly head Mollie's eyes were held by the expression on Meg's face. She was looking at Clan with an urgency, a piercing quality in her gaze. Then suddenly she averted her face and stepped back into the shadows of the house.

"Clan, I want Benjie put to bed. We'll bring his supper to him," Mollie said as they stepped onto the broad porch.

"Put him in his an' Tim's old room," Bet added quickly. "I can see he needs ter rest."

Mollie followed Clan and Benjie upstairs, her medicine pouch over her shoulder. Once in the bedroom, Mollie and Clan stripped the breeches off Benjie, and he gave a great sigh of relief as she straightened the sheet over him.

"After supper, I'll check the bandage and put on a new one," Mollie told him. When she returned to the big room downstairs, it was swarming with people. Ben Delanty had come in with Squint Burleson and Sean. Ben had already been told of his son's death, and Bet was now comforting him. Clan and Sean hugged each other unashamedly. Sean was quick to take advantage of the situation and plant a warm kiss on Mollie's lips.

"Life has been empty with you gone, *querida mia,*" he said. "Now you have returned, and when I get back from Corpus with me supplies, I will come courtin' whether ye will or not!" His laugh was so infectious that Mollie had to join in. He was quite as handsome as his brother, and Mollie had the feeling he was much more settled, despite his youth. But there was his liaison with the inscrutable Meg that she could not explain away.

Clan was glad to see Meg, an old friend, and he congratulated her on escaping the famine. He caught Deidre in his arms and tossed her into the air. The child gasped with delight and gave him a moist kiss on the cheek.

"She looks remarkably like me brother." He grinned at Meg, something of a challenge in his face. "If I didn't know better..." he trailed off, laughing. It made his handsome face even more appealing.

Meg made no reply. Her great gray eyes met Clan's merry blue ones and, as always, her expression was unreadable.

Ynez took Mollie, Rose, and Aunt Kate with her to the kitchen to show them the woven basket on the floor. In it was the tiny baby son of Ynez and Fernando Hernandez.

"He eez so good all zee time, I breeng heem wiz me every day!" Ynez said proudly, as her friends exclaimed over his beauty and happy disposition.

"He eez Fernando too, but we call heem Nando," his mother said, beaming. "I take heem home weez me when I finish here, an' he an' heez papa an' me, we all have supper together."

When dark had fallen, they all sat around a supper table laden with the bounty of the Delanty ranch. There was roast beef, broiled chicken, an enormous pink smoked ham, green spring beans swimming in rich pork fat, crowder peas, sliced red tomatoes, yams, and great, smoking Irish potatoes. There were bowls of three kinds of squash and a platter of fluffy cornbread, with a bowl of golden, fresh-churned butter beside it.

Bet had taken a steaming plate up to Benjie earlier and came down saying her son was eating heartily. Mollie felt heartened, for he had lost weight as they traveled.

Sean and Clan were seated together at the table, and Mollie sat between Squint Burleson and Rose. Next to Rose was the silent but sharply observant Meg and her cheerful little daughter. Kate was next to Clan, while Ben and Bet occupied the head and foot of the table respectively.

As they filled their plates, Squint asked brusquely, "Did you shoot anything—game or man—or did you miss 'em all, Miss Mollie?"

Mollie smiled at the man who had taught her the use of guns. "To tell you the truth, Squint, I wasn't quick enough when that awful Mexican soldier kidnapped me out on the plains beyond the house. And when I was with Colonel Almonte's people, I killed a rabbit, but skinning and cleaning it was such a mess, I didn't try for any more game."

"She saved many a life," Clan put in.

"Humph," Squint said. "Well, she's best at that, I reckon."

"Bet, I can tell you about Benjie an' Tim at that last battle." Clan's blue eyes were directly on Bet. "We'd fought all day—February twenty-third it was, a day I'll never ferget—and the battle was seesawin' back an' forth. We guerrillas an' th' rangers went from one part o' the field to another, wherever th' fightin' was heaviest. We suffered casualties then—but not th' twins. Then, at last, as th' sun was low in th' sky, Chance an' I, wi' two rangers an' Tim an' Benjie, saw a small troop o' young Americans near th' foothills o' th' mountains. They were bein' pushed back under th' onslaught of a big force o' Santa Anna's men." Bitterness touched the easy Irish brogue. "They had a piece o' artillery to augment their firepower, an' they were slaughterin' th' untried American troops."

All eyes were on Clan, including Meg's. Mollie, who had already heard from Chance exactly how the twins had been wounded, felt her heart beat heavily as she remembered.

"We rode, all six o' us, ter aid those hard-pressed Americans. Tim an' Benjie, faster'n all o' us, were in front. They charged th' artillery first, fer it was causin' so many casualties. They swept down on it, just th' two o' them at full gallop, firin' as they went. Though they were under a hail o' fire, they took that artillery out, killin' all th' Mexican soldiers manning it."

He paused. Bet's face had grown whiter as she caught her lower lip in her teeth. Meg Moriarty's great eyes never left Clan's face.

"I never saw such courage, Bet." Clan's voice was measured. "Tim an' Benjie knew they would certainly be wounded an' probably killed. But they saved many American lives by their act. Your Tim took out th' last two gunners *after* he was wounded." There was a long pause before he finished. "We turned th' captured artillery on th' enemy."

"Good lads," Squint said gruffly.

"We couldn't have taken out th' artillery wi'out 'em," Clan said quietly. "An' wi' th' heavy fire from it... likely we would all ha' been killed."

"I should've been wi' ye," Sean said darkly, his voice troubled, "instead o' tendin' me crops an' buildin' me house."

Meg tore her eyes from Clan and looked at Sean without a trace of sympathy.

"No, brother," Clan replied quickly. "Some must stay an' tend th' land—or th' woods take it back an' nothin's won, fer the soldiers have naught ter come back to."

"Aye," Ben said, "that's a great truth, Clan. Wi'out th' men to keep the land, 'twould all go fer naught."

Bet dabbed at her eyes with her apron once more, then lifted her chin determinedly. "'Tis so excitin', wi' Rose wed ter that dashin' Colonel Almonte." She smiled tremulously at Rose. "An' we've the pleasure of lookin' forward ter another baby in th' house in July. Ah, Kate an' Rose, me darlin's—an' Mollie, who's like a daughter ter me. It's almost like we were never apart. Ye must stay wi' us always!"

"I'll stay... 'til Rose has her baby, for I promised her." Mollie smiled. "But then it's Corpus Christi and independence for Kate and me. Isn't it, Kate?" she gave her aunt a challenging glance.

"Ter be sure," Kate said sturdily.

"You an' yer independence," Bet said scornfully. "Ye'd be twice as independent right here, an' ye'd work as hard here as ye ever did in Ireland, only 'twould be of yer own choosin'. We need someone who knows medicine in these parts. Why, people would come from all around, once the word got out, and ye could pick up plenty o' money, Mollie!"

"Mollie's one in a million," Clan agreed, his eyes intense on her. "So beautiful an' so wise too. In fact, Bet, I intend ter marry her afore July! Right now, she won't have me"—his quick grin was reckless—"but I'm hard ter discourage, an' by July, I'll have won her heart!"

There was an uncomfortable silence. Mollie saw Meg's lightly tanned face grow white and sick. The breath went out of her as a sudden realization struck her. *Oh, I've been so wrong about Sean! It was Clan!*

"I've th' same idea meself, brother," Sean said coolly, "an' I'll give ye a run fer yer money between now an' July."

Clan's face darkened, and Mollie remembered the legendary brawls between the brothers in Ireland, despite the united front they presented and the love they bore each other.

She looked away from them. Remembering Chance's dark head bent to her breast, she knew a sudden throb of pity for Meg. Like Mollie, she had given her love to a man who did not return it.

"Aye, Mollie has two to choose from," Meg spoke up abruptly, her face still white. "Two of Ireland's finest. 'Twill be a hard choice."

"Not for me," Mollie said lightly. "I'm going to Corpus Christi with Aunt Kate."

"Ah, ye'll change yer mind," Ben said, chuckling, "long afore that, Mollie darlin'." His kind-brown eyes, now with a permanent look of sadness in them, nevertheless twinkled with affection.

"Ye'll be needin' to know how to handle a gun, while you're here anyway, Miss Kate." Squint said, to everyone's surprise. "Miss Mollie can tell you I'm a good teacher."

"Indeed I can," Mollie said, thankful she was no longer the subject of conversation. "He's wonderful, Aunt Kate, and he's right. We should all know how to handle firearms."

The rivalry between Clan and Sean was not mentioned again, but it hung in the air as the conversation turned to crops. It had rained a lot in April, and more was promised in the coming month. According to Sean, the O'Connor acres were expected to yield a good crop of cotton, corn, and potatoes. He had a fine vegetable garden as well, thanks to Meg's efforts. He smiled at her as he spoke, but she did not return his warmth.

"An' I'm goin' ter Corpus termorrow ter buy fruit

trees and more seed and ter try ter hire two more men," Sean continued, his eyes seeking Mollie's. "Meg an' Deedee were ter stay here because we've had Indians come in on us twice in th' last month." His eyes went to his brother and they were hard. "But wi' me brother comin' ter stay wi' us, I think they'll be safe at home."

"Them Injuns don't come to the Delanty ranch no more," Squint remarked, his admiring eyes on Kate. "They know we've got men here who won't put up with their mischief."

"I know." Sean sighed. "When I've hired more workers, I expect they'll leave us alone. But right now there's only Ramon Lopez an' his seventeen-year-old brother Juan, an' when the Indians come, they hide out in the woods. Ramon's mother was killed an' scalped by Indians when he an' his brother were little —right in front o' them, while they were hidin' out in th' chaparral."

"We'll go home with Clan tomorrow, " Meg said quietly. "It's so dark and late, I think we should accept the Delantys' hospitality for tonight, don't you, Sean?"

Clan gave his brother a brooding glance before his eyes swung to Mollie. Bet had risen and was picking up the empty plates.

"I think that's wise," she said, going toward the kitchen. At the door, she met Ynez who took the plates as Bet came back for more. Mollie, Rose, and Kate began to help.

"Mollie"—Sean spoke in a rush—"ye can be independent if ye marry me. Ye'll have yer own household an' duties as great as those ye'd find in Corpus." He paused, looking at Meg as he added slowly, "No one is ever free of responsibility ter someone."

"She will be when she marries." Clan's voice was coaxing. "Mollie, I'd let ye do as ever ye please."

Squint looked at the two men and remarked sourly, "'Pears to me like you two are making Miss Mollie powerful uncomfortable. If she say she don't want to marry right now, it oughta be enough."

"But I love Mollie," Clan said quietly.

"And *I* love Mollie," Sean echoed. "I can't give her up without a fight."

Meg looked at the two brothers, and her mouth went down at one corner. Her eyes were hard now, and fury burned behind them.

Mollie, filled with the painful knowledge that she loved Chance Delanty—and that he did not want her —spoke thickly. "And I tell you I will *not* marry! You'd both better find other prospects."

"Nay, ye'll marry, an' ye'll marry me, Mollie darlin'. Wait an' see." Clan spoke with winning conviction, and all his charm was in his smile.

"We've six bedrooms upstairs and one down here on 'tother side o' the hall. Room fer all o' us, do we double up a bit," Bet told them as they sipped a last cup of coffee over Ynez's peach pie.

Mollie left the table then, going upstairs to check on Benjie. She was relieved to find that his wound, despite his unusual activity, had not reopened. She put a heavy coating of emollient on it and a fresh bandage.

"I'll be glad when I don't have ter take me breeches off fer you ter treat that knee," he grumbled. "I've lost all me modesty around ye."

"You'd better get it back, because I won't have to bandage it too much longer," she said, laughing.

As she went into the dark hall, she was met by Bet carrying a lighted candle in a tall glass chimney. The shadows in Bet's tired blue eyes cried louder than words of her grief for Tim Delanty.

"I'm goin' ter put you in Chance's bedroom. It's next ter Benjie an' Tim's—I mean Benjie's. 'Tis awful big, but if Benjie should need ye in th' night—"

"Yes. I've been sleeping in the wagon beside him at night all the way here," Mollie said, "so I could tend him."

In the dark room, Bet lit two more candles, one on the washstand and one on the bedside table, revealing bedroom walls of rough-hewn pine logs, carefully chinked with a mixture of clay and mud. The huge bed, which was extra wide and long—Chance had made it for himself—was the same as Mollie remembered, and

the handmade chairs and hooked rugs were neatly
cleaned and dusted. The high windows were open, and
the night air sent the sweet scents of May through
them. Mollie recognized the fragrance of wild honey-
suckle, wildflowers, and curiously, roses, which must
have come from the carefully tended flower beds of
Ynez, Josephina, and Elena. The fragrance of pine
threaded the mixture.

"I had Alessandro bring up all yer bundles, colleen.
They're there beside the bed."

"Thank you, Bet dear." Mollie realized suddenly
that she was very tired. "I know the others will want
to sit and talk awhile, but it's been a long hard trip for
me, Bet. Tell them I decided to call it a day."

Bet smiled. "Ye'd be surprised. I think th' others are
ready ter call it enough fer one day too. I'm goin' ter let
ye sleep late in th' mornin', child," she added. "'Tis
somethin' ye deserve fer sittin' up nights wi' me Benjie."

Mollie washed up in the bowl on the washstand,
promising herself the luxury of a full bath in the big
wooden tub the next evening.

When she slipped between the coarse cotton sheets
of Chance's bed, she found the feather-filled mattress
and feather pillows an extravagance of comfort difficult to believe after the months spent on her hard bedroll. All too readily, she could imagine Chance's big,
hard body lying next to hers, and the thought set her
heart pounding.

Fool! Chance had called her a fool, and he had been
right. Why couldn't he have said, just once during
those terrible, wonderful moments they made love to
each other, "I love you, Mollie." Ah, but he had not. He
had wanted her, but he did not love her. And not loving
her, he would never want to marry her. How blithely,
how airily she had said, "I'm not marriage minded!"
And she had believed it. Chance had heard it, and he
had believed it. That was why he was so free in taking
her love. But she knew now that every time she had
given herself to him, she had given him her love. Yes,
Mollie O'Meara was a first-class fool.

She tossed in the luxury of the featherbed, and sleep would not come. The old moon slowly rose, lopsided now as it peered in the room seeking her out. She got up and went to the window, folding her arms across the sill as she had done that long-ago dawn in Corpus Christi when she was waiting for Chance to come for her.

Where was he now? He might even be dead in the far reaches of southern Mexico. Or, if still alive, in terrible danger. It made her sick to think of it. Slow, hot tears burned her eyes.

It was then she heard the door open softly behind her. She wheeled about swiftly to see a white shape coming toward the empty bed. It was a woman in a long, white nightgown. Rose? Kate? Bet? As her eyes took in the long fall of black hair, she realized it was someone else who felt among the covers for her.

"I'm over here, Meg," she said softly. "By the window."

The figure straightened, and the moon threw a flash of light on the long knife Meg held in her hand.

Chapter 22

"Did you come to kill me because of Clan?" Mollie asked as Meg stood poised over the empty bed.

The woman turned, saw her, and approached slowly. "If I have to. Clan is mine! I bore his daughter and followed him to the New World with a fortune to offer him."

"When he knows of your fortune, maybe he'll marry you. I hope to God he does, for *I'll* never marry him."

"Ah, you say that! But I know his winning ways, and he is so bonny..."

She sounded curiously like her small, sunny daughter. "You'll weaken, and he'll have you."

"Would it convince you if I told you I love another?" Strangely, Mollie knew no fear, only pity. Meg was evil without knowing she was evil, and for that reason alone, she was to be pitied.

Meg paused, the long knife glinting in her hand, her pale eyes shining.

"I don't believe you. You've said marriage was not for you."

357

"That was brave talk. I'd marry soon enough if the man I love asked me."

"Who is it? Why won't he?"

"I can't tell you."

"I don't believe you," Meg said flatly.

"I'll never marry Clan." Mollie's voice was as flat and cold as Meg's

There was a long silence between them. Then Meg stroked the knife along her thigh against the cotton cloth of her nightgown.

"If you do," she said slowly, "if you make love to him, I'll surely kill you, no matter the cost to me."

Mollie shrugged. "He's going home to Sean's with you in the morning. You'll have a whole week with him alone in the house. Show him your fortune; I know he has none. You may marry him yet, Meg."

The silence drew out once more. "Remember what I said to you," Meg said. "I will kill you no matter the cost, if you let Clan convince you."

Mollie was weary. Her own thoughts of Chance had depressed her terribly, and she knew she would go to Corpus Christi a lonely, unfulfilled woman, for there could never be another man for her.

"I know something of how you feel," she said bitterly, "because the man I love does not love me."

"What a lie! You're afraid of me and my knife. And well you should be, for I'll make good on my promise. Believe it!"

"Go to bed, Meg," Mollie said tiredly. "And woo Clan in the week you have him alone to yourself."

The week slipped by. Sean stopped on his way home and paid Bet back with a sack of white flour and three pounds of coffee.

Mollie was still depressed. She thought of Chance too much, and no matter how she busied herself making a new batch of medicine and refilling her supply of medicinal herbs and emollients, he intruded on her thoughts. She had been cool to Sean, so cool that he had left early, puzzled and hurt by her lack of cordiality.

Probably I'll be one of those pinched, thin women who pine all their lives after one man, she told herself scornfully.

She thought of July and the journey back to Corpus. She had already asked Squint if he would escort her and her aunt, and he had agreed with alacrity. He was taking Kate down to the river every day and showing her how to handle both pistol and rifle. He had even cajoled her into wearing breeches and learning to ride astride with him when he went out to check the livestock.

This latter accomplishment had amazed both Mollie and Rose, for they had believed that no one could get Kate into breeches. She had grumbled about it but insisted that she wanted to learn to ride and see all of Chance's rangeland, and she had implied that Squint was crabby and wouldn't take her if she wore a skirt.

"Says I'll spook th' cows inter a stampede wi' skirts," she had complained. "He says he hasn't much use fer women, so he's doin' me a great favor by teachin' me these things. Says he's doin' it fer Mollie, on account of she patched up his hand."

The second week in May, Clan came to call. Mollie's reception of him was chilly, but he was not easily discouraged. He asked her to take a short ride with him along the river. She agreed reluctantly because he said he had something important to discuss with her. She saddled up her mare Colleen, and they set off beside the cool, clear water.

It was a beautiful morning, and the birds were filling the trees along the river with clear, crystal music. The air smelled even sweeter than it had when Mollie first arrived from Mexico, all the fragrances coming to a summer height before the dry heat of the southwest set in.

"Now, what is it that is so important for us to discuss?" Mollie asked coolly after they had talked about the day, the beauty of the river, and how each ranch was doing.

"I wanted ter come afore this," Clan said soberly, "but I couldn't get away from Meg. She follows me about like me own shadow. An' I told her long ago there was nothin' fer us together."

"Nothing but Dierdre and love!"

"So she told ye that, did she?"

"I guessed it before she told me. It was obvious from the way she looked at you." Had Mollie been that obvious when she looked at Chance? she wondered, for she had looked at him so often—as often as he came into sight.

"Will ye not let me have a fair trial, Mollie darlin'? Will ye not listen ter my side o' th' story?"

"How can you explain away or justify a child who cannot claim her own father? Or a woman who loves you desperately enough to follow you to the New World and live in your brother's house until she could find you?"

"An' did she tell ye that she sought me out in the barn on her husband's property, in the tavern where I stayed the night in Sharavogue, throwin' herself at me because her husband Bill was as old as her father?" A hunted look came into his eyes, and the weary sadness of his finely sculpted face struck her afresh. "An' did she tell ye she smothered Bill an' took his sack o' gold ter come ter th' New World? She has murder on her hands—I could never love her."

"My God! I didn't know she'd killed her husband! But that doesn't justify your leaving your child a bastard. How can that be forgivable?"

"How do ye forgive what life does ter us, Mollie? Only God can forgive that. You think I planned Dierdre—or worse, the murder done by her mother? Ah, ye know better than that, lass, for a cruel man I'm not."

They had stopped the horses, and now he helped her down. They sat on the bank, watching the horses crop the lush green grass that grew back from the edge of the river.

Looking into his clear blue eyes, Mollie knew he was speaking the truth. He was not a cruel man, but he was cursed with a magnetism that drives women to forget everything in pursuit of him.

"Ye may find it hard ter believe, Mollie, but Meg threw herself in me way at every turn—cryin' an' beggin' fer the comfort the old man she married couldn't give her, so old was he that he had no love left in his dried-up body."

He reached out and caught her hand, and in his eyes was the desire she had seen so often in Chance's.

"There must have been more than Meg who sought you, followed after you—and you never turned them away, did you, Clan?" But there was no accusation in her words. The ghost of Ireland was in the warm, southwestern air, and Mollie's heart was softened by the remembrance of the way Chance had looked at her in Bet's cottage when first he saw her. Her heart beat faster with the memory, and the early summer about them wrought a magic of its own.

"No," he said slowly, "I never turned them away. And I made each o' them happy for a little while. But they claimed more o' me than I could give—for me heart belonged to you, Mollie darlin'. It was yours, I think, even when ye were a child, runnin' through the gorse, playin' in th' burn, lookin' at me with those beautiful eyes o' yours."

His hand reached out and caught hers again, then slipped gently, tenderly up her bare arm where her shirtsleeve was rolled up. For a moment it felt like Chance's touch. It *was* Chance's touch—and all the more desirable because she knew she could never be with him again. Tears gathered in her eyes, tears for the loss of Chance and tears of pity for Clan, so handsome, wanting a passion she could never give him.

"Why, yer cryin'! Mollie, there's nothin' ter cry about—I'm offerin' ye marriage! Sean'll get over it, an' we'll make us a place next ter his."

"No, Clan." She pulled her arm away and dried her tears. "I can't marry you without love."

"But ye'll come ter love me, Mollie," he pleaded. "Give me a chance." With sudden desperation, he turned and pulled her down on the thickly tufted grass. She struggled to rise, but he loomed over her, forcing her down beneath him. The fresh green fragrance of crushed clover rose and filled her lungs.

Before she could utter a single cry, he spoke fiercely. "Ah, Mollie darlin', I want ye so, an I love ye wi' all me soul!"

He brought his head down and his mouth covered hers. All the terror of that long-ago moment in the copse beyond Arderin shook her once more. Chance was far away. There was no one to save her now.

Writhing under his heavily muscled body, she tore away from his kiss—a kiss that carried all his passion, all his heartbreak at her rejection.

"No, Clan. No!"

His head above her blotted out the trees that sheltered them from the late morning sun, but she heard the small, dry sob that came from directly behind him. Lost in the turbulence of his emotions, Clan apparently heard nothing.

Then, as Mollie looked up, she saw his handsome face suddenly contort. As he rolled half off her, above him she saw Meg Moriarty, her black hair swinging wildly, her arm upraised, the long knife gleaming bloodily in the sunlight before she drove it home once more.

Clan's breath went out of him, and he heaved reflexively off Mollie, turning to face Meg above him, her blade aloft once more. He caught her arm then and twisted it, catching the hand holding the knife and imprisoning it in his own.

He turned it slowly inward against her, and she came down on the point that was bright with his blood.

Under Mollie's unbelieving eyes, the blade sank into Meg, the hilt resting just under her left breast. Unlike Clan, who was still moving, Meg fell without a word to the ground beside Mollie.

I couldn't get away from Meg. She follows me about like me own shadow.

Slowly Clan pulled himself away from the two women and sank to his knees. His eyes were on Mollie as he reached a hand to her. She looked at it in stunned disbelief. Then she looked down at her white shirt. Two drops of bright blood lay on it, brilliant against the whiteness. Clan's or Meg's? She shook her head in a shocked refusal to accept what her eyes told her.

Clan whispered hoarsely, "Take me hand, Mollie." The words rattled in his throat and chest as he tried to draw a deep breath.

Numbly, Mollie took his hand, crouching before the kneeling man. He squeezed her hand painfully. Then suddenly he smiled, the famous O'Connor Irish smile that could coax a bird off a branch.

"Ah, Mollie darlin', I loved ye so. An' I never had ye, not even the once."

His hand loosened and slowly his knees gave way. He fell backward to lie staring sightlessly up at the tall tree above them. Leaves shaken by the late May wind rustled softly, a requiem to those who had fallen.

There was a flutter of wings and Mollie looked up, still dazed. A cardinal, red as the blood beside her, peered at her from a leafy branch. He gave one beautiful, liquid note of song, then spread his wings and darted away.

Slowly, Mollie rose to her feet and stood looking down at Meg, at where the knife handle nestled beneath her rounded bosom.

She turned even more slowly and went to the two horses, grazing undisturbed a few yards away. Had Meg followed them on foot? She must have, hiding behind the brush and the thick tree trunks. Mollie shook her head and, holding the reins of the two horses, turned to retrace their steps to the Delanty house on foot.

The wind, rising a little and cooler now, swept mournfully through the leaves above her, lifted her hair and caressed her cheek. In her heart Clan's words echoed with sadness. *How do you forgive what life does to us, Mollie? Only God can forgive that.*

They found the horse Meg had ridden from the O'Connor place when she followed Clan. Squint and Ben came upon the mare when they started out to ride to Sean with the news of his brother's and Meg's death. The animal was tied in a small stand of trees just a few yards from the Delanty house.

No one pressed Mollie for details after she told them that Meg had followed them to the river and launched her attack on Clan. And almost no one was surprised when she told all of them that Dierdre was Clan's daughter. Only Bet, when Sean O'Connor confirmed it, wept afresh with surprise. In her innocence, Bet had always refused to see the family resemblance, despite Mollie's long-ago suggestion that the beautiful child was Sean's.

Later Squint, with the help of Ben and the three vaqueros, built simple wooden coffins, and Clan and Meg were buried on the O'Connor farm. Sean chose a spot several hundred yards from his house and fenced it to serve as a family cemetery.

Dierdre cried hard at her mother's burial, and she was the only one who asked Mollie questions about her mother's death. Dierdre spent three nights at the Delanty house while Sean put things in order.

Mollie answered the five-year-old's questions with the truth; that her mother had killed Clan O'Connor with her long knife and then he had turned it on her. And when the child asked her why, Mollie replied, *"Because Clan hurt her."*

"Why would bonny Clan hurt my mother? Why would my mother use her knife on him? I loved bonny Clan, and he loved me.

"You must wait until you grow up to understand that, Deedee."

"Bonny Sean says he will be my papa for always, Mollie."

"Ah, Deedee," Mollie replied, hiding her tears behind a smile, "he will be the best papa a little girl ever had!"

After that, Dierdre asked no more questions. But her haunted blue eyes with faint blue shadows beneath them reminded Mollie of Clan so vividly that, after the child had left with Sean, she went to her room and cried for the first time since the terrible tragedy.

She wept silently, her face muffled in a pillow, her fingers wringing and twisting in the quilt. Not because she had loved the man, for she had not. But he had loved her. He had loved her the way she loved Chance Delanty, helplessly, passionately, and without real hope. She knew it now.

She wept until she could weep no more, and she didn't go down to supper. Instead, Bet and Kate tiptoed in and whispered over her while she feigned sleep.

"Poor child's asleep," Bet murmured.

"Let her sleep. Her face looks swollen. Maybe she's cried at last."

"Thank God for that. 'Tis terrible when ye can't cry," Bet replied feelingly. "I was that way after I first heard about me Tim"

"An' I about me Rose marryin' that...that man." Kate's voice faded as they went out the door, closing it quietly behind them.

For a long time after they left, Mollie lay with her eyes open, staring up at the rough-beamed ceiling in the fading light.

Dierdre was with her uncle where she belonged. The child had wanted to stay with Mollie, but Sean had told her sorrowfully that he would be too lonely without her. Dierdre had clung to him, her tears spilling afresh, and they had gone together to the big log house farther up the Nueces.

Mollie rose and poured water into the bowl from the pitcher on the washstand. She began to bathe her tear-streaked face. Well, I'll stay until Rose has her baby, she thought. Then, Kate and I will go so far away that maybe, just maybe, I can forget Chance.

Forget him? Her little laugh was a sob in her throat. How could she forget him when she knew she would never be whole again? Always, now, she would go to bed empty and hungry for him. Yet she had given herself to him—and he had never once said, "I love you, Mollie."

Could she have made him love her? Now she re-

membered the times she had cut him with sharp
words, had flung "I hate you!" at him. Too late, too
late! She had lost him, and she ached with a premonition that she would never see him again.

She dried her face and hands and turned away from
the washstand. Then she went downstairs to join the
others.

It was July nineteenth, and even under the heavily
leaved oak tree the midmorning sun was hot. It was
going to be a scorching day, Mollie thought, wiping her
forehead with the back of her hand as she curried her
mare. She should have worn her broad-brimmed hat.
Instead, she had tied her long hair back with a blue
grosgrain ribbon, and her tresses hung down her back
in a gleaming black tumble.

Tomorrow she and Squint would set out for Corpus
Christi. Despite tears and arguments from the others,
she would leave in the early morning.

She glanced up idly, and her gaze was caught by a
rider coming up from the river. He was on a big red
gelding, and two pack horses followed him. Her eyes
narrowed. Tall in the saddle, broad of shoulder, and
lean of hip, he reminded her sharply of Chance Delanty. His right arm was in a sling, and a white bandage covered his dark forehead under the brim of a hat
pulled low.

Her heart leaped, then settled to a quick, heavy
thud. That lean tall body! It could belong only to one
man—the *only* man who could tear her heart with just
the sound of his low, vibrant voice.

Her hand holding the currycomb slowed, and she
swallowed hard as disbelief gave way slowly to realization. It *was* Chance! She stood poised, frozen into stillness. Only her heart moved, the wild beat of it pulsing
in every vein.

He had seen her from a distance she knew, for he
rode steadily toward her. When he stopped the gelding
beside Colleen and looked down at her for a long, still
moment, at last she was able to speak.

"You made it back, after all," she said inadequately.

"And you're still here, after all." The deep, husky voice slipped over her, warm and smooth, melting her feigned indifference.

"Is the war over?"

"Very nearly. My horse was shot out from under me at Cerro Gordo in mid-April when General Scott took the city."

"Is that where you were wounded?" Anxiety crept into her voice in spite of her feigned coolness.

"No. That happened last month in a skirmish outside Chapultepec. Another horse was shot from under me and I broke my arm. A bullet grazed my head."

"I thought surely the war would be over before you returned."

"Scott's going on to take Mexico City after Chapultepec. He may already have done it; then it'll be over. It's a matter of days now, if there's enough of the Mexican government left to make a peace treaty."

"You came all this way wounded and alone?"

"I wasn't much use to Jose with a broken arm, so he sent me home with a long letter to Rose. How is she?"

"She had a fine eight-pound boy on the tenth. He looks just like the colonel. Incidentally, I delivered all your messages to Ben and Bet, but she's going to argue with you about the money for the land you're giving them. As for me, I've served my term, and Squint's escorting me to Corpus Christi tomorrow at dawn."

"You and Kate?"

Mollie laughed derisively. "My aunt is in love with Squint Burleson—and so changed, she's forgiven Rose and is an absolute fool over the baby. No, I'll be going alone."

Chance's shoulders shook with sudden laughter. "Kate and Squint. Now there's a pair. I can't believe it."

"Squint's taking me mainly, I think, so he can fetch a priest who'll baptize Rose's baby and marry him and Kate afterward. His Presbyterian leanings are apparently forgotten. He's becoming a good Catholic."

"There's no need for Squint to leave. I'll take you

back to Corpus and get the priest." His jaw was tight, his vivid eyes on her accusing.

"You need medical attention yourself," she said defensively, fighting a wholly irrational desire to reach up and take the angry, tanned face in her hands, pull it down to her, and shower it with kisses. My God, that would confirm everything Chance had ever thought of her! "A good hot bath and bed for twenty-four hours."

"Will you stay and see to my wounds?" His eyes searched her face. "Mind you, you don't owe me a thing. It would be strictly a favor for which I'll pay the going rate. Cayetana patched me up the best she could, but I haven't seen a doctor and I've been on the road for over a month."

Mollie was silent, fighting for control of her runaway heart. The cicadas in the trees about them were loud in the silence, adding to the summer somnolence.

He sighed. "Ah, well. Knowing how you feel about me, I shouldn't ask. Forget it, Mollie."

"I'll not forget it," she blazed suddenly. "And you don't have the least idea of how I feel."

"About me, I do," he said bitterly. "You've told me often enough that you hate me." He slid from his saddle and added irrelevantly, "I miss Beau—he was a great horse. But I've learned the hard way not to give anything . . . anyone all my love."

"You didn't suffer any other wounds, did you?" Mollie asked, hiding her apprehension.

"None that show, anyway. I'd better get these horses into the stables and unpack. They're as tired as I am."

"I'll help." She took Colleen by the bridle and pulled her along as they went through the corral gate and into the stables.

"You could get Squint or one of the men to help," he said.

"They're out riding herd and tending crops. Besides, I want to do it and see that you follow my instructions. When we get to the house, I'll look at that arm and the spot where the bullet grazed your head."

"It hasn't healed— Does this mean you'll stay?" His

eyes on hers were piercing now, and a muscle in his jaw tightened.

Again she made no answer; inexplicably, her throat was tight and she fought down tears as she put Colleen in the first stall and closed the gate. Then she began unpacking the first of his packhorses, avoiding his intense scrutiny.

He began unstrapping the saddle on the gelding. "I rubbed him down last night. All he needs is food and rest," he said, putting the horse in the next stall. With one hand he began to loosen the straps on the second pack animal.

"How did you manage all this with a broken arm?"

"Not very well."

"I can see that Cayetana splinted it well. Where was the break?"

"The upper right arm. Damn, but it's awkward! I've bathed in rivers all the way, and it's hell working around it in the water."

He finished unpacking the horse and came to help her. He stood so near she could smell the clean heat from his body, feel his nearness keenly. She did not move away, and they brushed against each other while unstrapping the bundles.

Her breath grew shorter, for the powerful urge to touch and be touched by him flared up and ran like fire through her veins. He was looking at her as they worked. She could feel his gaze, but she did not meet it.

"Mollie," he said huskily, "look at me."

She shook her head. "I can't," she whispered. She knew her yearning would show in her eyes, for she longed for the passion only he could stir in her. She wanted the man—and for the rest of her life she would want him, desire him, love him. Pride kept her head down. He must never know what he had done in bringing a proud woman to her knees.

"Mollie, do you hate me so? Leave me a little pride," he said low.

"Pride!" she burst out. "You're the proudest, most arrogant man I ever met, and you ask *me* to leave *you*

pride—when you've humbled mine time after time!"
Mollie faced him then, less than a foot away, her blue
eyes stormy and revealing.

"You've bedded me like any trollop to be bought in a
brothel—more than once—and gone on your way! I
know you don't love me, and that's why—why—" Just
in time she stopped the rush of words. She could not
say that that was why she was leaving. Mollie was
still a prideful woman, and she was determined to rebuild that pride. Telling him would be an admission of
her love for him, and he must never, never know how
deeply he had humbled her.

He caught her arm with his left hand, pulling her
close, forcing her to look into his face. His eyes burned
her like blue fire.

"I never took you as a trollop! I've loved you since
the moment you rushed into Bet's cottage in Arderin,
bursting to confide in her and unable to because I was
there. I've wanted you longer than I've ever wanted
any woman, and I thought I could make you love me. I
was wrong—" He broke off, trying to control his rage,
and Mollie stared into his eyes, dumbfounded as realization tore her heart.

"I visualized us as a team," he went on, his voice
lower now, "each needing and loving the other, each
independent yet commited to the future of this ranch."
He paused, his eyes brilliant with the echo of hopes
and dreams. "Did you know the future of this ranch is
unlimited, now that the Mexican question will be settled? Cotton and beef—everyone in the world needs
them—and you and I together could reap a reward in
hundreds of thousands of dollars . . . raise our children
to inherit and carry on after us!" He caught himself,
and his face suddenly went blank.

She could only look up into his face, silenced by the
powerful emotion that strangled speech and filled her
eyes with tears.

"But I've a pride of my own, Mollie O'Meara." He
drew a long breath. "So you can leave tomorrow, knowing you've left a man who loved you as deeply and ten-

derly as any man could. If your pride has suffered, that should restore it. Another scalp to your belt, miss."

He turned away from her, pulling the two pack-horses to empty stalls. With a loud slap on each rump, he turned them in, where they could get at the filled troughs. When he turned back, Mollie was standing where he had left her, lips parted, eyes shining with tears.

He came to her slowly, almost hesitantly, taking her trembling chin in his hand and tilting her face up to his so he could look closely into her eyes.

"Well, I'll be damned," he whispered huskily. "Pride. It's been a wall between us all the time, Mollie darling."

Her arms flew about his waist, and she put her curly black head against his chest, breathing in the warm, masculine scent of him, shivering as the promise of passion built within her.

"Looks like Squint can go alone tomorrow morning to bring back a priest"— he laughed softly—"for a baptism and *two* weddings."

"Yes, yes," she whispered, able at last to admit it. "Oh, Chance, I love you so. Let me share that future— give you those children—" She was silenced again, this time by his mouth, closing over hers.

Epilogue

Mexico City was attacked and taken by American troops on September 14, 1847. Santa Anna, escaping from the city, briefly continued desultory warfare. But on April 5, 1848, having resigned the presidency, he received permission to retire from the country and sailed for Jamaica, going from there to Venezuela.

In 1853, he was recalled and elected president of Mexico once more. However, within one year and after setting up an odious despotism, he proclaimed himself president for life, with the title of Serene Highness and with the right to nominate his successor.

Revolution followed in March, 1854, and when he saw his cause was lost, Santa Anna fled the capital on August 9, 1855, and found refuge in Cuba, Venezuela, and Saint Thomas. In his absence, he was tried and condemned for treason, and his estates were confiscated.

He returned to Mexico during the French occupation in 1864, but was not permitted to remain. In 1867, he again returned, but was once more exiled and went to live in the United States. Finally, after the death of

Juarez and the amnesty of 1874, he was permitted to reside in his own country, where he ended his career in poverty and obscurity.

Don Jose Almonte never caught up with the elusive dictator, but his estates were returned to him, and he brought his bride and his young son back to his enormous hacienda. He and his wife had three daughters after young Jose was born. Dona Rose was a gracious and beautiful wife to him, but she returned once a year to the Delanty ranch on the Nueces to visit the Delantys, her mother and Squint Burleson, and her young half brother, Peter Burleson.

Ben, Bet, and Benjie Delanty built a big house on the large tract of land they purchased from Ben's brother. There they established a fine ranch and even finer orchards.

As for Mollie and Chance Delanty, they established an empire in the deep southwestern part of Texas, raising blooded horses and cattle and the finest cotton to be found in that part of the country. They had four sons and two daughters, who eventually inherited one of the largest and most legendary ranches in the southwest. It remains so today.

The Timeless Romances
of New York Times Bestselling Author

JOHANNA LINDSEY